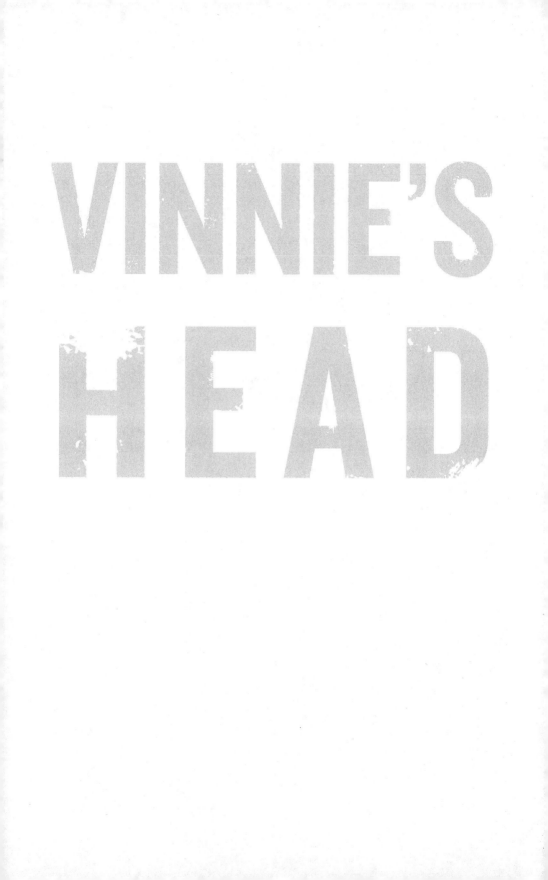

VINNIE'S HEAD

VINNIE'S HEAD

MARC LECARD

ST. MARTIN'S MINOTAUR 🏛 NEW YORK

This is a work of fiction. All of the characters, organizations, and events portrayed in this novel are either products of the author's imagination or are used fictitiously.

www.minotaurbooks.com

ISBN-13: 978-0-312-36021-4
ISBN-10: 0-312-36021-5

First Edition: March 2007

10 9 8 7 6 5 4 3 2 1

FOR DAN HOOKER

ACKNOWLEDGMENTS

Thanks to my agent, Ashley Grayson, for sticking with me, and to my editor, Michael Homler, for his subtle critique and understanding, and for fighting the good fight. Thanks also to Kenneth J. Silver and the production team at St. Martin's for combing out my verbal tics, eccentricities, and straight-up errors, and for making me look good. And thanks to Dave Gordon and Kim Rawdin, *compañeros*, old friends, funny guys.

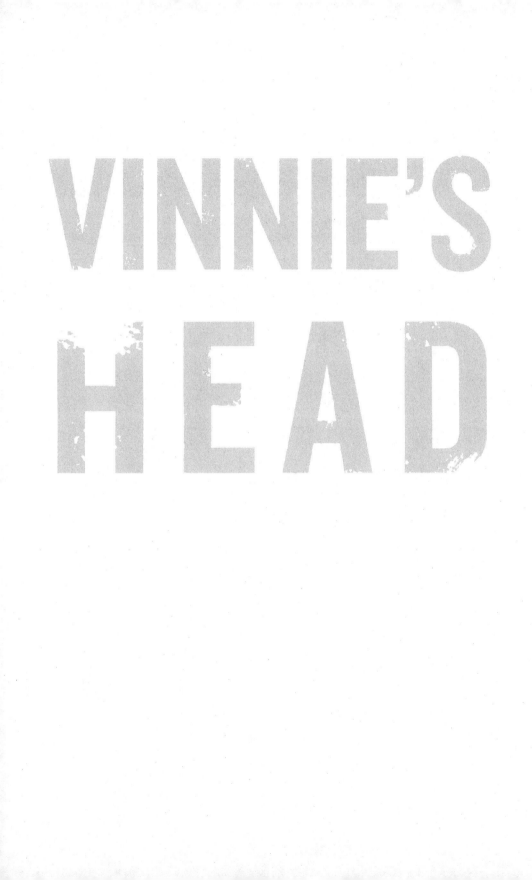

CHAPTER ONE

I SNAGGED VINNIE'S HEAD while I was out fishing for flounder off the end of the town dock in Comapogue, down there on the South Shore of Long Island between Lindenhurst and Copiague. At first, I thought I had hung up on an old tire or an outboard, maybe a drowned refrigerator.

"Oh fuck." No matter how I pulled and yanked on it, the fishing line didn't move an inch.

"Fuck me," I said for variety. I had only the one flounder rig—two hooks with little orange balls on them, a brass spreader, and a yellow sinker. The pole wasn't even mine; I found it in the shed in the backyard. The old guy who owned it would never know it was gone—this is what I told myself.

I gave the line another tug. The rod bent double, but whatever it was I'd hung up on didn't budge. So I backed up, holding the rod out straight to break the line without fucking up the borrowed pole. Then, with a little give, an *uudge* like a tooth sliding out of a novocained gum, the line came loose. As I reeled in, I could feel there was something still on it, dragging the rod tip down. It felt like I had a concrete block on. I kept reeling.

The head coming up looked like a head. That is, it came up crown-first, hair streaming out around it, just like the head of a living person coming up from a dive. But this was a lonely head, without a body to keep it company.

The second-worst thing about the head was that it didn't surprise me. Seeing it dangling from Mr. Colucci's flounder rig with the little orange plastic balls above the hooks, I realized I had been expecting something like this to happen. Not sunken heads exactly. But I had been asking myself what would happen next, and how could things get any worse, any more fucked up than they were already.

Never ask yourself that.

I lifted the head onto the dock, quick as if it were a flounder and might get away, worrying that the line would snap. The head bounced over the rails and onto the splintery wooden boards, then rolled to a stop against a creosote-smeared piling.

The head had been cut off clean, right under the chin. One of the flounder hooks had snagged under an ear; the other dug into the scalp. Crabs had been at it; the eyes were gone, parts missing to the bone here and there. The cheeks were all sucked in and hollow-looking. It was a mess. But the very worst thing about the head was that I recognized it.

It was Vinnie's head.

Water was running off his black hair, which was all mashed down on his skull and hanging every which way. Vinnie would have hated that; he spent a lot of time on his hair, getting it just right. The parts of his face the crabs had left showed three or four days of stubble. I remembered reading something about how hair and fingernails keep growing after you die, and I wondered if that was what was happening.

I stared at the head. It was hard to look at, but it was Vinnie all right. Some kind of sea creature crawled out his left eye socket and hung there, waving back and forth.

Vinnie looked a lot worse than he had just a few days ago when I saw him and his girlfriend off to the airport.

I panicked. I heaved up on the rod, thinking to jerk the head back in the water so I wouldn't have to look at it anymore. But I must have moved too quickly; the hook pulled out of the left ear, a piece of the scalp peeled loose, and the head fell on the dock, rolling up to my foot.

So I would have to touch it after all. Just pick it up like a fish and drop it over the side, I told myself. I bent over and reached out my hand, but I couldn't bring myself to grab the wet hair, which was like seaweed now more than hair.

This is where you puke, I thought. I was breathing heavily, sweat rolling down the back of my neck.

I checked back behind me down the dock to see if anybody was looking. There was no one there. At the street end of the dock, there were a couple of parked cars, but the way the sun was setting, I couldn't see through the windows because of the glare. I tried to remember whether the cars had been there when I came, and whether there was anybody in them, but my mind was blank.

My foot nudged the head and it moved a little. That freaked me out. Leave it, I thought, just leave it on the dock and walk away. But suppose someone was watching; suppose someone saw me and told the cops. They would certainly want to talk to me about the head. And I was anxious not to talk to cops at the time—about anything. And I knew they would come looking for me if I came to their attention. Something like Vinnie's head would probably bring me to their attention.

Leave it. Call the cops from a pay phone. No one will see you. Just get out of here, my mind was telling me. I looked around again and saw some old buster walking his dog, heading toward the end of the dock. That's when I made my next bad judgment call.

Along with the borrowed fishing rod, I had brought a black plastic trash bag with me to hold all the flounder I was going to catch. Now I took it out of my jacket pocket, unrolled it, and held the mouth of it open as I nudged the head into it with my foot. That was hard. Even with boot leather, I hated to touch the thing. It rolled into the trash bag like a bowling ball, with just a little wobble. I twisted the mouth of the bag on itself, tied it off. Just in time, because now the old guy and his dog were walking up to me.

"Catch anything?" the old guy asked. His dog, an old beagle, was sniffing the bag and grunting; the old guy tugged him away from it.

"Just one," I said.

The old guy nodded wisely. "Yeah, they used to be a lot of 'em around here. Now you can't catch a damn thing. Nothin' but trash."

"You got that right," I said, and smiled as nicely as I could.

"You do catch anything," the old guy continued, "you can't even eat it. It's all poisoned from pollution."

"It's not the way it used to be," I said. I began to hop from leg to leg, as if I needed to take a leak.

"That's right, that's right, too many laws now—you can't eat this, can't catch that," the old guy said, as if agreeing with something I'd brought up. "An' there's no fish left anyway."

"Well, I better get home and clean this guy." I hefted the trash bag; that was a bad idea. You could see the shape in it was not a fish.

The old guy didn't seem to notice. The beagle's eyes, though, followed the bag intently.

"Well, take care of yourself, young man," the old guy said. "And good luck." The beagle tilted its head up and began to howl; the old guy turned around and started whacking on it with the end of the leash. "Stop that, Henry. You stop that! What is wrong with you?"

I left the two of them there and started back to Vinnie's house.

When I was halfway down the first block from the dock, one of the parked cars behind me suddenly started up and turned on its lights. I nearly shat from paranoia. My neck muscles tensed up as I tried to keep myself from looking around. Then the car drove by me, not slow, not fast, heading toward Montauk Highway.

I let my held breath out in a big rush and used all my willpower to keep from breaking into a jog. There was no one around, no one to see me. It was dinnertime, getting dark, lights on in all the houses, people sitting down to eat, not looking out the window for guys carrying severed heads in plastic trash bags down the street.

Carrying the head was a problem, though. If I held the bag loosely, by the neck, the head would bounce against my legs as I walked. If I gripped it higher up, the bag stopped swinging, but I could feel the head against my hand. That was nasty. There was no comfortable way to carry it.

It was just as well I didn't have far to go.

Now a couple of questions will probably occur to most people here. One, why didn't I call the cops to come and get the head? Well, as I said earlier, I was not eager to talk to the police. I thought that no matter how the conversation started out, sooner or later it would come round to the fact that I had missed my court date, jumped bail, and was a fugitive from justice. Carrying Vinnie's head around in a garbage bag might not impress them much, either.

Then, too, it was Vinnie's head. Vinnie had been a good friend to me. My best friend, I guess. I couldn't bring myself to just drop his head in a Dumpster, even if that had been a good idea.

"You are so fucking stupid," I said to myself out loud as I walked up the street. Talking to myself again—a bad habit. "Just so fucking dumb. Can't you do anything right?"

And then, of course, there were the people who had shot all the window glass out of Vinnie's McMansion on the North Shore. Whoever the fuck they were. I would have minded this less if I hadn't been sleeping on Vinnie's couch at the time.

So I had every incentive to stay out of the news for a while.

I was carrying the trash bag over my shoulder like Santa Claus; with every step, the head bounced against my back. Vinnie's house—his parents' house, really—was just a couple blocks from the dock. I had been staying in his garage ever since I had to leave his North Shore house after I missed my court date. And it was shot to pieces. Did I mention that? Needless to say, Vinnie wasn't there. He had told me he was going to South America on business.

The whole thing about missing my court date had nothing to do with Vinnie at all. It was just bad luck. Here's the way it started.

I had just gotten out of county in Riverhead, where I was doing two weeks for no visible means of support. (This was bullshit, by the way—I was living in my car, which may not look like much but is definitely visible.) I stopped in Vinnie's cousin's tavern, the HiLite, to wash the taste of jail out of my mouth. I could run a tab there—they knew me. But when I went out to my car, my lights were still on, burning pretty dimly, though. Not enough juice left to start.

Now what I should've done, I should have gone back in the tavern and asked if anybody had cables, could jump me. That's what I should have done. But I was in a hurry, and pretty drunk and fucked up, I guess. Not thinking clearly. So instead of asking for help, I helped myself to the battery from the car next to me. I was just borrowing it; I meant to return it. But before I could get it installed, the guy whose car it was from came out of the bar. He and his friends beat the crap out of me. We all went back to county for disturbing the peace, and disorderly, and some other stuff. Another thirty days. A hard thirty, too; every time those guys saw me, they would hit me again, and after a while, other guys in the jail began to take a poke at me, too, just for fun. It became a kind of fad. Another week and I would have been unable to walk out when my time was up.

That's not the reason I skipped out on my court date, either. Maybe being punch-drunk had something to do with it. But the bad stuff, the really bad stuff, went down after I got out of county the second time.

(It occurred to me more than once that I should just move to Riverhead, so I wouldn't have so far to go when I got out of jail. Believe me, I know guys who have done this.)

I got a ride back to Comapogue from somebody I met in the joint. My car was still in back of the HiLite, the battery still dead, and I didn't have a fucking nickel. I had the guy drop me off by the nail salon where my old girlfriend worked. I hoped she wouldn't be too upset to see me, but at this point I had nowhere else to go.

The nail salon was a tiny little hole-in-the-wall—I suppose you don't need a lot of room to do nails—without a shadow in it, bright light shining everywhere. The nail girls all looked up quick and startled when I walked in, like browsing okapi on the Nature Channel when the lion walks into the picture. Then they went back to whatever they were doing. Except for Linda Scopolomini, my old girlfriend; she looked up, down, and then up again. She didn't seem real pleased to see me.

I gave a casual wave to reassure her. She looked at me and shook her head, shooting her eyes toward the babe whose nails she was working on. I understood; I sat down in a chair and picked up a magazine, ready to wait as long as it took.

After a few minutes, Linda came over and sat next to me.

"Johnnie, what are you *doin'* here?" she said in a strange, strangled voice. It was as if she was trying to shout at me, but so no one else would hear. "I axed you not to bother me at work. And where have you been, anyway? You haven't called me in six months."

Linda is a beautiful girl, and I had been in love with her since high school. She still wears her hair up, though, in a big bouffant do, like it was 1962. Her mother has the same hairstyle. It is really terrifying to eat dinner with the two of them. Their hairdos loom over you like a pair of floats from the Macy's parade.

Linda's hair hung over me now, and it disturbed my thought process. I found it hard to speak. Also her smell—after a while without a woman, her smell of soaps and makeup and girl went right to my brain.

Finally, I managed to pull my scattered head together and explain my situation. "Linda, I just got out of jail. And Linda, I really need a place to crash, at least for tonight. I'll get out in the morning, I promise, but right now I have nowhere else to go. I need you."

She stared back at me, frowning and fooling with stray curls of hair escaping from under her bouffant puff. After a while, she said in a quieter voice, "Okay, Johnnie, okay. You can stay on the couch. But just for tonight, all right? And don't think you can come back after six months, you never call me once, and then just everything will be the same as it was. Because it's not."

"I understand."

"Okay, good. Now get *outta* here. I get off work at five-thirty. Come back then and meet me. . . . No, wait. . . . Why don't you meet me at the Coma-Linden Diner? At around six o'clock?"

"Sure. Uh, Linda, I don't have any money for, like, a cup of coffee. If you could . . ."

"Jesus Christ," she said, "you never change." But she gave me five bucks.

———

It was hours until Linda got off. Now I had five bucks, but that wouldn't buy much, not even a pack of smokes. Better save it for the diner, I thought.

I mooched up side streets toward Sunrise Highway, in the direction of the diner, wasting time, thinking about Linda, wishing I had a cigarette. Then, as if angels had suddenly answered my prayers, I saw a pack of Marlboro Lights lying on the sidewalk in front of me, still wrapped in cellophane.

I bent down and picked up the pack with extreme caution, expecting some kind of joke—a fishing line attached, cigarettes jerking down the sidewalk as I followed—but nothing happened. The cellophane was intact. I zipped the pack open; everything seemed to be in order.

Of course, I had no fucking matches.

Now, I said to myself, if angels are really looking out for my bad habits, there would be a book of matches on the ground. I looked around: no matchbooks. But there was a box lying in the entrance to the parking lot about six feet ahead of me that looked familiar somehow. I went over and picked it up: a box of matchbooks, the kind store owners put next to the register for their customers to take.

Yes, it was spooky. Too fucking spooky. Cue the *Twilight Zone* theme.

A few feet beyond the matches lay another pack of cigarettes, Kools this time. I began to get suspicious again—*Candid Camera*, reality TV, some elaborate practical joke? Not angels, probably. But I picked up the Kools without incident, and scanned the parking lot. There was a trail of trash leading across it. Following it, I picked up two more packs of smokes and saw a strange assortment of things: slices of pastrami and smoked turkey breast—one of my favorites—Swiss cheese, American cheese, globs of potato salad, a bag of chips, chewing gum, kaiser rolls. It looked like a lunch wagon had sprung a leak.

The trail of delicatessen seemed to lead toward a Mercury Montego parked in the back corner of the lot. I walked toward it, keeping my head down, looking for more cigarettes. When I was about ten feet away, the driver's window rolled down.

"Yo, douche bag! The fuck you doin' here?"

And I recognized the voice of my lawyer.

I walked over to the car—a big mistake. Bug Rankin, the public defender for my ugliest conviction, the display of obscene materials one, was at the wheel. I hadn't seen or heard from him in a year, since he lost my case after the bookstore bust.

Rankin popped open the passenger door. "Get in, douche bag! How you been?"

I peered into the Montego. There were two guys in the backseat holding bags of groceries.

"My partners," Rankin said, "Hector and Alfredo."

"How you doin', man?" The Spanish guy leaned forward and shook my hand. The other guy just sat and stared at me around the cartons of cigarettes sticking up out of his shopping bag.

"Hector, Alfredo, hey," I said, sliding into the front seat next to Rankin. I had a feeling of doom come over me like a wet raincoat, but it was like I was helpless. It's always that way.

"Want somethin' to eat?" Hector offered. "Make yourself a san'wich, man." He handed me a large uncut roll of turkey breast and an open loaf of white bread.

The other guy, Alfredo, leaned forward now.

"He calls you 'douche bag'?" he said, tilting his head toward Rankin. "That's your *name*?"

"My name's LoDuco, Johnnie LoDuco. He just calls me that," I said.

Rankin grinned. "Low Douche Bag."

Alfredo still seemed bothered. "And you let him? You let him call you that?"

"But I wasn't part of it!" I complained to the lawyer assigned to me. "I only stopped to talk to Rankin! I had nothing to do with stealing the cigarettes!"

The public defender glanced up at me; he looked tired, very, very tired.

"I believe you, Johnnie," he said. "I really do. Because it seems like the kind of pointless, fucked-up thing that would happen to someone like you. But you have to understand that no one else—*no one else*—will ever believe it."

"Rankin will back me up," I said. "Ask him! He'll tell you I just walked up to shoot the shit five minutes before it all went down."

The PD held up his pen like a chinning bar and rested his chin on it, looking at me.

"I did ask Rankin."

"And?"

"He says it was all your idea, that they just wanted something to eat, and it was you who suggested going back for the cigarettes."

I was nearly speechless.

"Fuck. Shit."

"I think if this case goes to trial," the PD said, "there is a risk all four of you will get the max. But I'll talk to the DA, see if I can make a deal."

He told me that would probably be one year on a plea bargain, out in eight months if I behaved myself, and that I would be lucky if it wasn't more.

"Your record's not bad," he told me, speed-reading through the contents of a manila folder. "No priors." No serious felonies, he meant. He glanced up. "But it's not good, either. It doesn't inspire confidence."

"Of course, these charges—B and E, criminal trespass, possession of stolen property—are felonies. We are not talking two weeks in county for this."

By "we," of course, he meant me.

My sheet was small stuff, aside from the one conviction for displaying obscene materials. Okay, that: I sold an underage kid a stroke book at the time when our local assemblyman was pushing a hot political campaign against porn. I got crucified. The owner of the adult store I worked at knew somebody or paid somebody, or both. He got off. I got time in county, and my picture in the papers as a smut peddler.

The PD gathered up his papers, shot a look at his watch, and was out the door. He paused, one hand on the door frame.

"I should be able to cut a deal," he said. "The DA wants Rankin bad, since he is like an officer of the court, and they want to make an example. Maybe, who knows, they won't go after you so hard."

"Let's hope not," I said. He nodded briskly and disappeared.

"Five years! Five fucking years!"

"It was the best I could do," the PD said. "I don't know what's with them; they really have a bug up their ass for this Rankin. You got the overflow. It just wasn't your lucky day." He looked down at his notebook, paused, and scribbled something, something almost certainly about his next case. I was history as far as he was concerned. He looked up, like he was surprised to see me still sitting there.

"Okay, we don't take the deal. We let it go to trial," he said. "Look, you never know with juries. Maybe they'll feel sorry for you. Maybe you'll get off. And even if they do convict, it's all up to the judge. He might reject their recommendations, give you less time."

"Or more," I said. I was not optimistic.

The PD shrugged. He glanced wistfully at the door. "Johnnie, what's the difference? If you don't go down for this, it'll be something else, right? Time is your destiny."

My arraignment sucked, too. I was tired of sitting around in jail, waiting for someone to hit me in the face. But the DA convinced the judge I was a flight risk—I could have told him my car wouldn't get me very far—and my bail was set at $100,000.

This was a little more than I had on me at the time.

"Trial's scheduled for next month," the PD informed me. "Look, three, four weeks in county, you're used to it, right? You've been there before."

"I've been there before," I said, "and I don't like it."

The PD shrugged. "What can I say, Johnnie? Maybe someone will bail you out."

"No, Johnnie, I can't, I just can't! I want to, but I can't," Linda Scopolomini said. "I want to help you, Johnnie. But where would I get that kind of money?"

I knew she would say that.

"You don't need to. Just go to a bail guy, a bondsman. He'll lend the money. All you got to do is put something up to secure it," I told her. "Linda, look, I can't just sit around here waiting for my trial. I have to be out in the world, organizing my defense." Whatever that would be. "Besides, I think my life is in danger."

"Oh Johnnie!" She started to sob. "I want to help you, really."

"What if you use the house as collateral?"

"The house? I can't do that. It isn't mine! Besides, my mom has a second mortgage on it already, and she took out lots of cash."

Sunlight broke through the clouds.

"Your mom! Could she lend me the money?"

There was a long silence.

"Johnnie, I don't think so," Linda said after a while. She had stopped sobbing. "Mom and her new boyfriend went to Atlantic City after she took out the mortgage. She's been really weird since they got back. She won't tell me, but Johnnie, I don't think there is any money. I think they lost it all."

Fuck.

"Johnnie, I'm sorry, I really am." There was another long pause, filled with Linda's wet breathing. I was out of ideas.

"Johnnie, be careful, okay? Take care of yourself," Linda said. "I'll come visit you in jail. Okay?"

"Sure. Okay."

She hung up.

So after this, it was very depressing to meet Rankin and his compadres as they were heading out the door.

"Hey, too bad, Johnnie, too bad," Bug Rankin said, patting me on the back. "I'll make some calls, I get outside, see if I can help you."

I knew he wouldn't.

"How did you assholes make bail, anyway?" I asked.

Bug Rankin shrugged.

"DA only asked for five thousand. I thought we'd get out on personal recog, because I am like an officer of the court, but no such luck. Still, not so bad, huh? Depends on who you know."

Unfortunately, I didn't know anybody.

"It was easy, man," Hector put it. "No problem. I spend more money on clothes, you know?"

So after all this, I was surprised when a deputy came over to my bunk and told me to get my things.

I didn't have any things, so that part was easy.

"What's up?" I asked, expecting something fucked. But I was wrong for once.

"You're out, LoDuco. Somebody went your bail." He turned around and walked away before I could ask any more questions. I scurried after him.

The clerk who signed me out didn't know much more.

"You don't even know who bailed you out?" This fact seemed to reach him through his boredom and disgust. He shook his head and almost smiled. "That's amazing."

"But you know, right?" I asked him. He shrugged.

"The bond came from Canetti's. Ask him."

Donnie Canetti, the bail bondsman, had a chest that stretched his T-shirt to capacity, a bald head, and a Fu Manchu mustache. He looked more like a pizza chef than like anyone connected to the court system. He was looking at me with real disgust.

"I told him he was a fucking idiot," Canetti said. "But he didn't listen to me."

"Who was it?" I asked for about the third time, but Canetti wasn't ready to tell me yet.

"But it's not just the money. It's more than that," Canetti said, for probably the first time in his life. He shook his head as if it were surrounded by biting gnats. "I know the guy. I trust him. I know he's good for it. I don't have a problem with that. It's you I have a problem with."

He stared at me some more, his eyes glistening. I think for fifty cents he would have belted me across the mouth.

The problem was, I knew Canetti from way back. He'd been friends with my father. He had known me for a long time and had already formed his opinion.

"It's that, I look at you, and I think, A guy like this, he won't come back. *You won't come back.* Even if you want to, you won't show. A guy like you. Even if you want to, you mean to, it doesn't make any difference. You'll find some way to fuck it up. You'll forget or get lost or something. I *know* this. I told him this. And then I am out a hundred thousand dollars. And your friend loses his house. What do I want with a fucking house?"

Canetti stared at me with deep unhappiness.

"My dad always spoke well of you," I said.

This did nothing to cheer him up.

"Your father. Your father, Christ, if he could see you, he'd be turning in his grave."

What could I say to that? I shrugged.

"Spinning like a fucking crankshaft. You piece of shit." Canetti was getting worked up, carried away by his own eloquence. Tiny foam bubbles flecked the corners of his mouth. "You worthless piece of shit. You know that?"

I shrugged again.

"Who was it, Canetti? Who paid for my bail? That's all I want to know. Can't you just tell me?"

Canetti glared at me, looked away, sighed.

"He asked me not to tell you. I don't blame him. I wouldn't want you coming around to where I live, fucking my life up. I wouldn't want you to know where I live."

"I don't know where you live," I pointed out.

"I know your parents since we were kids," he said, pointing a fat sausagelike finger at my chest. His eyes popped out and started glistening again. "Remember, scumbag, I know where *you* live! I know where you drink. I know where you park. When you scratch your balls, I know how many times. I can find you in a minute. So *you will show up.* You will."

"Of course," I said.

"*Of course,*" he repeated. The two words seemed to make him sick.

Just then, the door burst open and a large guy came into the room. He was tall, about six three or four; each shoulder looked capable of filling Canetti's T-shirt by itself. The big guy had a strange haircut, shaved up on the sides and back, a wad of hair left on top. It looked like a divot on top of a flesh-colored bowling ball. He had a skimpy little soul patch that started in the middle of his chin and didn't quite get to the bottom.

Canetti's eyes glinted happily. "Stosh!" he said.

The large guy nodded. "Canetti. Got something for you."

"Sure, sure, in a minute" Canetti said. "I want you to meet some-one. Stosh, meet Johnnie LoDuco. Johnnie, Stosh Budjynski." He waved his hands between us, graceful as a party host welcoming someone onto his yacht.

Stosh turned his eyes on me. I could see him take me in, analyze me, categorize me, and dismiss me, all in seconds. It was scary to see that much beef apparently connected to a brain.

"Pleasure," Stosh said in a quiet, furry voice. He held out an enormous fucking hand.

"Johnnie, I hope, I really hope this is the last time you ever have to meet Stosh," Canetti said.

"Same here," I said. "No offense. Really, nice to meet you, Stosh. You work for Mr. Canetti?"

"Sometimes." Stosh shook hands very carefully. I appreciated that.

"Stosh is a bounty hunter, Johnnie," Canetti explained. He seemed to be enjoying life again. "But you will never meet him in his professional capacity, right?"

"Of course not."

Real jail time: I couldn't handle it. "I can do the time," I muttered to myself, trying it on like a con in the movies. But there was no point in pretending that I wasn't bummed. I could not do five years. I didn't think I could do five days anymore, after that whackfest in county.

In some ways, of course, jail was a natural for me. Sitting around on a bed or couch, doing nothing for days on end, pretty much described my lifestyle anyway. But the reality is that you are not left alone in jail. To be left alone, you have to work pretty hard and full-time at it. And I doubted that I had what it took to achieve jail solitude.

And while there is truth to the idea that we are all in prison anyway, that jail just shows you how much this is true, this point of view made me want to kill myself, not go to jail.

So I was pretty sure I would not show up in court. It was too bad about Donnie Canetti, an old friend of my dad. And my mystery benefactor, whoever he was. And really too bad about Stosh. But I felt I had no real choice. I wasn't living at my parents' house anymore anyway, though I put down that address, and it was still on my driver's license. My brothers had sold the place six months ago. I had no fixed address. I was nowhere—in so many ways.

I'll just take my chances with Stosh or whatever thug Canetti sends after me, I thought. Anything would be easier than more time inside. And if I ever found out who went my bail, I would pay him back. How, I wasn't clear on. But it's the thought that counts, right?

I mooched along the street between the bail-bond place and the courthouse, heading toward downtown Riverhead, not really going anywhere, just moving these hard possibilities through my head, getting used to them. Then someone spoke up right behind me.

"Hey, Johnnie!"

I knew that voice. I straightened up and turned around. Vinnie

McCloskey-Schmidt was standing there grinning at me like a demented car salesman.

"Johnnie boy, hey, how you doin'?" Vinnie didn't quite hug me,
but he grabbed each shoulder at arm's length and shook me back
and forth.

"Vinnie, hey, how you been?" I said, my voice wobbly from the
shoulder shaking. I hadn't seen Vinnie for a while; it seemed like we
kept running across each other at about two-year intervals. Of
course, Long Island's not that big a place, especially if you confine
your activities to the same five or six bars, supermarkets, and video
stores.

We had been good friends, really good, close friends, in high
school. I spent a lot of quality time sitting stoned on the couch in his
parents' den, watching TV with the sound turned off as Vinnie sup-
plied the dialogue and narration. They were always better than the
original movie. That, and stealing cars.

Vinnie and I liked to steal cars back then. Most of them we just
drove around in and left somewhere. Occasionally, we would be
moved by high spirits to drive one off a dock, or tear-ass across
sand dunes until the car became completely bogged down, then
bury it.

We were little assholes, that's for sure. But we never got caught.

Things had changed.

"What're you doin' in Riverhead?" I asked him. "You're not in
the court system, are you?"

Vinnie looked away, up toward the county jail complex.

"Nah, I'm looking after something for a cousin of mine," Vinnie
said. He had thousands of cousins, I remembered, all versions of
one another. "What about you?"

"Ah, Vinnie, you know," I said. I suddenly felt embarrassed. "I got
fucked. Fucked again. You know?"

Vinnie put his hand on my shoulder. "Sure, I understand. Look, you're done here, let's go get something to eat. My treat. Okay?"

Since I hadn't eaten anything but candy bars since I got out of jail, I wasn't about to turn him down.

CHAPTER TWO

AFTER LUNCH AT BERTOLLI'S Courthouse Diner—I had the veal parmigiana, which was pretty good—Vinnie drove me up to his new place. He lived up on the North Shore now, in a well-to-do kind of neighborhood, more like Westchester or New England than the part of Long Island we had grown up in.

There was basically just one road in Drunken Meadows, winding along the water. From time to time, I saw wooden street signs pointing down what looked like abandoned driveways leading into the woods. Vinnie said they were private roads. You couldn't see many houses, only trees and grass and water.

"Quaint," I muttered, and I meant it.

We drove by some nice houses, backed up against spectacular views of Long Island Sound, surrounded by a couple acres of lawn and hedge.

"Who lives around here?" I asked Vinnie.

He shrugged. "Doctors, lawyers, investors. CEOs. Murphy, the Dumpster king, has the house at the end of the road, near me. You can see his neon leprechaun at night."

Vinnie turned the Range Rover in at a driveway nearly at the end of the street. A long, low ranch-type house sat at the end of the drive; beyond it you could see the Sound, and beyond that Connecticut. And if you looked down the street, sure enough, you could see Murphy's green neon leprechaun on the roof of his house, twenty feet tall, waiting for night.

"Vinnie, you done good for yourself," I said.

Vinne grinned, then shrugged. "Yeah, pretty good. Not much like Comapogue, huh?"

Vinnie was doing computer stuff, high-tech stuff, he explained on the drive up from Riverhead. He made zillions during the dot-com boom, his start-up in Silicon Alley snapped up by venture capital before the paint was dry on the sign, well before it ever made a nickel. In fact, it never earned squat, but that didn't seem to bother anybody. Vinnie bought his house, cashed in his stock options, and watched from semiretirement as the industry all blew away like dry-ice fumes when the tech bubble burst.

"Now I'm starting over again, like a snail coming out of its shell," he told me.

"Brilliant," I said without sarcasm. "More Web stuff?"

Vinnie shook his head. "Nah, the crash scared all the money away from the Web. I'm programming again, writing software. That's how I started." He turned and grinned at me. "Bet you thought I was a geek, huh? In high school."

I shook my head in all honesty. I had never thought Vinnie was anything but a fucking genius the entire time I knew him, even when we were stealing cars. Everything he did, he did with flair, a style and touch that was all his own. I could only admire.

Vinnie's house was one of the modern kind that is all glass and stainless steel, about as comfortable as a morgue slab. I didn't say this, of course. The house was decorated mainly by its views, which were spectacular: endless blue water, framed by a few tree leaves and a small piece of lawn, maybe two or three acres of it.

We wandered around on the lawn like kings, sipping mixed drinks and admiring the view. A wooden bulkhead kept the grass from toppling into the Sound; Vinnie stood with one foot up on a piling, squinting out across the water. He sipped his drink; I sipped mine. Water sloshed against the bulkhead; wind tossed the tree branches around.

Neither of us said anything for a while. Then Vinnie looked over at me.

"Here we are, huh? The two of us." He grinned. "Can you believe it?"

I couldn't. But then, I wasn't really there, just a ghost of Vinnie's whim.

"Two worthless punks from the South Shore, I mean," Vinnie explained.

I nodded. "Fucking car thieves."

"Losers. Morons. Yet here we are." Vinnie giggled, choked on his drink. I began to laugh, too. It was ridiculous.

"What if they find out?" I said, beginning to giggle uncontrollably. We both knew who "they" were.

"They'll never find out," Vinnie said, choking on his laughter now. We leaned against each other, laughing helplessly, though a voice in my head kept nagging at me: What are you laughing at?

"Never," Vinnie said, wiping his mouth with the sleeve of his expensive suit.

"So how about you, Johnnie?" Vinnie said to me. "How are you? I mean, how are you really? What's been going on in your life since the last time I saw you?"

I had told him about my court date over lunch but held back the nasty details. Now I told him everything—about stealing the battery, going down with the cold cuts gang, Canetti, the mystery money-man, looming jail time, how I just couldn't go back to jail, what Stosh would probably do to me, how I didn't care.

When I finished, Vinnie looked at me with big concerned eyes.

"Maybe you'll get off."

"Vinnie." I was a little disappointed in him. Maybe I hadn't explained things carefully enough. "I won't get off."

Vinnie looked down into his drink for a while, frowning. We were sitting in big metal lawn furniture now—not the kind you buy in K mart, but solidly built stuff, probably worth more than my parents' house. The twisted metal in the chair back dug into me in a hundred places.

"No, if I were you, I would *not* go," Vinnie said, taking the little Japanese umbrella thing out of his drink and throwing it on the lawn. I had taken mine out right away. "I would definitely not go to jail." His eyes slid away from me; he stared at the fallen umbrella as if it might try to get away.

We stared at the umbrella together for a while. But something was bothering me, gnawing at the fringes of my brain like a starving mouse.

"Vinnie, was that you, that went my bail at Canetti's?"

I figured it had to be; I just didn't know anybody else with a house.

Vinnie watched the umbrella some more, then looked up at me with a tight little grin.

"Would I be advising you to jump bail if I'd paid for it?"

I laughed nervously. "No, I guess not."

"I don't throw money away like that."

I knew it was him, though; who else could it be? I didn't want to embarrass the guy, but I didn't want him to lose his house on my account.

"Yeah, well, I would hate to stiff this guy, whoever he is," I stumbled on delicately. "But I just can't go back to jail."

Vinnie squinted up at me, serious and thoughtful.

"It's your call. Tell you what, though. Why don't you come stay here?" he said. "At my house. Until you decide what to do. You know, Johnnie, I might be able to help you."

I liked the idea. I had already decided what not to do, but deciding to actually do something might take some time. Vinnie's glass palace would be a nice place to spend that time.

"Sure," I said, "and thanks, man."

The sun went down. The bugs came out and chased us into the house. My forehead was covered with lumps from mosquito bites. It felt like I was about to sprout devil horns. The bugs seemed to leave Vinnie alone, for some reason.

Everything in Vinnie's house was made of metal and glass, even the chairs. The big dining room table we were sitting at was all stainless steel, with a thick slab of green glass for a top. It looked good, I have to say. But I had never been so uncomfortable, not since my parents made me go to church. The metal chairs were harder than church pews; my ass was permanently asleep, perhaps broken for life.

The table was set like for dinner at a restaurant, with folded napkins, clear glass plates, five or six forks at each place.

"Why all the forks?" I hated to display my ignorance, but I can never keep my mouth shut.

"The fuck knows," Vinnie said. He wasn't engaged by the forks. "Jennifer likes the table set. I think it's just to intimidate people."

He was sticking one of the forks into a big squash or gourd thing on a plate in the middle of the table, surrounded by littler squash things, like a dog with puppies.

"Jennifer? Who's Jennifer?"

Vinnie had been slumping over in his chair as we talked, killing the squash. But now he straightened up.

"Jennifer Smeals. My girlfriend. I want you to meet her. She is very cool." He looked around the room as if he were seeing it for the first time.

"This whole house was her idea, you know," he told me. "She picked it out, decorated it. I would probably just've stayed in the apartment in Brooklyn."

I had been wondering about that.

"It impresses people," Vinnie said.

I was impressed. "It's got great views," I said.

We spent the rest of the night talking about me. I hated that. But Vinnie had taken up my case now. Now that he was thinking about it, he began to have lots of ideas.

"You're too serious, Johnnie," Vinnie said to me. "You take things too personal. You can't be too serious about Long Island and survive. Some places will destroy you the hard way: it's not like that here, not like Manhattan, or Miami, or Vegas. Nothing dramatic. Here you just go numb, a little at a time. Then one day, you wake up and you don't care anymore. Then you'll never get away. Believe me, I've seen it happen."

"I believe you," I told him. "But Vinnie, this is the thing: I was born numb."

He just shook his head. "No, no. Not you, Johnnie."

"Anyway, Vinnie, you're still here," I pointed out. "You're not numb. You're one of the least numb people I have ever known. Yet you're still here."

Vinnie smiled and ducked his head. "Ah, but not for long, Johnnie, not for long."

"What, you moving back into the city?"

"Uh-uh. South America. I got a business deal to do down there. Paraguay. When I finish that up, I don't know. I thought I might look around down there, maybe stay there awhile. Maybe permanently." He became thoughtful again, jabbing the fork into the ornamental squash thing until it finally broke into pieces. He pushed the whole mess away from him; it nearly fell on the floor. Vinnie didn't seem to notice.

"I want to set up something down there," he said, "maybe move all my operations there. I've been thinking this through. And it just occurred to me that you could come with me! Take you down there, get you out of the country, set you up in Paraguay."

"Paraguay," I said. I had only the vaguest idea where Paraguay was.

"Yeah!" Vinnie was warming up to his idea now, his eyes getting wider, his gestures broader. "You know, the thing about Paraguay is, they don't have any extradition treaty with the U.S."

I nodded. I remembered hearing something about that somewhere. That was why the place was full of Nazis and bank robbers.

"Now your beef is not very serious, the way you describe it," Vinnie went on. "I can't imagine they would even bother to look for you once you made it to Paraguay."

I hated to burst his balloon.

"Vinnie," I said, "I'm sorry, but I don't have any money. I don't know how to do anything. I don't even speak Spanish. What would I do in Paraguay?"

"You'd work for me," Vinnie said, filled with confidence. I had always admired Vinnie's certainty.

"What would I do?"

"Administrate. It's simple; I'll show you. You don't speak Spanish?"

I shook my head.

"Don't worry about it; you'll learn. Anyway, most of the people you'll be dealing with will understand English."

I wasn't so sure that would help. Since it would still be me who'd be speaking it to them, I mean.

"Vinnie, what is it exactly that you do now?" I asked him. "If you're not doing the Web thing anymore, I mean. Because I don't know anything about computers, you know."

"You won't have to. You'll administrate."

"Yeah, but what? I mean, what kind of business?"

Vinnie looked around the table; I think he wanted to start stabbing the squash again, but it was out of reach. Finally, he said, "It's a billing agency."

"A billing agency—you mean like debt collectors?" I did have some experience there, even if it was on the receiving end.

"No, no, credit card billing. Look."

I looked.

"I wrote this program," Vinnie said. "It's running on billing computers all over Long Island now."

"What does it do?"

"Look," Vinnie said again, "every time anyone on Long Island uses their credit card, a fraction of every dollar goes to a bank account. *My* bank account."

"Does it show up on their bill?"

Vinnie shook his head. "Nope. It's invisible. The amount is folded into the charge. But it's such a small amount, a few pennies, a dollar maybe, no one ever questions it."

"But just a couple pennies," I said. "That's not much."

"A couple pennies *on every credit card bill*," Vinnie said. He was getting quietly excited. "Johnnie, this is Long Island. There are two and a half million people living here. Exclusive of Queens and Brooklyn, I mean."

"Of course."

"Two and a half million people. And all they do is shop. Shop, shop, shop. That's all there is to do on Long Island. Boats, cars, washer/dryers, home theaters, security systems. Shop, shop, shop. Gas stations, Seven-Elevens, pork stores, nail salons—no limit. And every time anyone buys anything with a credit card, I get a penny, two pennies, a nickel." He sat back. "It adds up."

I thought about it. I could see Vinnie's point.

"About how much does it add up?"

"Lots."

" 'Lots'?"

"Lots and lots. Millions."

"Holy shit."

Vinnie nodded.

I kept adding in my head.

"Holy fucking shit."

Vinnie smiled broadly.

"And that's just Long Island. I have plans. I hope to expand to Jersey, Connecticut. The tristate area, Johnnie, the tristate area!"

"Man!"

"And after that, the whole fucking U.S.A.!"

"Wow," I marveled. "Paraguay?"

Vinnie shook his head. "Not Paraguay. Paraguay will be the billing center. I don't want to mess it up."

" 'Mess it up'?" My little brain chewed on this. "Vinnie, this billing, this two cents on every dollar thing."

He nodded expectantly.

"People don't know about it? They can't tell?"

He shook his head.

"What about the companies, the credit card companies? Do they know about it?"

Vinnie shook his head. He grinned.

"But what happens when they figure it out?"

"We'll be long gone," Vinnie said. "Safe and warm in Paraguay."

There was a dog on the glass-topped coffee table in Vinnie's living room, a plastic dog that looked somewhere between a bloodhound and a dachshund. The dog's head bobbed up and down when Vinnie picked it up.

"For Jennifer," Vinnie said thoughtfully. "I'd like you to meet her."

"I'd like to," I said. "What's she like?"

"Long black hair," Vinnie said. "A doctor. She's really smart. I like that in a woman. But sexy, too." He put the dog down. "I'd like you to meet all my friends, Johnnie. They could help you."

I nodded vigorously. I needed help.

"I know you're in trouble now. But that won't matter. It's small stuff. They are tolerant people. They recognize ability when they see it. That's what they value."

I wondered what they'd think when they saw me. But I let Vinnie continue saving me from my life. I didn't think he could do it, but I liked seeing him try.

"You, you're a poet, Johnnie," Vinnie said. "That's your problem. A poet in this world." Vinnie looked pensively at the bobbing-head dog figure, poking it with his index finger. "Whatever happened to that screenplay you were writing?"

"Oh, that," I said. "I discovered a problem with it."

"What was the problem?"

"It was a piece of shit."

Vinnie nodded, not disagreeing. After a while, he said, "Your poems were good, though. Remember those poems you wrote in high school?"

"Ah." It embarassed me to talk about this. "I stopped writing poems."

"Didn't you get something published, though? I thought I heard something like that."

"A couple books."

"What kind of books? Novels?"

"Novels." *Lesbian Cannibal Nuns* was one title. *The Sisterhood of the Tongue* was another. So bizarre, I was almost proud of them. *She-Male Vengeance* was more typical of my oeuvre. *The Dong Meister. Night Nurse in Bondage.* And so on down the tubes.

"Tell me the titles. I'll look out for them."

Fortunately, Vinnie was obviously not sincere, and I spared myself further humiliation by shining this on.

"I think I still have copies somewhere," I said. "I'll send you some."

"Autographed?" When Vinnie smiled the way he did now, you had to love him.

"You bet. Inscribed."

Though he seemed to have forgotten about it, it was Vinnie who had put me in touch with Fat Al Rugosa, the porno king of the South Shore, and kick-started my career as a pornographer and adult-bookstore clerk. Vinnie knew him somehow; Vinnie always knew everybody.

Writing stroke books was easy once I stopped using my own little jack-off fantasies and began using my imagination. The wilder the better—there was nothing I ever thought of that didn't have a group of sweaty wild-eyed fans somewhere, glad their personal perversions were finally being catered to.

Eating economy-size family-pack bottles of amphetamines helped, too. A couple weekends of frantic total typing, and voilà: a box of weird filth, for which Fat Al would see I got five hundred bucks.

"The clientele really likes your books," Fat Al told me once. He always referred to the furtive, silent men who lurched through his bookstores as "the clientele." "I can't keep 'em on the shelves."

"You should pay me more money, then," I pointed out.

Fat Al was honestly surprised by this.

"Are you out of your fucking mind? Do you know what my overhead is on these books? You don't like the money, go sell them somewhere else. See what you get."

Since I didn't know anybody else in the market for vile third-rate pornography, and since the books kept me in rent, amphetamines, and cigarettes, I was happy enough. We just left it there.

I woke up in Vinnie's guest room—one of several guest rooms, in fact; the house was way too big for just one guy—sat up in a panic, and looked wildly around, until I remembered where I was, and that no one was going to walk out of the toilet and punch me in the face.

The guest room was in the back of the house, facing the water. One whole wall was a sliding glass door that opened onto a redwood deck. Everything in the room—everything in the house—was clean and sharp, so new that it hurt you to look at it.

I showered and shaved in the perfect little bathroom and changed my worn-out, greasy clothes for some of Vinnie's. "We used to be the same size, right?" he had said to me as he handed me a pile of clothes the night before. Vinnie was carrying a little more weight now, although not that much. The clothes fit me okay.

There was a note from Vinnie on the glass-topped dining table:

"Johnnie: make yourself at home, okay? I have to do some meetings. Be back P.M. Later. Vinnie."

So, okay, I had the house to myself. All I had to do was stay inside and not annoy the neighbors. Stay inside and attract no attention at all. I figured I could handle it.

The big-screen TV had a bank of speakers attached to it for that vooming, moving-sound experience, and I had cranked the volume up to take maximum advantage of the technology. That was why, probably, I didn't hear the door open or hear anyone walk in. And why, when I looked up and saw a tall woman with long black hair suddenly standing over me like the angel of death, I freaked. I sat up, eyes wide, mouth open.

"Holy shit!"

Truly smooth and elegant.

I grabbed the remote and punched the volume down. The black-haired woman smiled.

"You must be Johnnie. Vincent told me about you. I didn't realize you were actually *living* here."

Looking at her standing on the Tuscan-tile floor in white high heels, her dress some sort of layered, see-through brown chiffon, very elegant, I felt as if I had known this woman all my life. In fact, I was sure I had seen her somewhere before; the shape of her face, with her long black hair hanging down around it, long white nose poking out like an accusing finger, nagged at synapses in my brain, but they refused to light up.

I smoothed down my hair and shut my gaping mouth.

"And you must be Jennifer," I managed to say. I had forgotten her last name already. Or maybe Vinnie hadn't told me yet.

Jennifer stopped smiling and walked briskly across the room.

"Vincent told me he'd be away today," she called out to me without turning around. "But I came over anyway, to meet you."

"Well, any friend of Vinnie's," I said lamely.

She came back with a pair of drinks, something tropical with rum in it. A little too much for the time of day, I thought, not that I cared. But for a change, I kept my mouth shut. The drinks had those umbrellas in them, confirming my theory that they were her idea.

"Well, cheers," Jennifer said, hoisting her glass and smiling. Her teeth were white, large, and even. I had never seen such nice teeth.

"Cheers," I said. "Here's to friendship."

"So, what do you do, Jennifer?" I asked. We had almost gotten to the bottom of our drinks without saying much, and the silence was starting to build. I hate that.

Jennifer didn't say anything right away. Instead, she looked me over in a pretty thorough way, as if she were thinking of buying me but wasn't sure I was worth the money. Finally, she said, "Didn't Vincent tell you?"

"He told me you were a doctor," I said. "He didn't say what kind."

"That's right. I was a doctor." Emphasis on *was*.

"You don't look like a doctor," I told her.

She didn't exactly smile, but her lips moved. "What do I look like?"

I shrugged. "I dunno. Like you work in a bank or something."

Now she did smile, a big white smile that lasted. It played over me like a heat ray.

"Very good, Johnnie, very good. I *am* a banker."

I felt like I had won the prize. It broke the ice, anyway. Jennifer took out a cigarette—Benson & Hedges menthol—offered me one. We lit up. It seemed vaguely illegal to smoke in that sterile house, as if angry nurses or security guards would jump out and make you stub it. I looked around for an ashtray but ended up tipping my ash into some kind of ornamental vase with a sprig of flowers in it.

"You've known Vincent a long time," Jennifer said.

"Yeah, since we were kids. We grew up together, in the same town, down in Comapogue. That's between Copiague and Lindenhurst."

Jennifer nodded and smiled. I got the feeling Vinnie had filled her in very thoroughly on my bio.

"Vincent talks about you a lot, you know," she said. "All the things you did together when you were kids."

Not all of them, I hoped.

"You mean a lot to him, Johnnie," Jennifer said. "You're his connection to the life he used to live. You remind him of how far he's come."

I wasn't completely happy about this, but I had to admit I was a good reminder of what not to do.

"Vincent means a lot to *me*, Johnnie," she went on, squinting at me through the menthol smoke.

I wanted to say "Me, too," but it got stuck in my throat and I coughed and nodded instead. Menthols aren't really my smoke of choice.

"I hope we can be friends, Johnnie," Jennifer said. "To each other. Like we both are to Vincent."

I made noises of general agreement, shrugging and squirming on the leather sofa. I would have paid her twenty bucks to change the subject.

We both sat there quietly for a while, concentrating on our cigarettes.

"So, what are you doing now, Johnnie?" she asked. "Beyond your current problems, I mean. Vincent filled me in on that. But what were you doing before this run of bad luck?"

"Oh, this and that," I said, uncomfortable. I am always the last person to know the answer to that question. "I used to work in a bookstore. I was thinking about going back to that." In Guam, or Malaysia, I thought, but not on Long Island, not with five years hanging over me.

"Has he told you about Paraguay yet?"

"Oh yeah. That is, he told me he might be moving there, and he might have some work for me. But we didn't get into the details."

Jennifer folded her legs and smiled at the point of her high heel, jogging it up and down. She kept her eyes on her shoe as she spoke.

"You know, Vincent thinks the world of you, Johnnie. He'd like to help you. I hope you'll let him." Finally, she looked up at me. "He likes to help people. That's one of the things that drives him."

I was interested by this concept. "You know, Jennifer, I haven't seen Vinnie in a long time," I reminded her. "What other things drive him? I mean, what is he doing now? What is he working on?"

"Hasn't he told you?"

"Well, he told me about the credit card billing thing," I said. She looked surprised for a split second, as if maybe he wasn't supposed to have told me about that, then recovered herself and smiled at me. She had those really good teeth.

"That's a part of it, yes. But not the most important part."

"Okay," I said, though millions of dollars accumulating two cents at a time seemed important to me. "What is?"

"Well," Jennifer said, and even I could hear the shitload of hesitation and qualification she was piling on, "he's working with international investors on a number of different projects now. All computer-related, of course."

"Of course. Software?"

She nodded. "And he's on the point of going out on his own, expanding into different areas—different markets."

"Different countries?"

She nodded again. "What he's setting up now could be a major undertaking." She leaned forward to stub out her cigarette, very nearly sliding off the couch. She unfolded her legs for balance; they were very nice legs, strong and shapely. I sucked the last of my drink out from around the ice cubes, trying to stay focused on what she was saying.

"Really major." She looked up at me to emphasize this. "And you could be part of it. Vincent wants you to be. Are you ready?"

"I think so," I said, which was, for me, a positive statement.

"But, like," I bumbled on, "I'm still not clear on what it is Vinnie wants me to do."

"He'll fill you in. All in good time. But first, he has to know if you're willing to be a part of this." She gave me the direct stare again, blanking out most of my thought process. "Are you a player?"

I was cool. I stared back at her a moment, slugged down the meltwater out of my drink, put the glass down on the glass-topped coffee table, and nodded.

"You bet," I said.

You wish, I thought.

Vinnie came home a couple hours later and scooped us both up—me and Jennifer. You could tell he liked having the two of us there. Vinnie is one of those people whose personality gets bigger the more people he has around him. I'm just the opposite. The more people around, the smaller I feel. If enough people came into the room, I think I would just disappear.

"I want you two to know each other!" Vinnie said, his arms around us. "I want you to love each other as much as I love both of you!"

Jennifer's smile was pretty weak. I think she was wondering how long it would take to warm up to me. As far as me loving Jennifer, what was the point? I found it pretty embarassing.

Vinnie dragged us to a new restaurant a couple towns over, right on the water. It was loud, crowded, and more expensive than anyplace I had ever eaten at in my life. I ordered duck in pomegranate sauce. I liked duck. But the food, when it finally came, was inedible. My duck leg was hard as the head on a rubber mallet. I couldn't tell if it was way overcooked or not cooked at all.

I looked up from my tough duck and glanced over at Vinnie and Jennifer. They weren't eating, either. Jennifer's steak was haggled into bits, but she wasn't putting any in her mouth. I could smell Vinnie's fish from where I was sitting; it had a nasty smell, like someone had spritzed it with ammonia.

"This is just the beginning, Johnnie," Vinnie said. I didn't think he meant the food.

A lot of the time that first week after I arrived at Drunken Meadows, both Vinnie and Jennifer were out of the house, busy somewhere, setting things up, "taking meetings," as Vinnie said. Meetings with who, he never told me. I was left to take care of myself. That meant I slept really late and watched daytime TV until my brain was numb.

I suppose I should have been learning Spanish or something, finding out more about computers than how to turn them on and off. But I figured I would have lots of time for that once we got to Paraguay.

CHAPTER THREE

VINNIE'S TELEVISION SITUATION WAS truly superb. There were TVs in every room. There was even a screen in the bathroom so you could watch on the shitter.

The best one, of course, was the TV in the living room, where I spent most of my time. Six feet tall and about an inch thick, it was hard to figure out what kept it upright. It looked like you could roll it up like a rug and carry it under your arm.

It was cool, too, to see the large-size figures on the screen, so much more real than anything in my life up to that point.

The morning after our big dinner, I was sacked out on the leather sofa—about the only thing in the room not made out of glass and steel. I wasn't really paying attention to what was on the screen; my mind was occupied with Vinnie's Paraguay offer. Of course I would take it; what else could I do? But I wondered about South America, Paraguay: Would I like it there? What was the weather like? Pizza and bagels—did they have everything bagels there? And could I remember more than a fistful of curse words in Spanish? I found myself wishing I'd paid more attention in Spanish class; that, of course, would have meant attending it once in a while. I picked up more Spanish in jail than I learned in four years of high school.

So at first, the woman flitting across the TV screen caught my eye without my conscious mind understanding why. It was like an itch in my brain. I began to focus on the screen again.

Some sort of infomercial was in progress; I could see that from the quality of the video, that strange effect where reality seems so much less convincing than good videography, so fake.

A man in a white coat was leaning over someone in a barber chair. Except that it looked like a doctor's office, with shiny metal tools and hypodermics laid out on a white cloth, medicine cabinets in the background.

Then a quick cut to the top of a guy's head. The voice-over was talking about how natural and undetectable it was, "it" obviously being a hair transplant of some sort. Then there were some quick cuts to smiling guys swimming, jogging, dancing with beautiful women in nightclubs, their hair thick and immobile.

"Our trained staff of medical specialists will see that your hair-replacement strategy is perfectly matched to your original hair shape, thickness, and color," the voice-over said. The screen showed the specialists bustling about in white coats, looking very serious. One of the white-coated figures was Jennifer Smeals. I knew I had seen her somewhere before.

"Sure, that was her." Vinnie frowned slightly, as if I were out of line to bring it up. "She used to work in a hospital, of course. But she had some problems and had to leave."

"Problems? What kind of problems?"

Vinnie shrugged dismissively. "Oh, drugs, some other stuff. She is a doctor, a *real* doctor. Look, anyone can fall down. It's how you pick yourself up and move on, right? You, of all people, should know that."

"I'm not criticizing her," I said. "I'm just curious is all."

"She had a drug problem," he explained. "That's what led her to do it."

"To do what?"

"She blackmailed the head of the hospital. She was supplying him. It's surprising how many physicians are addicts." Vinnie paused and rubbed his chin thoughtfully. "A real scourge, drugs."

I tried to nudge him back on track. "So he turned her in?" I asked.

Vinnie shook his head. "Oh no, she had him good. Too good. Like Marion Barry videos, the whole thing. The guy embezzled a ton of money from the hospital to pay her off, and he got caught. Everything came apart, and Jennifer got sucked into it. She was lucky; she was able to work with the DA as a witness to bring down the hospital guy. She only got two years, out in six months. But it was not good for her medical career."

"And that's how she ended up at the hair-replacement clinic? I thought she was some kind of banker."

"She *is* a banker," Vinnie said. "She left the clinic after the infomercial was made, went into financial services. A real loss to medicine. She was a genius at hair replacement, you know. Look at this." He bent his head down and rubbed a hand in his hair so that it all hung down every which way. "See that? Can you tell? Could you tell that's not my own hair?"

I could tell. I knew guys who had thicker hair on their backs. But it was hair, and it looked human, if a bit thin and scraggly, so I said, "No, I would never have known if you hadn't told me."

———

But Vinnie being Vinnie, I wasn't allowed to stay in my big-screen-TV cocoon for long.

The next day, when I had barely finished my breakfast—Dunkin' Donuts and coffee regular, which Jennifer had brought over—Vinnie rolled into the kitchen and stood there smiling at me, hyperreal and overwhelming, like a daytime TV talk-show host.

"Paraguay briefing," he announced. "Ten o'clock in the conference room. Be there or be square." He was gone before I had completely registered his appearance.

The conference room was in a part of the house I hadn't been in yet—the house was pretty big and sprawled all over the place. There was a long oval table, made out of wood for a change, and ten or a dozen chairs covered with Naugahyde or something that looked like leather but smelled like WD-40.

Vinnie stood at the head of the table. He was dressed up—suit and tie—hair combed, everything, as if Jennifer Smeals and I were a whole roomful of corporate money boys hanging on his every word.

Vinnie was explaining to us who we would be in the new life.

"You," he said, pointing to me, "you are Kenny Moleri, thirty-five years old, of Patchogue, New York. You were born the twenty-eighth of March, 1969. . . ."

"Hey, so was I!" I said brightly. Vinnie stood there as if someone had hit the pause button, waiting for me to finish. Jennifer looked at me with disgust.

When he saw I wasn't going to say anything else, Vinnie started again.

"Kenny Moleri, thirty-five, computer security adviser. You went to Pace College, got a degree in computer science. Did you ever get to college, Johnnie?"

I shrugged. "Two semesters at Suffolk Community. Make that one and a half."

"So you know what it's like. Remember that. You"—he pointed at Jennifer, who smiled uncertainly—"you are Melina Bain, chief financial officer of the company. You went to Harvard Business School." He tapped a pile of papers lying on the table. "Employed after that in several of Wall Street's top brokerages. Memorize these." He pushed the stack of papers over to her.

"Vincent, is all this really necessary?" Jennifer asked him, leafing through the stack in a depressed kind of way. "Why do we have to tell anyone what we're doing? Why can't we just do it?"

"People will wonder," Vinnie said. "People will talk. It's better to have a story."

"What if they see the story's bullshit?" I asked. That's how it usually worked for me.

"Then you have a second story. And a third in back of that."

I got it. "And one in back of that?"

Vinnie nodded. "Stories out the wazoo. No end in sight."

"What's your story, Vincent?" Jennifer asked.

"My story: I am Vincent McCloskey-Schmidt," Vinnie said. "Software inventor. Venture capitalist. I represent the chance for a poor, flea-bitten Third World country to climb on board the great American economic success train."

"And in back of that?" I was such a wiseass.

"Back of that?" Vinnie looked at me, a funny expression in his eyes. I wondered if he was thinking of hitting me.

"Back of that," Vinnie said, "I think I am Johnnie LoDuco." He grinned at me. So did Jennifer.

"Who is Johnnie LoDuco?" she said, sounding like a *Jeopardy* contestant. Then she broke up laughing.

So did Vinnie. So did I.

We laughed ourselves sick.

———

"Oh, by the way," Vinnie called to me as I was heading for the TV couch one morning. "There's some info I need from you."

"Sure, Vinnie," I said, plopping myself down in one of the glass slab chairs. "What is it? What do you need?"

"Date of birth, place of birth, eye color, Social Security, like that."

I scribbled it down. "This is for, like, an ID?"

"Something like that. A passport."

I stopped scribbling and looked up.

"Don't I have to, I don't know, fill out forms and go to the post office for that?"

"Not for this passport. Not for this guy. I'm having them done special, for all of us." He grinned, completely happy and full of himself. "Matching passports for the three of us."

"What about a photo?"

Vinnie snapped his fingers. "You're right. We'll need one." He rubbed his chin, looking thoughtful. It occurred to me right then that Vinnie was always real but that he always added another layer, too, an as-if, heightened reality, on top of the real reality. Vinnie in stereo, split-screen video, both halves starring Vinnie.

"Jennifer has a camera," he said, "a digital one. That's useful. I can put them right into Photoshop."

"You? You're making these passports?"

Vinnie grinned. "Just the photos. The hard stuff, the skill work, I've contracted that out. Trust me. The guy I'm using is good, an expert, a true artist. His work would fool the CIA. And in Paraguay, no one is going to look too hard at an American passport."

The photos, when I finally saw them:

Me, of course, I looked like shit, dorky, furtive, an obvious "Please step over here, sir" kind of guy.

Jennifer looked great, with a brilliant smile like a tooth model, much better than she looked in the infomercial.

Vinnie, too, looked of movie-star quality, his energy and charisma vibrating out of the tiny photograph.

We made a great team, except for me.

Time passed in a blur of TV shows broken up by occasional forays into the outer world for pizza, doughnuts, beer. My "legal difficulties," as Vinnie called them, passed by in the distance, like thunderstorms far out on the Sound, headed for Connecticut, not me.

Vinnie and Jennifer were gone almost all the time now, sometimes not coming back to the house for days. I was okay with that. Vinnie kept me topped up with cash—not a lot, but more than I needed. My wants were simple and few. Mostly, I napped, did a little fishing off the dock in back, checked out porn sites on the Web.

I hung out.

Finally, the big day had almost arrived, Departure Day, the day when Vinnie and Jennifer would go on ahead to set things up in Paraguay.

"When everything is cooking along," Vinnie informed me, "when the local authorities seem to accept us, when I've got the groundwork in place, then it's your moment. You arrive. You set the place in order."

"I administrate," I said.

"That's it," Vinnie said. "That will free up Jennifer and me to network, outreach, spread the word, and rope in investors while you hold down the fort."

I was still not at all clear what this involved. But I had faith now. What Vinnie said would come to pass. All I had to do was go along for the ride. Anyway, my options on Long Island were rapidly evaporating. I wondered how long it would take Stosh to come after me.

With any luck at all, I would be long gone in Paraguay before he got a line on my whereabouts.

When Vinnie got back from one of his "meetings," he was always glowing. His body seemed swollen, about to pull apart at the seams, like a fat caterpillar forcing its way out of a cocoon and emerging as a new, bigger, better Vinnie, with wings. A kind of emotional congestion hung around him. He oozed testosterone. His whole body was one big blood-filled exclamation point.

When he burst open the front door and sailed into the aquarium house the night before D-day, you could feel his excitement from across the room.

"Johnnie!" he cried when he saw me; he took both my hands and shook me back and forth, rocking me on my heels. "So good to see you! I'm so glad, Johnnie, so glad!"

Jennifer Smeals looked away and snubbed out a cigarette. I think he embarrassed her.

She stood up. "Vincent, I should get going. There're some details to wrap up at my place, and I still have some things to pack."

Vinnie reached out and scooped her in. We made a little circle, like something in a therapy session.

"Jenny, Jenny, you don't understand," Vinnie said. You could feel his body heat, like a space heater next to a pile of newspapers. Vinnie had two settings now: manic and more manic. He squeezed her until she nearly folded in two.

"Everything's changed!" he told her, us. "The plan I outlined to you is dead! There's a new deal! A new game in town!"

"You're not going to Paraguay?" I asked. I was disappointed, sure, but not completely surprised. I'd known something would go wrong, but thought I'd get a little more daydreaming time out of the deal before it dried up and blew away.

"No, no, now more than ever! Paraguay! Paraguay!" He gave me the same sort of hug he'd given Jennifer, then let me go. I staggered back.

"Jenny, go home, get ready!" he said. She unpeeled herself from him and stood there, rubbing a forearm.

"I am ready, basically. I was ready days ago. Vincent, what is going on?"

Vinnie was not someone to be slowed down by a pissed-off babe. He danced around the room in big circles, singing, "Paraguay, Para-guay," like a show tune. He whirled to a stop just in front of Jennifer.

"I'll tell you on the plane," he said, serious all of a sudden. "It changes everything, but everything stays the same. It's better this way. You'll see." He spun around to me, put his hand on my shoulder, and steered me to the other side of the room. Now he put on the solemn, slightly constipated look of a coach about to tell someone he was off the team.

"Johnnie," he said, "look, I hate to do this to you, but I have to kick you out of here. This place"—he looked around the room as if it sickened him—"I lease it; the lease runs out in a couple days."

"You don't own it?"

"Nah." He shook his head, as if actually owning houses was an idea he would never even consider. "Somebody else's moving in. This is a deal I set up a long time ago, and I can't change it now. But it doesn't matter. You can go stay in my old house."

I knew it well. "What, your parents' place? In Comapogue?"

Vinnie nodded vigorously, pleased to see I was keeping up.

"In Comapogue. That is, I rent out the house. Remember old Mr. Colucci, used to live next door to the plumber—what's his name?—Cromarty? He's living there now since his wife died. But there's an apartment. I made the garage over into a studio. There's nobody in it now. You can stay there." He held on to my shoulders and beamed at me. "This way, I know right where to find you."

I was shaken to realize that Vinnie didn't own the McMansion, and that I would have to give up the big-screen TV. But on the whole, the Comapogue plan had its appeal. It was much less conspicuous, for one thing, and besides, I knew the neighborhood.

"I'll be waiting for your call," I told him.

"It'll come," Vinnie said. "Sooner than you think. Be ready to leave at a moment's notice."

"I will be," I said. Easy for me to say. A paper grocery bag of socks and underwear doesn't take long to throw together.

Finally, Jennifer stormed over and dragged Vinnie off somewhere on last-minute errands. I was alone again after an exciting day.

I sank down in the leather sofa, the remote in one hand. My trial was coming up in a couple of days. Did I give a shit? I was going to Paraguay. I punched up the six-foot flat screen and cranked up the volume.

I missed the dawning of the big day by several hours; I slept until noon. There was no sign of either Jennifer or Vinnie when I got up.

Around 3:00 P.M., Jennifer Smeals walked in with a couple big suitcases, big enough to hold all the equipment for a good-size Pee Wee football team. She rolled each one into the house while I watched from the couch. When she had them all, she thanked me, very sarcastic.

"Thanks, Johnnie, thanks for your assistance."

I waved from the sofa. "Anytime."

"Where is Vincent?"

"Nobody here but me," I told her. She muttered something under her breath; it sounded to me like she said, "Nobody at all."

I was stung upright.

"You need a hand with that?"

"Fuck you, Johnnie," she told me. "Just leave them there. The car is coming for us at seven."

She poked around the house for a while, looking to see if Vincent was really hiding somewhere, I guess. From time to time, she looked in on me, but the sight seemed to repel her. Finally, she came to rest outside in one of the deck chairs and sat there, chain-smoking and staring at the Sound.

At the last possible second, Vinnie came back; he beat the limo by less than ten minutes.

I helped the driver hump the suitcases out to the car this time. The limousine driver got behind the wheel.

Vinnie appeared from back in the house somewhere and walked over to me. He was wearing a white suit and a colorful shirt, very tropical, in honor of Paraguay, I guess. He looked like a Puerto Rican gangster.

"Johnnie! Sit tight!" he said, holding on to my shoulders and shaking me. "You'll hear from me, okay, buddy? When we send for you, be ready."

"I'll be ready."

Jennifer Smeals was zipping in and out of the room, shrugging on her coat, fooling with her handbag. You could tell by her brisk, decisive movements that she was pissed off about something.

"Vincent, are you coming?" she called over, standing in the doorway. Vinnie nodded, waved.

"Gotta go, buddy," he told me. "Here's the key to the studio. You know where it is." I nodded. "Okay. You can stay here for a couple days, but check out by the first. Got it?"

I nodded again, feeling like the bobble-head dog on the table.

He clapped me on the shoulder and walked—practically skipped—to the door. Jennifer Smeals had already left the room in disgust.

Vinnie paused at the door, one finger in the air.

"Paraguay!" he said.

I raised my hand like an Indian chief in a cowboy movie.

"Paraguay," I said.

After Vinnie and Jennifer were driven off in the limo, I hung around outside, walking over the grounds. The driveway looped back to the street in a slow arc. It was paved with cobblestones, and walking on it was dicey, so I ended up on the lawn. Why cobblestones, anyway? I pondered. Did they really go with modern architecture that looked like a cross between a tropical-fish aquarium and an operating room? Did they convey such a powerful vibe of wealth that they were indispensable somehow, no matter what else was happening?

I hobbled to the street, looking up and down it with as much satisfaction as if I actually lived there. I lit up a cig.

It was getting dark, the sun a big red-orange blob descending on Jersey, the water blue-gray, with distant house lights. At the end of the street, Murphy's neon leprechaun burbled to life, casting a green glow down the wet leaves and black asphalt nearly as far as Vinnie's driveway. The neon mythical figure raised its big knobby stick in a farewell salute.

Headlights were coming up the road toward me. I could hear the shush of tires on wet leaves, and soon I could make out the vehicle, a stretch limo as big as a cruise ship. I was surprised when it slowed down, and apprehensive when it turned into Vinnie's driveway. What the fuck? Did they miss their flight? Had something else, something worse, gone wrong?

I flipped my cigarette into a storm drain and strolled back toward the house. By the time I got there, the stretch limo had parked and two guys had gotten out. There was room in it for plenty more, but you couldn't see a thing through the tinted glass.

The driver of the stretch was short and broad, with a powerful chest and shoulders and not much neck. He wore his light brown greasy hair fairly long, hooked over his ears. He seemed only capable of frowning. He frowned at me now.

The other guy had a thin, loose mouth, which hung open. His lips reminded me of earthworms on the sidewalk after a heavy rain. He had black streaky hair falling away from a comb-over, and wore a black leather car coat with a white shirt and tie. A car coat! I hadn't seen one since my dad threw his out when I was twelve.

"Who the fuck are you guys?" I asked.

The driver frowned harder. "We work for Mr. Malatesta. You work here?"

"I live here," I said, realizing it was true. True enough for these clowns anyway.

"We're here to pick up Johnnie LoDuco," Worm Lips said.

That made me twitch. I almost said, "Yo, that's me!" but at the last second, I remembered I was supposed to be Kenny Moleri.

"I'm sorry, Mr. LoDuco is away on business," I heard myself saying; I couldn't believe it was my voice. "I can relay a message to him." This is administrating, I thought.

The two of them stared at me. They seemed stunned. After a too-long silence, Worm Lips said to me, "And your name is?"

"Moleri, Kenny Moleri," I said, as we had agreed. "I'm a business associate of Mr. McCloskey-Schmidt." I could hear it all coming true as I said it.

"McCloskey-Schmidt? A business associate?" Worm Lips considered this a moment, then snapped his attention back to me.

"When is LoDuco coming back?"

I shrugged, spread my hands. "His trip is open-ended. It depends on how long it takes him to conduct his business."

"Where did he go?"

"Europe," I said, lying effortlessly. I wasn't sure why; Vinnie hadn't asked me to cover our tracks. But something in me wouldn't tell the truth to guys like Frown and Worm Lips. "Germany, Italy, maybe Hungary."

More staring.

"Hungary."

I nodded.

"Excuse me a moment," Worm Lips said, whipping out a cell phone and walking to the other side of the limo. I smiled sunnily at Frown, trying hard to hear what the other one was saying. I couldn't really, but I thought I heard the words *business associate*, the name Moleri.

Worm Lips listened to the cell phone for a long time without saying anything. He looked over at me a couple times in a way I didn't like at all. Frown stared at me without saying anything. Nobody was saying anything. I took out my cigarettes, offered one to Frown. He waved it off.

Worm Lips snapped his phone shut and came around the car. He jerked his head at Frown, who went and got behind the wheel.

"Mr. Moleri," Lips said to me, "just to confirm: Mr. LoDuco is away in Europe on business?"

I nodded.

"And you are a business associate of . . . Mr. McCloskey-Schmidt?" he said, as if he just couldn't believe it.

"That's right."

"And you'll be staying on here at this address?"

I nodded again. I even smiled. The breeze blew ash from my cigarette onto his car coat. Worm Lips didn't notice.

"We'll be in touch," he said, and climbed back in the limo.

The day after Vinnie and Jennifer left, I woke up on the sofa, my neck stiff from resting on the steel and leather armrest. The remote was on the floor, where it had fallen from my lifeless hand; the flat screen was black and still. It was gray and foggy outside the plate-glass windows, apparently early morning.

I lay there trying to decide which would be worse, the discomfort of cold steel and genuine leather against the back of my head or actually trying to stand up and function. Then I noticed something funny, something different. It took me a little while to sort out what it was.

I had forgotten to pull the curtains across Vinnie's front windows—good thing I didn't sleep naked. So I could clearly see that a tour bus had pulled up outside, right into Vinnie's driveway. It was about ten feet from the house. Maybe that's what woke me up, I thought.

A tour bus. I sat up, rubbed a hand through my hair, and squinted at it. Either a tour bus or one of those Greyhound bus–type RVs that country singers travel in. Either way, it was not usual to see one outside Vinnie's house.

Maybe the new tenant, I thought fuzzily. Vinnie hadn't mentioned that he was a country singer. Anyway, no one was due to show up for a couple days.

Then the telephone went off like a fire alarm. I twitched and shivered, but at least I was awake now. I picked up the unit near the couch.

"Hello?" I said, my voice cracking and fucked up from sleep.

"Get out of the house now," a woman's voice said.

I couldn't immediately take this in. "Huh?" I replied.

"Just do it," the voice said. "You know where to go. I'll contact you when I can." She hung up. The dial tone came back just as I remembered whose voice it was: Jennifer Smeals's.

The door of the tour bus opened and some people got out. All guys, about ten of them. All were carrying what looked like guns, large guns, very serious weaponry. They lined up in front of the house.

I thought I should probably go. I hopped over the back of the couch and was heading for the kitchen when they opened fire.

I felt like a bug on a dinner plate. There was absolutely nowhere to hide in Vinnie's house. I shimmied on my stomach across the tile floor toward the back of the house, glass shards flying all around me. I felt a couple shards bite into my flesh. Then I was out the sliding door from the dining room to the deck. Fortunately, the door was open. The glass flew out of it just as I got across the deck. Glass fragments fell into the shrubbery like hard rain.

I stayed down on my belly, moving worm-style over the short, thick blades of grass. Behind me, the weaponry had stopped roaring. I knew in a couple of minutes a guy would come walking over the lawn and put a bullet in the back of my head. I crawled faster. Really fast. I think I was whimpering.

When I got to the dock, I stopped crawling and rolled over it, right to the edge, and then into the water. I fell in like a sack of shit. I think you could have heard me in Connecticut. But maybe the gunmen were deafened by their own firepower. Anyway, nobody came to look.

As soon as I hit the water, I kicked off the bulkhead and swam under the surface as far as I could. I came up when I just couldn't stay down anymore, panted in some air, and sneaked a quick look back at Vinnie's house. I couldn't see anybody walking around; in fact, I think the tour bus was gone already. But I wasn't about to go back and check. No. I went back underwater and swam like a fucking duck toward the other side of the cove.

I spent the rest of daylight huddled in the back corner of somebody's boathouse, waiting for my clothes to dry. I wasn't anxious to show myself.

Once it was good and dark, I sneaked out between the houses and began to walk. Dogs barked at me; lights came on. But no one came out to hassle me. And nobody drove by and shot at me.

I knew where I was going: Vinnie's parents' house. I just didn't know how I was going to get there.

It was a good thing I fell asleep in front of *el tubo* with most of my clothes on, wallet and keys in pocket. Or else I would have been truly fucked. As it was, I was underdressed, and my shoes had dropped off somewhere, maybe while I was crawling on my belly through shards of plate glass, or maybe while I was swimming underwater. Or maybe they were still next to Vinnie's couch.

What I did, eventually, keeping to back streets, was get to the Long Island Railroad. Nobody seemed to care about the way I was dressed on the LIRR. I took a train into Jamaica, then caught another one back along the South Shore to Comapogue. It took a long fucking time. I could hardly breathe the whole trip, expecting someone to recognize me and shoot big pieces out of my body.

I finally got to Comapogue at about three o'clock in the morning, tired, smelly, wet, cold, barefoot, and nearly broke.

I could have found Vinnie's parents' house in the dark with my eyes closed. After all, I'd spent half my life there when I was a kid. I knew it as well or better than I knew my own parents' house.

Cutting across the pool table–sized patch of dead grass in front, hip-checking the statue of the Virgin Mary on the way and nearly knocking it over, I threw myself against the metal screen door to the garage. I felt like a drowning man who finally makes it in to the beach.

When my breathing slowed down a little and I thought I could stand up unsupported, I fished out the key Vinnie had given me and let myself in.

Vinnie had turned the garage into a pretty nice studio apartment. The walls were not painted, but Sheetrocked and spackled, except for one wall that was covered with knotty-pine paneling. The floor was concrete, but indoor/outdoor carpet covered most of it. A closet toilet. A plastic shower stall. A big sink, small stove, and refrigerator. A ratty, worn-out couch faced a really small TV on a brass cart. The set had rabbit ears with aluminum foil on them.

It was nice, for a garage, but it was still a garage and would never stop being one. I knew that on really hot days, you would get a whiff of motor oil and damp cement from under the rugs. Phantom cars would park on your chest.

I crawled onto the rat-ass couch and passed out. It had been a hard day.

When I came to, curled in the fetal position, my head was pressed into the armrest of the couch. It smelled of mildew and cat shit.

It took me awhile to figure out where I was. Not Drunken Meadows, anyway. I raised my head, cursing as pain wrenched through my neck, and looked around, scoping out the room. The first thing I saw was the tiny TV with the tinfoil flags on it. Definitely not Drunken Meadows.

By the time I made myself sit up, it had all come back to me.

There was a telephone on a milk crate next to the couch. Rubbing my hair around to assist thought and movement, I was staring right at it when it started ringing.

I picked it up without thinking.

"Hello?" I said. The thought raced through my mind: Hang up now, moron. But it was too late.

"Johnnie?" a voice said urgently. After a beat, I recognized Jennifer Smeals.

"Jennifer?" I croaked. "I thought you were on your way to Paraguay."

"*Paraguay.*" She sounded bitter. "I never got there."

"What happened?"

"I never got off the fucking island. Johnnie, listen, Vincent's disappeared."

"Was that you on the phone yesterday? At the Drunken Meadows place, I mean."

"What? Yes, of course it was me. Who else did you think it was? Johnnie, listen to me; try to concentrate: Vincent is gone. I don't know where he is."

"When?" I managed to croak. "When did this happen?"

"He left me at the terminal, at La Guardia," she said. "He told me to watch the suitcases, said he was going to make a call, that he'd be right back. I never saw him again."

"What did you do?"

"What did I do? What could I do? He had the tickets. He had the money. He had every fucking thing. I waited for an hour; then I went over and sat in the concourse to wait for him. I waited until our flight left. I waited till midnight. He never came back."

"Where have you been since?"

"Johnnie, it's a long story," Smeals said. She sounded hurried, a tiny gasp in her voice, under the words. "I'll tell you all about it some other time. Later, okay? I can't talk long. I'm on my cell. I'm afraid somebody'll pick it up."

"Somebody? Like who?"

There was a short, static-filled pause.

"Johnnie, I know there's a lot you don't know about the situation," Jennifer said. That was an understatement. "But I'll explain everything when I see you."

"You're coming here?"

"Not for a while. I can't say when. When I can. Johnnie, tell me the truth."

This seemed like a sudden change of subject.

"I always have," I said, which I think was true.

"Have you seen Vincent? Is he there with you? Tell me."

"He's not here. Jennifer, what is going on?"

But she had hung up on me.

After Jennifer's phone call, I sat on the couch in a daze for a while, unable to make any decision whatsoever, even just to stand up. Finally, my bladder forced me to move. Once I had staggered into the tiny bathroom—my ass bumped the wall behind me as I whizzed in the can—I was loosened up enough to stay on my feet. I took stock of my surroundings.

A cupboard over the sink was stuffed with instant ramen noodle containers, about fifty of them. Aside from these, there was only a half-full box of stale Cheerios and a jar of instant coffee, almost empty, though there was a lot of instant caked in the corners that could probably have been worked loose with a spoon.

I went with the ramen noodles. The only thing to boil water in was a chipped and rusty enameled saucepan, but I was hungry enough not to give a shit. I turned on the television and hunched over it, sucking down hot noodles. The TV got only one channel. I watched the end of a news program—nothing about houses being shot to pieces on the North Shore, but I had missed the beginning—and the shows that came after, funny pet videos, a documentary about heating oil, and a fishing show.

Once I'd eaten, I washed up, for the first time in forty-eight hours. I could smell myself, like a wet dog. That was bad.

There was something wrong with the shower. The water never really heated up, and it came out of the showerhead in a thin dribble, like a monkey pissing down a rope. The drain was all plugged up, and it smelled nasty, as if someone had shoved a salami down the drainpipe and left it there. In spite of the piss-poor water pressure, water built up and ran over the lip of the plastic stall and all over the floor of the garage. I decided right then not to take many showers.

My clothes, what was left of them, were piled in a damp, disgusting heap on the floor, shower overflow puddling around them. I couldn't face putting them back on. Luckily, Vinnie had left some clothes in a little closet space next to the shower stall—paint-stained jeans, a T-shirt, a pretty cool leather jacket, some high-tops. They fit okay. I was in good shape there.

So there I was. Where was I? Was I going to spend the rest of my life in Vinnie's parents' garage? What happened to the bodies of people who lived on nothing but ramen noodles?

It must have been the fishing show that put the idea into my head, that and the prospect of eating ramen noodles for the rest of my life. But from somewhere I got the idea to go fishing. Maybe it was being back in Comapogue; I used to go fishing a lot when I was a kid. In fact, I used to go fishing with Vinnie, back when this garage had a car in it, rakes and lawn mowers and fishing poles.

Carefully, I poked my head out the back door and checked out the situation. Immediately to my right, a glassed-in porch stuck out of the main part of the house. There was a Fort Apache stockade fence head-high around a little backyard with one tree and a garden shed. I headed to the shed.

The garden shed was a little green-and-white metal house up against the stockade fence. The door was unlocked. Inside, the shed was hot, like a sauna—if saunas ever smelled of gasoline, piss, and rotten grass clippings. Garden tools hung on the metal walls—hedge clippers, pruning shears and saws, a chain saw, enough cutlery to have a war. Leaning in one corner was a fishing pole, all rigged up with flounder spreaders.

I picked up the rod, looked it over. It had a crusty, salty look, like it hadn't been used in a year or two, but I figured it would probably work. I took it with me into the house.

I figured around sundown I would sneak down to the pier, scavenge some bait, clams or mussels, and catch my own dinner. I felt like Robinson fucking Crusoe.

It turned out to be a bad idea, of course. How was I supposed to know?

But you already know what I caught.

CHAPTER FOUR

IT WAS DARK WHEN I got back to the garage with Vinnie's head. I stumbled around, trying to manage the fishing pole and the trash bag, nearly losing both, loose flounder hooks waving around and snagging the asbestos shingles of the house, the back of my neck, the bag. Finally, somehow, I got the door open. Popping on the light switch with an elbow, I collapsed onto the floor with fishing equipment, head, everything, and tried to think of what to do next.

After a few minutes, I reached out with my foot and kicked the door closed. No sense giving the neighborhood a front-row seat on my agony.

The black plastic trash bag was spread out on the floor next to me, like a big pool of ink with a rock in the middle. I knew it wasn't a rock.

What would I do with the head? Put it in somebody's garbage can? Bad idea—that would certainly draw attention to the neighborhood. Bury it? Then a stray pooch might dig it up and go parading down the street with the head in his mouth. Same result. Only worse: There'd be a big hole in the backyard, with a trail of dirt, sea creatures, and rotten head pieces leading back to it like a trail of cold cuts.

I stood up, pretty shaky, tottered to the refrigerator, and opened the door. It was one of those apartment-size refrigerators, a square box about the size of an old-fashioned safe. This one held a quart of sour milk, a single can of beer—Old Milwaukee—and a half-used stick of margarine. The freezer compartment was only about six inches high. Even if I chopped out the thick frosting of ice, it was obviously too small to accept the head. I shoved the groceries aside, wrapped the trash bag around and around the head, and shoved the whole thing in. The wad of head and plastic took up most of one shelf.

Next morning, I woke up. That in itself felt like an accomplishment. The couch was lumpy and seemed to shift out from underneath me as if it were alive and trying to get away. The one blanket I could find was cheap and thin and smelled of motor oil.

Maybe the poor accommodations accounted for the very strange dream I'd had: Driving down Sunrise Highway with Bug Rankin and his buddies Hector and Alfredo, I suddenly realized we were on a railroad track and not the highway. They just laughed at me when I told them. But now a train was racing toward us. I pointed this out; they all laughed some more.

I know, you're thinking that my dream life was precisely like my real life (if that's what you'd call it), and the same thing occurred to me, even in the dream. But what happened next was a little different. I realized that the train up ahead was not coming toward us; we were racing toward it. And it wasn't a train, in any case; it was Vinnie's head, big as the Goodyear blimp, sitting at the end of the tracks with its mouth open. We were racing for its gullet. Vinnie looked a lot more like the laughing face on the side of the old Steeplechase in

Coney Island and less like Vinnie as the dream progressed. I could see where pieces had been eaten out of the face down to the bone. The head got bigger and bigger as we got closer to it. Rankin and his pals weren't laughing anymore; they were screaming. I started screaming, too.

Then I woke up.

It was still early. I got up, made some instant coffee, washed up in the sink—the shower was still plugged up from the day before. After a while, I began to feel almost half-awake.

There was a faint, funny odor in Vinnie's garage, like a distant whiff of human shit and rancid bacon. I knew what it was.

I looked desperately around the room for something to take my mind off what was in the refrigerator. There wasn't much.

What the fuck, I asked myself, am I going to do?

The fishing pole was still leaning up in the corner by the door, one hook stuck in a guide and the line reeled taut to keep it from swinging around and hooking any more heads. I couldn't remember doing that, but there it was.

I should take the pole back where I found it, I thought. That at least was something I could accomplish.

The garden shed hadn't changed any; it still smelled of rust and pee. I don't know what I'd expected, exactly—a row of heads hanging up in place of the garden tools, cops and detectives waiting with arrest warrants—but I felt that something should have changed. Everything else had, and for the worse. Why not the shed? But it was still the same. I put the pole back in it.

But then as I walked back to the garage, I saw something that gave me hope.

At the back of Vinnie's old house there was a glassed-in porch, what they call a "Florida room," with glass louvered windows over screens. The louvers were open and I could see into the porch. There was not much to see, of course: cast-iron lawn furniture without cushions, a folding lawn chair with plastic webbing, and a freezer.

A freezer. Mother of God: an old-fashioned chest freezer like they used to have in the better butcher shops.

I slid up to the porch door—almost all louvers—and tried the knob. The door opened. I stepped in.

When I opened it, the freezer was empty and smelled faintly of Freon. I found the plug behind it, right near a convenient wall outlet, and plugged it in. The freezer hummed away, refrigerant gurgling happily through the pipes.

Of course I won't keep the head here long, I thought as I stepped back to the garage. Old Mr. Colucci would never notice—obviously, he wasn't using the freezer—and as soon as I could get what I needed, I would throw the fucking thing back in the Great South Bay, where it belonged, Vinnie's head or not. This time, it would be wired to a concrete block, which is what they should have done in the first place. Whoever *they* were.

I felt a little uneasy, it's true. Guilty, maybe. Frightened, possibly. But not enough to keep Vinnie's head in the refrigerator another day longer than necessary.

In under a minute, I had whacked the trash bag/head combo into the freezer. It looked stark and obvious in the bottom of the freezer, with nothing else around it. I eased the freezer door shut and turned around to leave.

The house door opened and Mr. Colucci walked out.

He was wearing a tattered bathrobe and holding a cup of coffee. He didn't seem in the least surprised to see me.

"That you screaming in there last night?" he asked me, nodding vaguely toward the garage.

I nodded back, too stunned to speak.

"I thought so." He took a sip of coffee. "I says to myself, 'He's either jackin' off in there or somebody's killin' him.' You're still alive, so I guess it's the other one. You jackin' off in there?"

I shook my head.

Mr. Colucci looked at me, unsmiling. We stared at each other in silence for about a minute. Then he seemed to remember something.

"You took my pole," he said.

This I could deal with. "I brought it back," I said. "I put it back in the shed."

"Like I give a shit," Mr. Colucci said. "I never use the fuckin' thing." He slurped up more coffee. "Catch anything?"

"Nope."

"You catch anything, my rod, give me some. That's all. I don't care you use it, just bring it back. Okay?"

"Okay," I said.

It was surprising how secure putting Vinnie's head in Mr. Colucci's chest freezer made me feel. Looking at it from any point of view, it was still real chancy, iffy, bad. Old Colucci might lift the lid. He might notice the freezer was plugged in, unplug it, then, when the smell got really bad, lift the lid.

The trick was to keep him from lifting the lid.

I went back in the house, feeling satisfied—uneasy, but satisfied.

Things went okay for a couple days. My court date was ancient history now. If anyone was looking for me, they didn't find me. I stayed in the house a lot—not hard, since I had no money. Anyway, being on the street made me so nervous, I couldn't bring myself to do it very often. I found an industrial-strength box of nondairy creamers in little square foil packets in the back of the closet, and this saved me from many dangerous forays into the inhabited world. I discovered that mixing some of the powder in the packets with water created a drinking substance that resembled milk at least in appearance. I learned to love what I had. I watched TV a lot.

Every morning, I scooped up a *Newsday* from the side yard—Mr. Colucci had it delivered—and leafed through it, looking for any report of odd body parts washing up on Long Island. There was nothing all week. Then on Friday, I found an item on the second page of the local section about a man found dead of a heart attack on the Comapogue town dock. The notable thing about this was that the old man's dog—apparently the guy had been out walking his dog—had been cut clean in half. Police were investigating.

This was close to home. It made me nervous and thoughtful. It preyed on my mind.

When it got dark, I sneaked up to Montauk Highway, trying to think myself invisible, and ducked into the Kozy Korner Tavern. I needed a drink, and I needed to talk to another human being. Above all, I needed some idea of just what had happened on the town dock.

Eric, the bartender at the Kozy Korner, had a brother who was a Suffolk County cop. Eric liked to work his brother into conversations, whether it fit or not. This query was a natural for him.

"Eric," I said with a breezy wave, plopping myself down on a bar stool.

Eric stared at me without pleasure.

"LoDuco," he said, "your tab is not long, but it's old. How about it?"

"Can't right now, Eric," I said. I slipped a five onto the bar—I'd just borrowed it from Pete Fontana in the parking lot. "But I can pay my way from here."

Eric poured a glass of Rupert's for me without enthusiasm.

After some aimless preliminaries, I got down to the topic that interested me.

"Hey, did you hear about that guy they found on the town dock? With the dead dog? What was that all about?"

"Massive coronary," said Eric. "My brother's on the force. He was on the call. He said the guy looked like he'd died looking at something awful."

"Scared to death?"

Eric nodded.

"What kind of dog was it?" I asked him. He squinted back at me.

"What kind of *dog* was it? What do you care? What difference does that make?"

I shrugged. "I like dogs. I just wanted to know, that's all."

Eric shook his head. "You sorry fuckhead. It was a beagle."

"A beagle." I knew it would be.

"That's right. Cut clean in half. Like maybe with a sword, a samurai sword or something. Now who would do that, cut a dog in half? What kind of sick fuck does that?"

I kept monitoring the paper but never saw another body-part finding—no hands, no legs, no torso.

Naturally, no head.

No Jennifer, either. No dead girls, I mean. That was good. I was hoping she would call me again and explain some of the mysterious business going on with her and Vinnie. I wanted to know exactly how paranoid to be. The answer would turn out to be very, but I didn't know that yet. I was still living in a fool's paradise, me and my best friend's severed head.

I didn't look forward to telling her about Vinnie. Right then, I was sort of numb about it. It didn't seem real. But telling Jennifer would bring it home to me, and I knew what was coming would be bad.

———

I might never have found the roll of twenties if it weren't for the bugs.

Cockroaches. Cockroaches as big as mini dachshunds began crawling around the garage. I had tried to be pretty neat—for me, I mean—but I guess I was supporting them with my leftovers, the crumbs and shit I dropped on the floor without realizing it. They seemed to be doing well off me, living large.

I hate responsibility. And I hate fucking bugs.

There was a cabinet under the little sink with boxes and spray cans and retired sponges and all kinds of stuff. I went rummaging around under there, looking for a can of Raid or some Roach Motels or at least a flyswatter. While I was on my hands and knees, digging in the back of the cabinet, I knocked over a couple boxes. Dish detergent spilled out of one and landed all over the floor.

"God damn it." I picked the box up and tried to scoop the spilled soap back into it with the palm of my hand. There was something wedged in the opening, getting in the way, a piece of the box, I figured. But when I plucked it out, I saw that it was a roll of twenties.

I sat on the floor in the middle of the spilled soap and took the fat rubber band off the roll. It was as thick as a roll of toilet paper. I thumbed through it to see if the bills were all twenties, and they were. Crisp new twenties that had never been spent. I didn't count them closely, but there was at least five hundred dollars in the roll, maybe more.

Vinnie. That fucking Vinnie. I should have known he wouldn't let me down.

Christ knows how long they would have sat there before I found them—if I hadn't spilled the soap, I mean. You don't use a lot of dish soap on old ramen noodle containers. And I wasn't very good with doing the dishes, even normal dishes.

I looked up from my counting and saw three or four of the big roaches watching me from the cabinet. I guess there weren't any roach motels in there.

"You assholes are in big trouble," I told them. "I can buy Raid by the flat now."

Finally, Jennifer called me back.

"Johnnie, thank God you're there" was the first thing out of her mouth. It made me nervous; why shouldn't I be there?

"Jennifer," I said noncommitally.

"Have you heard from Vincent?"

Uh-oh. I couldn't bring myself to tell her right away. I considered just telling her no, I hadn't heard from him, which would have been true, technically. But instead, lamely, I tried to change the subject, to buy myself time.

"Have you called any of his businesss contacts in Paraguay?"

"Are you kidding? I haven't had time for that. Look, Johnnie, I've been *hiding*. I can't tell you why right now. Just believe me. There are people I need to avoid for a while."

" 'People'? What people?"

"People who want to hurt me."

"Do they want to hurt me, too?"

It seemed like a reasonable question, but it exasperated Jennifer.

"Johnnie, please don't be difficult. I'm all alone in this, and I need some help. I need *your* help."

She must really be in trouble, I thought.

"Johnnie, are you still there? Can you hear me?"

"Yeah," I said.

"I'm worried about Vincent. It isn't like him to just disappear like this. To just disappear and leave his friends in a mess. I'm worried something's happened to him."

There it was, unavoidable.

"Jennifer," I said slowly, "look, I have something to tell you."

"What?"

"I don't know how to tell you this."

"Tell me what? Johnnie, for Christ sake, spit it out!"

I took a deep, deep breath.

"I found Vinnie," I said.

"Vincent! Where is he? What happened to him? Is he all right?" Then, suddenly, she quieted down.

"Johnnie," she said, "what are you saying?"

"I found him, Jennifer. Part of him anyway. Jennifer, I found his head."

Long silence.

"I found his head, Jennifer. Vinnie's head. It was in the bay. I hooked it when I was out fishing for flounder."

More silence.

"His head," she repeated finally. She seemed calm so far. In my experience, women as tightly wrapped as Jennifer Smeals could unravel with a bang, like a golf ball with the tough outer covering removed, if things got to them. But Jennifer was a surprisingly tough babe.

She sure surprised me.

"Do you have it?" she asked me.

"Well, yes, I do," I stuttered. "I have it."

"You didn't tell anyone? You didn't call the cops?"

"You know I didn't. Are you kidding?"

"Where is it?"

"In the freezer. Right here." Close enough anyway.

Her voice was tight and urgent.

"Johnnie, listen to me. Stay right there. Don't go anywhere. Don't show yourself. There are people involved in this, *very heavy people*, and you don't want to come to their attention."

"I sorta guessed that."

"I will come to you," she said. "I know where the house is. I don't know if I can make it tonight. But wait for me, Johnnie. I'll be there as soon as I can. And Johnnie . . ."

"Yeah?"

"Don't let the head out of your sight. Okay?"

"No problem," I said, but she had already hung up.

Everyone handles shock and grief in their own way. Nevertheless, Jennifer seemed to take the news pretty coolly, as if she was not in the least surprised. Maybe that meant she already knew Vinnie was dead. And if she did, what implications did that have for my continued good health?

These were urgent questions.

Another question also posed itself. What, I asked myself, could Jennifer Smeals want with Vinnie's head? Why did she care if I had it? I knew they were close. But Jennifer didn't strike me as the sentimental, romantic type, someone who might hang on to the head of a former lover as a keepsake. That was definitely not her style.

The more I thought about it, the more disturbed and uneasy I became. My plans for the head were to get rid of it as soon as I could figure out a fuckup-proof way of doing so. Lose it and make it stay lost, I thought. But now Vinnie's head had value to someone.

Why?

I paced up and down as I thought about this, smoking too many cigarettes for someone on a limited income.

Was I missing something?

It was not an easy decision, but I decided that I had to take a good look at the head. The thought of doing this—of unwrapping the damp plastic bag from around it, the smell, parts coming off, leakage—was almost more than I could take. But something was going on that I didn't understand, and I thought maybe the answer lay with the head itself.

After our neighborly conversation the other day, I felt confident about letting myself in Mr. Colucci's house. I opened the porch door and stopped dead.

The freezer was gone. The fucking chest freezer with Vinnie's head in it was simply not there.

CHAPTER FIVE

I PANICKED. IT SHAMES me to remember this, but the first thing I did was to run out of the porch at top speed and tear around aimlessly in the backyard for a while. When I calmed down some, I went back onto the porch, gulping breath to work up resolution.

The chest freezer was gone, no doubt about it. You could see the rust stains where it had rested on the linoleum, and the darker tiles sunlight hadn't touched in twenty years. There were balls of dust and hair along the baseboard, like little gray shrunken heads.

I was hyperventilating now, close to passing out. I mashed down the buzzer by Mr. Colucci's inside back door; then when nothing happened, I began to pound on the door with my fists. I was not thinking clearly.

After a few minutes—I couldn't tell you how many—Mr. Colucci opened the door. He was in his bathrobe and carpet slippers, as usual. He seemed pale and shaky, and I wondered if he was drunk.

We stared at each other wildly for a minute, neither of us able to say anything. Then I gathered my thoughts and got to the point.

"Mr. Colucci, where is the fucking freezer you had here? Where did it go?"

Mr. Colucci looked at me in horror, his eyes wide as could be.

"The freezer!" he gasped. "Ah, Jesus Christ!" Then he dropped his head into his hands and began sobbing.

I realized I had a hold of him and was shaking him back and forth, and that this treatment might have contributed to his breakdown. I let him go. Mr. Colucci stood there and continued to sob.

"Ah, Jesus Christ!" was all I could get out of him for a while. I led him over to the painted metal sofa on the other side of the porch; it hung from springs and rocked back and forth. The sofa was covered with a drop cloth and smelled powerfully of mildew. We sat down on the drop cloth and rocked back and forth for a while.

The sobbing stopped in a couple minutes, and a couple minutes more and he was breathing normally again, though still shaky. I thought it would be okay to question him now.

"Mr. Colucci, you all right now?" The old geezer nodded. "What are you upset about? What is it?"

"My son, my son," he gasped. I thought he was talking to me, calling me his son, and had gone crazy or maybe was dying.

"What, what?" I whispered urgently.

"My son come here last night and took the freezer. He asked me could he have it, and I said, 'Sure, I don't use it.' He's a fisherman; he needs it for bait." I could hear that he was working up to a sob attack again.

"So your son took the freezer. Where did he take it?"

"To his house. He said he was going to put it in his garage, I think. But then Belinda . . ." He began to sob for real this time.

"Belinda? Who is Belinda?" I said as calmly as I could, though I was going seriously out of my mind.

"Belinda, my daughter-in-law. She calls me," said Colucci

through sobs. "She calls me this morning. She says she found a head in the freezer! She says I put it there, this head! She calls me a killer!"

So that was that. Time to go.

"Mr. Colucci, listen. Why did she think you had anything to do with it?"

"A fucking killer! That's what she calls me! Her own father-in-law!"

"Mr. Colucci, Mr. Colucci," I said, shaking him again. "What did she say? What about the head?"

He calmed down a little, sniffling. "She says it's my landlord's head, Vinnie. She recognizes him. She met him here, a couple times she was over. She says I must have killed him and put his head in the freezer."

Right. "Did she call the cops? What did she do?"

"She didn't call no cops. She says she wants the car."

"Car? What car?"

"My car. My good car, that I bought just last year! The bitch! The fucking prostitute!" He was hyperventilating now, too, but I was afraid of interrupting his concentration, so I didn't interfere.

"If I give her the car, she gives me the head. That's what she said to me, imagine! I don't know about no fucking head, I tell her. And then she hangs up. And now what am I supposed to do?"

I sat there, rocking back and forth for a while, thinking.

"She tell your son about this?" I asked him. He shook his head.

"You tell him?" No again.

I thought some more.

After a few minute's silence while I desperately tried to think of something, Colucci said, "You think we should call the cops?"

Now it was my turn to shake my head.

"Unh-uh. No way. They might believe her and put your ass in

jail," I told him. "You never know who they'll believe." This was pure bullshit, but the old man bought it. He stared at the floor, just about shaking with fear and anger.

"What the fuck am I goin' to do?" he whimpered. I felt sorry for the old fart. I had been saying the same thing not long ago.

"You know, I think you should go and talk to her, right now," I said. "Straighten things out."

"Talk to her?"

"Yeah. This is obviously a bad misunderstanding. Talk to her. Work it out with her."

"Go up and see her?" Mr. Colucci said beseechingly.

I nodded forcefully.

"I'll drive," I said.

Mr. Colucci came out in about twenty minutes. He was dressed in tan shorts and a white shirt. He looked pretty sharp for an old guy. He took me by the arm and walked me around the other side of the house. He had the Cadillac there, sitting under a canvas tarp. The tarp was spotted with bird shit and little black splatters from a wild cherry tree that grew just over the fence in the neighbor's yard.

"I never drive it anymore anyway," he said sadly, looking at the shit-spotted tarp.

I peeled the canvas back. The Caddy was clean and shiny, only a couple years old. It was worth way more than the house. I wondered how old Colucci got his hands on it.

"Nice car," I told him. "You buy it new?"

Mr. Colucci nodded. "When my wife passed away, I got the insurance money. She was a wonderful woman. She woulda loved this car." His eyes were tearing up again, thinking about his dead wife. Then his jaw set and his eyelids came down a little. I could see where his thoughts were heading.

"Belinda, that fucking bitch," he muttered. "She's not gonna get this car."

The daughter-in-law lived out in Wading River. I used to get taken up there when I was a little kid, to buy corn and peaches from farm stands. It was the ass end of nowhere then. Now it was the new hot spot for big ugly houses.

The Caddy drove like a dream. I took Sunrise to the William Floyd Parkway, and we drove up through the pines, not talking. Then after a few miles of silence and looking out the window, Mr. Colucci finally let me know what was on his mind.

"I can't figure it out, a fucking head. Only thing I can think of, he must of got in bad with the mob, maybe borrowed too much, something like that."

"Seems extreme, though," I said. "Don't they usually, like, break a leg or some fingers?"

Mr. Colucci didn't hear me; he was lost in speculation. After a while, he turned to me.

"What about you, you . . . connected?" He sounded nervous and apologetic.

I shook my head. "Not me. I don't know anyone in the Mafia. I've never even watched *The Sopranos*."

We drove along in silence.

"What about you?" I asked him after a while. He shook his head without looking at me.

"I wish I was in the fucking Mafia, I tell you that!" Mr. Colucci said. "I know what I'd do to that bitch, my daughter-in-law!" He mimed holding a rifle or shotgun, then the kick as he fired it, the barrel rising up. He was pretty good; I could almost hear the report.

"That fucking bitch!" he said again.

We pulled up in front of his daughter-in-law's, a big new house in a new development of big new houses just like it. There were no trees; the landscaping hadn't grown in yet, and only some of the houses had sod lawns so far. The place looked pretty bare and scrubby, though very clean.

The daughter-in-law, Belinda, opened the double doors before the door chime finished its little tune. She glared out at us.

"You murdering cocksucker," she said. "I know what you want."

"Belinda, please, I didn't kill nobody," Mr. Colucci said pleadingly. "Let us in, please. Let's talk about this."

Belinda looked me up and down. Her eyelids hung heavily over large soupy brown eyes outlined with a couple pounds of mascara. The corners of her wide mouth turned down. Black hair was ratted into a kind of crest on top of her head, and it was quivering with some sort of fight-or-flight reaction. The muscles in her jaw bulged like golf balls as she chewed her gum.

"Who's this? Your fucking bodyguard?" she said. Her skin was tight with fat and muscle; it was obvious that she could kick the shit out of the two of us.

"My neighbor, Johnnie, he drove me up," Colucci said.

"You're in this together," Belinda theorized. Colucci shook his head.

"Belinda, we're not *in* anything. We didn't *do* anything. You got this all wrong."

Belinda shook her big bonce. "I got the head. Explain the head."

"That's what you say," I said. They both turned and stared at me. It was the first time I'd opened my mouth. "Where is this head?"

"You want your head, it's in the garage, where I found it," Belinda said. Talking had made her makeup crack in spots; her face was beginning to look like the floor of a sump in a summer drought.

"Well, let's take a look," I said.

There were two doors to the garage, but it would have held at least four cars, maybe more, and maybe a boat, too. It was bigger than the house I grew up in.

Belinda punched one garage door open with a remote as we walked up the steep driveway—she wouldn't let us in through the house. Old Colucci was puffing and panting by the time we got to the top.

But there was the chest freezer, off to one side of the garage near some weight-lifting equipment and a rack of fishing rods. My heart gave a thump; I was very glad to see it.

"When Sal brought the freezer back from your place, it was fucking filthy," Belinda said to us accusingly. "So I thought I would clean it up a little, maybe put some frozen stuff from Costco in there, not just his bait fish."

"I haven't used it in years," Colucci pleaded. "That's why it was so dirty."

Belinda ignored this. "So I go to clean out the inside. And I find this!" She flipped open the freezer. I saw it was filled with frozen moss bunker now, and some squid, halfway to the top.

Belinda rooted around in the bait and pulled out a black plastic trash bag. I was so glad to see it again, I could have hugged her.

"This!" Belinda shouted, holding the trash bag up and shaking it in our faces. She must have been holding it wrong; I could have given her some pointers. Anyway, when she shook the bag, the head bounced out and rolled up against Mr. Colucci's shoes. He stared down at it in horror.

The head didn't look any better than when I had last seen it. White frost clung to it in spots—freezer burn, it occurred to me—but at least it didn't smell.

"Will you close the fucking door?" I asked Belinda.

"You close it," she said, shoving the remote at Mr. Colucci. "I don't care if everyone sees what I'm doing. *I've* got nothing to hide."

But I noticed she moved over between the head and the open door, blocking the view from the street pretty effectively.

Mr. Colucci took the remote without looking at it. His eyes were still fixed on the head leaning up against his shoes.

"What did your husband say when he saw the head?" I asked Belinda, testing her. She glared at me, snapping her gum. Then she shrugged.

"He didn't see it. He didn't look inside the bag. I told him it was Salisbury steaks from Costco. He hates Salisbury steaks."

"Okay, right," I said, "let's talk. What do you want?"

"I want the Cadillac," she said. "Give me the car, I give you the head. No cops, no questions asked."

"So you don't care where the head came from?"

Belinda shrugged. "It's none of my business what you guys are up to. I just want what's mine. You give me the car, you get the head."

"It's not my car to give," I said. We both turned and looked at Mr. Colucci. He was pale and sweating, clutching the garage-door opener like a piece of the true cross. He didn't seem to notice me and Belinda staring at him.

I thought I'd try a little subtle intimidation on her.

"Belinda," I said, "how do you think this head got there?"

She shrugged, just barely moving her shoulders. She stared at me with pure disgust.

"I have no idear."

"This head could be yours," I said.

She didn't actually spit. "Give me a fucking break."

"You don't know what you're getting into."

"I'm getting into the Cadillac. Like right now. Or do I call the cops? You can pile your bullshit on them."

I sighed, gave it up, and leaned forward and whispered to Belinda. "Wait a few years and you'll inherit the Caddy anyway."

She glared back at me. "That old piece of shit is never going to die," she said in a voice you could've heard back in Comapogue. "I'm sick of waiting on him. I want it now."

"Look, take the car, as far as I'm concerned. Just give me the head," I told her. "I'll drive Mr. Colucci home; we'll come back with the ownership papers."

"Oh no," Belinda said. "The head stays here. Come back with the papers. Give me the keys. Then you get the head."

"How do I know you won't keep it?" I said.

"How do I know you'll come back?" Belinda came closer to me, thrusting out her big tits like weapons, frowning and grimacing like a pro wrestler getting ready for a rope dive.

The garage door suddenly rolled down a foot or so; the noise made us both jump and turn around. Mr. Colucci was punching wildly at the buttons on the door opener.

"The fuckin' thing, the fuckin' thing," he muttered, mashing down all the buttons at once. Both garage doors began to shoot up and down, moving a foot or so in each direction. The overhead light flashed on and off.

While Belinda was distracted by Mr. Colucci's wigged-out per-formance, I reached down and made a grab for the head. I was closer to it now, and Colucci had backed off it a bit. But Belinda saw me move before I quite reached it.

"Oh no," she yelled. "Get the fuck outta there." She made a dive at the head, or at me—I couldn't be sure which. I grabbed her wrists to keep her from picking up the head. She was strong. Together, we wrestled each other around the garage, Belinda cursing and spit-ting, trying to bite or head-butt me. I just held on. Old Colucci stepped out of our way when we got near him, like a dancer on a crowded dance floor, but otherwise he ignored us. He kept mashing on the door opener. The garage doors kept going up and down, up and down. I figured Colucci must have busted the door opener somehow.

Then one of us—Belinda, I think—gave the head a good soccer-style kick. It spun out the garage door and rolled down the driveway, coming to rest against the rear wheel of the Cadillac. I slipped on something—a piece of the head, maybe, or some frozen menhaden—and we both went down.

We rolled around on the garage floor for a while, neither able to outmotor the other. Through Belinda's heavy breathing I could hear the whir and rumble of the garage doors, which were still traveling up and down, up and down.

Belinda had me down now, right in the doorway, her long blue nails—with little silver stars on them, I saw—digging into my wrists. In seconds, she would break free, and I didn't want to know what she would do to me then. Panic gave me strength; I twisted one leg under me, pushed off, and somehow flipped Belinda over. Her head whacked into the concrete with a satisfying *donk*.

I sensed rather than heard the descent of the garage door, and jumped back out of the way. At just that moment, Belinda pushed herself up off the floor, growling like a sick mandrill. The descending garage door caught her right on the larynx. She went down, her head whacking against the ground again, and the door settled on her throat.

I rushed over to Colucci and grabbed the remote away from him. "Give me the fucking thing."

When I moved the garage door up, Belinda popped up, both hands at her throat, and began running in circles around the garage. I discreetly lowered the door again.

Belinda was making noises now like a garbage disposal trying to digest a pork rib. I wondered for a second whether I should try to help her or just go for the head.

"Fuck it," I said, and headed for the side door—I didn't want to open the garage doors again and give the neighborhood a good look at what was going on. Grab the head, throw it in the trunk, and just drive away, I told myself. We would have the head, Colucci his car. Belinda got *ugazz'*. A satisfying resolution.

Just then, I heard a sort of sigh, and turned around just in time to see Mr. Colucci slowly sink to the floor. His face was blue around the mouth; his eyes were closed. He was holding on to himself with both arms, as if he was trying to keep himself warm.

I knelt down and felt his pulse. It was still there, but feeble and irregular, like a moth beating against a screen door. He was barely breathing.

This was a heart attack; I knew that much. But what should I do? I'd read articles about resuscitation more than once, tried to remember the drill. I'd known I would have to use it sometime. But all I could bring to mind was the Heimlich maneuver.

"Press fifteen, breathe five," I chanted, pushing down on Mr. Colucci's chest as I had seen people do so many times on TV. Or was it other way around? I forced breath into the old man's leathery mouth, pushed down on his breastbone. No response.

He was gone. Even that last screen-door moth had flown away.

I got up, shaking and wobbly, and walked over to where Belinda was lying in a tangle of fishing equipment. She looked bad, a lot worse than Colucci. Her eyes were wide open, staring, and her tongue was sticking out. Her face was a nasty blue-black that in patches matched her nails. She was really fucking dead.

So this was not good.

When I could think again, I went out to get the head—that was obviously the first order of business. The side door opened onto a laundry room with a sliding glass door to the backyard. Within seconds, I was through the cedar gate in the fence and jogging down the driveway. The head was still there, leaning up against the rear wheel of the Cadillac, its empty eye sockets aimed at the little cupola on top of the garage. I scooped it up—I was getting used to the head by now and wasn't squeamish—and looked around to see if we were busted.

Belinda and her old man lived in a circle-shaped dead-end street, with five or six identical houses around it, five or six identical driveways raying down to the curb. I scoped out the neighbors' houses, but nothing moved; not so much as a curtain twitched. In fact, I didn't see any curtains. I wondered if the houses were even inhabited. There was no way to tell. Probably the owners were in Manhattan, seventy miles away, working to pay down their big mortgages, and wouldn't be home until midnight.

As I stood there holding the head by its cold, wet hair, looking around Dawn Court, it occurred to me that the circle of asphalt and big houses looked like those little target circles in a pinball game that the big steel ball bearing disappears into. Suddenly, I had the eerie feeling that the whole fucking development, all of Heirloom Farm Estates, was really one big pinball table, all the little courts and circles and lanes and drives. I could feel it all at once, sense the shape of it, feel the click of the counter, the clunk of the spring-loaded plunger, the shift of the ground as the player tried to English the ball in.

My only questions: Was I the ball bearing or just one of those rubber posts it caroms off of? And if so, what was the ball, and where was it right now? And who was the player?

I shook off the strange vision and walked back up the driveway, Vinnie's head bumping against my leg.

Mr. Colucci and Belinda were still there, of course. I knew they would be. But I was looking for something to put the head in. I couldn't see driving back with it on the seat next to me; even on Long Island, someone was sure to notice. Belinda's old man was a fisherman; he had to have a cooler.

Sure enough, there were five or six big ones in a row, up on a shelf by the fishing rods. I stepped over Belinda and yanked the biggest one down. The head fit, with room to spare; I filled up the extra space with frozen moss bunker to help keep the head cold.

Next, I had to decide what to do with Belinda and Mr. Colucci. I had sudden doubts—suppose he wasn't really dead? What did I know? But when I felt him again, he was already getting cold. Belinda, there was no question about.

I was in shit up to my neck, no doubt about it. But there was no reason for me to appear in all this. If I were to ditch Mr. Colucci's Cadillac somewhere—bury it maybe, like Vinnie and I used to do—there would be nothing to connect me to all these bodies.

Then I had the brilliant idea to leave the head there, too. All my worries would be over, stuffed in a freezer in Wading River.

The more I thought about it, though, the more I could see how it would go. Eventually, no matter how much he preferred to avoid her, Sal would miss Belinda. He'd look for her, call her friends, call the in-laws, then the cops. Sooner or later, someone would open the freezer—probably Sal, next weekend, when he went fishing to get away from all the fuss—and there they all would be: his wife, my next-door neighbor, dead and stiff. Not to mention old Colucci's landlord's head in a plastic garbage bag. *My* landlord. *My* friend (they would find this out). It would certainly bring the heat down on Vinnie's parents' house, sooner or later. I wanted to avoid heat. And I had nowhere else to go.

Plus, Jennifer Smeals wanted me to hang on to the head, for mysterious reasons of her own.

And, most important, it was not just any old severed head. It was *Vinnie's* head.

I ended up putting Belinda and Mr. Colucci in the chest freezer—Belinda first—and covering them up with frozen bunker. They just fit. I had lots of bait left over; I put as much as I could on top of Vinnie's head, then filled up another cooler. Even so, there were a dozen or so fish, which I ended up just chucking in the trunk, on top of the two coolers. I didn't plan on keeping the Cadillac, and I wanted to remove all signs of activity from the garage. It would be awhile anyway before anyone thought to look in the freezer. Or so I hoped.

———————

I dropped off the coolers at the Comapogue house, hoping nothing would begin to melt for a while, and went to ditch the Caddy. That went pretty well; I wiped it down and left it in the parking lot of a major mall. The parking lot was vast, and there were always cars in it, day and night. It would be weeks before anyone noticed an extra Cadillac, if they ever did.

The head was more of a problem. The cooler had kept it nice and frozen, but I knew that wouldn't last for ever. Some of the fish on top were already getting a little soft.

Then I had one of my brilliant inspirations. The freezer part of the little refrigerator in the apartment wouldn't hold the head, true, but it would hold an ice cube tray. So I went into the ice-making business. I broke into Colucci's place and took the ice tray from his freezer. Together with the occasional bag I boosted from the local deli's outside ice chest, I managed to keep the cooler full and the head firmly frozen. The meltwater, I collected every day from a spigot conveniently located at one end of the cooler. I dumped it on Mr. Colucci's tomato plants, which flourished.

I got almost a week out of this plan.

I knew it couldn't go on forever though, and it didn't.

A couple days after the incidents up in Wading River, I made a sortie up to the deli a few blocks away, where I bought half a dozen eggs and stole a candy bar and a bag of ice. A gaggle of women, young and old—dog walkers, leaf rakers, busybodies, housewives—were standing under the streetlight on the corner when I got back to the house. It was impossible to avoid them, and I wanted to find out what people were saying anyway, so I walked over and said, "Hello, ladies."

They turned their eager laser eyes on me.

"Oh, hoy," one of them said. "You're Vinnie's friend that's living in the garage."

I had really thought that no one knew I was there; I should have known better. These babes knew everything.

"A cousin," I said. "Hey, what's all the commotion?"

"Didn't you hear? Old Mr. Colucci's dead; he was *murdered*. His daughter-in-law, too," one old harridan said. She sounded almost glad.

They were all incredibly stirred up by the news, easily the biggest thing that had ever happened on the block. From where we were standing, you could see the house. From time to time, the women would take a quick peek over at it, as if they expected murderers to walk out the front door at any moment.

"I heard they arrested the husband," another old babe said.

"Oh my Gawd, his own son!"

"I bet he hired someone to kill his wife, and poor Mr. Colucci just got in the way!"

"The wrong place at the wrong time!"

"I mean, no one would kill their own father!"

"But why hire someone to kill her?"

"For the insurance, dummy!"

"He's your neighbor. Didn't you know him?" one old babe asked me suspiciously.

I hoped they would think the sweat I could feel dripping down my forehead was from the summer heat.

"Talked to him a couple times. Nice old guy. Didn't really know him," I said. They nodded, taking this under advisement.

"Well, there's more to it than they're telling," the suspicious old babe said. "You can bet on that."

"So true," I said.

A young housewife with a sweet face and a ridiculous hairdo pointed at my grocery bag.

"Yaw ice is dripping."

I looked down. Meltwater from the ice bag had dripped down my pant leg and was filling up my shoe. Normally, I would have cursed and danced around a little, but the presence of so many housewives made me be good.

"Fucking shit," I whispered, then, louder: "Well, ladies, nice talking to you. I better get going." I began to walk away, then turned back. "Say, do any of you have any ice I could borrow?" I held up the dripping bag of ice. "I go through a lot."

"What, are you havin' a party?" one of them asked.

"Something like that," I said.

In the end, I got three trays of cubes out of them, plus cups of coffee, more prying questions, and some mild flirtation. It was worth it. I filled up the refrigerator and the fish cooler with the spare ice. You can't have too much ice, I told myself.

Ice was becoming my life.

I was gloating over my stash of cubes when someone started knocking on the front door, a sharp, quick rap that sounded like cops to me. You're being paranoid, I told myself; it's probably just the ice ladies with more cubes. I lifted a corner of the curtain over the garage windows farthest from the door and peeked out. At the end of the driveway, a tan Ford Crown Victoria was parked. A four-foot-long whip antenna grew from the rear fender. The car screamed undercover police vehicle.

When I started breathing again, I tried to come up with a plan. Walk outside, engage the cops in talk? Lurk inside, wait for them to break down the door? Hide in the bathroom until they left?

Eventually, I just opened the door. A very bored but polite cop stood there in a black raincoat. He had a long, sallow face, a big nose, and enormous dark bags under his eyes.

"Good morning, sir, sorry to bother you," he said. He didn't look sorry, but I thanked him anyway.

The raincoat cop consulted a notebook. "Sir, I'd just like to ask you a few questions, if you don't mind."

I nodded. What else could I do?

"Are you Mr. Vincent McCloskey-Schmidt?" the cop asked.

I shook my head. But I couldn't remember who I was supposed to be anymore. Recent events had driven my fake name right out of my head.

"Uh-uh, nope," I said smoothly. "I'm—my name is Johnnie Mc-Closkey."

The cop gave me a quick look, his eyes squinting up. Was he laughing at me? It was hard to tell, what with that face.

"What is this all about?" I asked, because I knew it was expected of me. "Can I see some ID?"

He flashed me his badge.

"Detective Carbone," he said. "Homicide."

Detective Carbone stared at me for a while, just to unsettle me, I think. It would have worked better if I hadn't already been so unsettled.

"Your next-door neighbor, Mr. Colucci?" he said.

"Yeah?" I prompted, trying to convince myself I didn't know where he was going with this.

"They found him in Wading River this morning," Carbone said, watching me carefully.

"*Found* him? What do you mean?"

"Mr. Colucci is dead," Carbone told me.

"The old man? Oh shit! I can't believe it! When did this happen?" I sounded pretty real, I think. I couldn't really believe any of the stuff that had happened in the last few weeks anyway, so it wasn't that hard to act surprised.

Carbone and I stared at each other in silence for a while.

"Mind if I come in?" he asked.

I nearly shat. But I backed up and let him in.

Carbone's eyes tracked over the crappy little room and then stopped at the door that led into Colucci's place.

"Okay if I look around?" Carbone asked.

"Sure, no problem. Be my guest."

Carbone made a beeline for the door.

The cooler—*the cooler*—was sitting on an end table right by the door to Colucci's place. I had a little plastic bucket positioned under the spigots to catch any drips.

"Watch, don't spill the bucket," I told him.

He moved the bucket out of the way with the side of his foot.

"Where does this door go?" he asked.

"To Mr. Colucci's house. But it's locked from the other side."

Carbone rattled the handle. "Got a key?"

I shook my head.

He inspected the door pretty closely, then walked around the room again.

I couldn't take it anymore.

"Look, what happened to Mr. Colucci? How did he die? Did somebody kill him?"

Carbone looked at me sharply. Oh fuck, I thought, what is wrong with me? I guess I was trying too hard for realism.

" 'Kill him'? Why do you say that?" he asked me.

"I don't know. I wondered why you'd be here if he, like, just died."

"Nobody killed him." His eyes roamed over the studio. There really wasn't much to see. I willed him not to look at the cooler.

"How well did you know Belinda Colucci-Hahn?" Carbone asked suddenly.

"Who? I don't know her at all," I managed to say, but I could feel my eyes giving me away; they must have been as wide as Belinda's when she'd collapsed under the fishing poles.

Carbone looked at me speculatively. He looked almost interested.

"You Irish?"

I shook my head. "Italian." Then remembered I was supposed to be a McCloskey. Oh fuck.

"McCloskey, that's Italian?" Carbone said.

"My mother is Sicilian," I said, which was true. "My dad's half Italian, on his mother's side. I think of myself as Italian, you know?"

"*Eh, paisan*," Carbone said. "Close enough." He took out his little chewed-up notebook again and jotted something down. He seemed very pleased with himself. The motherfucker was almost grinning.

"You look Italian, why I asked. How long you been living here?"

"Not long. A couple months," I said, lying.

He wrote that down.

At last, Carbone got tired of poking around in the studio. I was wishing I had left the head up in Wading River. Then it would have been his problem, not mine. And where the fuck was Jennifer? She was the one wanted the head so bad.

Carbone drifted slowly toward the door. When he got there, he turned around and stared at me with his dead, soft-boiled eyes. The bags under them looked painted on.

"You remember anything you want to tell me, let me know, okay?" He held out a business card. "Give me a call. Okay, Johnnie? I'll be in touch."

He slumped through the door. I stood there holding his card, wondering how exactly he made the name Johnnie sound like Lo-Duco.

CHAPTER SIX

CARBONE'S VISIT MADE ME think about pulling up stakes, maybe leaving the island, getting away from it all and letting the situation cool off a little. I slept on the thought, though, and that turned out to be another mistake.

The very next morning when I went out to steal Mr. Colucci's *Newsday*, wondering how long it would be before they stopped delivery, there was a big shiny black stretch limo parked right in front of the house. You didn't see many such vehicles in my old neighborhood, except maybe on prom night or for weddings. Something told me that finding one parked right in front of Vinnie's parents' house was probably a bad omen.

The stretch had tinted glass windows, so I couldn't see who, if anyone, was inside. I wasn't kept in suspense long. The doors swung open, giving me a quick glimpse of white leather interior, like a lined coffin. Then Frown and Worm Lips got out.

Worm Lips smiled. That was bad; if he'd known how it made him look, he wouldn't have done that. I split a watermelon with a machete once; I forget why—drunk, probably. But the watermelon had had the same smile after I hacked into it.

"Good morning, Mr. Moleri," Worm Lips said warmly.

"I'm sorry, you're mistaking me for someone else," I said. "That's not my name."

"Moleri, McCloskey, whatever the fuck your name is, get in the fucking car," Frown grunted out. Somehow he had gotten around behind me, between me and the house.

"Mr. Malatesta would like to see you," Worm Lips said smoothly. He held open the door of the stretch limo with a little bow. I felt like a prom date.

"I know you two have business to discuss," Worm Lips added.

This was too cute. It irked me.

"You know, you would make a good parking valet," I told Worm Lips. "I know somebody owns a restaurant. I could get you a job, when your boss goes down. It could happen sooner than you think."

"Shut your mouth," Frown said. He had a hold of my upper arm.

"This is an abduction," I told them. Then I started to whoop and scream like a car alarm. "Fire! Fire!"

That rocked them, but not for very long—a second, maybe. Frown pushed me into the car cop-style, arm and the crown of the head, and jumped in after me. Doors slammed. The stretch pulled away from the curb.

Through the tinted glass I watched the crappy little houses of Comapogue disappear behind me.

Frown and Lips sat one on either side of me, crowding me. Worm Lips looked out the window. I was afraid he might try to smile again, so I avoided eye contact. Frown stared at the seat in front of him. His eyes were empty, with nothing at all going on behind them, as if someone had turned him off at the main. None of us said anything. There was a driver, too, of course, but all I could see of him was a thick neck in a cheap suit. A Plexiglas partition shut off the driver's seat from our part of the limo, like in the better NYC cabs.

We drove up to Sunrise Highway, drove east for a while, then turned north. The stretch got off the Sagtikos at Pulaski, drove up through some beat-to-shit towns of small shabby houses, then turned north again, toward the water. The streets got narrower, the trees got thicker, and the houses got bigger and not so shabby.

Now we were passing gates, big cast-iron gates like the entrance to Hell. At each gate, I expected the limo to turn in and deposit me at the entrance to one of the big old houses I could dimly make out lurking back behind the trees. But the stretch kept going. We went over the hill, away from the river, down toward the Sound shore.

Finally, almost to the water, we came to a big plot of open land at the end of a short run of asphalt. In the middle of about six acres of mud and tan dirt stood a big, big house, a sort of Colonial/neo-Victorian contemporary home scaled to the size of a covered-mall shopping center. It stuck up out of the dirt as if it had been dropped there by helicopter five minutes ago. The house had a strangely fake look, like something in Disney World or Vegas. There were no trees anywhere near it, though off to one side there was a pile of logs and dirt. Near the driveway, a slow-moving lawn crew was unrolling sod in long green strips. They had a lot of ground still to cover.

There was some sort of twisted metal arching over the driveway, held up by skinny brick pillars on either side. It was like a gate in a fence, but with no fence. We drove under it and up the driveway, which ended suddenly at a big pool of brown water. There was no garage. Big square flagstones led from the driveway across the dirt to the front door of the house, looking like pizza boxes floating in sewage.

"We're home," Worm Lips said sweetly. He and Frown helped me out of the car with the same care and solicitude they would have shown their senile old grandmother.

"Watch out the mud, you dumb fuck," Frown told me.

"You should talk," I said. "Look at your shoes."

Frown frowned at his oxfords. They were streaked with mud and clay.

Worm Lips pursed his lips, shook his head.

"You'll never get that off."

A big chesty guy in a dark suit swung the front door open when Worm Lips pressed the buzzer. More big guys in dark suits were standing around inside the house. They were everywhere. This seemed to be where they made big guys in suits, or at least warehoused them.

Everything about Malatesta's house was supersized. The windows went from floor to ceiling, and every ceiling was about twenty feet high. All the doors were double ones.

One peculiar thing about the house was that there was hardly any furniture in it. Guys in suits—even the movers wore them, apparently—were wrestling sofas and tables and big wooden boxes through the halls, but there wasn't much in place to show for their efforts. Everything smelled of wet paint. I thought I would be sick soon.

Frown and Worm Lips marched me down a big hall with doors on both sides and then stopped suddenly. Worm Lips reached over and pulled one of the big doors open; Frown gave me a shove that sent me hopping on one foot halfway across the parquet floor.

"Wait here, scumbag," Worm Lips said.

They disappeared, which was a relief.

Like most of the rooms in Malatesta's mansion, this one was short on furniture. At one end of the room, close to a fireplace big enough for a family of six to camp in, there was a white shag rug with a couple of big chairs on it. Two big arched windows looked out over acres of mud and construction debris toward a swamp with a distant slice of blue water behind it.

I went over to the windows, wondering if I could slip out and get away. I was wearing a T-shirt, jeans, and high-tops, so I thought maybe I could pass for one of the lawn crew. But the big windows didn't seem to open.

Sighing, I hiked across the vast expanse of parquet to the rug island. The chairs were big, way too big for most humans. When I sat down in one, my feet didn't quite touch the floor; I could feel the chair back looming over me like the Chrysler Building. The chair was carved all over, everywhere, with dragons and half bird, half lion things. The arms ended in big human heads, with wild staring eyes and long beards that became the arm supports. I was trying to think of who the faces reminded me of when Malatesta came into the room.

Malatesta was short and wide. He looked a little like Napoléon Bonaparte, but fatter and dumber, with a buzz cut. Like everyone else in the place, he was dressed in a dark suit. I knew I should have felt seriously intimidated, not to say underdressed. But something about him, a residual goofiness, reminded me of people I'd hung out with in high school. I think it was his overbite and the way his eyeballs bulged out.

I stood up, pushing myself out of the chair. One of the bearded heads stayed in my hand when I stood up. I looked down at the wooden head; the head stared back at me, wild. Right then, I realized who it reminded me of—Belinda Colucci-Hahn, but with a beard.

Malatesta stared at me and the wooden head in disbelief. Then, to my relief, he decided to ignore what had just happened.

"Mr. Moleri," he said, stepping forward with his hand out, giving me a do-over. I stuck the bearded Belinda head back on the chair—you could see the little wooden peg it went on—and shook his hand. If he wanted me to be Kenny Moleri, then I'd be Kenny Moleri until further notice.

We both sat down in the big uncomfortable chairs. I was quietly pleased to see that Malatesta's legs ended about two inches short of the floor. We looked like two grade-school kids waiting for the principal.

Malatesta seemed to realize that sitting in the big chair was giving away his advantage. He jumped up and walked over to one of the big windows, his hands clasped behind his back. Suddenly, he turned around, like a teacher trying to catch somebody out.

"Mr. Moleri, I'll get right down to business," he said. "I want my money back. I want it back now, no bullshit, no excuses. If you don't give it back to me, I'm going to kill you. Slow and ugly. So save us both the trouble. Tell me: Where is it?"

Slow and Ugly, I thought, I already met them. Unfortunately, I had no idea what money Malatesta was talking about. I didn't think he would like me saying that, so instead, I asked him, "Those your guys shot up the house in Drunken Meadows?"

"That," Malatesta said, dismissing the complete ruination of Vinnie's house with a wave of his hand. "That was just a warning. A wake-up call. To let you understand this is serious business."

Serious business. Getting killed was pretty serious—so serious, my mind became completely blank. I couldn't even think of a halfway plausible lie, not that it would have done any good. I had no idea what to lie about.

So I stared at Malatesta, and he stared back at me. We stared at each other for quite a while.

Finally, he got fed up.

"Look," he said, "this doesn't have to be hard." He exposed his teeth momentarily in a little smile that was more like a facial tic. I figured he thought it was reassuring. I was not reassured.

"We can do it the easy way," he said between smile tics.

"What's the easy way?" I asked. I wondered if it would seem easy to me. I didn't think so.

"Just tell me where you put the money. That's all. Tell me where it is. I'll do the rest. You won't have to do a thing. No revenge, nothing. You walk away. Just tell me."

"That's great. That's really a great idea. Just tell you. I would tell you. I really would." I could feel a long free-form babble performance rising up from somewhere deep in my brain, uncontrollable. "I'd *like* to tell you."

Malatesta raised his eyebrows, his smile flickering like a broken neon sign. He nodded. His right hand made half circles in the air, over and over, to encourage me to spit it out.

"But I don't know," I said. "I don't know where it is."

He kept looking at me expectantly, as if he thought I was going to jump up and say, Hey, I was only kidding. But I didn't say anything.

We stared at each other some more. I could feel drops of sweat running under my shirt, down my spine, and into my ass crack. I noticed that Malatesta was sweating, too. In fact, he looked as sick as I felt.

Suddenly, Malatesta leaned over and put his fists against his forehead. He beat on his head a few times, then straightened up.

"Look, Moleri, McCloskey, whatever the fuck your name is supposed to be. You may think this is a game, that you can play it and win. You may think. But it's not."

"I'm sorry," I said meekly, interrupting him, "but I'd like to clear up a misconception. Before it goes any further."

This stalled him. " 'A misconception'?"

I nodded. "I am not who you seem to think I am. I know what I told"—I almost said "Worm Lips," but stopped myself in time—"your . . . representative. But my name is not Moleri. I'm really Johnnie LoDuco. That was just a game, those other names. I'm not playing anymore. So let's be straight with each other. Okay?"

During my little speech, Malatesta had been looking at me as if he couldn't believe what he was hearing. Now he shook his head disgustedly.

" 'Let's be straight with each other,' " he mocked. "Don't give me that bullshit. Johnnie LoDuco is dead."

This was news to me.

"Dead? How do you know?" At this point, I was open to being convinced of anything.

"LoDuco is dead. You killed him. You think I don't know that? You think I'm fucking stupid?"

Malatesta watched me narrowly to see if I'd agree with him. When he saw that I was temporarily incapable of talking, he went on.

"Look, just stop the bullshit, okay? I know. I know everything. Your guy told me all about you.

"You think I don't know. But I know. Vinnie McCloskey-Schmidt, what a fake name that is. You could have at least come up with something halfway believable.

"I found out. You know how? He told me. He told me every-thing, your guy, all about you, what you were planning. He sold you out, Moleri. Then he disappears, the money disappears, you think I don't know what happened?

"He came clean to me, you know? He felt bad. Maybe he was scared . . . I don't know. But he confessed what you were doing—the money, the banks, everything. He was going to help me catch you. He turned you up, Moleri.

"He told me his real name, Johnnie LoDuco. He told me how you planted him here, how you had this plan to rip me off. Now he's gone, and I'm supposed to think he ran off with the money. But I know better."

Malatesta lurched to a halt and stood there, glaring at me under his low, heavy brows.

I sat there going over this news in my head. It was hard to process. Finally, I gave up. I thought I would sum things up.

"Well, here we are," I said.

We were walking down one of the big halls in Malatesta's McMansion. I couldn't remember how we'd gotten there. My mind was functioning at less than full capacity. I was still trying to figure out if I was dead or not.

Malatesta had his arm around my shoulder. He gave me a squeeze, then leaned over to whisper in my ear.

"You can understand my problem," he said.

I nodded.

"I want that money back. More than I want to kill you. Though it's close."

"It must be a terrible dilemma," I said. I couldn't help myself.

"It's not just the insult, the betrayal of trust," Malatesta went on.

"It's the money," I said, thinking, Keep your fucking mouth shut, idiot.

Malatesta gave my shoulder another squeeze.

"It's the money," he agreed. "A lot of money. But if you get it back to me, we'll call it quits."

"Even-steven?"

He shot me a weird look but repeated, "Even-steven."

"But what if I don't know?" I babbled. "What if I really don't know where the money is?"

"That would be too bad. We'd have nothing to talk about then." He shook me back and forth by the shoulders, reminding me of Vinnie. "You want to keep on talking, don't you?"

I nodded. I did.

"Then you'll get me the money?"

I nodded again.

"All of it?"

"Sure."

"All twelve million?"

Twelve million. Vinnie had done himself proud. It did occur to me that it might be difficult to come up with twelve million dollars. But at that point I would have said anything just to get the fuck out of there.

"No problem," I said. "I'll bring it to you."

We came to a big double door. Two guys in suits pulled it open as we came up to it, revealing acres of mud, with Worm Lips and Frown in the foreground, the big stretch limo behind them.

Malatesta paused on the stoop, stroking his chin with a stubby thumb. I could see his beard had come in blue; he had a five o'clock shadow like a swipe of motor oil on his cheeks. His thumbnail shone pinkly.

"All right," he said after a few chin strokes. "I'll have Petey take you home. But remember, if you don't get in touch with us, then we'll get in touch with you."

"Don't even worry about it," I said.

"You'll wish we hadn't."

"You won't have to," I said as reassuringly as I could.

Malatesta held out his hand; shaking it felt like gripping a wet paper bag of bread sticks.

"A pleasure doing business with you, Mr. Moleri," he said. "You have one week."

My luck didn't last a week. It ran out as soon as Worm Lips and Frown drove me back to Vinnie's garage. They were supernice to me, helping me out of the car and into the house. I wasn't real happy about their inviting themselves in, but I was in no position to say anything.

They certainly knew how to party.

"Where is it, numbnuts?" The fist smashed into the side of my head, causing my cheek to slap against the wall and bounce back.

"I don't know," I tried to say. The blood running out of my mouth made me hard to understand.

"What was that?" A hand in my hair jerked my head back. "What did you say? 'I don't know'?" Whack. " 'I don't know'? Don't tell me that." Whack.

"You better tell us where the money is, Kenny," Worm Lips said. He was leaning over the stove in the garage studio, fiddling with the burners, still wearing the black leather car coat. "Hughie will beat your head flat if you don't." He pronounced the name "Youee."

"You'll never find out, then," I said. Whack.

"Very true." Both burners burst into blue-and-yellow flames. Worm Lips was laying out some silverware on the stovetop.

"I'm glad you have gas," he said. "An electric stove's not so good to work with. I guess it has its uses, for like direct application. But it just doesn't heat things up as well as gas." He was leaning some butter knives and a spatula into the blue gas flames, holding them with a barbecue mitt that had WORLD'S GREATEST CHEF stitched on the back.

Worm Lips glanced over at us. Frown was holding me against the wall, his fist cocked back, ready to whack me again.

"Put him in the chair, Hughie," Worm Lips said quietly. "Let him clean up a little."

Frown jerked me across the floor and threw me into a little white-painted kitchen chair. He tossed me a roll of toilet paper, which somehow I caught.

"Here it is," Worm Lips explained to me patiently. "We need to know where the money is. Right now. Not next week."

"Your boss said I had a week."

Worm Lips shook his head sadly.

"Yes, I know. That's the way he is. But we want it now. Right now."

"And if I really don't know where the money is?" I asked. My nose was bleeding like a faucet, and I was trying to stuff a wad of toilet paper up one nostril.

"Then, my friend," Worm Lips said sadly, "we are going to have to make you very uncomfortable. Because we just cannot believe that you don't know your own business."

"What if I don't? What if I told you my partner stiffed me and I don't have any of your money?"

Worm Lips stared at me impassively.

"I expected you to say something like that. But I just can't believe it," he said. "That's why I'm heating up this silverware." He took the butter knife out of the flame and held it up. It glowed red. "When I'm done with this, I'll look around. I bet I find something interesting to use. You'd be surprised how many household implements can be used to cause intense, unbearable pain."

Worm Lips looked at me coyly.

I imagined the red-hot butter knife against my cheek—or somewhere else. That brought me to my feet.

"You can't do this, you—"

Frown picked me up by my shirtfront and slammed me into the

wall. The wad of toilet paper unrolled like a scroll, but it stayed partially wedged in my left nostril.

"Careful, Hughie," I panted, "you'll wake the neighbors."

Worm Lips thought this was really funny. "Wiseass," he said. "I don't think anything's going to wake up Mr. Colucci now."

I was just about to say something to this when Frown hit me in the stomach. Instead of talking, I slid down and sat on the floor, retching.

"Yeah, we know about that," Worm Lips went on. "We are plugged into the cops. Surprised?"

"Nothing surprises me anymore," I said through seriously swollen lips.

Worm Lips looked at me sadly.

"Put him back in the chair, Hughie."

"Wait, wait!" I said.

Frown's enormous fist thudded into my kidneys a few more times. Then he said, "What? What's that?"

"Wait!"

"You have something you want to tell us, Moleri?" Worm Lips asked. I nodded, blood dripping down my chin.

I can't remember what I had planned to say. More bullshit, of course—I didn't have anything else. But before I could get it out, whatever it was, the back door smacked open and Stosh Budjynski stepped into the room, pointing a shotgun at us.

Everyone in the room froze, like we were playing some kind of kids' game, Frown with one hamlike fist cocked back to whack me, Worm Lips holding the red-hot butter knife like a symphony conductor's baton, me covered with blood and toilet paper.

"Sorry," the big bounty hunter said to Worm Lips and Frown. "I knocked, but nobody answered." He nodded in my direction. "You can break his legs or whatever it is you want to do after he gets out of jail. But now he's mine. I'm taking him back."

Worm Lips and Frown straightened up, slowly processing this new information.

"But what if we don't want you to?" Frown asked Stosh. The bounty hunter just looked at him. The shotgun in his hand didn't waver; it was pointed at Frown's crotch.

"Come on," Stosh said, looking at me. He waved the shotgun toward the door, like a pointer. "Don't make me hurt you."

That was funny.

The instant the shotgun barrel moved away from his crotch, Frown threw himself to his right, diving sideways through the air like an Olympic gymnast, bringing out a revolver from somewhere, pointing it at the big bounty hunter. I had seen this dive before—in Hong Kong movies, I think. It had always worked for John Woo and Chow Yun-Fat.

His movements calm and steady, the bounty hunter tracked his dive with the shotgun and blew Frown's head clean off.

"That was really stupid," the bounty hunter said to no one in particular. "Jee-sus, what a fucking idiot." He seemed amazed, almost awestruck by the depths of Frown's stupidity. "You're not going to do anything like that, are you?" he asked Worm Lips beseechingly, waving the shotgun at him.

"No," Worm Lips said in a hoarse whisper. He cleared his throat. "No, sir."

"Then let's go." This was meant for me. "*You*," he said to Worm Lips, "you better lie on the floor, put your hands behind your head." Worm Lips got down on the floor and put his hands behind his head. The bounty hunter reached out, picked me up off the floor, and spun me around. I felt him grab my arms, twist them behind me one after the other, and snap a pair of handcuffs on my wrists—all with one hand. Then, with me in front of him and the shotgun pointed at the ceiling, we backed out through the ruined back door.

Stosh drag-marched me around the side of the garage. I was glad it was dark now and no one in the neighborhood could see this latest humiliation. Worm Lips didn't follow us. I wondered how long he would lie there on the floor with his hands on his head. Days, maybe.

"Look at you. You're a fucking mess," Stosh said when we came under the streetlight. "I got here just in time, huh?" I didn't bother to say anything. It was hard to talk anyway.

Stosh tossed me in the front seat of his car, a fairly old Toyota sedan. My head came up hard against the dashboard. By the time my mind cleared, the big man was behind the wheel and we were driving toward Riverhead. Back to jail.

Stosh seemed pleased with himself.

"I told Canetti this one'd be harder than it looked," he said to me. "You may be a punk-ass loser with no game, but you hang around with some nasty people."

"Nice job on Frown," I said by way of thanking him.

"What, the kung fu diver with the little handgun?" The bounty hunter shook his head bemusedly. "I still don't believe that guy back there. How fucking dumb was that? What made him pull a move like that in front of a shotgun?"

"People drive like that around here, too," I told him. "Unexpected moves, I mean. Not smart."

The bounty hunter looked over at me. He didn't say anything, but it was clear he thought I lacked standing to talk about smart.

"Will they come after you now? Malatesta's people?" I asked him, with the forlorn hope of bringing him down a little.

But Stosh was nonchalant.

"Nah. This's just byplay. They'll clean it up and it will be like nothing ever happened. For me. For you, yes, they will come after you. But they will have to wait till you get out of jail."

"What about the cops?" I asked. I was sincerely concerned. That garage was where I *lived*.

Stoshbo looked at me pityingly.

"*The cops*," he said. "You poor dumb fuck. That's the last thing you should be worrying about."

"So you're not going to call it in?"

The big galoot shook his head. "Not my job. My job is you."

We drove in silence for a long time. Finally, I couldn't take it anymore.

"So Stosh," I said, "how did you find me?"

Stosh stared out over the steering wheel, obviously considering whether it was worth his time to talk to me. Finally, he said, "Easy. You used to live in that neighborhood, numskull. Or did you forget? I asked around. Plenty of people who remember you still live around there. Half the people in Comapogue knew you were living in Vinnie's garage."

"It's nice to know you're remembered."

Stosh squinted at me. "You're a real little wiseass, aren't you? No wonder everyone wants to kill you."

"Who wants to kill me?"

"Well, the obvious—those assholes back at your place. And whoever killed your friend Vinnie wants your ass as well is what I'm hearing."

Whoa—this was a lot of information at once. "You knew about that? About Vinnie? How did you hear about it?"

"It's on the street. I have a lot of contacts—got to in my line of work."

" 'Contacts'—who?"

Stosh shook his head. "Confidential information. You wouldn't know them anyway."

I mused on this.

"Why did he get killed?" I asked. I really wanted to know.

"What I heard on the street, he owed money, big-time. He set up a scam, ripped off some guy, then tried to hang on to the money for himself. Stupid. His creditors got to him and pulled all his teeth out, trying to get him to talk."

"Talk about what?" I asked. I rubbed my jaw, trying not to imagine what it would feel like to have all your teeth yanked out without novocaine.

Stosh shrugged his enormous shoulders. "Money, what else? Where he put the money he was holding out on them. But my guess is he didn't tell them. They're still mad. They still seem to be after you, for instance. If I were you, now, I'd tell them where the money is. Won't do you any good anyway. Filet mignon's hard to eat without teeth."

"I hate steak," I told him. "Anyhow, I'm going to jail."

Stosh nodded. "You sure are. But they can get to you in jail. You'll need teeth, even in the joint."

"There's a problem with that, though," I said.

"What's that?"

"I really don't know. I really have no fucking idea where the money is. I don't know what they're talking about."

"Oh yeah?" Stosh seemed to find this richly comic. "They'll never believe you, though. You know that."

I nodded. "No one ever does."

"I'll send you some straws in the can."

We drove on through the Long Island night. Stosh worked us toward the LIE, taking obscure side roads. It started to rain again. I stared glumly out the window at acres of tombstones, one industrial park after another, endless parking lots, shitty little houses.

We jumped on the expressway at Straight Path.

Were these mysterious sources of Stosh's talking about Mala-testa? Who thought I had killed Vinnie. Or was there another group of people Vinnie had ripped off? And if so, had he told them about me? And if he had, would they come after me?

The answers: Maybe. Most likely. Probably. Without a doubt.

A car one lane over suddenly shot in front of us without signaling, forcing Stosh to hammer the brakes.

"Fucking *ass*hole!" Stosh said.

"See what I mean about the driving here?" I said. "It's real random."

The other car—I couldn't see exactly what make it was in the dark, but it had that ass-in-the-air look of a relatively recent model—now shot back into the lane next to us and fell behind. Then it was up with us again, nearly touching our left front fender. The rain was really slapping down now, and a head-high mist of water bounced up from the roadway.

Stosh cut the wheel, braked, and swore. He shot me a look filled with unpleasantness.

"I think these are friends of yours," he said. The other car side-swiped us; we swerved up onto the shoulder, then back on the road.

"I wish I was in the goddamned truck," Stosh muttered. Twisting a hand over his left arm, he reached into a flap on the door and came out with an evil-looking handgun.

"Look, steer with both hands, okay?" I said. "You're making me nervous."

Another sideswipe. We slid across two lanes, rode up on the far side of the shoulder, up against the retaining wall, paint scraping off in a shower of sparks, then slid back the other way.

These were no friends of mine.

Stosh rolled down his window and stuck the handgun out. The car beside us dropped back, and Stosh leaned his head out, following it. A big-ass semi passed us on the right with a whoosh like a jet plane. Then the other car rear-ended us, good and hard.

"Holy shit!" I heard Stosh yell, right before I blacked out from fear.

CHAPTER SEVEN

I COULDN'T HAVE BEEN out that long; the wheels on Stosh's car were still rotating when I came to. The car was lying on its side on the shoulder; I seemed to be outside it. I was still handcuffed. Stosh was nowhere in sight.

Jennifer Smeals was bending over me.

"Johnnie, can you walk? Get up, get up!" She pulled on my arm. I got to my feet and then immediately fell down again. I had no idea what was going on.

"Johnnie, get up!" Jennifer hissed at me, then said, "Oh shit!" as she discovered I was handcuffed.

She pushed me over to the passenger side of a red Miata, opened the door, and shoved me in. My head whacked the gearshift before I could straighten up. When I had squirmed myself upright, I noticed that the top of the Miata was down, and it was still raining.

Jennifer suddenly reappeared and jumped in the driver's seat. She tossed a fat bunch of keys into my lap—right in the balls—put the car in gear, and took off. By the time I was tracking again, she had gotten on the LIE, westbound, and was breaking all present and future speeding regulations.

The top was still down, and the rain lashed into me like metal wires. It hurt, but it revived me a little. I sat up slowly. Pain shot through various parts of me. I tried to rub the top of my head where it had whacked the gearshift. The chain of the handcuffs caught on the tip of my nose.

"Jennifer," I yelped, "what the fuck?"

She glanced over at me. "You okay?"

"Not really," I whined. "What happened?"

"Sorry about the top," she apologized. We had to bellow at each other in the rush of air and rainwater. "Things happened so fast, I didn't have time to put it up."

She pulled off to the side, jumped out of the car, and in about fifteen seconds had the top up. I wasn't much help.

With the top snugged home, it was quiet enough to talk.

"You were following me?"

She nodded. "I was coming to see you. But just as I got there, I saw those guys in the limo pull up. I waited. I didn't know what else to do. Then the big guy came. He brought you out. I followed."

"Was that you cut us off?"

She shook her head; wet hair stuck to her cheekbone.

"Not me."

"Who was it, then?"

"No idea. Maybe it was just an accident."

I was losing my belief in anything that was "just an accident." I was worried that Worm Lips's buddies were involved, and that they might be right behind us.

"What happened to Stosh?" I asked.

"The big guy? I put him out."

I had to consider this. Big muscular Stosh; tall but thin and delicate Jennifer. I supposed the car accident had incapacitated him somehow.

"Dead?"

Emphatic head shaking from Jennifer. "Just out."

"How?"

"Ether," she said. "A spray can of ether."

"Huh?"

"I put the big guy down with ether. I carry a spray can in my purse. For emergencies."

What kind of emergencies did you need a can of ether for? I thought, but I said, "Was he hurt?" I was conflicted about Stosh. He had saved my ass, true. But he had this obsession with taking me back to jail, and I had to disagree with him there.

"I don't know," Jennifer said cooly. "He was awake, anyway. But groggy. Couldn't get his seat belt off, so maybe he was hurt somehow. I put the mask on him and gassed him out. Took ten seconds. I gave him another spritz when I went back for the keys."

Now I remembered. She was a doctor of some kind.

"I saw you on TV."

"Oh, yeah, you saw the infomercial," she said. She didn't look pleased. "I look like shit in that. Videotape makes you look fat, with, like, golf ball skin."

We drove through the rain in silence for a while. There weren't that many cars on the LIE, for a change. I looked behind us, but all I could see were a few pairs of headlights, not close at all.

By now, we had put Suffolk County behind us and were deep into Nassau—not that you could tell from looking at it.

After about a half hour of driving in the rain, Jennifer cut across three lanes and shot off the expressway, heading south toward Hicksville.

I was beginning to calm down—just a little. Hicksville is not noted for scenic beauty, but it really looked good to me now. I was not dead yet. I was not even in jail. Things were looking up.

That's when I noticed the car following us. It wasn't hard to make it; we were almost the only traffic on the street now.

Jennifer swung the Miata in a sharp left turn up a side street. Looking over my shoulder, I saw headlights as the car behind us made the same turn.

"Jennifer," I mumbled, "I think—"

"I know," she said, hunched down over the steering wheel. "That guy followed us off the LIE. I'll see if I can lose him." She cut the wheel and we shot into a gas station, heading toward the back, where the bathrooms usually are, then bumping over the curb and going through what looked like a vacant lot. Big weeds whacked at the windows. I bounced up and down like a sack of shit. I was glad we were in a convertible. A metal roof would have permanently flattened the top of my skull.

We lurched over another curb and into the street just as a pair of headlights came jolting past the gas station and into the vacant lot.

"He's right behind us, Jennifer," I said.

Just then, the headlights disappeared. There was that whumping sound of sheet metal crumpling up that usually comes at the end of a long brake-squeal noise.

"Building site. Must've gone in the foundation," Jennifer said with satisfaction. "Too bad. You have to know where it is."

"Cool," I said with total sincerity.

We cut through some side streets for a while, then back onto a main drag.

"Is this smart?" I asked her. She didn't say anything. Suddenly, she pulled a two-wheel turn into a motel parking lot, drove around the back, and braked. The car rocked on its springs. My head rocked on my neck; I felt like Vinnie's bobble-head dog.

It was pitch-black behind the motel. I could see a lamp with a cone-shaped metal shade somewhere up ahead, lighting up a door like a spotlight onstage, but the light from it didn't reach us.

Jennifer leaned over, retrieved Stosh's key ring from the floorboards, and unlocked my handcuffs.

"There!" she said. "Maybe we can put them back on later."

I had no idea what she was talking about. I just sat there, afraid to move. But Jennifer jumped out of the car and walked off into the darkness.

She came back when she saw I was still sitting there.

"Come on, get out. We're here."

"Where is 'here'?" I asked.

"This is where I've been staying. It's safe, at least for now. It belongs to a guy I know."

"He won't mind my being here?"

"He won't even know," Jennifer said.

It wasn't much brighter in the hall of the motel than it had been out back. There was a ratty brown carpet that smelled of dog, and I could see a row of closed doors. A yellowy shadeless bulb overhead was the only light. It looked like a mental institution, or maybe a small private prison.

Jennifer must've noticed me sniffing and staring; she said, "How do you like my new place, Johnnie?" Her smile was all crooked.

"It's okay," I said noncommittally.

"The good thing about it is that nobody knows I'm here," she said. "At least not the people who are looking for Vinnie. That son of a bitch."

"Who, Vinnie?"

"He set us up, Johnnie," Jennifer Smeals said. "You and me. His girlfriend and his best friend."

"Well, we weren't that close anymore," I replied, demurring. "I mean, I haven't seen him that much in the last year or so."

"Oh, don't make excuses for him. He set us up, and then he took off and left us holding the bag."

"Yeah, and the bag has his head in it," I said, trying to restore some perspective.

We stopped in front of a door. Jennifer took out another key—she seemed to have an endless supply—and unlocked the door.

"My little home away from home," she said, waving me inside. "What do you think?"

"Looks like a motel room in Hell," I said.

It was like a suite, really, several rooms at the back of the motel. Jennifer said it was where the motel manager usually lived. But he had gotten busted for selling crack to motel guests, and they hadn't found a replacement yet. The guy who owned the place let her stay there, Jennifer told me. He owed her, she said, but she didn't say why. I guessed he was someone from her old drug-honking, black-mailing pre-Vinnie hospital days.

"But the place is safe now," she said. *Now?* What did she mean by "now"? Why wasn't it safe *before*?

It was in my mind to ask her this, and more, but she turned away from me and began fussing with things on the kitchen counter.

"You want some coffee?" she asked, filling up a kettle. "Why don't I make some, and meanwhile you can take a shower, wash up, get yourself together. You look like shit."

I came out of the bathroom wearing a terry-cloth robe that belonged to Jennifer, I guess. It fit all right but was cut kind of low in front. And it was short—really short. I felt stupid and self-conscious, but a little sexy at the same time, in a weird kind of way. It was almost cross-dressing, right? But not quite.

Jennifer's eyes lit up when she saw me walk in wearing her robe.

"You are a hairy one," she said, grinning. "Vinnie was like that, too, black hair all over his chest, like a gorilla."

"Jennifer," I began. I didn't have anything in my head; I didn't know where I was going with this, if anywhere. But she cut it short. She must have sensed something.

"Johnnie, no. Don't even think about it," she said. Her smile was gone, like a snapped rubber band. "Don't even think about thinking about it." She put two coffee cups down on the dining table.

"Jennifer, I don't," I said. "I wasn't–"

"Johnnie, just shut up and sit down. Please."

We sat at the table drinking coffee. It tasted great, so much better than caked-up instant scrapings. Neither of us said anything for a long time. Jennifer drank the last of her coffee, then sat there playing with her mug, turning it this way and that, looking into it.

After a while she said, "So, Vinnie is really dead. It's so hard to hold on to that."

"What do you think happened? Who killed him?" I asked.

Jennifer didn't answer me right away, just looked back into her coffee cup.

"They must've gotten to him right at the airport," she said. "I can see how it would have happened. In the men's room, probably. Or maybe they crowded him at a phone booth, put a gun on him, walked him out of the terminal."

She sounded like she'd done things like that herself. Not for the first time, I wondered about Jennifer Smeals. Where had she come from? What had she been into? Did I really want to know the answers to these questions?

"I guess they were following us the whole time," Jennifer said.

She sniffed. I wondered if she was about to start crying. She didn't seem the type.

"Vincent always thought he was so fucking smart," she said. "He thought he could use his moves on anybody, that nobody could keep up with him."

I looked into my cup, too. There was nothing inspirational there. "His moves didn't work on Malatesta, huh?" I said.

Jennifer snorted. "*Malatesta*. Malatesta is as deep in the shit as we are. Malatesta's a goof. He never could have come up on Vincent. It's the people he's responsible to that I'm worried about."

This was news to me. I was still plenty worried about Malatesta. It was depressing to think that there were people he was scared of, that didn't like us much, either.

I sat and brooded for a while. There were so many things about this I didn't understand, I could hardly open my mouth. What I needed was to grow a couple extra heads so they could all talk at once, asking Jennifer all the things that were bothering me.

Finally, one urgent question shouldered its way to the front of my brain.

"Why did you call me up and tell me to leave Vinnie's house? What was that all about? I mean, how did you know those guys were coming?"

She gave me a funny look.

"Johnnie, I was all alone. I had nowhere to go. I burned all my bridges before we left." She made a sour mouth. "And people—they were looking for me. The same people, probably, who got to Vincent. You see what they did to him."

I thought about beheading and painful, nongentle tooth extraction. These things were bad things, true. But they didn't really answer my question.

I opened my mouth to ask it again, but Jennifer jumped up as if the kitchen chair had ejected her.

"You want some more coffee?" she said. "It's pretty good, isn't it?"

Well, it was good, and I said so. She came around the table and got my coffee cup, giving me a little shoulder squeeze at the same time. I felt her bare leg brush mine as she leaned over to get the cup. My mind, if that's what it was, went blank again.

"How did you meet Vinnie?" I was honestly curious. Jennifer didn't seem like anyone Vinnie would have known back when we were in high school. But obviously a lot had changed since then.

"He was a patient of mine," she said. Her eyes got sad and shiny as she looked into the past, which was full of Vinnie. "Normally, I do not date patients. You really can't. But Vincent got to me. He was really something. That charm of his, it just drilled right into you. He colonized you. And before you knew it, you didn't want to get rid of him anymore."

"This was when you were at the hospital," I asked, "or at the hair place?"

Jennifer slid me a low, mean look. "The hair-treatment center. He was really, deeply upset about losing his hair, you know. I never saw him like that. Most things rolled over him, never touched him, never fazed him. But his hair, that did it."

"I can't imagine Vinnie bald."

"Neither could he. Vincent had a lot of personalities, a lot of different people inside him. But none of them was bald."

We were both quiet for a while, listening to the resonance of the past tense as applied to Vincent McCloskey-Schmidt.

"He never made it to Paraguay," I said, sighing.

"That would have been fun, huh? Can you imagine how Vincent would have made out down there?" Jennifer's eyes shone. "That place is so corrupt and backward, it makes Long Island look like DisneyWorld. He would've had a field day."

"He told me he wanted to leave Paraguay out of it," I reminded her. "Paraguay was going to be the billing center, the refuge." I could hear Vinnie's voice in my head, as loud as my own. "He had no plans to run the credit card scam down there."

Jennifer frowned.

"Credit card scam? What are you talking about? That wasn't part of it."

"But, but," I babbled, "wasn't that the big plan? Isn't that where the money came from?"

"He told you that?" Her eyes narrowed with scorn and disbelief. They clearly said, Putz. Sap. Moron.

"I had no reason to disbelieve him," I said.

"No, I suppose not. It *is* true that Vincent got his hands on a program like that, a thief program that would skim a penny or two from every transaction it conducted. But he never did anything with it, beyond testing it out at his local deli."

"What deli was that?" I asked.

"The one up the street from where he used to live. Where he grew up. He even took me there once," she said in wonderment. "Boy, that was quite a date."

I nodded. That was my local deli, too, Bruno's, the one nearest my house in Comapogue. I'd been going there all my life.

"He only ever realized about seventy dollars from it, you know," Jennifer said to me.

Some of it probably mine, I thought, from my cigarette and beer money. Oh well. All that ice I had boosted from Bruno made up for some of it.

"Okay, but if that's the case, then where did all the money come from? I mean, I'm assuming there is money in this somewhere. Real money."

Jennifer nodded. "Real money, Johnnie."

"I mean, you don't cut someone's head off for cigarette money," I continued.

As if I had reminded her, Jennifer reached into a pocket of her dressing gown and fished out a pack of cigarettes—Marlboro Lights this time.

"Want one?"

I hooked a smoke out of the proffered pack. We lit up.

Jennifer leaned back in her chair, blowing smoke and looking thoughtful. I could see she was wondering just how much I needed to know.

"Malatesta really trusted Vincent," she said through the smoke. "Anyone would, and Malatesta . . . well, a lot of people are smarter than Malatesta."

"A few Cheerios short of a bowl?" I suggested. She nodded.

"He let Vincent run everything for him. It started out with just the computer part of it. But Vincent ended up with his fingers in everything."

" 'Everything'? What would that be? What did Malatesta have going?"

"A couple things." She stubbed her cig out in the coffee cup. "The big thing was the boiler room."

"Boiler room?"

"Malatesta was selling stocks, crappy, worthless stocks. Over the phone, and online, too. He had a Web site. That's how Vincent got involved."

I smiled ruefully, shaking my head. "Yeah, Vinnie, he was always Mr. Programmer."

Jennifer looked at me with what even I recognized as utter disbelief.

"*Mr. Programmer?* Vincent couldn't program a VCR. He used to have to have his secretary turn his computer on for him in the morning."

"But, but," I said, "in high school, he was always Mr. Computer. He talked about it all the time."

Now Jennifer smiled, and I realized this was something she didn't do so much when she was happy as when she was about to put it to other people.

"He *told* you about it. I'm sure he did. But did you ever see him sit down at a computer and write code?"

I shook my head.

"Would you know computer code if it came up and bit you in the ass?"

I shook my head again.

"Johnnie," Jennifer said in what I was beginning to recognize as her "poor dumb Johnnie" voice—she'd used it on Vinnie sometimes, too—"Vincent was very good at just one thing: convincing people of pure bullshit. He was really, really good at that. He was the best. He hired people to do the rest."

"The gambling and the porn sites were key," Jennifer told me. "They started to bring in more than the shitty stocks. Then Vincent had his big idea. He started selling stock for the gambling and porn sites. Except he forgot to tell anyone—the SEC, Malatesta, people who might have been interested to know."

"What did he do, keep the money?"

"He would have," Jennifer said. "One hundred percent of the proceeds. But Malatesta found out. If he was smart, he would have killed Vincent right then. But Malatesta is not smart. He let Vincent talk him into partnering up on it. Malatesta got to keep most of the revenue; Vincent only got a commission."

This jibed with what Malatesta had told me, though leaving out the part where Vinnie'd said he was me.

"That doesn't sound so bad," I commented. "Malatesta gets most of the money. Isn't that what he wants?"

Jennifer nodded, lighting up another Marlboro. The problem with those light cigarettes is that you end up smoking twice as many.

"It might have all been okay. Except that Malatesta never got the money. Somehow, Vincent siphoned it all away. Even I don't know how he did that. Malatesta didn't even realize it at first. But he sure knows now.

"But the bad thing," Jennifer went on, "the really bad part in all this: Malatesta didn't try to keep it to himself. He told the people he works for."

"They didn't approve?"

Jennifer shrugged. "They don't give a shit how the money comes in, so long as it does. But telling them about the scam raised their expectations. And now Malatesta has to disappoint them. From what I've heard, they hate being disappointed."

I reached inside the bathrobe and scratched my chest thoughtfully.

"Is there really that kind of money in porno and gambling sites? Enough to cause all this trouble?"

"Maybe," Jennifer said. "Maybe not. But that doesn't matter. Because the whole thing was a scam from the inception. There was no reality to it. Vincent made it all up—the stocks, the documentation, fake histories, everything. It wouldn't have stood up to even a quick double check, of course. But most people were too greedy to check. That's how Vincent made his money."

"How did he work it?"

"Paid off the original investors with the proceeds from the new ones. Keeping most of it for himself, of course. A basic Ponzi scheme. A cheap-ass, unimaginative hustle," Jennifer said with disgust.

"Not what you'd expect from Vinnie," I offered. She looked at me with pity and scorn.

"You never really knew him," she said, "not like I did. His ideas were all ridiculous, pitiful. Only his presentation was great." Her look softened. "He really was good at that, though. At making you think he was somebody. He had charm; he was persuasive—he could make you believe anything."

We devoted some more quiet time to considering the life of Mr. McCloskey-Schmidt.

I couldn't believe it myself. None of it sounded like the Vinnie I knew. Well, maybe the stealing part. That fit. But something was missing from the picture. I wondered if Jennifer knew and was keeping it from me. She would, I figured, if she did. But it was always possible she didn't have all the facts herself. This would explain why she was so suddenly interested in me. Everyone always seems to think I know something. Maybe it's my eyes.

"So how much money are we talking here?"

Jennifer narrowed her eyes at me.

"Lots."

I'd heard that before.

" 'Lots'? How much is lots?"

"Millions," she said. "Try two million on for size. It was at least that the last time I looked. And I wouldn't put it past Vincent to have hidden some even from me. Bless his little heart."

This was not exactly what I'd heard from Malatesta, but I figured Jennifer wanted to keep a little something in reserve, for emergencies. A kind of financial can of ether.

"Why didn't Malatesta just kill me?" I asked her. "When he had me in his house, I mean."

"Obviously, he wants the money more than he wants your skinny little ass," Jennifer explained graciously. "And too, maybe he thinks you'll go to the money, and then he can follow you to it." From the hard, probing looks she was giving me, I could see Jennifer might be thinking the same thing.

"He thinks I killed Vinnie," I said sadly. "He thinks I cut off my best friend's head and took his money."

Jennifer shot me a strange slit-eyed look. "You didn't tell him about the head, did you? About finding it?"

I shook my head. "It didn't come up."

"Where is it now?" she asked.

"Back at the house, Vinnie's parents' house," I said. "I'm not going back for it, that's for sure." That much seemed clear to me.

"You've got to go back for it," Jennifer Smeals said.

"Huh? What?"

"The head. You've got to go back for it." She turned toward me, eyes wide. "The head is important. I can't tell you why now. But we have to have it."

So there it was. The whole thing was out in the open, lying between us like a corpse on an autopsy table.

Jennifer eyed me carefully, hoping to see how I was processing all this information.

"You hungry?" she asked. "You want something to eat? I could scramble up some eggs."

In spite of the events of the last twelve hours, the talking, the beating, the talking, the car wreck, more talking, in spite of the coffee cups on the table filled with sludge and dead cigarettes, in spite of the phantom head looming over everything, I was suddenly hungry—really hungry.

"Let me do it," I said, and jumped up. I'm a pretty good cook, actually, one of the few things everyone agrees I am good at. Diving into the refrigerator I came up with half an onion and a wrinkled-up green pepper, some eggs. The cupboard coughed up garlic powder, Parmesan sawdust in a green cardboard tube, oregano. We were in business.

"Stand back, Jennifer."

She didn't stand back, exactly, but followed me around the kitchen as I threw things together. Trying to help, I thought. We kept bumping into each other. It had a Laurel and Hardy aspect. But it was sexy, too, in a weird way.

After we scarfed down the omelettes—they turned out pretty good for a last-minute desperation fry—I cleaned off the table and started washing up.

"You should start your own restaurant, Johnnie," Jennifer said. She was leaning in next to me. Her dressing gown hung open, and I could see her tits. She pressed against me once, very lightly, maybe accidentally. I felt her bones under the skin.

"Jennifer," I said helplessly.

I put a hand on her shoulder and pulled her toward me. She stiffened and resisted, but then I heard a little sigh.

"Is this what you want, Johnnie?" she asked, letting me pull her over.

There was not much under her gown, nothing under my robe but me. I leaned over and kissed her.

We did that for a while.

The robes had fallen to the floor, and we were skin against skin, panting and slithering over each other. I was completely gone. Suddenly, she stepped back, held me at arm's length, and gave me that very serious appraising look she had. Then she seemed to arrive at a decision. She backed up some more and held out her hands to me.

"Johnnie, come here."

I went to her. She walked backward into the bedroom, leading me by the hands. When we got to the bed, she sat down on it and made me sit next to her.

There was a pause, filled with ragged breathing—mine, I guess.

"You should know this, Johnnie," she said, leaning against me and fooling with my hair. "I am into different things."

This was more talking than I was ready for, but I said, as required, " 'Things'? What things?"

Jennifer smiled, the crooked one again. She bent over—the curve of her bare back almost made me pass out—and reached under the bed, pulling out a small black case. When she opened it, I saw that it was lined with red velvet and contained ropes, chains, handcuffs, and some other things—ball gags, dildos, straps.

"Different," I muttered.

"This can't surprise you, Johnnie." She grinned. "Vincent told me all about you, those novels of yours. He made me read one."

"Oh yeah? Which one? Did you like it?"

"I like this." She surged up, snapped a cuff on my wrist, and attached the other to the headboard.

Soon she had me spread-eagled on the bed, naked, cuffed, and chained. She sat on top of me, fastening a ball gag in my mouth. When she finished, she sat back, admiring her handiwork.

"You know, Johnnie," she said, "I *am* into this." I could see from her eyes that she was telling the truth.

"But not with you." Jennifer jumped up and danced away from the bed. "Not with you and not now. Sleep tight, Johnnie." In two seconds, she was out the door.

Five minutes later, she came back and tossed a blanket over me.

"If you piss on my mattress, I'll beat the snot out of you," she whispered. "Sweet dreams."

She turned off the light and the door snapped shut behind her.

Early the next morning, Jennifer came in and freed me from the bed. I sat up, rubbing my wrists.

"You could just say no, you know," I whined. "You didn't have to fucking trick me like that."

"Johnnie, look, I'm sorry," she said. She was being nice to me this morning. I could see that was the plan. "I don't know what I was thinking. I just couldn't deal, so many things have been happening. I'm sorry. I just flipped out, I guess. You're a nice-looking guy, but . . ."

That *but.*

"Where the fuck are my clothes?" I said, not in a particularly good mood.

"On the floor by the bed," Jennifer told me on her way out the door. "You want some coffee?"

"Coffee!" I yelled after her. "A lot of coffee." I began to perk up at the thought of it. I have a forgiving nature. "With real milk," I added, remembering the water and powdered nondairy creamer I'd been drinking the past couple of weeks. "And sugar. Lots of sugar."

"You got it."

My clothes were there, lying in a pile on the floor, where she had tossed them. They smelled bad, which was only natural, since I'd been wearing them for a week. A tough week at that. I began putting them on—I was used to dirty clothes at this point—but stopped at the socks. I couldn't do the socks; they were foul beyond description, and seemed to be turning into some kind of jelly.

I looked around the motel manager's room. There was a chest of drawers against the wall, and when I opened it, it was full of socks. I felt like I'd broken it at a slot machine. I yanked open the other drawers, finding underwear—boxers, which I don't usually go for, but acceptable in the circumstances—and undershirts. These must belong to the guy who runs the motel, I thought, Jennifer's friend. But he won't mind if I borrow some. He probably will never know.

With the new underwear on, I felt much better, crisper and more defined. But the thought of slipping back into my greasy pants was even less attractive than before.

Next to the head of the bed was a closet door. Behind that door, I told myself, are shirts, trousers, suits, and ties. I decided to push my luck and steal some more fresh clothes if I could. Maybe they would even fit me.

I opened the closet door. That is, I went to open the closet door, but it was stuck, jammed against the carpet, maybe. I gave it a good tug. The door swung open.

Hanging from a coat hook on the inside of the door was a guy in his socks and Skivvies. He was stuck up on the hook by virtue of the tie around his neck. His eyes were bugging out and his face was that blue color of Belinda Colucci-Hahn's nails.

"The fuck?" I said, displaying my usual insight.

Jennifer was right behind me, carrying cups of coffee. I hadn't heard her come in. I think she had been hoping to head me off so I wouldn't open the closet, but I had been too quick for her.

"This is the guy owns the motel," she said by way of introduction.

"Owned," I said. "What happened to him?"

"I thought he was all right," Jennifer said, staring at the hanging stiff as if she wanted to take a bite out of it. I hoped I'd never catch her looking at me like that. "He set me up in this place. I was grateful. If Malatesta's boys had found me at that point, it would have been all over."

As I contemplated the stiff, I rubbed my jaw where the late Frown had been whacking on me. "But what happened? Did they get him?"

She shook her head, still staring at the dead guy. He wore boxer shorts with little cars on them, classic Chevies, and had a nasty little Clark Gable mustache.

"The little shit just got greedy, I guess," she said. "He told me if I didn't fuck him, he would turn me over to the guys who were follow-ing me."

"You should have fucked him," I said helplessly, experiencing my usual instant regret.

"I did fuck him," Jennifer said. "But I knew I couldn't trust him anymore. The minute he stopped panting, the little shit would have been on the phone to Malatesta. I could tell." Now she smiled, and it scared me more than her angry, hungry look. "I told him the tie around the neck was a sex thing." She grinned and glanced over at me. "It is, you know, for some people."

"Not for me," I said, though I had written about such things. "Not for him, either, I guess."

"Don't worry about him," Jennifer said. "If I didn't kill him, somebody else would've. He was a king-size asshole."

I looked at the guy hanging there. He was starting to get ripe. He smelled, in fact, like an open sewer. In spite of my time with the head, I wasn't quite used to that. I reached over and swung the door shut; it moved easily. The motel must've tilted in that direction.

"So I guess we can't stay here," I said, half-hoping she would say, No, of course we can. But she said, "You got that right. Finish get-ting dressed, Johnnie. We have heads to fetch."

We sat around the suite the rest of the day. There wasn't much day-light left—and I had slept pretty long, in spite of the handcuffs. But both of us thought, on mature consideration, that head fetching was better done in the dark.

We didn't talk a lot—I was still pretty pissed about the night be-fore. My pride was wounded. We watched a fair amount of TV.

When it finally got dark enough, we climbed into the red Miata—it was a pretty cool little car, though conspicuous. Jennifer had put on a head scarf and glasses, a sort of Jacqueline Kennedy Onassis look. I was dressed for breaking and entering, courtesy of the dead motel guy.

Before she started the car, Jennifer sat staring at the steering wheel for a minute. It looked really staged; even I could see that. She was having a "sudden thought."

Sure enough, she turned to me and said earnestly, "Johnnie, Vincent told me he'd hidden some money somewhere—someplace on the island. Getaway money, emergency money. To use if we got in trouble."

"Oh, yeah," I said. I could see myself double-reflected in her sunglasses, looking small and far away.

"Do you know where it is?"

"Oh yeah." I nodded. "I found it."

"Fantastic!" Jennifer Smeals breathed out a big sigh of relief. She turned the ignition and fired up the Miata. We tooled through Hicksville and turned north, heading back toward the LIE.

"How much did he leave?" she asked once we were on the expressway.

"Oh, five or so," I said, "I didn't really count it."

"Five." Jennifer gnawed her lip. "There has to be more."

"That's all there was," I told her. "You need some now?"

She shot me a funny look. "No, I'm okay. But Johnnie, maybe you should let me have it, for safekeeping."

"What, all of it?" She nodded, watching me carefully.

"Okay, I guess," I said. After all, it was Vinnie's money, not mine. "Just let me have a couple twenties, for, like, expenses."

Jennifer smiled. It was a nice smile this time, not a mean one. She leaned over and pecked me on the cheek.

"You're cute, Johnnie, you know that? Where is it?"

I was still fixed on the "cute" part. The previous night came back into my head, forcefully, the early parts at least.

"Where is what?"

"The money," she said patiently. "Where is the money?"

"Oh, that. Back at Vinnie's parents' house, under the sink."

"Shit," she said. "I should've thought of that."

"Well, it doesn't matter. I can grab it when I take the head."

She brightened up a lot. "That's right. We'll be all set."

"Set for what?" I asked, really wanting to know.

"To get out of here. Before it all blows apart."

It seemed to me like it had already blown apart pretty good, and I said so. Jennifer looked at me pityingly.

"Malatesta and his little goons are nothing to what's going to come down, believe me, Johnnie. You don't want to be around when his employers find out the money they were counting on is not on the table anymore."

"Who are these guys?" I whined. "Where do they come from? What do they want from me? Are they Mafia?"

Jennifer was scornful. "The *Mafia*. The Mafia doesn't have that kind of push. Not anymore. The people we're dealing with use the Mafia as errand boys."

"Who?" I asked. "Who, *who*?" I sounded like a demented cartoon owl.

Jennifer shrugged. " 'The cartel,' Vincent called them. International investors. We'll probably never know for sure who's behind it—shell companies, banks, accommodation addresses, funds laundered through legitimate businesses—you could never get through it all. The Mafia may even be part of it, but a small part. But whoever they are, they expect a return on their investment."

"Can't we talk to them, negotiate? If they're like businessmen."

Jennifer shook her head. "Johnnie, you don't understand how things work," she told me. "It's not the mob anymore. It's not even that personal. It's not even any one organization. There's a whole class of people now that make up a kind of shadow army—mercenaries, muscle, thugs, killers for hire. Where do they come from? The Colombians, the Russians, Serbs, South Africans, the old-time Mafia. Out-of-work armies. These guys are everywhere. They transcend the old crime organizations. There's enough work in the world, they can live off whoever hires them. And in the new economy—the *real* new economy, not what you read about in the papers—the money needs them."

"I don't get it," I said. She turned her head slightly, and the wind ripped her reply away; it sounded something like "fucking idiot."

As Jennifer Smeals's bright red Miata tooled down the streets of my old neighborhood toward Vinnie's parents' house, I began to get increasingly nervous. It was something like the feeling I had when I was seven years old, waiting in the wings of the grade-school auditorium for my cue in the class play. Except now, of course, the stakes were higher. Now I ran the risk of being shot at, having the crap kicked out of me, or, at best, getting shoved around and thrown in the back of a squad car. I was walking back into the garage apartment, filled with heads and headless bodies, dead fish, probably a good deal of meltwater from my ice collection. I was not happy about this.

The Miata slowed down at the head of the block. I could see Vinnie's parents' house at the other end of the street, just past the streetlight.

"Get out here," Jennifer said. "I'll drive around, come by and pick you up. I don't think they're watching the house anymore, but you never know. Don't take your time about it."

"What about the cops?"

Jennifer shrugged. "The least of our worries. Come on, get out."

I got out. No part of me wanted to, but I knew she would push me out if I didn't.

The stretch of sidewalk from the corner to Vinnie's parents' house was endless, and I cringed like a bug each time I had to walk through the glow cast by a streetlight. But finally I reached the house, scooted around the back, and let myself in. I didn't even need the key, thanks to Stosh; the door was hanging by a hinge.

It was dark inside. I tried to navigate by memory, but I immediately tripped and fell, landing, fortunately, on the sofa bed.

At least I knew where I was now. I groped around for the lamp I remembered being next to the sofa bed, found it, and flipped it on.

Frown was gone. Most of him anyway. I had half-expected to see his body still stretched out where it had fallen. I wouldn't have been surprised to find Worm Lips still lying on the floor, either, with his hands behind his head, waiting for Stosh to get farther away. But he was gone, too.

Parts of Frown were still with us, however, mostly sprayed out along the wall. Little brain pieces hung down from the zone of red splatter.

The realization slowly sifted through me: The cops had already been here, carted away bodies, and cleaned up a little. And if that was so, they'd be back, were maybe watching the place at this moment. My entire body broke out in a cold sweat. And if they'd taken Frown away, they'd have found the head, and taken that, too.

Feeling sick to my stomach, I thrashed over to the other side of the room, then pulled up short.

There they were, the beauties: two coolers sitting side by side, right where I had left them. The bucket I had left to catch the drip from the cooler spout was full to the brim, and the studio smelled like a bait shop. But it could have been worse—much worse. I hefted the cooler, felt the weight of it. Nice and full.

Just then, headlights scraped over the curtained garage-door windows, and I realized I was taking too goddamn long. I grabbed the cooler and fled, only just remembering to grab the roll of twenties from beneath the sink and snap off the light as I left.

———

Feeling my way through the pitch-dark side yard, I saw a car zoom by on the street, not Jennifer's, but a late-model Chrysler. I couldn't see the driver, could just make out a hunched silhouette at the wheel. I felt relatively safe in the cool darkness by the side of the house. A big hedge, some kind of evergreen, grew along the boundary between the houses, bulging over the top of Vinnie's parents' stockade fence and blocking out the light from the street. No one could see me there. I crouched down and waited for the red Miata to cruise by.

After about ten minutes, I stood up and stretched, then sat on the cooler gingerly. It held me fine and was a lot more comfortable than squatting. That was a good thing, too, because I had a long wait ahead of me.

After another ten minutes or so, I crept up to the edge of the house and peeked around the corner. The street was empty. The night was still and windless. In the distance, up on Montauk Highway, I could hear cars shushing by, sirens, trucks, traffic. But closer to home, silence. Specifically, no humming Miata pulled up to take me and Vinnie's head out of there.

After what felt like hours and hours but was probably only one, or less, I began to feel panic burbling up in me, starting in my legs and shooting out the top of my head. I was a Roman candle of pure panic.

Every couple of minutes, I walked to the end of the house and peered around. After a few dozen repetitions, this didn't work anymore, and I had to walk all the way into the street and look up and down the block to soothe the anxiety burbling in my belly.

Aside from one car creeping by two blocks down the street, I didn't see a fucking thing. No Miata, no Jennifer Smeals, nothing.

I began to sink into despair, unable to move, perched on top of the cooler by the side of the house. I knew that night was sliding toward day, though I didn't have the slightest clue as to what time it was. It felt like next week, next year, another century. I knew that when day finally arrived, I would be conspicuous, sitting in the side yard of a house that didn't belong to me, squatting on a cooler filled with bait fish and my best friend's sconce.

She wasn't coming. Something had obviously happened to Jennifer, probably, given the circumstances, something bad. I had to face it and get myself out of there before something just as bad happened to me.

It took awhile longer before the overwhelming terror of waiting there balanced out the fear of walking on the streets in plain sight. But eventually, just sitting there seemed worse than almost anything I could think of. I picked up the cooler and began to walk.

First, I walked around the block to see if maybe she was parked somewhere nearby, waiting for me. Nada. I didn't meet anybody, and I don't think anyone saw me.

Walking around and around the block until something happened seemed like a bad plan. I headed up to Montauk, thinking, Grab a taxi. Just get off the streets.

But by the time I got up to Montauk—the main thoroughfare on that part of the island—there were no cabs in sight, hardly any traffic of any kind. I bounced back and forth between feeling glad there were no cars filled with thugs observing me and a feeling of total naked exposure, like a cockroach on an operating table.

I walked aimlessly up the highway, heading west, toward Hicksville, Jennifer, and relative safety. But I didn't have a hope of making it on foot.

Then I almost walked into a bus stop signpost. The buses on Long Island don't run very often and don't really go anywhere. But I thought if I could somehow get to the Hicksville LIRR station, I could find Jennifer's secret motel again. Anyway, I'd have a better chance on the bus than I would on foot.

There was even a bench for prospective bus riders. I sat down to wait again.

Two hours later—two hours of sweating, trembling terror—I saw the bus coming toward me. I shot to my feet, waving, just in case the driver decided not to stop. It's been known to happen. The bus pulled in; the door sighed open.

Frantically, I scrabbled in my pockets for exact change. I barely had enough. I grabbed my transfer and walked to the back, the cooler whacking against the seats as I went. Fortunately, there was hardly anybody on the bus.

We cruised along, making good time, occasionally stopping to pick up more passengers. I was beginning to feel better as we got closer to Hicksville, thinking I might get back in one piece after all. Then I saw Worm Lips.

What was worse was that he saw me, too. A black stretch Caddy pulled up next to the bus as we waited at a stoplight. Someone was leaning out the passenger window like a German shepherd, staring up the road. I recognized the top of Worm Lips's head. Then for some reason, maybe signaled by the buzzing of panic in my head, Worm Lips looked up. Our eyes met. A nasty writhing smile spread slowly over Worm Lips's features.

When the light changed, he pulled his head in, taking a last look at me. Glancing through the rear window of the bus, I saw the Caddy pull in behind us.

This was fucked. It looked as if there was no possibility of escape now. I wondered what Malatesta and his goons would think of Vinnie's head. They would never believe I'd had nothing to do with it. They would just think I killed him to take whatever it was he had taken from them.

Then, to make things worse, the traffic began to slow down. Craning my neck out the window, I could see a thick stream of cars ahead of us; there was no traffic at all in the opposite direction. I saw bright lights in the distance, the whirling red strobes of emergency vehicles and cop cars, and what looked like smoke.

Horns began to honk as the traffic slowed to a crawl. Some cars pulled out of line in smoking U-turns and blasted back the other way. Others drove up onto the shoulder, even the sidewalk, trying to navigate around the trouble. When they saw they couldn't, they tried to force their way back into the traffic stream, creating even more snarling, honking, and yelling.

I had the pleasure of seeing a beefy big-wheel truck, body raised up about four feet off its springs, muscle its way back into line just in front of Worm Lips's Caddy. Both Worm Lips and the driver were leaning out the windows of the stretch, screaming and cursing at the truck. The driver of the big truck ignored them. As the truck cut in front of them, its left rear bumper scraped a long swatch of paint off the Caddy's front fender.

I ran up to the front of the bus. "Let me off here," I said to the driver, who was frozen in disgust and hopelessness. Without a glance in my direction, he popped open the doors and I scuttled out, hoping the monster truck would block Worm Lips's line of sight.

Keeping my head down, I walked quickly up the street toward the blinking red lights. Normally, carrying a cooler full of severed body parts is not something you want to do around officers of the law, but even the cops seemed a better deal than Worm Lips and company.

But when I got up to the accident, no one paid any attention to me at all, and I could see why. The wreck was a three-way collision between a fuel-oil tanker, a sewage-pumping truck—what we used to call "the honey wagon," which pumps out Porta-Potties at games and job sites—and a late-model Chrysler sedan. Both the tanker and the truck were on their sides, and reeking black fluid was pouring into the street, oil mixing with shit, a volatile combination.

Just as I came abreast of the tangle of vehicles, I heard one of the rescue workers shouting through his bullhorn, "Get back! Get back!"

I figured this must mean me, as well. I took off running, the cooler under one arm like a big square football.

I had gone about half a block when—*whump*!—a flash told me the oil tanker had gone up. The concussion propelled me down the street like a toy. I was running and half-falling, until I tripped over the curb in front of a small strip mall. Somehow I kept a grip on the cooler.

There was a lot of yelling, and the sound of sirens and car horns behind me. I didn't wait to find out what was happening.

CHAPTER EIGHT

ALL OF THE STOREFRONTS in the strip mall were dark, except for a video store. The sign in the window said they were open 24/7; I pushed the door open and walked in, not daring to look behind me.

As I walked in, the girl at the cash register jerked her head up and sneered in my general direction.

"We close in fifteen minutes," she informed me.

"Close? The sign said you're open twenty-four/seven," I pointed out.

"Not tonight. We close six hours for cleanup."

"Okay, but even if you close for just six hours, it's not exactly twenty-four/seven, is it? That's like false advertising."

The girl shrugged and went back to reading her magazine. She wouldn't even sneer at me anymore.

I knew better than to push it. "Can I leave this here?" I asked, holding up the cooler. Some wild thought of abandoning it rumbled through my head. Just walk out the back door, leave it with the video punks, and let it be their problem, I told myself. But there was no back door that I could see.

The girl at the register actually looked at me now, but nothing in particular showed on her face. She nodded, though, so I put the cooler down alongside the register stand, out of traffic.

I thought I should justify my presence while I desperately tried to think of what to do next, so I browsed the racks. None of the videos looked good to me. I had been out of it so long, I didn't know a thing about the new releases. It seemed as if either I had already seen every other video in the store or I never wanted to see them in this life. My choices were, as they often seemed to be, way reduced.

Finally, I settled on an old black-and-white cowboy movie from the fifties, the video equivalent of comfort food, and a cheesy horror movie made in the Philippines and dubbed. I carried these up to the counter.

Part of me—the part that still had any sense—couldn't believe I was actually going to rent a movie, but I figured what the hell. If I ever got back to Jennifer's motel/morgue, I had no plans on ever leaving it again. The videos would give me something to do. And since I thought I would probably be dead soon, I didn't worry too much about them being returned late.

Did Jennifer's motel suite even have a VCR? I wasn't sure—of this and many other things. But motels always have VCRs, right?

The girl at the register was typical in her complete lack of interest in the customers or the job itself, but her appearance set her apart from most Long Island retail help. For one thing, her hairdo was different. She wore dreadlocks tied up with little bits of string, the strands leaning this way and that. On a black woman, this might have looked good; on this girl, it looked as if someone had dropped a plate of dead baby snakes on her head.

"I like your hair," I told her.

She looked up at me with a lack of curiosity usually only encountered in shellfish. The oversized black horn-rims she wore were tilted rakishly to one side. Her nipples made hard little bumps in her black leotard. I guess she was cold. She didn't say anything, just reached out and processed the videos.

I didn't have a card and had to apply for one. This took time, which was good. Every second off the street, out of sight of Worm Lips, was good.

The girl paused when she came to the Philippine horror flick and glanced up at me through her horn-rims.

"This's a good one," she said, hefting the tape. Then she swiped it and tossed both tapes on the counter.

End of brief encounter. I picked up the videos, grabbed the cooler, and headed out. But just as the automatic door began to swing open, I saw Worm Lips's pale, ugly face in profile, framed in the open passenger window of a car that was driving slowly through the parking lot.

I backed away from the door, which, after a moment, swung shut again. Then I walked back to the counter.

The girl in the black horn-rims was waiting on another customer, so I stood there, bouncing up and down on my heels, sighing, and drumming on the counter with my fingers until she finished with him. Both the girl and the customer glared at me. Finally, they were done. I leaned forward.

"Excuse me, is there a back door to this place?"

She looked at me more intently, annoyance changing to something almost like interest.

"Sure. Why?" she said. "See somebody you want to avoid?"

Through the plate-glass window I heard the chunk of a car door slamming. "I think they want to hurt me," I blurted out.

"Who?"

"Those guys out there. In the black Caddy."

This seemed weak to me, so I added, almost truthfully, "They've already tried to kill me twice."

She stared at me for another second. Then she stood up.

"C'mon," she said to me, "Bob, take the register." Bob, a shave-headed youth who was sullenly sorting returned videos behind her, nodded without looking up.

I followed after her, not daring to look around. We zipped be-tween the rows of shelving toward the back of the store, then sud-denly ducked through a curtain into a little side room.

"Adult section," the girl explained.

There was someone in the adult section, a bald guy in a tweed suit, who looked up at us, alarmed.

The girl in the glasses went over to one of the floor-to-ceiling video shelves that completely covered the walls of the little room. The shelves were loaded with porn of every description, catering to every taste. In spite of the urgency of the situation, my eyes roved over the titles. I still felt a professional curiosity.

The girl saw me and grinned a bit. "No time for that now," she reminded me as she reached around behind one of the shelves. Some sort of catch released, and the whole shelf swung forward on hinges. There was a metal door behind the shelf, which the girl swung open, revealing a staircase heading down into darkness.

"Is there some kind of trouble?" the man in the tweed suit asked.

"You better go out this way, too, Mr. Minetti," she said to him. "You never know." Mr. Minetti looked at her, glanced at me and then at the curtain behind me, and headed down the dark staircase as if he'd done it a hundred times.

"This goes to the basements under the stores," the girl said. "Turn left at the bottom and stay close to the wall. There're two more doors. They should be open. After the second door, go up the stairs. That's the bakery. They're used to this. They'll let you out."

"Out where?" I asked.

"Parking lot right behind the bakery. Don't worry, you can't see the back door of Video Palace from there. Just go into the parking lot. There's a gray Honda Civic with lots of bumper stickers on it. That's mine. It's open—lock's busted. Get in. I'll be out as soon as I can."

"Out? Honda?" I babbled, but she had run back through the curtain.

I didn't wait. The stairs were unlit, but at the bottom I could see a faint red glow. Following that brought me to a door, then another door. I stumbled around in the dark, bumping against things and cursing, and finally found another staircase. This led me up to a small, bright room where men in white were working at long wooden tables. The bakery. One of the men, husky and unshaven, went over to a windowless metal door in the rear wall and held it open for me.

"Enjoy yourself," he said to me as I ducked through.

The Honda was easy to spot. About twenty or thirty bumper stickers obliterated the rear fender and most of the window. I tried the door; it opened. I got in the back, sat there nervously for about two seconds, then lay down flat. If there had been a blanket or a tarp back there, I would have hauled it over me.

After about twenty minutes, the door opened and the girl with snakes on her head jumped in.

"You all right back there?" she asked.

"Fine," I said, my voice muffled by my jacket, which I had pulled up over my head.

"Well, put your seat belt on. And hang on to that cooler."

The girl in the horn-rims was a good, fast driver. I felt the Honda—there was no way I was actually going to look—slide out of the parking lot and zip away.

We zipped around for a while. Every time we stopped for a traffic light, I almost puked, expecting doors to open and thug arms to reach in for me. And every time we pulled away again, I felt reborn.

I approved of this girl's notion of average highway speed. She drove like a maniac.

"Hey, backseat! Yo!" the girl called out. I grunted in response.

"You can come out now. Nobody's following us."

Cautiously, I lowered my jacket and looked around. "How can you be sure?"

"I back-streeted it. There was no one behind us or even near. Now we're on the LIE. Nobody close."

I peered around suspiciously, but she seemed to be right.

"What's your name?" she asked me.

"Johnnie. You?"

"Patrice. That's the part I use anyway. Patrice Mooney. Where you going, Johnnie?"

"Hicksville. Take me to Hicksville."

"Okay. Where in Hicksville?"

"Near the train station. I forget the address, but I'll know it when I see it."

Now that it looked as if I was going to escape, I began to wonder what I was escaping to. Jennifer's motel, after all, was not exactly a safe haven, crowded as it was with dead guys in their shorts, and right on the main street in a town where the people who were looking for us had every reason to look again. But I had nowhere else to go.

Patrice seemed to be enjoying herself. She drove right by the Hicksville exit. My head whipped around and I was about to stutter out an objection, but then I realized she must have done it on purpose. She had; two exits later, she cut and drifted between cars and just made it off the expressway. Nobody followed us.

"Whoo-ee!" she yelped. "That was fun!"

She was a great driver. We crept through back streets and housing developments, nosing back toward Hicksville. But something was bothering me.

"Why did you do that? Help me like that? Back in the store, I mean."

Patrice smiled but kept her eyes on the road. That alone told me she was not a local.

"I was bored. You know?"

I did, and said so.

"Really, really bored," Patrice said. "I've been waiting for something to happen. Something. Anything. And I thought maybe you were it." She looked at me out of the corners of her eyes. "Are you?"

I did feel like I was it, it in a game of tag—tag played by guys with automatic weapons and baseball bats.

"Got me" was all I said, however.

"Sometimes you've just got to go with it, with whatever's happening," Patrice said to the windshield. "You get your chance to change things, and you just take it."

There was no response I could make to this. Such things had never happened to me. Or at least I hadn't noticed.

We drove along without talking for a while, strip malls whizzing past on both sides.

"That guy back there, the bald guy. Who is he?" I asked, more to fill the silence than out of curiosity.

"Mr. Minetti? Oh, he's the high school principal. He's in there all the time. He's afraid the PTA will see him leaving with *Debbie Does Dallas*, so I always let him out the bakery way. The wanker," she said smugly.

"*Wanker*, that's British. You English?"

She smiled over at me, looking pleased to be taken for a Brit, but shook her head no.

"You're not from around here, though," I said. "I can tell. Where're you from?"

"Delaware," she said. "But I went to high school here. A couple years anyway."

"Like it here?"

She shook her head again, a lot harder this time. "I hate it."

"Delaware is better?"

The girl in the horn-rims drove along in silence for a while, concentrating on the road. Then she glanced over at me.

"Answer one of my questions instead," she said.

"Okay."

"Why were those guys after you? What did you do to them?"

"They think I know something I don't."

Patrice thought about this.

"What's in the cooler? Got anything to drink in there?"

I shook my head. "Fish. Fish on ice."

"Why are you carrying fish around at midnight?"

I couldn't answer this, so I said nothing. She said nothing in return. We drove in silence past the distant neon and sodium lights of Long Island's shopping malls and parking lots.

"How do I know they weren't cops?" Patrice said a few blocks later. "And how do I know you're not some kind of serial killer?"

"Those guys in the car, did they look like cops? Did you get a good look at them?"

She nodded. "Actually, I did. I went over to the window and checked them out. They were just sitting in the car, you know. I don't think they were going to come into the store at all."

"They didn't look like cops, though, did they?"

Patrice shook her head.

"Not even undercover cops?"

She shook her head again, harder this time, so that the baby snakes flopped from side to side and her horn-rims came off one ear.

"No way they were cops. They looked like rejects from a *Sopranos* casting call."

"And if I was a serial killer, I'd have a head in the cooler, or something. Wouldn't I? But I've got fish instead."

Patrice laughed. She sounded relieved.

"You're a serial fisherman," she said.

We got back to Hicksville without incident, and I managed to direct her to the train station. Then my memory gave out.

"Drive around, okay?" I instructed her. "It's somewhere right around here."

The Hicksville streets had a gray, drab, almost unbelievably oppressive atmosphere, like a memory extracted from the mind of a mental patient. All the houses, all the streets looked the same to me. Then, as we drove by a line of strip malls and used-car lots, we passed a brightly lit entry into a long, low white motel, and something clicked.

"This is it."

We pulled in and drove around behind the motel. This was definitely the place.

Patrice looked at me expectantly, but I made no move to get out of the car.

We sat there, a beat, two beats, three, frozen in time. Soon it would be impossible to move ever again.

"You getting out?" Patrice asked. She didn't sound impatient or pissed off, but I detected a slight edge of regret to her voice. I think that's when I began to fall in love with her. But I said, "Uh, Patrice, can I ask a favor of you? Could you, like, just drive around the parking lot, so I can see if my friend's car is there?"

She looked at me blankly, the shellfish thing, then put the Honda in gear.

"Sure," she said.

We cruised the parking lot without seeing the red Miata or the black Caddy. While I was desperately trying to think of what to do next, Patrice pulled the Honda around the back and parked near the rear door.

"Stay here, Johnnie," she said, opening the door and getting out.

"I'll walk inside, see if everything looks okay." Before I could say anything or express my admiration in any way, she was gone.

In just a few minutes, she was back. She jumped in the car, started it up, and backed out without saying a word. She jammed the Honda—as much as you can jam a Honda—around corners and up streets until we were on the other side of the railroad tracks.

Neither of us spoke a word. I knew something bad was up there in the motel suite, but I didn't really want to know what.

We drove all the way up to Jericho Turnpike before Patrice told me what she'd seen.

"The back door was open a crack," she said, "so I walked in. The place was empty, and quiet. I walked right down the hall, just like I was visiting someone. And I saw the suite door wasn't closed all the way. So I listened for a minute, then stuck my head in. Johnnie, your friend's apartment was trashed!"

Fuck.

"What do you mean, 'trashed'?" I said stupidly.

"Trashed, as in drawers pulled out, things turned over, everything a mess. Somebody even cut the couch cushions to shreds and pulled out all the stuffing."

Fucking hell. My last refuge, my only friend. What was I going to do now? It was just me and the head.

And Patrice, of course.

"Patrice, did you see—I mean, was she—"

Patrice shook her head. "I didn't see anybody lying around. I couldn't see very far, and there was no way I was going in. But I think if her car's not there, your friend is okay."

That was something. But how was I going to get in touch with Jennifer and give her the fucking head?

"Patrice," I said, "thanks for going in there and checking that out."

She shrugged. "No problem. Nobody knows what I look like. Your friends, I mean. Whoever they are."

Whoever they are.

"I mean, you'd do the same for me, right?" she asked.

"Sure," I said.

You're kidding me, I thought.

We were still driving, east now, Patrice cutting through Westbury down to Sunrise, me slouched down in the passenger seat, knees on the dashboard, collar up around my ears.

"Where are we going anyway?"

"My place. Unless you've got a better idea."

I didn't have any ideas at all, so I let it happen.

Patrice's place, as it turned out, was not all that far from where Vinnie and I grew up. She was staying in an apartment behind a split-level home in Massapequa Park, in a cul-de-sac in back of the Sunrise Mall, near the county line.

"It's my aunt's house," she told me as we pulled in the driveway of a big white-shingled Colonial, its two-car garage sticking out, with a basketball hoop above the doors. "I get cheap rent, and she leaves me alone, pretty much."

"Cool," I said.

The little apartment had a separate entrance. Patrice and I surged in like a couple coming home with the groceries; I put the cooler down on the kitchen table.

"Whew!" Patrice whistled, leaning against the counter. "How did we get here?"

I shrugged. I never knew the answer to that one.

"Want a beer?"

I was feeling frisky, now that I knew I wasn't going to die right away.

"Patrice, let me explain to you. Locally, *beer* has two syllables, not one. Bee-uh."

"Bee-uh."

"Okay, okay, but slur the syllables together more; there's, like, a link between them, a *nyyah*."

"Beeuh," she said, but laughing so she could barely get it out.

"Great, that's great. You sound like you come from Wantagh."

"*Fucking* Wantagh."

Just then, there was a knock at the door, a sharp rap on the glass. I could see a middle-aged woman standing there trying to see in. She had on black horn-rims that came to little points in the corners, just like Patrice's. They made her look old, while Patrice's made her look young. Go figure.

"Oh fuck," Patrice whispered. "Aunt Vivienne."

Aunt Vivienne rapped on the glass again, quick, polite little raps. Patrice pulled the door open.

"Oh, you're home!" Aunt Vivienne said, as if she'd just noticed. She stared at me over the tops of her horn-rims. Her hairdo framed her head like a fur helmet. I knew from looking at it that even in a gale-force wind, not a single hair would blow out of place.

"Is this your young man?" she asked Patrice.

"This is my friend Johnnie, Aunt Vivienne."

"So pleased to meet you, Johnnie. I'm always telling Patrice she doesn't get out enough. You can't meet someone if you never go out!" Aunt Vivienne bent over my hand, smiling dementedly, and shook it while she checked me out.

"This is true," I muttered.

"Do you live around here?" Aunt Vivienne said. "What do you do?"

"Aunt Vivienne, please!" Patrice said.

"Actually, I just got out of jail," I said.

"I can't believe you said that to her."

Patrice was lying on her belly along the sofa, resting her chin on her hands and kicking her bare feet in the air. She looked about fourteen years old.

"I wasn't trying to be funny," I protested. "It's just the truth, that's all."

"Her face, Johnnie, did you see her face?"

"I was looking right at it."

"She just came right apart. That should teach her, the nosy old bitch. She's probably on the phone to my mother right now."

"Is that bad?"

Patrice shook her head. "I don't give a shit." She studied me in silence for a while.

"What were you in jail for?" she asked. "I mean, is that okay to ask? I don't want to invade your space like Aunt Vivienne."

"No, it's okay; I don't mind. But it's a long story."

"That's all right," Patrice said. "I love stories. The longer the better."

"I mean it. A really long story."

"That's cool."

"This will take awhile," I said. I meant it as my final warning.

"Go for it," Patrice said.

So I told her. I told her everything, starting with Bug Rankin and the cold cuts gang, Vinnie, flounder fishing, the head. I told her about Mr. Colucci, and Belinda, and Stosh, about Frown and Worm Lips, and Jennifer, and the hanging motel manager. I didn't know how else to tell it, how to leave anything out and still have it make sense.

Of course, even with every detail in place, it made no sense.

When I had finished, Patrice just sat there staring at the arm of the sofa for a minute. She rested her chin in her hands, thinking. Then she looked up at me as if she had forgotten I was there.

"Whoa," she said. "Is all that real? Or are you just tripping on me?"

"Too real," I said. I sounded stupid to myself, uncool, like a high school teacher trying to be hip. I realized that Patrice was making me feel old, the first time I had ever felt that way. She was like somebody's kid sister you've known all your life, who you suddenly realize has become totally foxy and totally contemptuous of you, all in about twenty-four hours.

Except that Patrice still seemed to like me—so far. At least she hadn't jumped up and run screaming out of the apartment. Not everyone would calmly accept the presence of an ice-cooled head in their kitchen, but she seemed to be taking it in stride.

I could see that she was reviewing what I'd just told her in her mind, turning the pieces of information over and over like bargains on a sale table.

"What are you going to do now?" she asked me after a while. She lay there waiting for me to answer, playing with one of the baby snakes.

"Try to contact Jennifer Smeals, I guess," I told her. "Find some way to get the head to her."

Patrice sat up on the sofa and stared at the cooler; I had moved it onto the floor over by the refrigerator.

"So it's in there."

I nodded. "Sure is."

"Why does she want it, your friend? I mean, you'd think she'd be glad to be rid of it."

"I know I would. But she didn't tell me why. She just said we need it."

"Maybe to prove to these guys, the gangster guys, that your friend is really dead."

"Maybe. But that puts me in a shitty place."

"Why?"

"Because these guys think I was working with Vinnie. They figure I probably know where the money is that Vinnie is supposed to
have taken. But they can't be sure he wasn't gaming me, as well. If
they know Vinnie is dead, they've got to think I've killed him and
have the money myself."

"Why do they think you know about it?"

I shrugged. "Vinnie must have told them."

"Some friend."

"No, he had his reasons, I'm sure," I said. I didn't like hearing
her criticize Vinnie. "He was always planning something. This plan
just didn't come off before they got to him."

Patrice was frowning, looking confused. I didn't blame her.

"But wait, if these gangsters think you killed Vinnie, that means
they didn't kill him. So who did?"

"Jennifer says Vinnie was involved with more than these guys.
She also thinks there are guys behind these guys, mob guys, I mean.
Powerful guys. Who maybe they killed Vinnie."

"That still doesn't make sense. You know what I think? I think
she killed him." Patrice rested her arms on her knees and put her
chin on them. Her eyes roamed over my face. "Killed him and cut
him up. I don't know why she wants the head, but I bet once you
give it to her, she kills you, too."

Someone rapped on the window glass again. Then again. Patrice
raised her head up, then let it fall back into her arms.

"I don't believe this," she muttered.

I went over and opened the door for Aunt Vivienne. She was
carrying a TV tray with some drinks and sandwiches on it. Her eyes
roamed over the apartment as if she was afraid we'd redecorated it
while she was gone.

"I brought you some sandwiches, Patrice," Aunt Vivienne said.

Her voice was loud and nasal, like some kind of power tool. "And so-das. I didn't know if you wanted Pepsi or Coke, so I brought both. Is that okay?"

Patrice groaned. I took the tray from Aunt Vivienne.

"Thank you very much," I said.

"Isn't he polite!" Aunt Vivienne stared at me with big hungry eyes, her mouth slightly open.

"Tell me, Johnnie," she said. "How was it in jail? Was it very bad for you?"

This embarrassed me. "Not so bad, no," I said. Except for the face punching, of course, but I didn't bring that up.

"Do you need a job?" Aunt Vivienne said. "Because if you do, I might be able to help you. I have a friend whose husband runs a trucking company. He's always looking for someone. He doesn't mind hiring"—Aunt Vivienne reddened slightly—"ex-cons. And too, I have some work around the house I need done, yard work, and roof repairs. Now my husband's gone, the house needs a man's touch."

Her voice during the last part of this segued into a kind of coy laughing tone, and she actually primped her hair on one side. The hair bent up like aluminum foil and stayed that way.

"I'm sorry about your—husband," I said. I almost said "your old man" but caught myself.

Patrice jumped up from the table and took the tray from me.

"Thanks for the sandwiches, Aunt Vivienne," she said. "We're fine now. Thanks. Thanks. Thanks." Pressing the edge of the TV tray against Aunt Vivienne's belly, Patrice forced her out the door backward.

Aunt Vivienne stood on the stoop, in the glow of the porchlight. Moths flew around her head and bumped into her hairdo. She seemed bewildered, like someone just returned to earth by space aliens.

"Well, let me know if you need anything, kids," she said vaguely, and stumbled back to the house.

"I. Don't. Believe. It. I just don't believe it. She was hitting on you! Hitting on you, right in front of me!" Patrice was storming up and down the kitchen. She threw the sandwiches into the garbage, paper plates and all, and dumped the sodas in the sink.

I watched her sadly; those sandwiches had looked good to me. "Patrice, I don't think—" I began, but she cut me off.

"Well, I think. I saw what she was doing. Ever since my uncle died, she's just been out of control. But this is too much."

"Well, you can't blame her," I said. This wasn't coming out right. "I mean, living alone and everything. Not me, I mean, but just being lonely."

Patrice puffed out her cheeks and plumped herself down next to me on the sofa bed. She leaned back on her arms and looked over at me.

"No, I guess not. You can't really blame her." She leaned forward; a long stretch of her, from knee to mid-thigh, pressed against me. "I don't blame her."

I was already up against the arm of the sofa, so there was nowhere I could move to. Patrice's leg was warm against me, and I could smell her, a little soapy clean-girl smell. Up to now, I had been much too freaked out to really pay attention to Patrice as a woman; plus, she was so much younger than I was. But now I could see that she was really quite attractive, in spite of the weird hair. By the way her breasts hung against her leotard, I could see she didn't have a bra on. She was wearing tight black pants of some kind that only went partway down her legs, and her legs were strong and shapely. My head began to spin. I leaned toward her.

Patrice jumped up off the sofa bed and went over to the sink. She began rinsing out the plastic glasses Aunt Vivienne had brought the sodas in.

"So, what are you doing tonight?" she asked, her back to me. "Where are you going to stay?" She threw the plastic glasses she had just washed into the garbage.

"I don't have anyplace," I said, which was true.

"You can stay here." She still didn't look around.

"Sure. I can sleep on the floor."

She turned around.

"You can sleep on the sofa if you want. It turns into a bed."

"No, I can't do that. Where are you going to sleep?"

"On the sofa."

Patrice smiled at me, a little uncertain under the crown of baby snakes.

"If that's okay with you," she said.

Making love to Patrice was intense. At one point—she was on top— her hair snakes began to thump rhythmically into my face, like little blackjacks, until I thought they would knock me unconscious. But I toughed it out, rolled us over, and we kept at it in a new position, half on, half off the couch.

Like I said, it was intense.

Some time later, we were resting. Patrice rolled over and dug her chin into my shoulder. A piece of her hair dangled down and tickled my ear.

"Hey," I said to her. "A man can't get any sleep around here."

Patrice grinned lazily. "That was pretty pornographic, huh?" she said.

I agreed. "And how. Like something in one of my porno novels."

"Porno!" Patrice propped herself up on an elbow. "You write porno? That's so cool." She seemed delighted.

I demurred. "Well, I used to. I haven't written any in a long time."

"You should, you should! I love pornos. What ones did you write?"

I told her some of the titles.

"*The Sisterhood of the Tongue*! I read that!" She gave me a long, searching look. "I bet you are into some weird and freaky stuff, huh?"

"Not really. I just write it." This was true. In my career of fornication, I had pretty much stuck to the standard moves.

Patrice leered at me. It was plain she didn't take my statement at face value.

"I'm open to all kinds of things myself, you know," she told me. "You'd be surprised."

I was.

"Whoa," I said when I'd recovered some. "My my."

Patrice grinned wickedly and bit my shoulder.

"You are a wild girl," I told her.

She rubbed her forehead against my upper arm.

"You got that right," she said. She bit me again, a little lower down.

"Ow. I wouldn't've thought, you know, looking at you," I started to say, but even I could tell this was going in the wrong direction.

It was too late, though. Patrice shot upright.

"*Look*ing at me? What is that supposed to mean?"

I shrugged and squirmed. "Oh, you know, the hair, the glasses. I thought you were probably, like, a lesbian."

Patrice made an indignant noise, all puffed breath and lip sound, and bounced on the bed, too pissed off to speak.

"Or something," I said hurriedly, "Some young cool chick who would never be into a guy like me, I mean."

"You are such a loser," Patrice said, and not for the last time.

———

Breakfast the next morning was a relaxed affair. Aunt Vivienne did not reappear. Patrice buzzed around the tiny kitchen area making eggs, coffee, toast, dressed in a somewhat long T-shirt. I watched attentively for those moments when the shirt rode up over her naked ass.

"You want orange juice?"

"Please."

Patrice bending over and reaching into the back of the refrigerator was a sight for the ages.

I was in such total blissed-out stupor, after a night of love play and a feast of eggs and buttered toast—remember my diet for the last few weeks had consisted mostly of ramen noodles—that I had almost completely forgotten about the head.

"I want to see it," Patrice said out of nowhere. She plunked down a plate covered with eggs and toast in front of me.

I was stunned. "See what?" For a split second, I thought maybe she was talking about my penis.

"The head. I want to see the head."

"What for?"

"I've never seen a head before. A cut-off one, I mean." Her eyes were shining.

I wondered if this was some weird sex thing with her.

"Look, Patrice," I said. "It's pretty nasty. I mean, it's been kicked around a lot. It doesn't look very good."

"I'm okay with that. I'm ready for it," Patrice said. "Besides, maybe we can figure out why your friend wants to get her hands on it. Like maybe there's a piece of microfilm hidden in one of the teeth, or something like that."

I didn't know how to tell her about the teeth.

"Patrice, I don't know," I said. I sounded like my mother.

"I do," Patrice said, sounding very definite. "Show it to me."

I shrugged; what else was there to do? "It's in the cooler, under the fish."

But it wasn't.

The cooler was filled—entirely—with half-thawed moss bunker. I had taken the wrong one.

CHAPTER NINE

I WAS STANDING IN front of Vinnie's parents' house again, late at night, just outside the cone of light from the streetlight by the garage. It was still hot; locusts buzzed in the trees. An on-again, off-again wind blew low-tide stink down the street. There was no sign of Worm Lips, Stosh, the cops, or anyone else.

This was getting repetitive. I felt like my tape kept getting rewound to this point and that I would never get beyond it, just always end up back here at the curb, a cooler full of moss bunker in my hand.

At least it was better than being in jail.

But only just.

I looked over my shoulder at Patrice, who was parked across the street in her Honda. I could make out her silhouette; from her arm motions, I guessed she was urging me to hurry up and get it over with.

Mentally, I shrugged, then trudged around to the back door to the garage studio. I fished around in my pockets and came up with the key Vinnie had given me, several rewinds ago. Then I remembered that I wouldn't need it; the door was just wedged in the frame, thanks to Stosh. Carefully, trying to make as little noise as possible, I held the door so it wouldn't fall on top of me, then slowly pushed it open.

It occurred to me that it had gotten quiet all of a sudden, really quiet. I couldn't hear the locusts anymore. In fact, I couldn't hear anything. The world had become one big ball of quiet. It felt like my ears were stuffed with cotton wool.

It also occurred to me that I was lying down on the grass. I wondered why I was doing that. I looked up, but nothing I saw made any sense to me. Trees, parked cars, lights coming on in houses across the street, heads sticking out of windows—all played out in silence, like a TV with the sound off. I saw Patrice standing over me like the giant in *Attack of the 50-foot Woman*, looking concerned. Arms came out of somewhere and helped me stand up. I turned around to face Vinnie's parents' house.

It rocked me to see that instead of a one-story asbestos-shingled home with garage, lawn, and a statue of the Virgin Mary in a little grotto by the front door, there was only a twisted pile of boards. The house had been peeled open like an orange by a big hungry hand. There was crap all over the lawn, stuff everywhere—shingles, glass, pieces of furniture. How did this happen? I wondered.

I staggered a step or two toward the house and almost fell. Patrice put out a hand to steady me. Looking down at what I almost tripped over, I saw that it was a large red-and-white Coleman cooler. The lid must have come off when I tripped over it. Vinnie's head was lying on the lawn next to it, sitting in the mouth of a black plastic trash bag.

I remembered now. This was what I had come here for. I bent over and scooped up the head.

Somehow I was back in the Honda, the head in my lap. Patrice was driving. We weren't in Comapogue anymore.

She looked over at me, still concerned.

"You feeling any better now?"

"Whoa," I said. My voice sounded strange to me, far away and echoey. I sat there and thought about that for a while; then I tried again.

"What the fuck just happened?"

"Johnnie, the house blew up!" Patrice said. "I thought you were dead." Her voice was all choked up.

Things began to come back to me in fragments, like falling house pieces.

"The head!" I said. "Where is it?"

"It's in your lap."

Right, I knew that. Gently, I lowered the head to the floor of the Honda. The thighs of my jeans were damp where it had been lying. It was too dark in the car to see it well, but I could tell from the stench that filled the Honda that the head was in worse shape than when I had last seen it.

Patrice coughed and cranked open her window. I did the same. As I wound it down, I realized I was looking up at the door of a truck, which filled my vision entirely. I tilted my head back; it was like looking up the side of an ocean liner. The truck seemed awfully close. I could have reached out and opened the door.

"Johnnie, throw something over the head before somebody sees it!" Patrice said. I turned away from the window and rooted around in the backseat, which was piled high with stuff, and found a damp beach towel.

"Okay to use this?"

Patrice nodded. She was green around the gills.

"Maybe it will help with the smell," she said.

I draped the beach towel over the head. It did help with the stench, at least a little, but it was still pretty strong.

An engine roared, gears clashed, and suddenly the truck door was back, filling the window. It was no more than six inches from us. Nervously, I remembered the car that had run Stosh off the road. Different car, yes, but same driver? Same plan?

"Asshole!" Patrice said throatily. "He nearly sideswiped us!"

The truck gunned out ahead of us and we got a good look at it: a big brown GM pickup, full-size, not a mini, and about twenty years old. The truck was raised up on its suspension and had outsized tires and thick wheels.

"Do you think he saw the head?" Patrice asked.

"Nah. Too dark," I reassured her. "But keep an eye on this guy. Try and stay away from him. I don't want to be in any more car accidents."

The brown truck disappeared in the traffic up ahead without making any more moves toward us. The loud buzzing of pure paranoia in my head began to die down.

But now that my head was beginning to settle down, I realized I had no idea where we were or where we were going.

"On the LIE, heading east," Patrice told me.

"Where are we going?"

Patrice shrugged. "Anywhere. Nowhere. I just wanted to get away from that place before anyone showed up and began asking questions."

"Well, okay. But we probably should head back to your place."

Patrice didn't answer. She was driving with her head down by the top of the steering wheel, as if she expected something to crash through the windshield at any moment. She looked miserable.

We drove awhile in silence. I was relieved to see the Bay Shore exit shoot by, and some familiar gas stations and shopping centers along the frontage roads. I had been so disoriented that I wouldn't have been totally surprised if we were in California.

More silence.

I could tell, now that my brain was working again, more or less, that Patrice had something she wanted to say, something she was having a hard time bringing up. I tried hard to think of some way either to prevent this or at least make it happen sooner. But as usual when it came to man-woman talking, my mind went into vapor lock.

Finally, she got it out on her own. "Johnnie, why don't you just get rid of it?"

"What, the head?"

"What else do you think I mean? Just chuck it in the water somewhere, back where you found it. Get rid of it. Let somebody else worry about the fucking thing."

I thought about it.

"But we just got it back. Besides, Jennifer says the head is important."

"Then let her worry about it. Throw it away, then tell her where it is. Let her go get it."

"I don't know how to get in touch with her. Anyway, it's Vinnie's head, I can't just . . . just chuck it away like a piece of garbage."

"Johnnie, it *is* a piece of garbage. Can't you smell it? It's going to fall apart soon."

She was right.

"You're right. We've gotta get it back on ice soon as we can."

Patrice looked over at me in this pained way, made a kind of gasping noise, as if she were trying to inhale and exhale at the same time, and beat her hands on the steering wheel.

I put the head in the freezer compartment of Patrice's refrigerator. It was in there all by itself. There was plenty of room, since Patrice refused to keep any of her food in the same compartment, even after I wrapped the head in a fresh trash bag. We had to eat nothing but frozen pizza and tofu dogs for a week. A stack of other frozen items slowly thawed in the back of her refrigerator.

Patrice was a little sulky.

"I still don't know why you don't just get rid of it," she said.

"Patrice, look, I don't want to hear another word on the subject," I said, hearing my old man's voice echoing in my head.

That was really the wrong thing to have said, and I knew it as the words rolled helplessly out of my mouth. Patrice didn't actually explode, but words came shooting out of her like balls of fire from a Roman candle—one of those defective ones that shoots sideways and all over the place, and everyone has to hit the deck, and the table-cloth on the picnic table catches fire.

I can't remember what she said word for word, so I won't try to reproduce it exactly. But the general trend of her remarks was that I was a moron, an unenlightened patriarchal pig moron who secretly hated women but wasn't going to lay his sick archaic thinking on her. That if I wanted to take my fucking head out of her freezer and get the fuck out of her apartment, I was very welcome to do so. She had tried to be patient with me and help me out, but if I didn't appreciate what she had done for me, I could just get the fuck out and leave her alone.

I sat there and took it. It occurred to me that Patrice's old man was probably a lot like mine, said the same kinds of things at the dinner table and so forth, and that this speech of hers, this fucking aria of resentment, had been waiting a long time to come out. But then maybe I deserved it.

In any case, I didn't say a word until awhile after she was done yelling. When I judged the time was right, I said, "Look, Patrice. I'm sorry."

"You're *sorry*? Is that all you've got to say? You're *sorry*?"

"I'm real sorry. I didn't mean to talk like that. You know, I try to be sensitive, I do. But I have a thick skull"—and here I rapped myself on the forehead dramatically—"and it just doesn't get through. But I try."

"You *try.*" she repeated with deep sarcasm. She was still mad, but I could see she was beginning to wind down.

I shrugged, meaning to convey the impression of a simple guy who did the best he could but got misunderstood sometimes.

"Asshole," Patrice said. A smile started tugging at her lips like a fish on the line, and though she fought it, I could see it coming on.

Raving and screaming seemed to have sated Patrice.

"Johnnie, you know what?" she asked.

"No, what?"

"We just had our first fight."

Pure terror washed over me. I couldn't even consider the broader implications of this statement. All I could think of was that this was some kind of anniversary, a date I would be expected to remember always. And I knew I would always forget.

"Well, you know, not really. I mean, when we were in the car before, driving back from Vinnie's parents' house, that was a fight, wasn't it?" I said hopefully.

She shook her head. "That was not a fight. But I'm glad about one thing, you know? That when we do fight, we manage to resolve something, work something out."

What she meant, I think, is that she'd won. But this time I had the sense not to say anything.

After the house blew up, and with the head safely stashed in her freezer, Patrice and I spent some quality time together, getting to know each other. She seemed to think that now we had fucked each other and fought with each other, we were practically married. This made me nervous, but only a little.

After going in to work a couple of times, Patrice just stopped going. "I was so sick of that place anyway," she said. "You have no idea."

It was nice. I almost forgot the situation I was in. We just lay around, watched TV, listened to music, screwed like mink on Viagra. It was a vacation. Only the tofu-dog and frozen spinach dinners reminded me of what was waiting in the freezer, slowly developing a bad case of freezer burn.

This lasted for several days.

There was a computer sitting on Patrice's desk—I say desk, but it was a hollow-core door resting on two two-drawer filing cabinets. Patrice spent some time every day sitting in front of the screen, reading her e-mail, she said, and surfing the Web. I got the impression that before we got together, she used to spend most of her time online.

I was sitting on the bed, smoking—in spite of all her health-food ideas, Patrice still smoked, and she didn't mind me lighting up. She smoked those clove cigarettes, nasty shit, much worse than my Camel Lights. God knows what they were doing to her lungs.

Patrice was at the computer, rattling at the keyboard, squinting at the screen.

"How do you spell your last name, Johnnie?"

"LoDuco," I told her. "*L-O-D-U-C-O.*"

More tapping and rattling. Then she said, "Hey."

"What?"

"Come look."

I jumped off the sofa bed and peeked over her shoulder.

"Look what I found."

It was an interesting Web page all right. The first thing you noticed were the naked babes crawling around the logo at the top of the page. Many, many naked women. Very soon after, you saw the photos farther down the page, and what people were doing in them.

"Porn site," I said calmly. After all, I was a pro, a sleaze master from way back. "So?"

"Look at this item in the sidebar." Patrice clicked on a listing I didn't have time to read before the page opened. There were no pictures on the new page, just text. I was a bit disappointed.

"Recognize it?" Patrice asked me. I read on.

"Holy shit!" I said reverently. "That's my novel!"

"*The Sisterhood of the Tongue*! You didn't tell me your books were online! This is so cool!"

I hadn't told her, only because I didn't know myself. I wasn't surprised, though. I had sold the porno novels for a flat fee, signed away all conceivable rights to my boss, Fat Al Rugosa, the adult-bookstore king of the South Shore. I never thought the books would have a future. Who knew? Anyway, at the time I needed the money with crawling, groveling desperation.

My hand on top of hers, I clicked and scrolled through my old novel. I remembered it, too, every word. I remembered it much better than I remembered most of the horrible things that had happened to me while I was writing it.

I straightened up. "That's it. It's just an excerpt. If you want to read the rest, they make you pay."

"Here," Patrice said, "let me see." She shouldered me away from the monitor and began tapping on the keyboard again. As she typed, she hummed and muttered to herself. Once in a while, there would be a recognizable word or two—" 'At's right" or "There you go"—before she lapsed back into baby talk. She tapped away, babbling and cursing, until I got bored and lay back down on the couch.

After about ten minutes, she yelped out, "I'm in!"

I went back to looking over her shoulder. She had somehow gotten into the paid area of the porno site without paying.

"How did you do that?" I asked her.

"Porno sites are easy," Patrice said in a tough little voice I had never heard her use before. "I've hacked into some rough pages, government pages."

"What, like the FBI, CIA?"

"Worse than that. The IRS."

I was impressed and said so.

"Scared the shit out of myself," she admitted.

"Why'd you do it?"

"To see if I could. I never do anything when I hack into a site, you know. I'm just doing it to see if I can, and to find out what's so important that they have to hide it behind a wall of tricky codes."

"Say, you're pretty smart. If you can do computer stuff like this, what are you doing working in a video store?"

Patrice looked down at her feet, as if I had caught her out in some misdemeanor.

"I'm not sure, you know, if I want to commit to all that—school, a job, nine to five," she said. "For me, working on computers is fun, a blast. I'm good at it. But if I had to do it for a living, for some fucking corporation, that would change everything."

"You'd make lots of money," I pointed out. "You could go out on your own, be a consultant. Lots of people do."

She peered at me under half-lowered eyelids.

"Like your friend Vinnie."

"Vinnie did good with it," I said, at the same time thinking of what Jennifer had told me about Vinnie's lack of computer skills. "You should see his house—what used to be his house. You should have seen his house before they shot the walls out of it. It was really something, a trilevel aquarium the size of a small warehouse."

"Yeah, before they shot the walls out. Before they cut his head off and threw it in the Great South Bay."

"Well, but that didn't—that had nothing to do with his computer skills," I sputtered. "That was the people he got involved with."

"I don't know, Johnnie. I think it did have to do with his computer skills. I think he was consulting for some rough people, doing Web design for them maybe, and he fucked them over in some way. I think that's why they killed him."

"Are you saying that the mob has its own Web site?"

"Not the mob. But somebody, maybe the guys who put up this porn site."

It almost made sense. "How did you find this site anyway? How do you know Vinnie had anything to do with it?"

"I don't. But it's a good guess. I found it by searching your name on the Web, Johnnie," she said. "I found a whole world of things just by using your name. Look at this." She jumped back a few screens to her search results. They filled the screen and jumped to the next page.

"What has all this got to do with me?"

"Your name is in every one of these sites," she said. "In there somewhere. The porno site's easy; they gave you author credit for *The Sisterhood*."

"No royalties, though," I complained. I thought of Fat Al, spending the money my books made, probably thousands.

Patrice bent over the screen, her face intent, mouth open a little, a look you might have if you were trying to spear a cockroach with a fork before it got to the edge of the table. She clicked open another Web site. The screen filled up with brightly colored animated playing cards and roulette wheels. In a minute, you could hear an audio of casino sounds—wheels spinning, slots whirring, buzzer going off, payoffs tumbling into cups.

Patrice laughed like a little girl. "Gambling site!"

"Once again, what has this got to do with me?"

"Sshhh." She began tapping and talking to herself again, so I went outside and smoked a couple Camels. It was a nice warm night, humid, but with a little breeze to keep it off you. Looking over toward the main house, I could see Aunt Vivienne through a big picture window. She was sitting in front of the TV, eating popcorn, her face blue-white in the glow from the tube. Neighborhood dogs barked; tires spun in the distance. I whacked a mosquito on my neck, stubbed out my cigarette against the side of the house, and went back in.

Patrice was still sitting at the computer, leaning into it, her body tense, her face pressed against the screen. She didn't turn around, but I knew she'd heard me come in, because she called out to me.

"Johnnie!"

"Yo."

"Do you have a nickname?"

Well, I did have a couple, although none I cared to recall. People were always coming up with names to call me. I don't know why. The name Johnnie is not so hard to remember.

"What do you want to know for?" I shot back.

"*Johnnie!* Don't be difficult. This is important."

I put my hands on her shoulders and peeked at the screen over the top of her head. She ignored me completely, her eyes focused on the monitor.

"What's so important about it?"

"Look at what I found this time."

The page she had on the screen was different from the porn and gambling sites we had been looking at. There were no pictures, for one thing, just a lot of text, very staid, blue-and-white background, discreet logo.

The type at the head of the page read "International Investors Bank of the Cayman Islands, Ltd."

"Whoa," I muttered. "You found that searching my name?"

Patrice nodded. "Do you have an account there or something?"

"Patrice, it must be some other LoDuco. I don't have a bank ac-

count anywhere. I've never been to the Cayman Islands. I don't even
know where they are."

"In the Caribbean. Johnnie, look, someone used your name in
here somewhere, or else my search wouldn't have pulled it up. Maybe
as an account holder, or someone with access. But it's in there somewhere."

This was way over my head. "You lost me, Patrice," I told her.

"It is possible," she said in her new, serious voice, "that someone
else built your name into the structure of this page, but I don't think
so. I think it's your buddy Vinnie, playing games.

"Johnnie, see this tab here, the one that says 'Accounts'?" I nodded. She was talking to me in a patient, "poor dumb Johnnie" voice
that reminded me a little too much of Jennifer Smeals, but I took it
without complaining.

"Yeah," I said in a voice choked with suppressed whining.

Patrice clicked on the tab. A little window swam up.

"What's your Social Security number?"

I told her.

"Now I need a password. See?"

"So try my name again."

Patrice typed. "Nada. Johnnie, I can only take so many shots at
this. Pages like this, especially a bank's, have some limit on how
many passwords you can try."

"You do this all the time, right?" I asked. "So how do you usually
come up with a password?"

"I wrote a program that generates passwords and tries them out.
But I don't think that would work here. Anyway, I bet it would set off
some kind of security and we'd get shut down."

"But you think you can get in with my name, or nickname, or
something?"

"I can just feel it. Johnnie, your friend Vinnie had something to do with this. Who else would use your name? Who else you know would be involved in all this stuff—gambling, porn, a Caymans bank?"

It made sense, I guess.

"Try *lodouchebag*," I told her.

"Low—*what?*" She giggled.

"*Douchebag*. People called me that sometimes in high school. Vinnie called me 'douche bag' when he was making fun of me."

A grin all over her face, Patrice typed. "Too long," she said, then added, "Wait."

The little window she had been typing in disappeared. The stupid little clock face that told you things were working appeared on the screen.

"I think we're in," Patrice whispered.

A text page suddenly opened up. It looked different from the fancy design of the other pages. The typeface was generic, crude. Numbers ran down the middle of the page, long numbers.

"Bank accounts," Patrice explained. "I tried *lodouchebag*, but it didn't all fit. I tried a few more combinations, and *bon-ng-ngg*." Patrice made a vibrating gong sound, pretty realistically, I thought.

"So what was the password?"

"*Douchebag*. But with your first initial. The password is *jdouchebag*."

"Fucking Vinnie," I said.

The whole Web experience made me very thoughtful. If Vinnie had made those porn and gambling sites—that is, if Jennifer's assessment was wrong and Vinnie really had known what he was doing—then maybe the fact that my name was all over them, built into them, as Patrice said, was no accident, and no joke. Maybe it was a clue. A message from beyond the grave.

Maybe it was a gift.

I thought about it carefully most of the night—I didn't sleep much. Then at breakfast, I brought it up.

"Patrice," I said, "you can get into this bank site to look around. But can you get into it and . . . do something?"

"Make a withdrawal, you mean," she said. I nodded.

"Well," she said dubiously, "I could try."

When I was a little kid, my parents took me to the Automat in New York City. I don't mean we went in just for that; they must've taken me to a movie or a Broadway show or something. But what stays in my head is the Automat. Horn & Hardart: I can see it clearly. You got a tray, walked past a wall of glass doors. Behind each door was a food item, a sandwich or a slice of pie, as if on display in a museum: "Foods of the Recent Past." You put in a coin; the doors opened; you took your food item. I thought it was the coolest thing I had ever seen. I couldn't wait to grow up and become an adult with change in my pockets and the ability to go into the city and go to Horn & Hardart. It seemed to make the whole prospect of adulthood more bearable.

Of course, by the time I got old enough to do anything about it, they didn't have Horn & Hardart Automats anymore.

But now Patrice and I were inside the accounts pages for the International Investors Bank of the Cayman Islands. It was like walking through the vaults of a bank with a cafeteria tray in your hands. One of the little doors had our money behind it. My money. The money Vinnie had stashed there in my name.

Patrice was swimming in a sea of numbers on the computer screen. I was in awe.

"Johnnie," she said without looking at me, still tapping away at the keyboard, "I need another password!"

"What do you need another password for?"

"It's asking for one, a secret word. You need just a four-character password, like a PIN number at your ATM. It's probably a word only you would know, to identify yourself. Like your mother's maiden name, your dog's name, something like that."

"I don't have a dog."

My mind, such as it was, raced.

"Try the name Vinnie," I suggested.

Patrice looked at me sadly. "That has six letters."

"Even if you spell it with a *y*?"

"With a *y*, it has five."

I thought about it.

"Try *head*."

Patrice tapped the keyboard without enthusiasm. But after a few seconds, she straightened up, looking surprised.

"We're in," she said.

"You're a rich man, Johnnie LoDuco."

Patrice was scrolling through pages of numbers faster than I could follow. The screen behind the numbers was a soothing light blue, like something in a doctor's waiting room. The numbers themselves were a darker blue. The color scheme tore at your eyes; I could feel a headache coming on.

"All that's in my account?"

She nodded.

"How much?"

"These're all deposits," she told me. "I don't see any withdrawals."

"Yet."

"Here." She had reached the bottom of the page. "That's your total, as of—let's see. Well, the last deposit was two months ago."

Even a math moron like myself could see that it was a big, important figure. I counted the zeros, my lips moving, then counted them again.

"Holy shit."

Patrice nodded. "You can say that again."

"That's twelve million fucking dollars."

Patrice smiled.

"Very good, Johnnie. you figured that out all by yourself."

Leaving Patrice to do her work, I walked up to the store, bought some smokes and a six-pack, then went back to the house, sat on the stoop, smoked Camel Lights, drank beer, and thought. I thought of Vinnie, pumping funds into an account in my name. Ill-gotten funds, it went without saying. Funds he ripped off, or somehow diverted, from his employer. *Embezzled* was the word I was looking for. No wonder they'd gotten mad at him.

I thought about what I could do with twelve million dollars. If I had realized there was that kind of money in porno, I might have stuck with the industry.

After a while, the bugs got to me even through the Camel smoke. I went inside and drank beer at the kitchen table, being quiet so as not to disturb Patrice.

I knew the money probably hadn't started out as a gift, that he was hiding money he stole, putting it under my name, and that if they hadn't caught up with him, I never would have seen a nickel. But I could also imagine Vinnie dropping little clues, building little road maps into his pages, grinning to himself, the asshole, and wondering if I would be smart enough to figure things out.

How much is twelve million dollars divided by the rest of my life, assuming I live beyond next week, that is? I wondered. How much would that be in a year? Would I ever have to work again? Would there be any reason to leave the house? I was still trying to work out the math, scribbling in pencil on the side of a grocery bag, when Patrice screamed behind me.

It was more of a yell or roar than a scream, really. She had pushed herself back from the computer and was pulling on her hair and screeching.

"I can't do it! I can't do it! I can't do it anymore!"

"Whoa, Patrice, calm down! What's the matter?"

"I can't get anywhere with this site. I just keep bouncing back. It's crazy. I can't break it. I don't understand."

She looked at me with hot, angry eyes. "Whoever built this site was a motherfucker. The security is airtight. I cannot get inside."

"Hey, don't look at me like that. It's not my fault."

"I'm sorry, Johnnie. I can't do this anymore. Not tonight. My brain feels like a bag of wet cat litter. It was easier to get into the IRS than this."

I looked at Patrice, who was all stressed and pale, compulsively pulling at a tuft of hair above her left ear. I could hear her synapses frying from where I sat. I jumped out of my chair and gave her a hug. She collapsed against me, leaning her head on my shoulder.

After a while, she straightened up and pushed me away.

"You know, Johnnie, maybe we're going about this the wrong way," she said.

"What do you mean?"

"Well, it's your account. It's in your name. You know the passwords. Maybe we should do this the normal, regular way."

"Which is what? I walk up to a teller window in the Caymans and ask politely for twelve million dollars?"

She shook her head as if her hair were on fire.

"No no no no no. There's a form, an online form for transferring funds, that the bank uses. We could fill it out, submit it. See if they honor it."

"And if they don't?"

She shrugged. "We try hacking in again. But it could work. Even if there're more passwords involved, we can probably guess them. I think I'm beginning to see the way your friend's mind worked."

I thought about this. "So I just fill out this form, we send it in, and the bank gives us money? Without ever seeing us?"

Patrice nodded. "More or less. There's bound to be more verification steps, but I bet we can come up with the answers."

"And then they transfer the money. All twelve million?"

"Let's start small, okay? Let's try, I don't know, five thousand. Transfer five thousand dollars to your account."

"Great. There's one problem."

Patrice squinted at me, her head tilted to one side. "What?"

"I don't have a bank account."

"For Christ's sake, Johnnie, open one! It's not hard." She jumped up, rubbing her eyes. "I'm sorry, I don't mean to yell at you. But all this stuff is really stressing me out."

"All this money stuff, yeah," I said soothingly. "Who ever knew having twelve million dollars in the bank could be so stressful?"

"And the head! Have you forgotten you have your friend's head in my freezer?"

I had forgotten.

"We can get out of here, Johnnie," Patrice said. "We can take this money and go somewhere. You and I. You'll take me with you, won't you, Johnnie?" She looked at me beseechingly.

"Are you kidding?" I said. "No way I'm letting you get away." And as I heard myself say it, I knew it was true.

"We can go somewhere. Together," Patrice whispered. "Blow off Long Island, maybe even leave the country. Go somewhere nice and have fun."

All this was something I had been considering for a while. Believe me. "Look, Patrice," I said, "maybe we should go down there. Where the bank is, I mean. Maybe I should just walk in there and ask for the money."

She stared at me, and I saw that she was crying again, her eyes all red and puffy, rimmed with drops.

"I thought you just said how stupid that was, to walk in and ask for it."

"Well, but maybe not. Maybe if we're right there, on the spot, it will go better. Quicker, anyway. And quicker is good."

Patrice stood there wiping at her eyes, waiting for me to continue, so I did.

"Anyway, if we hang around here, sooner or later they're going to find us. The guys who killed Vinnie, I mean. They think I know something. They think I know where the money is."

"Johnnie," Patrice said, "you do know where the money is."

"Uh, right. So that's a very good reason not to be here."

"I have an aunt in Boca Raton," Patrice said. "We could go down and stay with her for a while. She's always asking me to visit." She looked at me appraisingly. "And if we spiffed you up, cut your hair, shaved you, and put you in a suit, you might look acceptable."

"Hey, now wait a minute," I said.

"You might look like somebody who has twelve million dollars in a Caribbean bank account," Patrice went on. She was cheering up.

"Well, it could work," I said.

I woke up next morning, cringing as usual once I realized I was awake, unwilling to open my eyes and begin another day of difficulties and humiliations. Then I remembered the money.

My eyes snapped open. The studio apartment was filled with sun, morning sun. Island sun. Caribbean island sun. The room was filled with the special glow that comes from a really serious amount of money.

Patrice was snuggled into my arm, pretending to be asleep, but I could tell she wasn't.

"Hey! You awake?"

She grinned. Without opening her eyes, she said, "Good morning, Johnnie Millionaire."

"We'll go to my aunt's first," Patrice was explaining. She had it all worked out.

"Lie low for a little bit. Look behind us. Make sure no one is looking for us. Then we'll slip over to the Caymans and collect the money."

She sounded like she'd been faking money out of banks her entire short life.

"If they give it to us," I said, always the downer.

"I've been thinking about that," said Patrice. "We have to look the part. Not just the suit and tie, I mean. We can't just walk up and stuff the money into a couple of grocery bags. We've got to look like some kind of legitimate businesspeople. Or even illegitimate. But serious, for real."

"How do we do that?"

"We've got to have a business. Business cards, a Web site, maybe even a mailing address."

"Huh?"

"Like a post office box. And we need a bank account to transfer the money to."

I thought about this. It all sounded like good sense.

"They'll be watching for us, though," Patrice said doubtfully. "They'll be waiting for us to make a move on the money."

I hadn't thought of that, but it seemed pretty fucking likely.

"Disguises?" I suggested. "I could dye my hair. I always wanted to be a blond."

Patrice shook her head.

"No, you have to look like yourself if you're going to walk in there and get the money. For twelve million, I bet they ask for picture ID. Maybe we could fake something, I don't know. But we should think of something else."

For a change, I thought of something: There was one flaw in Patrice's reasoning.

"Patrice," I began. I hated to burst her bubble—and mine.

"Johnnie."

"Vinnie set up these accounts in my name?"

"Okay," she said, waiting for the punch line.

"He was pretending to be me. I mean, he probably told the bank he was me."

"And?"

"If I want to walk up to a teller window and withdraw twelve million dollars, then I'll have to look like him, not me."

"Fuck." Patrice gnawed her lip, looking thoughtful. "Do you? I mean, could you pass for Vinnie?"

I thought about it. We were about the same size, and we both had black hair. But there the resemblance ended.

"Probably not. Maybe if I grew a beard."

"You didn't tell me Vinnie had a beard."

"He didn't. But guys with beards tend to look alike. It might work."

We both knew it wouldn't.

"Well, we could try that, I guess." Patrice didn't seem totally into the plan. "But look, Johnnie, here's another thing: At some point if you go down there, however you finesse the appearance thing, they're going to want a signature. If this was Vinnie pretending to be you, the signature they have on file is going to be his. Can you forge Vinnie's signature?"

"Forge Vinnie forging my name, you mean?" I doubted it. I couldn't remember ever seeing Vinnie's handwriting, at least not since high school, when he let me copy his test answers.

A thought came to me.

"Maybe he was forging my handwriting," I suggested.

"Why would he do that? The bank has never seen your handwriting."

"I don't know. As a disguise? As a joke? Vinnie did stuff like that."

"There's got to be some way to find out. Maybe I could take a job there, as a teller or something, and snoop around. Or maybe I'll be able to get deeper into the bank site eventually. Maybe they have some signature-recognition software I can fuck around with. Oh, I don't know, I don't know!"

Patrice frowned as she thought about it. I looked at her, and the money and the head in the freezer dropped out of my reality completely. She looked so good to me, frowning and chewing on her lower lip, that I felt as if somebody had punched an eject button under the kitchen table and my chair was being launched into space. I held on tight.

"All we can do," I said, falling under the empowering influence of her presence, "is try."

Patrice stopped chewing and frowning. She stared at me, looking very serious, like a little kid. Then she broke out in a big white smile.

"That's right, Johnnie," she said. "We can try."

So it was settled. Patrice called her aunt and let her know we would be in the area. The aunt performed to spec and invited us to stay with her. Patrice would close out her bank account; I would use the roll of twenties from Vinnie's box of laundry detergent to get us to Florida. Patrice's Honda might just make it all the way; if not, we had enough spare change to hop a Greyhound.

It was pretty exciting. I had never thought about actually leaving Long Island before, not seriously. It just hadn't seemed possible. Now a whole new life in a whole new place with a brand-new person opened up in front of me. I didn't have much to regret, or much to leave behind: my car, still parked in back of the HiLite Bar and Grill in Riverhead; my nice leather jacket, now in the ruins of Vinnie's glass mansion; my bail bond; an outstanding warrant or two. Nothing I would miss. I gave some thought to changing my name, but that could wait until we cashed out.

So things were definitely looking up. There was only one little speed bump in the road to a new life.

"You've got to get rid of that fucking head, Johnnie," Patrice informed me.

CHAPTER TEN

WE BEGAN TO GET ready for the big Florida trip. Packing didn't take me very long, since I didn't have much—just the business suit we'd bought at a local thrift store, a couple of shirts one of Patrice's old boyfriends had left in her closet, a package of underwear and some socks I'd shoplifted from a department store at the mall. But though I tried to ignore her and ride it out, Patrice kept after me about the head.

"We can't take it with us. Are you kidding? You're not serious, are you? I am not riding down to Florida with a severed head in the trunk. No. No no no." Patrice paused for breath, leaning on the kitchen table. I had an interesting view down the front of her blouse.

"Stop looking at my tits and pay attention to what I'm saying." Her mini dreadlocks were hanging down around her head; she looked like a sea anemone.

"I am paying attention," I said.

"So what are you going to do about it?"

I looked down at the table, then at the toes of my new thrift shop boots, which stretched out in front of me. But there was no escape.

"Okay, okay," I said. "I'll get rid of it. But you have to help."

———

The plan was to put the head back where I'd found it. This involved wiring it to a concrete block, something that should have been done in the first place.

Getting the concrete block was easy. There was a stack at the side of the garage from some past or future remodeling project; we borrowed one. There was a roll of copper wire in the garage; we took that, too. But putting all this together with the head was harder than it looked. And sloppier.

I covered the kitchen floor—a square of linoleum tile that defined part of the studio—with old newspapers, like I did for cleaning fish. Then we took the trash bag out of the freezer and the head out of the bag.

The head sat there, tilted over to one side. It looked bad. It didn't look human anymore. Frost clung to the cheekbones and eyebrows.

Patrice stared at the head a long time. I got the impression she hadn't really believed I had Vinnie's head in a Hefty bag in her refrigerator. But here was the evidence.

"Is that real?" she asked.

I knew what she meant. It didn't look real, but like a cheap rubber Halloween mask, one of the full-head kind. But nastier, of course.

"It's real all right," I said. "I wish to Christ it wasn't. I wish I'd left the fucking thing on the dock for the cops to find."

"Why didn't you?"

All I could do was shrug. "It's Vinnie's head, you know, Vinnie, my friend. I grew up with him. I couldn't just leave it there."

Patrice looked at me with what I think was total disbelief. She shook her head.

"Johnnie, you've got to let go. It's not going to do Vinnie any good if you carry his head around for the rest of your life. It's not going to do us any good. Let's just get it out of here."

We got down to it, wrapping the wire around the head. The plan was to wire it securely to the concrete block. But it was no use. The wire just squished off the face, bringing pieces of skin and cartilage with it.

The smell was getting bad again as the head warmed up.

Patrice looked at the head thoughtfully. "You know what we have to do, don't you, Johnnie?"

I knew. I didn't say anything, though. I was hoping maybe Patrice would just do it.

"Come on," she said. "Help me." She knelt down next to Vinnie's head and looked back at me. "Come on," she said again.

So together we passed the wire through the mouth, out the nose, through the space where the throat had been, out the mouth again. It was nasty, let me tell you. But it gripped. I could have picked the head up and swung it around the room by the wire.

Patrice was not real squeamish—obviously—but even she looked a little pale now. We washed our hands very thoroughly at the sink, leaning against each other. We used every last speck of borax in the white metal hand dispenser that stuck out over the sink.

"Did you notice," she said while we were drying our hands on the one towel, "that all the teeth were gone?"

I knew about the teeth. "Maybe they fell out in the water. Maybe the crabs got 'em," I said without conviction.

Patrice looked at me scornfully. "*Crabs.* No, I think someone pulled them out. To make it harder to identify."

"Or maybe"—I hated to think about this, much less say it—"somebody pulled them out, trying to get him to talk." I could just see Frown and Worm Lips doing that with a big pair of rusty pliers.

Patrice wiped her hands thoughtfully on the towel. She had been drying them for about five minutes, and I was beginning to be afraid she'd rub all the skin off her hands.

"He didn't talk, though, did he? I mean, the money's still there in the bank. In your name."

I nodded. Then a terrible thought occurred to me.

"Oh shit, Patrice, maybe they need me to get at the money! Malatesta, those guys, the guys who are after me. Maybe that's why they didn't just shoot me."

Patrice frowned. "I think they *were* following you, hoping you'd lead them to it. And they're still out there. That just means we have to be tricky. That's also why we have to get the fuck out of here as soon as we can."

Another thought struck me.

"What about Jennifer Smeals?"

"What about her?"

"She said the head was important and not to get rid of it. What if she finds me? What do I tell her?"

"Tell her where it is. Tell her to go find it herself."

"Huh." That appealed to me. "I could lend her my fishing rod."

We took the head back where I'd found it, to the fishing pier in Comapogue. We got there about three o'clock in the morning, after driving all over Long Island, doubling back, getting on and off the LIE, waiting in people's driveways, turning up side streets, cutting through the vast empty parking lots of suburban megamalls, just to see if anyone was following us. Nada. No one. We were all alone.

A storm had come in and it had started to rain, which was good, since it kept people off the streets—even the kind of people who might be up and about in Comapogue at 3:00 A.M. It was a warm rain on a warm wind, blowing up from the Carolinas, and it rocked the wires between the telephone poles, swayed the streetlights, and tossed whitecaps onto the pier.

It was a great night for getting rid of your best friend's head.

We dragged the trash bag with the head and concrete block in it up to the railing.

"Let's take it over where the canal comes in," I yelled through the wind and rain. "It's deeper there."

"Sshhh!" Patrice held up a hand. "A car!"

We crouched down in the shadow of the pier railing, leaning against each other, the head between us. A car drove through the intersection a block up the street from where we were, tires shushing on the rain-wet asphalt. It didn't stop or even slow down.

Patrice whuffed out a big breath. "Nobody we know."

"Okay. Let's get this done."

Somehow we got the bag up on the railing, then swung it over.

"Give it some momentum," I said. "so we can get it far out." We swung it back and forth.

"Count of three: one, two . . . oh fuck."

The concrete block ripped through the bag and splashed in the water about three feet from the dock. We peered into the water but couldn't see a thing. Little phosphorescent jellyfish glowed bluely in the disturbed water.

"That's okay," I said. "It's pretty deep here. We should be okay."

"Oh God," Patrice moaned. "This is making me so crazy."

We got back in the car and drove around some more, just to be certain we were alone. We were. It felt good to be without the head, I must admit. I felt light and free, ready to roll. Caymans, here we come.

We drove along Montauk Highway all the way to Moriches, then

turned around and went back west, then north into deep middle island, feeling our way back home. As far as we could tell, we were still
unpursued.

All the driving, and the incredible relief at being rid of the head
(though I still felt a twinge of guilt for chucking Vinnie into the bay),
had built up a raging, churning storm in my belly. Slowly, I realized
it was hunger.

"You hungry?" I asked Patrice.

"Oh yeah. Really, really hungry."

The diners on Long Island have one thing going for them: pre-
dictability. The food is never very good, or very bad. You can count
on it, just as you can count on there being at least one Greek special
on the menu. The way the last few weeks had been for me, I had no
objection to a little reliability. I was sick of change.

I couldn't figure out if the LoTyde Diner was retro sleaze or a real
fifties-era grease palace that had never been redecorated. The
grease part was authentic anyway.

"Oh, thank God!" Patrice said when she saw the neon diner sign
up ahead. "I am so ready for this."

The sun hadn't started to come up yet, but there were already
plenty of people in the diner, people out all night like us, I guess, and
guys on their way to work. Patrice and I made our way to a U-shaped,
salmon-and-turquoise Naughahyde booth at the far end of the diner.
There was a small jukebox built into the table, and I leafed through
the selections without finding anything I wanted to hear. It was too
early for music anyway.

Patrice disappeared behind a tall plastic-covered menu. "What're
you having?"

"Just a coffee for me, maybe a Danish."

"*I'm* having eggs, two eggs, over easy. With toast and hash browns, and bacon. Or sausage. Bacon *and* sausage. I am having *breakfast*," Patrice said. She sounded as if she had just invented it.

"I thought you were a vegetarian."

She smirked. "Not today. I just lapsed."

"Throwing heads off piers will do that to you."

The waitress showed up and took our orders. We sat and waited in silence for the food to come, too hungry and crazed from the night's activities to talk much. I hated the waiting part. I never know what to do, where to look, when I'm just sitting around. I always feel like there's a spotlight on me.

I sat there and twitched for a while. Patrice seemed okay, happily looking around the crowded diner, out the window, reading ahead in the menu, so that if we came back she would know what to order.

"Look," I said, "I'm going to get the paper."

"Have fun."

I stopped off in the men's room and wasted some time looking for a cigarette machine. I guess they don't have them anymore, probably because it takes so long to put seven dollars in the slot one coin at a time. When I finally got back with a copy of *Newsday*, Patrice was staring down at the place mat. She had twisted all the napkins into tight little cylinders as thick as drinking straws. She looked up at me with big worried eyes as I sat down.

"What's up?" I asked, concerned.

Patrice looked quickly over her shoulder, then turned back, frowning.

"That guy," she said.

"What guy?" I whipped my head around in terror.

"Don't look at him! Over there, on the other side of the diner. He watched you when you went to get the paper. And I caught him looking over at me. I think he's following us."

Carefully this time, I worked my head around, first looking out the window at the pork stores and pizza parlors across the street, then casually scoping out the diner patrons.

"What, that big guy in the sunglasses?"

"I know I've seen him before. That hat. Who wears hats like that around here?"

It *was* strange headgear for Long Island or anywhere, a round camo hat with a floppy brim. The big guy was entirely in camouflage, which made him stand out like a Humvee at a go-cart rally. Maybe more. And even though the sun was now officially up, it was too gray and early to be wearing sunglasses outdoors, much less inside a diner.

"Maybe he's a hunter."

"Johnnie, it's the middle of summer. Nobody's hunting now. Get a grip. He's following us. Oh no!"

"What is it?"

"He's coming over!"

Sure enough, when I twisted around again, I was looking right into a pair of mirrored shades under the weird camo hat. Bits of rusty blond hair stuck out from under the hat.

The big man grinned.

"Hello, folks," he said. "Mind if I join you?" Before either of us could say anything, he slid in next to Patrice.

A weird smell came off the big man, twisting through the good diner smells of bacon and coffee. I couldn't pin it down. I flashed on tiled rooms, disinfectant. Formaldehyde?

Maybe the guy was a taxidermist.

Patrice edged as far away from the guy as she could get and still stay at the table.

The big man folded his hands on the tabletop and beamed at us. He looked as if he was about to try to sell us insurance, or lead us in prayer.

Before the big guy could say anything, Patrice spoke up. "You've been following us," she said accusingly. "I saw you."

The big man nodded approvingly. "Very good. You're paying attention. Demonstrates alertness, an important quality. Yes, I *have* been following you."

"How did you stay with us?" Patrice asked. "We did everything; we made damn sure nobody was following us."

"I didn't. You lost me in the first fifteen minutes. You are very good at that."

"So how?"

"Patience," the big dude said smugly. "I knew you'd be back this way. You have patterns, habits. Probably unconscious. When you get near your house, you start to fall into them. You always get off the LIE at the same exit, for example."

"This diner is nowhere near there," Patrice objected.

The big man shrugged. "I got lucky. Middle Country Road is another one of your patterns. You always take it. I cruised it for a couple hours. Saw you drive by. Here we are."

It was depressing to find out we were so easy, after all our hard work. Depressing, and a little scary. If this guy could find us so quickly, who else might get lucky?

I decided to meet trouble head-on.

"You from Malatesta?" I asked him. The shades flashed as he turned toward me.

"Malatesta? No, I'm not from anyone. I represent my own interests."

"And what are those?" Patrice asked.

The big guy folded his hands on the table in front of him. They were big hands, even for a large guy like him, very clean and scrubbed-looking. He leaned toward us earnestly, bending down over his hands. He looked like he was praying.

"I know what you have," he said.

Patrice and I said nothing. For one thing, we still weren't sure what he meant—the head or the money? We didn't have either, of course. Anymore. Or not yet.

Besides, my mind had gone blank. I wouldn't have known what to say even if I'd known for sure what he was talking about. I stared at our reflections in the mirrored shades; they looked weirdly stretched out and distorted.

When he saw we weren't going to respond, the big guy sat back.

"I know what you have," he repeated. "I saw you reel it in."

That rocked me. I thought back to that evening; there had been no one in sight, I was sure of it.

Maybe "reel it in" was just a figure of speech.

"Look, I have no idea what you're talking about," I said half-heartedly. Even to myself, I sounded unconvincing.

"A head is hard to hide," he said.

Now Patrice leaned forward. "I don't know what you think you saw. You must have been hallucinating. But if you don't get up and go away and leave us alone, I'm having the manager call the cops."

A slow smile spread over the big guy's features, like spilled motor oil over a garage floor.

"You won't do that. Not after all the trouble you've taken to avoid them. Why, you shouldn't even be out here in public. You're taking a big risk. Anyone could see you. *I* saw you. You should be more careful. Let me help you."

"Why should *you* help *us*?" Patrice said, her eyes all squinted up with suspicion.

"You have something I want," the big man said simply.

More silence. The mirrored shades tracked from me to Patrice and back again.

"You have what I want," the big guy said again. "I have what you need—experience, practice, know-how. I have been where you are now. I can help you. Trust me."

"Why should we?" Patrice asked him.

The big man sighed. "Look, I think we're going about this the wrong way. Let me order something. We can eat and talk. Then we'll all feel better. I know you'll see things my way when you've considered them carefully."

"What is your way?"

"You have it," Mirrored Shades said. "I want it." He picked up a menu. "Look! Soft-shell crab special! You can't get that all the time."

The waitress showed up with our food—where the fuck had she been all this time?—and the big guy put in his order with her. There was a glaze on Patrice's fried eggs; my coffee was only lukewarm. The big guy beamed at us happily, sun glinting off his shades.

But we were hungry, *really, really* hungry. Shrugging physically and mentally, I dug in, Patrice likewise.

The big guy picked up the soft-shell crab sandwich and bit into it. The ends of the bread rose up like angel wings; crab legs flopped out on both sides and hung down, dripping butter. Patrice and I watched in silence, fascinated. It was like something out of a horror movie.

"Good, huh?" Patrice asked. The big guy smiled happily, mouth full of crab.

I thought about what crabs had done to Vinnie's head—were probably doing to it right now—and was glad I'd ordered a Danish.

Eventually, all our plates were empty, every last fleck of egg and crab wiped up with pieces of wheat toast and Wonder bread. The little square jelly packets were empty. The coffee was cold. The waitress was nowhere in sight.

The man in the mirrored shades smiled at us greasily. There was a shred of crabmeat on his chin. I could feel the tense silence coming back in like a tide. I couldn't stand it.

"Look, just who are you anyway?" I blurted. Patrice looked at me sadly.

The big man smiled even more broadly.

"I'm your guardian angel," he said.

His name was Bogdan, he told us. Bogdan O'Reilly.

"Bogdan," Patrice said. "Is that Gaelic or something?"

"Slavic," the big guy said. "My mom's Croatian. My dad was Irish."

He was a private investigator. He showed us his license when Patrice said she didn't believe it. Neither one of us had ever seen a real PI's license, but the paper he showed us was convincing.

He wanted the head.

"I saw you that evening," he said to me. "I saw you pull it in. You *hid* it!" He smiled triumphantly. "Many people—most people—would have left it on the dock and called the cops."

"Look," I said to Bogdan, trying to make myself sound rock-solid, tough, sure of myself. "Okay, you're right. We had the head. *Had* it. We don't have it, not anymore. We got rid of it."

Bogdan's face got stiff and corpselike. His face set. It was like watching something cook through the little window in the oven door.

"You got rid of it," he said softly. I nodded.

He stared at me through the mirrored shades. There was a spell of silence. Patrice scooted along the seat and pressed herself up against me.

"Where?" Bogdan whispered after a while.

"Johnnie! Don't tell him!" Patrice said urgently.

"Don't worry," I told her. And to Bogdan, I said, "Where we can find it again if we want to. Where you could find it if we told you where to look."

"Will you tell me?"

"Maybe. Maybe not. It depends." In spite of holding all the cards, sitting in the driver's seat, I felt like my advantage was slipping away from me as Bogdan stared at me through his sunglasses.

" 'Depends,' " he repeated. "*Depends*. On what I can do for you."

"Bogdan," Patrice said, "I don't think you can do anything for us. Except maybe leave us alone. Why don't you just go away?"

Bogdan took off his sunglasses and rubbed at his eyes. Before he whipped the glasses back on, I got a look at his eyes. They were big, pop-eyed, and blue.

"Well, I do have some leverage in this," he said. "After all, a simple anonymous phone call would have the cops poking around your house. Eh? And I bet you forgot to clean up everything. Right? There's always something you forget."

I tried to keep my face blank, but my mind was racing through Patrice's apartment, trying to find something we had overlooked. I knew Patrice was doing the same thing.

Bogdan smiled. "But don't worry. It doesn't have to be like that. There are plenty of other people following you. Did you know that?"

Patrice and I shook our heads, she with complete sincerity.

"I had to get in line most nights," Bogdan said. "It would be simple to give you up to one of them. Whoever they are. They don't appear to be very nice people." He reached over and popped me on the arm. "But don't worry, Johnnie! They haven't been close to you in a while, not since you hooked up with Patrice here."

Patrice frowned. I don't think she liked him using her name.

"But I'm not out to hurt you guys. Really! I'm not!" He held out his hands as if fending us off. We must have looked doubtful. "I'm the only thing between you and some ugly people. I've been protecting you. If it weren't for me, you would be dead or in jail now."

A thought came to me. "Was that you on the LIE the other night? You the one drove Stosh off the road?"

He looked at me and grinned. "I've been watching over you," he said, "keeping you safe. Now all I want in return is what you are trying to get rid of anyway. Is that too much to ask?"

"You bet it is!" Patrice had been quiet for a while, but now she let him have it.

"This is a setup, Johnnie," she said to me, but she was looking at Bogdan. "This guy, even if he's what he says he is, is working for your friend Jennifer Smeals, or that mob guy you told me about. There is no way we can trust him."

Bogdan sighed. Patrice sat there and glared at him, leaning on her folded arms.

"I don't know, Patrice. Why not tell him where it is?" I said. "I mean, what do we care? That's all behind us now. Let him have it."

"Now you're talking," Bogdan said.

"Sure, we'll tell him," Patrice said. "We can send him a post-card."

The big guy looked up alertly. "You guys are going away?"

Whoops. "To Canada," I said, simultaneously with Patrice's "To Mexico."

"Mexico, I mean," I added lamely.

The big guy nodded wisely. "A tropical island where you'll be safe from the law," he said slowly, as if reading it off a teleprompter with transmission problems. "Tahiti? Tonga? Palau? Palau's nice."

"It doesn't matter to you where we're going," Patrice said impatiently. "If we promise to give you what you want, will you go away?"

"I will, if that's what you really want. But Patrice, you know, given your situation, you should think about whether you can do it all on your own."

"Maybe he's right, Patrice," I said nervously. She grimaced, wouldn't look at me.

The big man stood up suddenly and tossed his napkin (he had tucked it into his shirt, like a fat tie) on the table. "Look, let's talk. We'll negotiate. Let's go to my place and work this out."

"Your place! No way! I don't think so!"

"Okay. Your place," Bogdan said. "I know where it is. I've spent the last few nights parked up the block."

I could see this didn't sit well with Patrice, the thought of this guy being out there all the while we were getting to know each other.

"Patrice," I whined. "Let's talk to him. What have we got to lose?"

She wouldn't look at me. I could tell she was pissed but that she was going along with it—whatever it was.

I could see that she was really uncomfortable with taking Bogdan to her house, though, even if he had practically been living there already. When we got out to the parking lot, she stopped in her tracks, looking unhappy. "Look, Bogdan," she said, "we don't have to go anywhere. We can talk in the car. Get in. I'll drive us around."

"Fine with me." Bogdan shrugged.

Patrice jumped behind the wheel of her Civic; I got in the front seat next to her, and Bogdan wedged himself in the back.

We drove around at random for a while, Patrice grumpy and noncommunicative, Bogdan silent and smirking, waiting us out. The tension got thick pretty quickly.

"So, Bogdan," I said after about five minutes of heavy silence, by way of a conversation starter. "You want this head?"

"Yes, now that you are through with it," he said graciously.

"What could you possibly want with a severed head?" Patrice asked, frowning and hunching over the wheel.

"For my collection," Bogdan said.

"Collection? You collect heads?"

"Like shrunken heads, from the Amazon?" I put in lamely.

Bogdan shook his head gently. "No. Oh no, nothing like that. Full-size heads, mostly female, mostly adult."

"And where do you get these heads?" Patrice asked. She examined him carefully in the rearview mirror as he spoke.

"I used to harvest them myself," Bogdan said dreamily. "Back in the day. Before I took an early retirement."

"You were a medical student?" I asked. "A mortician? Something like that?"

"No," said Bogdan. "Oh no. I was purely freelance, an amateur. Though don't think when I call myself an amateur I mean to indicate a lack of skill. I was very skilled, very good at what I did. As evidenced by the fact that I am here to tell you about it."

"You killed people and cut off their heads," Patrice said.

Bogdan nodded.

Silence fell—as much silence as you get in a seventeen-year-old Civic with a dicey transmission anyway.

After a while I said, "So Bogdan, why do you need this head you think we have? Why don't you just harvest another one?"

"I told you: I'm retired. A forced retirement. I can no longer pursue my old calling."

"Why not?"

"They almost caught me," he said. "I had to stop. They came to my house, talked to my mother! My poor mother. They were that close. A cop named Carbone, a homicide detective, was hanging around all the time. Everywhere I went, I would see his ugly face."

"I know Carbone," I said. Bogdan was right about the face.

"He was a homicide cop, then," Bogdan said. "I understand they busted him down to school-crossing guard after the case against me blew up."

"How did that happen?"

"They put me on trial!" He said it as if that were the final insult.

"So they did catch you," Patrice said.

"They arrested me, yes. But they couldn't prove a thing; they had no hard evidence, none. All purely circumstantial. And badly presented! The prosecution blew it. The jury was out only half an hour. A verdict of not guilty! I walked."

I could see he was getting worked up, remembering his days of glory. That made me nervous.

"They had to back off and leave me and my mother alone," Bogdan went on. "But they never stopped watching me entirely. I knew that. So I retired."

"I remember reading about that," Patrice said. "The trial. I couldn't believe they let you go. You're that guy, the one they called the Headhunter in the papers."

"That's me, all right," Bogdan said cheerily. "They fucked up. Big time. The cops really screwed the pooch. No jury would have believed them."

"So now you're a free man, Bogdan," Patrice said. I was beginning to feel left out. I had no memory of Bogdan's case. Patrice was an expert, it sounded like.

"Double jeopardy," Bogdan said smugly. "Now they can't try me again for the same crime."

"And you don't," Patrice said, cautiously, "you never—I mean, don't you get a feeling sometimes like you want to do it again? Like maybe you just can't help yourself and you have to go out and cut off somebody's head?"

I wished to fuck Patrice would not say things like that. She freaked me out. She always had a way of pushing things to the edge, and then over. Bogdan got real quiet; we could hear him breathing, like a big out-of-breath dog.

"I have my collection," he said. "And my memories."

"I bet."

"What about your collection? Did the cops just let you have it back?" I asked, not so much to change the subject—there was no getting away from it—as to lighten the tone a bit. I was afraid Patrice would drive Bogdan into some kind of flashback, or remission, or whatever the term would be for a serial killer who suddenly rediscovered his old joy in decapitation.

"They never found it," Bogdan said, the smugness starting to come back into his voice. "The morons."

"You must have hidden it good," I said. He nodded.

"I knew they would look in the most obvious places. They did. And after they looked in the most obvious place, the place any child of twelve would look, I moved my collection there. They never went back."

"Bogdan, that was really smart," I said. Patrice and Bogdan both looked at me funny.

"So you don't do it anymore," Patrice said.

Bogdan nodded. "I stopped."

"Just like that?"

He nodded again, more vigorously this time. "All the experts say that doesn't happen, that once someone like me kills, he will kill again, helplessly, in the same pattern. But I was smarter than the experts. I fooled them. I broke the pattern."

Patrice stopped talking to concentrate on her driving—we had drifted down close to the water now, and run into some heavy fog coming in off the Great South Bay. Something darted across the roadway in front of us—a dog, a raccoon. The Civic fishtailed as Patrice swerved to avoid it.

We swooshed through the fog. Car headlights appeared out of it like ugly repressed memories, then vanished into the fog behind us.

Patrice and I kept our mouths shut, staring out into the foggy street.

"So your history doesn't really build up a lot of trust, Bogdan," I pointed out after some more silent driving through the fog.

"It should," he said. "It explains why I'm interested in the head. It lets you know I'm working for myself and not these people who want to do you harm."

"It lets me know you want to cut off our heads," Patrice put in.

"I keep telling you that I'm retired. What do I have to do to convince you?"

"You can't," Patrice said.

Bogdan grew thoughtful.

"Look," he said, "I guess I'll have to be straight with you."

"What a good idea," Patrice replied.

"I didn't get involved in this purely on my own hook," Bogdan continued. "At least not initially. I was hired to watch over you, keep tabs on you."

"By who?" I wanted to know, but I had an idea. It had to be Jennifer.

"I never met him," Bogdan said. "He never told me his name. I wouldn't have believed him anyway. It was obvious he didn't want to appear in this. He spoke to me over the phone, gave me my instructions that way. The retainer was left on my doorstep, in twenties, in a cardboard box. He told me where I could find you."

"And what did he tell you to do? Kill us?" Patrice asked.

Bogdan shook his head. "Just watch you, and make sure nothing happened to you, and report to him regularly. Except that after that first instruction, I never heard from him again."

The fog had lifted, or else we had driven out of it. I recognized some buildings and realized we were in Amityville, almost to Patrice's house.

Bogdan stuck his big head between me and Patrice. "Hey, you know, I live right near here. Why don't you two come over for a visit?"

"Yeah, Bogdan." Patrice sneered at him. "We could hang out, look at your collection. Before we become part of it."

"No, I'm serious," Bogdan said. He seemed a little offended. "I could introduce you to my mom. She'd love to meet you."

"You live with your mother? Figures," Patrice said.

"Hey, go easy on the guy," I said, surprised to find myself defending Bogdan. But to tell the truth, I felt grateful for being rescued from Stosh. And if he had really wanted to cut my head off, he'd had plenty of opportunities and hadn't taken them.

" 'Go easy on the guy,' " Patrice mocked in a gobbling, stupid-sounding voice. (Did I really sound like that?) "Johnnie, can't you see that this asshole is just trying to lure us into his secret dungeon so he can torture us to death and cut off our heads?"

"You're not very trusting, Patrice," Bogdan said.

"You know, Patrice, I've been thinking," I said, annoyed to hear her sigh with exasperation. It's amazing how much sarcasm she could pack into a nonverbal sound. "And what I think is, we need help. We need all the help we can get. We are, like, a step ahead of these assholes chasing us. . . ."

"Not even that," Bogdan put in.

"And we could use someone to watch our back. That's all."

Patrice didn't say anything, which I took as a good sign.

"So far, everything this guy has done has helped us," I pointed out.

"Everything he *says* he's done," said Patrice. I took this for a halfway concession.

"If not Bogdan, then who?" I said.

"Actually, I've done more than I told you," Bogdan said. "Much more than you realize."

When Patrice whacked the steering wheel so that the horn let out a sharp *blatt*, I knew I had convinced her.

"Okay. All right, okay. But Johnnie, I just want to say this: If you end up hanging from his rearview mirror with your lips sewn shut, don't blame me."

"I'm retired," Bogdan said for about the eight hundredth time. "Anyway, I don't shrink them." He turned to me. "You guys will love my mom. She is the world's greatest cook!"

Bogdan's house, when we got there, was a rickety old place, wood shingles stained almost black by years of rain and car exhaust, set back behind a brick wall and an overgrown yard just off the County Line Road. It figured someone like Bogdan would live there. Bogdan hopped out to open a cast-iron gate in the brick wall, unlooping a padlocked chain holding it closed.

"Look at him," Patrice whispered to me. "Look at that fucking guy."

"Igor," I said. Patrice giggled. "The fog, the gate, the chain . . . he is Igor, no doubt about it."

"What are we doing here?" Patrice asked. But it was too late to change our minds; Igor/Bogdan was waving us in. Patrice gunned it

down the short driveway, forcing Bogdan to jump out of the way.
He popped back anyway and ran around to the driver's side to hold
the door open for Patrice, grinning like a maniac—which, of course,
he was.

"Come on in and meet Mom," he said.

Bogdan the Headhunter pronounced his first name in an elaborately
foreign way, like "Bohgue-dahn," but not his mom. She called him
"Danny Boy."

She was in the kitchen when we barged in. The place was unbelievably hot; pots and pans steamed on the stove. It must have been
a hundred degrees in there. Mom O'Reilly wore a red apron with
white ruffles, and two enormous magenta fluffy slippers. She
smiled brightly at us as we tromped through the house.

"Are your friends coming to breakfast, Danny Boy?" she cooed
at him.

"No, Moms. They're here on business."

Bogdan herded us through the kitchen and up dark, narrow
stairs to his room. He paused dramatically a moment, hand on the
doorknob, then pushed the door open and waved us in.

I don't know what I was expecting; I had never seen the child-
hood room of a serial killer before. But whatever I had in mind, this
wasn't it; this was just a room: a few paperback books and maga-
zines on a table by the bed, some dusty college pennants on the wall,
a model airplane hanging from the ceiling. It could have been any
depressing little boy's room that had been kept locked up since the
kid went away to college. Except that Bogdan was still there,
plopped down in a big armchair that was the only other furniture in
the room aside from the bed. The only things at all weird were a
couple of big samurai-type swords hanging on the wall. They looked
like the real deal.

Gingerly, we sat down on the bed.

"What do you think of Mom?" Bogdan asked.

"Nice lady," I volunteered. "Cooking up a storm."

"She's very sentimental," Bogdan told us. "You know, she kept my father's body in their bed after he died, for three years, before somebody found out and called the cops."

"Where did she sleep?" Patrice asked. She looked uneasily at the bed she was sitting on.

"Oh, she usually falls asleep in the La-Z-Boy in front of the TV anyway," Bogdan said. "Otherwise, she slept where she usually slept."

We squirmed to think of it.

"Didn't he smell?" I asked.

"Only at first. After a while, you didn't notice. The body mummified all by itself. This place has special properties, you know," he informed us. "Like some catacombs you may have read about in Rome and elsewhere, where the bodies mummify. The county line runs right through the middle of the house."

"I didn't know political boundaries had metaphysical properties," I said, wishing as usual that I hadn't. Patrice peered at me oddly.

"This house has special properties," Bogdan repeated. I let it go. Or I meant to let it go. But something must have showed on my face, some skeptical wrinkle, a laugh line of doubt.

Bogdan became agitated. "Look. Let me show you." He jumped up from the chair and squeezed past the bed.

Bogdan's bedroom was in the attic story, and the walls were angled in from about shoulder height up, following the roofline. The lower part of the wall was covered in cheap paneling, a knotty-pine veneer with shallow lines imitating planks in it. In the upper corner, there was a small piece of wood, the size of a cigar butt—a kind of toggle. You could see the lines where the paneling didn't quite match up. Bogdan twisted the toggle and a big piece of paneling lifted right out.

"My collection," he announced.

Not for the first or last time, Patrice and I were left speechless.

Bogdan's collection consisted of about six whole heads, dried up and leathery, hanging from little hooks in a piece of perforated Masonite. The neck parts were all raggedy and stringy. It looked like Bogdan had gnawed the heads off. In addition to the heads, there was what looked like a scalp, a long blond scalp, but no other body parts, thank Christ.

It was a solemn moment for all of us. I could see that Bogdan was moved. He had taken the sunglasses off and stashed them somewhere, and his bulging blue eyes were glazed-looking.

"You realize what this means?" he said in a husky voice.

"That you killed six people and cut their heads off and kept them?"

"Eight, actually," Bogdan said. He didn't seem perturbed in any way. "I didn't keep the heads at first. But as I became more comfortable with the process, I began to take the time to, well, keep trophies. But that's not what I meant to say."

"You were going to say?" I prompted; I couldn't take the thought of a long pause in the conversation, with only those heads to fill it.

"What I meant," he said, "was that this is a turning point in our relationship. I don't show this to just anybody. In fact, I have never done so before tonight. To anyone. And now there's no turning back."

"You can trust us," I said nervously.

"Oh, I know. I can tell," Bogdan said. "Otherwise, we wouldn't have come so far so fast. Head or no head." He put the square of paneling back in place and twisted the little toggle. Only when I breathed out did I realize I had been holding my breath.

———

After the unveiling of Bogdan's collection, there didn't seem to be a whole fuck of a lot to say. In a panic to avoid one of the long, menacing silences that were becoming such a prominent feature of our relationship, I scanned the room desperately. When I came to the samurai swords hanging on the wall, a nickel dropped.

"Say, Bogdan," I said, "was that you?"

Both he and Patrice looked at me in a way I was coming to recognize. The "What the fuck is he talking about?" look.

"The old guy and the beagle," I explained. "On the town dock. The guy who died of a heart attack when somebody cut his dog in half."

"Oh. Oh yeah," he said. "That was me. How did you guess?"

"The swords made me think of it. Plus, I know now you were hanging around."

"It wasn't supposed to happen like that, actually," Bogdan said thoughtfully. "I just meant to throw a scare into him." He glanced up at us, looking a little guilty, I thought.

"What is this?" Patrice put in, squinting angrily. "You cut a dog in half with a sword?"

"I was working for his brother," Bogdan explained. "The old guy owed him some money from a house they sold. A lot of money, actually. But I never thought he would croak."

"Shit happens, Bogdan," I said, reassuring him. Patrice threw up her hands but didn't say anything.

"It's just as well, as it turned out," Bogdan said. "If I hadn't been shadowing that guy, I might have missed you reeling in the head."

"I didn't see you." I'd gone over it a hundred times in my mind while we were driving around, and I couldn't figure out where he'd been.

Bogdan grinned, pleased with his shadowing technique. "In a parked car. Up the block. With a night scope. I was getting a fix on the dock, because I knew the old fart would come walking his dog out there, like he did every evening. And I saw you pull it in. Quite a catch."

I lowered my head modestly.

"I saw you think about throwing it back," Bogdan continued. "And I saw you shove it in the bag, then lie to the old man about it. That's when I knew there was more in this gig for me than just money."

So there was no getting around it: The head was back on the table.

"If we give you this head," I began—Patrice made an exasperated noise, but I ignored her—"what will you give us?"

"Freedom," said Bogdan. "Freedom from guilt, freedom from worry. One less thing to worry about. You have a lot on your plate right now. You don't need a head, as well."

I nodded my head slowly, reluctantly. Even Patrice was quiet at this point.

"What about the rest of the stuff on the plate? Can you help us there?"

"I can. I've dealt with these people before. I believe I can deflect them."

I wasn't so sure. Guys chasing twelve million dollars in stolen money require a lot of deflection.

Seeing the doubt in my eyes, Bogdan hurried to clarify. "Long enough, anyway, for you two to get away. If I don't . . ." He paused, looking from me to Patrice and back. "If I don't, I sincerely doubt that you will make it."

I hated to admit it, but I agreed with Bogdan there.

"Okay, Bogdan," I said, "You win. We'll tell you where the head is."

"Johnnie!" Patrice whispered to me warningly, and to Bogdan: "We'll tell you where it is, but not now."

"Why not now?" Bogdan asked. "I've told you everything. You know all my secrets."

"We don't know you well enough," Patrice said. Mentally, I begged to differ; I knew as much as I wanted to know.

"But after all our talk!"

"Look, Bogdan," I said, "the head's in a safe place. No one will find it where we stashed it. And when we get away safely, that will prove you held up your end."

Bogdan watched me eagerly, like a dog watching someone eat a hamburger.

"Then I get the head?"

I nodded. "Then you get the head."

Bogdan's mom invited us to eat again as we were leaving, but our appetites had been spoiled, probably forever. We just thanked her and left.

We drove Bogdan back to the diner. His truck was parked around back—a big-wheeled brown Jimmy. I recognized it all right.

Bogdan stood there in the parking lot, staring at us with big dog eyes and plucking at his fat lower lip. He seemed filled with uncertainty.

"You will keep up your end of the bargain?" he asked us.

"Trust us, Bogdan," I urged. The big serial killer smiled, showing off a mouthful of big white teeth like veteran's tombstones.

"Oh, I do, I do trust you both. Honestly, I am glad we came together like this. I feel a bond."

Patrice smiled at him full force. She was so pretty. I could see Bogdan felt it, too. It probably made him want to cut her head off and eat the rest of her, but he felt it.

"Me, too," she told Bogdan, pinning him in place with her smile. "Ciao for now, Bodgan."

"We'll talk."

"You bet."

The big serial killer lurched over to his truck, jumped in, and drove away in a spray of gravel.

"Man."

We sat in the front seat of Patrice's car, not talking, not moving, while Bogdan drove out of sight.

Patrice kept staring after his disappearing pickup for a long time, a weird expression on her face.

"Bogdan," she said, stretching the name out. "Booohg-dahhhn."

"That is one sick fuck," I said.

"You got that right."

"What do you think? Should we tell him where it is? The head, I mean."

Patrice twisted around and stared at me.

"Are you out of your mind? Would you let him have Vinnie's head? Your best friend? For his sick little skull museum? No way. No way we can trust that head chopper for a minute."

"But suppose he calls the cops? Or sells us out to Malatesta?"

"It won't matter. If he thinks we're going to tell him where the head is, that will hold him. We don't actually have to tell him. That was really brilliant, Johnnie."

"Oh, yeah, well . . ." I basked in the praise. I admit I wasn't used to it. I think I blushed.

"Anyway, let the big asshole tell the cops," Patrice continued. "What do we care? We are going to leave here tonight. We'll clean up. Don't worry. There won't be anything for the cops to find. Even if he does call them, they'll just think it was a wacko phone attack—which any call from Bogdan would be."

One thing worried me, though.

"Malatesta. Malatesta will come looking for us. You know he will. Even if Bogdan can slow him up, that won't last forever."

"That is why we have to leave tonight, right now, before this all comes unstuck. Tonight!"

"So we leave your place tonight? I'm not really packed or anything." I felt a little sick to my stomach thinking about it, but I could see Patrice was right.

She thought so, too.

"You don't have anything to pack. Tonight, Johnnie. Tonight."

We got back to Patrice's place in a few minutes. It was horrible to think that Bogdan lived so close to us, but in another way, I was glad it wasn't a long ride. The late hours we had been keeping had taken a lot out of me. I had gotten no sleep at all. My eyes felt like someone had taken a power sander to them.

Bogdan had spooked us, that's for sure. We kept looking around jerkily, like paranoid nutcases. Patrice dropped her house key when she tried to open the door.

"Oh *fuck*!"

"Ssshhh!" I whispered.

"Don't ssshhh me, Johnnie!" She got the door open and we stepped in, glad to be out of the glare of daylight.

"Anyway," she said, "we don't have to be quiet. We're home."

Home. I looked around the tiny apartment, thinking this would be the last time I'd see it. I hadn't lived there that long—though it seemed like months—but leaving a place is always a heavy moment.

And important things had happened to me there. Like love, and finding twelve million dollars.

"We'll get some sleep," Patrice was saying, "just a couple hours. Well, maybe three or four. But no more than that. Then we pack and go."

"Patrice."

"What?"

I was frozen. I could hardly talk, but I made my lips move.

"What's that on the kitchen table?"

Patrice and I stared at the black plastic trash bag. The bag bulged in the middle, a melon-size mound, and the folds and wrinkles around the bulge clearly outlined the shape of a human head.

We stared at the bag a long time in silence.

"Fucking Bogdan," I said after a while.

Patrice shook her head, like she was trying to get water out of her hair.

"Not Bogdan. He would keep it."

I went over to the table and hefted the garbage bag. I don't know exactly what I was thinking. A hallucination? A bag of groceries from Aunt Vivienne? But it felt like a head, and it made a nasty thump when I put the bag down, a sound I had become too familiar with.

Patrice was still standing in the same spot, but one hand was twisting and pulling at her snake dreads as if it had a mind of its own.

"Do you think it's, like, a cursed thing, that it brings bad luck to whoever has it?" she asked in an awed voice. "I mean, like to every-body that touches it?"

"You'd better hope not," I said. "I touched it. You touched it. Right now, it's sitting on your kitchen table." I stared at the head, too, wondering if I could ever get rid of it. "Besides, I never heard of a lucky severed head."

"Something very freaky is going on here," Patrice said.

I took her by the arm and pulled her toward the door.

"Where are we going?"

"C'mon," I said, my throat hoarse and sore, for some reason. "We can't stay here with this thing. Let's go."

Just then, the phone rang.

CHAPTER ELEVEN

I HAD A BAD feeling. "Don't answer it!" I shouted to Patrice, but it was too late. There's something about a ringing phone: You just have to answer it, even if you know it will blow up when you pick up the receiver.

Patrice picked up the receiver and listened for a few seconds. Then she held it out to me.

"It's for you," she said calmly.

I was not calm. I grabbed the phone from Patrice and screamed into the mouthpiece, "Who is this? What do you want?"

"Calm down, Johnnie," Jennifer Smeals said. "I have been looking everywhere for you."

"Oh, hi, Jennifer," I said in my best casual manner, hoping my voice wasn't shaking too noticeably.

"Hi, Johnnie. Where are you?"

"At a friend's," I said weakly.

Patrice grabbed my wrist and whispered, "Don't tell her where I live!"

"Johnnie, look," Jennifer said. "I only care about the one thing. Do you still have it?"

"Have what?" I stuttered. I meant it, too. My mind had gone blank and I had no idea what she was talking about.

"You know what I mean. Johnnie, please, don't be an asshole. Do you still have the head?"

I stared at the plastic garbage bag on Patrice's kitchen table, confirming its head-shaped bulge. Streams of salt water had run off the bag and onto the Formica tabletop and the floor. The kitchen smelled like a boat dock. There was a shred of bright green seaweed in a little puddle on the table.

"It's right here, I think."

"You *think*? What do you mean, you think? Do you still have it or not?"

"Well, it's in a bag on the table here," I told her. "But I haven't looked in the bag yet. It looks like there's a head in it."

Jennifer was silent for a long time, taking this in. Then she said, with an obvious restraint that I could only admire, "Look in it, Johnnie. Look in the bag, please."

I looked.

"Yeah, it's in there all right," I told Jennifer.

"Okay, good. That's good. Johnnie, I need it. I need it now. Where are you?"

I put my hand over the phone and looked at Patrice. "She wants the head," I whispered.

"Great. Give it to her," Patrice whispered back.

"What about Bogdan?"

"Tell him Jennifer has it."

I liked this idea. "Let them work it out, huh?"

Patrice nodded.

"Should I have her come here? To pick it up?"

"No, no. What are you, crazy? Don't let her come here!"

"Okay, okay." Then a brilliant thought came to me. "Bogdan's."

Patrice nodded vigorously, shaking her dreads.

I took my hand off the receiver and Jennifer's agitated voice jumped out at me like a rat from a hole.

"Don't fuck around with me, LoDuco! I don't have time for this!"

"Sorry, sorry," I said, trying to reassure her. "Look, Jennifer, where are you?"

"I'm at Malatesta's."

Oh shit.

"Is he there?"

"Not at the moment."

"Can you . . . get away?" For a dizzy moment, I felt like I was asking her to sneak out on a date.

"Look, Johnnie," Jennifer said, "it's like this: Malatesta doesn't believe me. I told him that Vincent is dead, but now he thinks it's a fake, a scam, that Vincent faked his own disappearance to throw him off. He wants to see the head. Then, he says, maybe he'll believe me. And, maybe, he and I will be quits."

As I slowly began to realize that I was about to get rid of Vinnie's head again, my own head got lighter—lighter than usual, I mean. With the head in Jennifer's care, I could go down to the Caymans with a clear conscience and rifle the account Vinnie had set up under my name. Jennifer would be happy; Malatesta would be happy; Patrice would be happy. Maybe even Bogdan would be happy. He could visit the head on weekends.

"So how can I get it to you?" I asked Jennifer.

"Bring it here," she said in a flat, controlled voice. I understood why the control: She thought I might be leery of visiting Malatesta. She was right.

"Uh-uh," I said, "no way. I am not walking into Malatesta's house with a head in a bag. Or in any way at all. No. You better think of something else."

Jennifer was silent. I could hear her pissed-off breathing.

"Look, Jennifer," I said when I figured she was open to any suggestion, "I have this friend."

"You are such an asshole, I'm surprised you have any friends."

I ignored this. "He lives on the South Shore, not far—" Patrice gave my ankle a swift kick. "Not far . . . from the water. So anyway, we could meet there."

More silence as she thought about this; then: "Tell me how to get there."

I gave her a time and some pretty clear directions. I was about to hang up, when something occured to me. "How did you get this number, anyway?"

"You sent it to me in an e-mail, Johnnie," Jennifer said. "Didn't you?"

"No," I said.

"Well, somebody did," she said, and hung up.

I let out a heartfelt whuff of breath.

Patrice stared thoughtfully at the head-shaped mound dripping on the table.

"There must be something inside it," she said. "Microfilm in a tooth, say, like in a spy movie."

"There are no teeth," I pointed out.

"I know, I know. I mean *like* that, something hidden in it. Or else why would your friend want to get her hands on it so bad?"

"You don't think there's any truth in the Malatesta story? That he thinks Vinnie's death is just a scam, that is?"

Patrice shook her head.

"He didn't think that when you saw him. Why should he think it now? I think your crafty friend Jennifer just doesn't want you to know the real reason she needs to get her hands on it."

We stared at the head together for a while.

"Well?" I asked. "Do you want to look?"

"No. I don't give a shit what's in it. Let her have it. Just let's get this over with and get off the island. I want to start our new life."

I was afraid Bogdan would be disappointed to lose the head, but he was cool with Jennifer's visit when I called up to give him the rundown.

"She was there first, Bogdan," I explained to him.

"Maybe when she's finished with it, she'll allow me to have it," he said calmly.

" 'Finished with it'? What do you mean?" I had a gruesome mental image of Jennifer playing with the head like a beach ball.

There was a slight pause as Bogdan thought about my stupidity. Then he patiently explained: "I don't think she wants it for the same reasons I do. There must be some other reason, something hidden in it, maybe a tattoo in code. She can have the information; all I want is the head."

"Yeah, Patrice thinks it's something like that." But there was another thing still bothering me. "Bogdan, look."

"Yes?"

"You didn't put the head on Patrice's kitchen table, did you?"

"Of course not. You know I wouldn't do that. Besides, you were with me all day."

"Well, I didn't think so. But if you didn't, who did?"

Bogdan sighed heavily. "Johnnie, I've told you before: You've got a crowd of people following you. It could have been any one of them."

Waiting in line, heads swinging in shopping bags like smoked hams.

"But why?"

"I can't even guess." Then he did. "Maybe to keep it in play. Like throwing a soccer ball in from out of bounds."

I tried to picture that particular ball game. It made as much sense as anything did lately.

"Bogdan, look," I said, getting back to business. "We're coming over. Tonight. Jennifer Smeals is going to meet us at your place at ten. All right?"

"I'd better make some preparations," Bogdan muttered thoughtfully. I didn't want to think too hard about what they might be.

"Later, Bogdan," I said.

I drove. Patrice sat next to me, scrunched down in the seat, her knees braced against the dashboard. She was in a good mood, humming and singing little songs under her breath.

"Bogdan Bogdan Bogdan," she sang. "Jenny Jenny Jenny."

"Yeah," I replied.

"Maybe Bogdan will fall in love with her," Patrice said dreamily. "Maybe he'll harvest her little head for his collection."

"He's retired, remember."

"Maybe they'll fall in love with each *other*," she said, sitting up, as if this was some great idea that had just occurred to her. "Maybe they'll get married and raise little Bogdans and Jennifers."

I shuddered. "Great. Can you imagine? They can sit around the day-care center sawing the heads off dolls."

"And their little playmates," Patrice added. "And when we go to visit them in the home for the criminally insane, we can tell them we knew their parents well. We can sell our stories to the tabs."

" 'I Knew Junior Killer's Dad.' "

" 'Pre-Pube Head Hunters Tell All.' "

" 'The Secret History of the Head-Chopping Toddlers.' "

I felt great, warm and happy, as if I'd just killed a bottle of good whiskey. We drove south, down toward the Great South Bay and Bogdan's mama's house. Beyond the bay, I knew, were Jones Beach and Fire Island. And beyond them lay the big green Atlantic, going on forever south of here, a long stretch of ocean with, somewhere, islands in it. Islands with my name on them.

Bogdan himself answered the door.

"Where's your mom?" I asked him.

"Out," Bogdan whispered, peering around the edge of the screen door. "At her bingo game. Where's your friend?"

"Hi, Bogdan," Patrice said brightly, giving him a little wave.

"Your other friend, I meant," he said. "The one who's supposed to come here."

"She'll be here any minute," I said.

He nodded as if he doubted it. His eyes caught on the black Hefty bag in my right hand.

"You have it?"

"Right here." I held the bag up. The head swung gently back and forth.

Bogdan didn't say anything, but I could tell he was moved. He ushered us in the house to wait for Jennifer. I could hear his breathing, raspy and urgent.

We sat down in Bogdan's prim living room to wait, Patrice and I on the love seat, Bogdan in his mother's La-Z-Boy. I put the head in the bag down on the coffee table between us—carefully, so it wouldn't roll off. For some reason, Bogdan avoided looking at it. I hoped the special mummifying effect of the house would kick in before the head heated up and began to reek.

It was hard to start a conversation. Nobody tried. The floor of the little living room was covered with beige wall-to-wall carpet. It smelled damp; you could catch a hint of sweat socks in the mix, and dog. The rest of the furniture was huddled in the middle of the floor, like pioneer wagons circled against the Indians. A TV set resting on a brass cart on wheels stood against the wall across from the couch. The windows were small and heavily curtained. Even in the daytime, the room would have been too dark to read in, almost too dark to see in.

Bogdan breathed. We all breathed.

As I sat there holding on to the arm of the love seat as if it were about to become airborne, I had the feeling that the room was becoming pressurized, like a jetliner or a diving bell, the air forced in by powerful pumps, the psychic tension turned up full and then some.

Then the doorbell went off, a classic "Avon calling" dingdong. Jennifer Smeals had arrived.

Bogdan opened the door, the perfect host. I thought he was going to bow.

Jennifer Smeals stood on the stoop, peering in at us suspiciously.

"Johnnie?" she called out.

"Yo, right here," I replied.

She came into the house slowly and carefully, ready to bolt at a moment's notice.

Bogdan stared at her without expression. Beads of sweat on his forehead glistened in the lamplight coming through the open door.

"Please come in," he said in a scratchy, resonant kind of radio announcer's voice I had never heard him use before.

Jennifer didn't even look at him. She walked warily over to the TV set, her eyes scanning the room constantly. The wet black plastic trash bag on the coffee table caught her attention.

"Is that it?" she asked. I nodded.

"Let's get going, then," she said, all business all the time. She marched over to the head and scooped up the bag, looking around at us. "Where can we work on this?"

What does "work" mean in this context? I wondered.

"This way," Bogdan said, still the perfect host. "Downstairs. I have a workshop set up."

"I bet," Patrice muttered under her breath.

Following Bogdan, we trooped down the narrow stairs to the basement. I whacked my head on the overhang, but nobody noticed.

Along one wall, there was a hefty workbench like the one my dad used to have, with a Masonite Peg-Board over it, lots of tools hanging from the little hooks. At a glance, they were the same tools my dad'd had—hammers, levels, screwdrivers. There seemed to be a lot of saws, though.

"Where are all the head-chopping things?" Patrice asked sarcastically. Silently, Bogdan pulled open a big drawer under the workbench. I caught the gleam of cutlery.

Jennifer pushed past him and plunked the head down on the workbench.

"I won't need all that," she said briskly. She turned up the bag and let the head roll out onto the table. It didn't look good, but I was ready for that.

I was worried about Bogdan. He stood in a corner, staring, his breath whistling out his nose, and I knew the pressures on him were intense—the head itself, of course, but also Jennifer Smeals's alluring, intimidating presence. I could see the effect she was having on him. Maybe Patrice was right: These two could have little serial killers in their future together.

I was afraid it would all be too much for Bogdan and that he would crack. And who knew what might happen then, but it wouldn't be pretty.

Jennifer frowned at the head critically, as if it wasn't living up to her expectations. "You haven't been fucking around with this, have you?" she asked, peering closely at it and moving it around with a forefinger.

"Believe me, no," I said. Bogdan and Patrice shook their heads like guilty classmates, but it was wasted on Jennifer, who was still frowning down at the head.

She bent down and looked at the crown of the head carefully—she wasn't squeamish, I'll give her that. With her fingertips, she turned the head from side to side. Then she began to rummage through the remaining hair, like someone looking for a lost golf ball in deep grass.

After a couple minutes of this, she straightened up and gave a strangled cry of frustration and pure rage, then whacked the head right off the workbench.

"God damn it!" Jennifer Smeals yelled. "This isn't Vincent. This is the wrong fucking head!"

The head didn't go far; I think it was losing its bounce. It ended up leaning against the wall beside the washing machine. The concrete floor of Bogdan's basement had not been kind to the head, and it looked distinctly lopsided now.

Bogdan quietly bent down and picked up the head. He seemed shy and chastened somehow, as if the whole head examination had been his idea and it hadn't come off very well.

It hadn't. I couldn't argue with that. But it wasn't his fault.

Everyone stood around, embarrassed. We could all hear Jennifer Smeals's ragged end-of-a-sprint breathing.

"Well," I said cheerily, "I guess we're done here, huh? We better get going."

Bogdan didn't look up, just stood there dolefully holding the head. Jennifer, on the other hand, was glaring at me in her most pissed-off manner.

"LoDuco, you little shit," she said graciously, "I couldn't believe it until now. But now I think you and Vincent were in this together from the very beginning."

"Of course we were in this together," I said, confused, as usual. "We're all in it together."

"All this bullshit with the head was just a setup, a fake," she went on. "You and Vincent put together this whole elaborate fucking charade to fake me out of the picture so you could keep the money yourselves."

In a way, she was right, of course, though not the way she meant. I shrugged and held out my hands, not saying a word. Patrice stood up, too, and moved toward the door.

"So where is it?" Jennifer asked. "Where is the money? Where is he? *Vincent!*" Jennifer ripped around, staring pop-eyed with rage into the shadows of Bogdan's basement, as if she expected Vinnie to jump out of the clothes dryer.

Bogdan was sadly putting the head into the plastic garbage bag. He looked like he was putting away a bowling ball after losing the big tournament.

"Would they have showed you the head if they knew it wasn't the right one?" Bogdan asked quietly. We all turned to look at him.

"They're dumb," he said to Jennifer, nodding sideways toward me and Patrice. "But not that dumb."

Jennifer was not mollified. "I'm not so sure. I think that 'dumb guinea' thing he does is just an act to fool people into underestimating him."

I wish.

"I think you've all been taken in," Bogdan said. "I think your friend Vinnie is sitting on a beach somewhere, counting his money and laughing at you."

"But what about Stosh?" I said. "He knew all about it. And what about Malatesta?"

"All I know is that that isn't Vincent's head," Jennifer said. "And since that isn't Vincent's head, I'm fucked."

I saw Bogdan's head perk up. I think he liked the sound of "I'm fucked" coming from Jennifer Smeals. But I was confused.

"Why?"

Jennifer's eyes went carefully blank, and I knew she had accidentally said something that was true and now was going to get back to normal lying mode.

"Because," she said, "I told Malatesta I would bring him the head. To prove to him Vincent is really dead."

This confused me a lot more. "But he already thinks Vinnie is dead," I told her, "except, of course, he thinks Vinnie is me."

Both Bogdan and Patrice looked like they were in real pain now. Jennifer Smeals looked even blanker.

"He said if I brought back the head, he'd let me go," she said.

I still couldn't see why Malatesta would give a shit about the head. Unless, like Patrice thought, it had some kind of golden microfilm in it. I couldn't believe it wasn't Vinnie's head anyway. Maybe that was what Jennifer was lying about so hard. But why?

"Would Malatesta know it wasn't Vinnie's head? I knew Vinnie a lot better than Malatesta, and it fooled me. So just tell him it's the right head, and he'll believe you."

Then the nickel dropped. I always *was* slow.

"Hey, wait a minute. Why would he have to *let you go*? I mean, here you are, right?"

Jennifer Smeals looked blanker—really, really blank. She didn't say anything.

Uh-oh, I thought, and then, Oh shit.

"Of course, I could bring him you instead," she whispered, like she was talking to herself.

Just then, upstairs, the doorbell rang.

"Trick or treat." Worm Lips grinned.

The two guys on the stoop behind him didn't grin. They didn't look as if they ever grinned.

"Petey." Jennifer nodded briskly at him. I had forgotten that was the little fuck's name.

Worm Lips/Petey didn't waste any time on introductions.

"You got it?" he asked Jennifer. She shook her head.

"A problem's come up," she told him. "We have to talk."

Worm Lips—I just can't bring myself to call him Petey—smiled. It was not nice to see.

"*We* don't have to talk, Doctor," he said. "*You* have to talk." He held up his hand like a traffic cop when it looked like Jennifer was about to follow his advice. "And not to me, either. You know who you have to talk to, and what he wants to hear. If you can't tell him that, then don't tell him anything."

His eyes lit up as he looked over Jennifer's shoulders and saw the rest of us standing behind her.

"Hey, Kenny baby!" he said to me. "Long time no see, man. Is that your name today, Kenny?"

I didn't say anything. I was no longer that sure myself.

"Who are the rest of these yo-yos?" Worm Lips asked Jennifer.

Her lips twitched. "Friends of the bride." She turned to me. "Johnnie knows where the money is, don't you, Johnnie? He knows more than I do about it."

Worm Lips loved this. "We're being Johnnie today, huh? Johnnie, it seems like we had this discussion before. You remember?"

I nodded. "I remember. I still can't get the brain stains off the wall."

"I can help with that," Bogdan put in helpfully.

"Shut up. And *you* shut up." Worm Lips pointed to Bogdan. He took out a cigarette, stuck it in his mouth, and lit it without taking his eyes off us. His eyes narrowed as cigarette smoke and evil thoughts floated up into them.

"You told me you had no idea where the money was," he said reproachfully, looking at me. "You didn't even know what money we were talking about. Remember?"

I remembered. I had been telling the truth, of course, then. But now I did know where the money was. That was going to make not talking about it much harder.

"I still don't. Know where the money is, I mean," I explained.

Worm Lips stared through his cigarette smoke. "I think all of you have to come with me," he said finally. All of us froze when he said it, like squirrels just before they throw themselves into traffic. You could feel our mutual desire to jump in front of a car coming off us in waves.

"And don't even think about the back door," he added. "I have people there, too. I'm not as stupid as you are."

Worm Lips looked at us with disgust. He threw his half-finished cigarette over the cast-iron railing around the stoop and it landed in the driveway. I knew Mrs. O'Reilly wouldn't like that.

"My mom won't like that," Bogdan put in. Worm Lips shot him a look that was like a knife in the showers.

"Back to the house," he said. "The whole fucking sideshow. Back to the house." He took a step toward me. The group in the doorway backed up as one.

Before anything else could happen, a car pulled up outside the gate and honked, a white late-seventies Mercury. Bogdan's mom stuck her head out of the driver's window.

"Excuse me, but do you mind moving your car?" she called over pleasantly. "This is my driveway."

"Hi, Mom," Bogdan called back. Malatesta's boys looked at her without expression.

I could see Worm Lips was trying to decide whether or not to shoot her and maybe all of us. But eventually, he waved his hand impatiently at one of the muscle guys.

"Move the fucking car."

The goon jumped to it and backed the car across the street, then double-parked. Mrs. O'Reilly pulled into the driveway, opened the gate herself—none of us moved to help her—and drove back to the garage.

The goon who had moved the car appeared by the side of the stoop, looking up at Worm Lips. "She wants me to help her with the groceries."

Worm Lips looked like he was in acute abdominal pain, but he waved his hand resignedly. "Help her with the groceries."

The thug jogged off.

I noticed that somehow, in all the excitement caused by his mom's arrival, Bogdan had disappeared. He was light on his feet for a big man, that was for sure.

"Okay, that's it," Worm Lips said as we heard the garage door close on Mrs. O'Reilly. "Two of you are going to come with me—you, Johnnie, and the doctor. The other two—where's the big guy?"

"He had to take a leak," I told him.

"Well, I don't give a shit about him. We can come back for him and his mother if we have to. Nobody's going anywhere."

"I thought you said we were going with you," Patrice said. Too bad, because maybe he would have left her behind, as well.

"And you, miss, will ride with Camminiti here." One of the goons rotated his head slightly to look at Patrice. His expression never changed. "Camminiti, you follow us," Worm Lips said to the goon.

"All right, kiddies," Worm Lips called out. He was happy again. "Everybody on the bus!" He backed against the railing as we pushed past him to the waiting goons below. I thought about shoving him over the rail—it would have been easy. But nothing would have been accomplished except maybe I'd get shot. I let him live.

Arturo held open the door of the car—not the stretch limo I knew and loved, just an older Ford Crown Victoria that looked like something from a police auction. Camminiti raced across the street to the other car and jumped in.

Bending over to get in the Crown Victoria, I looked out the side window and saw Bogdan sit up in the backseat of the car across the street. He was dressed all in black and had a black ski mask on. But I recognized his outline. Who wouldn't?

Bogdan sat up behind Camminiti and put something around his neck. Camminiti put his hands up to his neck. No one on our side of the street seemed to notice.

"Nice night," I said to Arturo. He actually smiled, but he didn't say anything.

"Get in the fucking car," Worm Lips said from behind me. "Arturo, get in the backseat with asshole here. On the other side. I'll drive. Doctor, after you." He reached down and held the back door open for Jennifer, smiling like a parking valet angling for a big tip.

Arturo ran around to the other side to get in. Then he disappeared.

I peeked out the window at him and saw a big black knife with tape on the handle sticking in his neck.

Cool. I was filled with admiration.

Worm Lips had finally noticed something was wrong. He had his gun out and was crouching down behind the Crown Victoria, pointing his weapon over the trunk and looking around wildly.

"The fuck? Arturo!" Arturo didn't respond. He yelled out a few more names I guess went with the guys at the back door, with no immediate response.

I couldn't see Bogdan, either; his big sihouette had disappeared from the car across the street.

Jennifer stepped back out of the car and got behind Worm Lips. She moshed him over the head with something I saw her take from her purse. He went down. She bent over, collected his gun.

The front door of Bogdan's house opened and his mom stuck her head out.

"Danny, what's all the noise out here? Are you okay?"

"I'm fine, Mom," a voice called from somewhere back by the garage.

Bogdan's mom looked confused, but maybe she always looked like that. "Well, okay. But try not to make so much noise."

"We promise, Mom."

She went back inside.

Bogdan stepped out from behind the garage and trotted up to us. Patrice, who had just been standing on the sidewalk through all this, looked like someone coming out of a trance.

"Whoa, Bogdan," she said, looking around at the carnage.

I saw Jennifer Smeals put Worm Lips's gun in her purse. She smiled at me apologetically.

"Sorry, Johnnie. I had no choice back there."

I shrugged. "What anyone might have done." Any traitorous low-life bitch, I might have added.

"I can take care of the bodies," Bogdan said.

"I bet," Patrice said. She was still not warming to Bogdan.

Any minute, I was expecting to hear sirens, but there was nothing. The only person who seemed to have noticed the action was Bogdan's mom.

"Help me move these guys," Bogdan said to us. "Put them in the backseat of the Crown Victoria. Then drive it to the garage."

Patrice and I lugged Worm Lips and Arturo onto the backseat while Jennifer supervised. I didn't like that much. Bogdan went and got the other car.

Bumper-to-bumper, the cars filled the driveway of the O'Reilly residence. By a gate in the back fence, over behind the garage, were two more dead goons.

"Whoa, Bogdan!" Patrice said again.

Bogdan seemed quietly proud. I think he was glad to be back in business again.

Patrice and I helped Bogdan drag the dead goons behind the house. There was a metal door in a concrete lean-to against the house. When Bogdan bent down and opened it, I could see a slide, made up of hundreds of little wheels, like steel roller-skate wheels, going down into the darkness under his mom's house. The wheels had a well-worn, shiny look, as if they had seen a lot of use in their time.

We slid the goons into the basement. Still no sirens. I looked up, paranoid suddenly to be hefting corpses around like bags of groceries, but a high brick wall ran all around Bogdan's house, and none of his neighbors could see into his yard.

Trust Bogdan to know how to get rid of bodies.

He looked over at me now like a warehouse foreman. "Any more?"

"One," I panted. I was about done in from carrying goons. Dead bodies weigh more than you'd think. "Worm Lips. Last one."

"He's not dead," Jennifer said. "I put him out, that's all."

"Well, we better secure him," Bogdan said. "We don't want him coming after us or alerting his boss. The more time you have to get away from here, the better."

Thinking about Worm Lips being secured in Bogdan's basement, I almost felt sorry for the guy. Almost.

But when we went into the garage to pull him out of the car, Worm Lips was gone.

CHAPTER TWELVE

WE SAT AROUND THE kitchen table while Bogdan's mom bustled about, making us something to eat. Lugging goon bodies will build up an appetite.

Only Jennifer Smeals didn't seem hungry. She had hardly touched her plate of blueberry blintzes.

"They'll be back," she said to the table in general. "And I don't want to be here. Malatesta will be really pissed off now."

"What do you think he'll do?" I asked around a mouthful of blintz.

Jennifer shrugged. Bogdan's mom was leaning over the table, dishing out more blintzes. She was a cheery soul, but she put a damper on frank conversation.

When Mrs. O'Reilly's back was turned, Jennifer made a fist and finger pistol, firing it a few times. She mimed the recoil perfectly.

"Maybe save one of us. Just to talk to," she said.

"I had that conversation," I said.

"It'll be worse this time."

I didn't like to think about worse.

"Patrice?"

She shrugged. "Let's just get out of here as soon as we can. Not that it hasn't been fun."

"What about you, Bogdan?" I asked.

No shrugs for Bogdan. My man was solid.

"I'll stay here," he said. "Take care of Mom." Mom smiled over her shoulder at this; obviously, she had no idea what we were talking about. Or did she? Anyone who could produce an offspring like Bogdan must have some surprising sides to their personality, I figured.

"They'll come for you," Jennifer said in a serious voice. "You know that."

"I'm ready for that," Bogdan said. Looking at him, you had to believe it. "I look forward to it."

We all stood up at the same time.

"Oh, don't bother to clear the table, kids," Mrs. O'Reilly called. "I'll do it."

Now that we were on the move, I began to feel an incredible urgency. I thought of Worm Lips with his sore head, on the phone to Malatesta, calling in more goons, carloads of them. I wanted to be gone before they arrived. I was regretting the blintzes.

"Where's your car?" I asked Jennifer. She didn't answer.

"She came with them," Bogdan said, his response quicker than mine, though I would have figured it out in a minute.

Bogdan's sharpness got him a wry smile and sideways look from Jennifer. I saw him liking it. Go for it, Bogman, I thought.

She wouldn't be good for him, though. Too cold. Bogdan might be a twisted little serial killer, but he had passion, you could feel it, bubbling under the surface. Jennifer Smeals was ice all the way through.

"I could drive you," Bogdan offered.

"No, no thanks, I'm all right." Jennifer said. "I mean, I'd love to spend some more time. But I really have to get going."

"Well, we have lots of cars now. Take this one." Bogdan held out a set of keys. After a very slight hesitation, Jennifer snapped them up.

"Johnnie!" This from Patrice, who was standing over by the front door. She was so exasperated, she could only whisper. When I looked over at her, she began making eager little motions with her head and eyes out the door.

"Okay, right. Uh, look, Bogdan, we have to get going, too."

The big mass murderer stuck out his hand. I shook it—I'm not proud, and besides, he'd saved my ass, our asses, no doubt about it. Shaking it was like hanging on to a slab of two-by-six.

"Take care now," he said. "Watch your back."

Patrice and I scurried down the front steps, leaving Bogdan with his mom and the head.

"Oh my God. Oh my God. I can't believe it. I just can't believe it." In the relative safety of her Honda, Patrice let herself get hysterical. "Did you see him sliding those bodies down the chute? Like he'd been doing it all his life!"

"Did you see the way he looked at Jennifer?" I asked. "I know that look. That was the look of love."

We laughed until I thought I'd puke. But when I came back to the surface, I saw big tears streaming down Patrice's cheeks. She held on to the steering wheel as if it were a life preserver taking her over Niagara Falls.

"Johnnie," she said through the tears, "we are almost out of here. No more Bogdan, no more Jennifer. No more head!"

The tears were rolling down. I was confused. "Is that a bad thing?"

She shook her head, whipping the baby snakes. "It's a good thing. You're a good thing. Where did you come from?"

Jail, I almost said. Comapogue. But for once, I kept my mouth shut.

"You just drop into my life out of nowhere. My *life* was nowhere. Then all of a sudden, there you are. And it's like I was waiting for that to happen."

"Waiting for me to come into the video store with a severed head in a cooler."

She laughed and shook her head, spraying tears. "It was fish. Remember? You had a cooler full of fish, and you were being chased by assassins."

"Well, yeah, I was in a bad spot."

Something had puzzled me at the time, and it puzzled me now. "Patrice, why did you help me? I mean, why did you take me home and everything? Why not just kick me out in the motel parking lot and let me take my chances?"

"I don't know," she said. The tears had stopped. "It just happened. I just did it. Every day I just do things, things I don't really want to do, boring things. I get up, go to work, watch TV. I'm like a zombie, and I have no idea what I want to be different. Then you walked into the video store, and I knew you were something different."

I'm something different, that's for sure. "I think, though, in your position, I would've called the cops. Changed my phone number, the door locks, something."

"I love you, that's all," Patrice said. All of a sudden, she was crying again. "I love everything about you. I love the little acne scars in the pits of your cheeks."

"Whoa, hey!" I said, pulling away, actually offended.

"No, I mean it! Look at you: Your hair's all greasy, you haven't shaved, and your shirt is *so* dirty."

"Look, I'm sorry," I said. "I'll take a shower as soon as we get back to the apartment. We've been so busy lately, I haven't had a chance."

Patrice laughed. "But I love it!" she said. "It makes me hot. Johnnie, you are a bad boy. A bad, dirty boy. And that's what I like."

I couldn't believe it. The phrase "loves you for yourself" floated somewhere in my head, but I couldn't accept it. Even I didn't love me for what I was. If I was being honest with myself, deep down, I thought I was a worthless piece of shit. I was getting better, maybe, but I was pretty fucking slow at it.

"Patrice, you are a pervert, you know that?" I told her. "Anyway, I'm not a bad guy. I've just had some bad luck, that's all."

Patrice was not bad luck, of course. I think I fell in love with her when she went marching into that corpse motel to see if the coast was clear. It's hard to be sure, since there had been so many moments like that.

No point in telling her all this, of course.

She was smiling at me again, that twisted-up smile.

"You are a piece of work, LoDuco," she said.

We drove up to Sunrise Highway, right past Aunt Vivienne's. Patrice lived close to Bogdan; we could have been home in ten minutes if we'd felt like it. But we wanted to make sure we weren't being followed.

We could have saved ourselves the trouble.

Anyway, Patrice drove up Sunrise into Comapogue, the northern part, where the drive-in movie theater used to be, and the bowling alley. I hadn't been up there in a while and hardly recognized the place. It had always been crappy and ugly up there, even for Comapogue, but now it was like wall-to-wall ugly and ten times as busy, with parking lots and stores everywhere. The drive-in was gone.

We drove across a few of the shopping center parking lots and around the back, where there were vast stretches of empty asphalt, so we could check out behind us and spot anyone trying to tail us. Nada. A few back streets, another parking lot, a halfway main road back to Sunrise, all without spotting anybody. I felt good.

"We're getting professional at this."

Patrice laughed. "Maybe Bogdan will give us a job."

I knew the second we pulled into the cul-de-sac where Aunt Vivienne's house was that something was wrong, and I was right.

For one thing, there were too many cars in the little circle. One of them was parked in Vivienne's driveway, our driveway. The others were parked all over the place, sticking out every which way, like parking lot overflow at a wedding.

Patrice saw it, too, as we turned into the court.

"Uh-oh," she said, braking and starting to put the car into reverse.

But it was too late. Another car pulled right across the opening to the court. We were trapped.

"Fucking Jennifer," I said, and when Patrice gave me a puzzled look, I added, "It had to be her. The one who tipped them off, I mean."

"She doesn't know where I live," Patrice pointed out. "Maybe they followed us."

I suspected that this was the part of the movie where Worm Lips would get out of the car in the driveway and come over to us. That's exactly what happened.

"Hey, Johnnie, where you been?" he said, bending down, resting a forearm on the car door, squinting at me across Patrice. "What took you so long?"

I didn't say anything; neither did Patrice. She looked over her shoulder. I knew she was wondering if she could blast across the neighbor's yard, knock down the stupid little decorative fence they had, and get away.

But Worm Lips noticed this, too.

"Don't even think about it," he told us. "This is all over. Just park the car and get out."

"Where?" Patrice said. "You assholes are taking up all the parking spots."

"Fine, I'll shoot you right here, in the car. If that's okay with you." Worm Lips reached under his jacket, not taking his eyes off us.

Various large guys got out of the cars scattered around the cul-de-sac and came over to stand around with their arms folded and stare at me.

"We should have left straight from Bogdan's," I muttered.

Patrice looked over at me sadly. "Johnnie," she whispered. But whatever she might have been going to add to that never got said.

Just then, a cell phone went off, a long, slow series of electronic beeps booping out "Way down upon the Swannee River."

We stared at Worm Lips, whose hand was frozen inside his jacket.

"Is that your phone?" Patrice asked him.

"It's not mine," I said, always trying to be helpful.

Worm Lips glared at us as if it was our fault his phone was ringing. Then he reached in another pocket, took the phone out, and answered it.

"Yuh? . . . Yuh. Uh-huh, right," Worm Lips said to the cell phone. "Yuh. Uh-huh. . . . What?" He walked a little ways up the street for some privacy, waving to the goons in the cars to come over and make sure we didn't get away. A couple of supersize thugs plodded over and stood, one by each door, their arms folded over their chests, staring at us.

Even I knew not to try making conversation.

Meanwhile, Worm Lips was pacing up and down the sidewalk, alternately listening intently to what the person on the other end was saying and yelling into the phone and waving his free arm around. Finally, he stopped pacing and waving and just stood there, listening and nodding his head. They can't see you, fuckhead, I thought.

Worm Lips folded up the phone and stood there a long time without doing anything.

I couldn't take it anymore. Leaning over Patrice, I yelled at him, "Hey! Yo! Worm Lips! Petey! What's going on? Are you going to shoot us, or what?"

A large hand was on my shoulder, dragging me away from the window.

"Please be quiet," said the enormous bearded person attached to the hand. He whacked me in the mouth, a short punch, but with plenty of oomph. I shut up.

Worm Lips looked stunned. Muttering something to himself, he walked back to the car and stuck his head in the window.

"Everything's changed," he said.

"Good," Patrice replied. "Because this sucks."

Worm Lips stared at us with more than professional dislike. He leaned in the window, Patrice angling away from him. His breath reeked of Marlboros and pizza and bad dental work.

"You little shitballs have caused me a lot of grief, you know that?" he said. "I don't know what this is all about, but I hope it ends up with you getting shot in the head. I hope so. Because I will really enjoy that."

"Who was that on the phone?" I asked him.

Worm Lips looked like he really hated what he was about to say.

"Here it is, kiddies," he said in a cloud of bad breath. "We are all going to leave now."

"What about us?" Patrice asked.

"You stay here. You don't matter," Worm Lips said. "Events have moved beyond you. You can stay here, or you can crawl up your own assholes and disappear. But I'll tell you this. When this is over, I'm coming back. And I'm going to shoot both of you, just for my own satisfaction."

"Does this mean we're not going to get to really know each other?" I asked him. "I was looking forward to that."

"Next time, LoDuco," Worm Lips shouted over his shoulder as he scurried away. "When next time comes, it's your ass."

"There is never going to be a next time," Patrice pointed out, but Worm Lips was out of hearing. He seemed plenty pissed off. Without looking at them, he waved the thugs back into their cars. The thugs hesitated for a moment—I could tell my guy had enjoyed whacking me and wanted to do it again. He gave me a regretful parting glance. Then he followed the other thugs as they all meekly got back in the cars. That's how it is when you're a thug. You just do as you're told.

Too bad, assholes, I thought. Maybe some other time.

"What was that all about?" Patrice asked me as the goon caravan fired up and drove out of Aunt Vivienne's cul-de-sac.

"Do you care?"

"No," she said. "Let's just get the goddamn suitcases and get out of here. Long Island's begun to creep me out."

"Can I make you something to take on the trip?" Aunt Vivienne was asking. "Something for the road?"

It sounded good to me, but Patrice just said, "No thanks, Aunt Vivienne. We'll get something in Canada."

We told her we were going to Canada. It seemed like a good idea not to tell her where we were really going, in case anybody thought to ask her.

"Canada," Aunt Vivienne said doubtfully. "What do they eat in Canada?"

"Canadian bacon?" I suggested. "Moose? Maybe they eat moose."

Patrice ignored us both, lugging a big suitcase to the car. I zipped over and opened the door for her.

"Bye, Aunt Vivienne. Thanks for everything." Patrice kissed her on the cheek.

"What'll I tell your mother if she calls?" Aunt Vivienne asked.

"That I'm happy, I'm having a wonderful time, and I'll be back soon."

But I could tell Aunt Vivienne wasn't buying this. There was something in the air. It definitely felt like the last time we'd all be together.

"Ciao, Aunt Vivienne," I said. "I'll look out for her." I could almost hear Patrice's eyes roll up inside her head.

Aunt Vivienne stood on the other side of the door, her hands against the screen, and I suddenly realized she wished she was going with us.

"Call," she yelled out to Patrice. "Write me a letter."

"Oh fuck!" Patrice rested her forehead on the steering wheel as if it was all suddenly too much.

"What is it?"

"I forgot something," she said. "I'll be right back." She jumped out of the car and disappeared into the house.

I leaned over and turned on the radio, glad she'd left the key in the ignition, but I couldn't find anything worth listening to. Yammering, bad rock and roll, yammering, oldies, yammering, yammering. I snapped it off and sat back.

It was peaceful in the Honda. I realized that this was the first time I had been alone, entirely alone, for days. I wasn't used to all that company. I let my head rest on the back of the seat and went over the bizarre events of the last few days.

We had caught some *z*'s after Worm Lips and his friends left. Just a couple hours. We had to, after our hard night's work at Bogdan's and that exhausting conversation with the goon caravan.

The car was packed with suitcases. Worm Lips and company had disappeared—who knew where or why. We were on our way. Finally. At long last. Things had been very weird lately, but they were definitely looking up. I let myself relax into warm thoughts of palm trees, beaches, and twelve million dollars in the bank.

A head suddenly appeared at the side window, right at my elbow. A large head, like a ham in a hairpiece. It was instantly joined by a large hand holding an even larger gun, which gleamed in the sunlight.

Stosh Budjynski grinned largely.

"Hiya, Johnnie boy. Didn't think you'd see me again, huh?"

"Christ Almighty, Stosh, it's only ten thousand fucking dollars," I said, exasperated. My hands were cuffed behind me; my ankles were tied up in some way I couldn't see. I was kneeling on the seat next to Stosh, facing the rear window, snugly seat-belted in place.

"It's not the money anymore, numbnuts," he said. "My reputation's on the line." He glared over at me. "And just so we understand each other: It must never be known that I got taken out by a woman. Even if she is a physician."

"Don't look at me like that. I won't say shit—not a word about it."

"I'll know if you do," he said, "and I'll come after you."

I considered this as we bumped along, my chin whacking occasionally into the headrest.

"You know, Stosh, you're pretty patriarchal," I told him. "It must be that Polish Catholic upbringing."

"You wiseass guinea fuck," he said. "What do you know about it?"

I enjoyed needling him, even in my present position, but I didn't want to piss him off too much while I was handcuffed to a car seat. So I let silence reign for a while, then introduced a change of subject.

"So, Stosh . . ."

"What is it, shithead?"

"How'd you find me this time?"

Stosh was quiet for a while, sticking out his lower lip a little, turning it over in his mind. The thoughts seemed to cause him no pleasure.

"I admit it was a bitch this time," he said eventually. "Even for me. You disappeared pretty good. I'll give you that, you little shit."

I didn't interrupt for a change, and he continued.

"So I gave it up for a while and worked on better things." He looked at me finally, though it was not a look of love. "Things that would make some money, rather than just waste my fucking time. But all the time, I was keeping tabs on Malatesta. I let his boys find you for me. So when the bees left the hive, I followed them. And here we are, Johnnie boy."

"I'm blown away, Stosh," I said, feeling the compulsion to talk myself into a beating again. "That metaphor, I mean, the bees, the hive. That's pure poetry. I didn't think you had it in you."

Luckily, he ignored me this time. In fact, he looked pleased with himself again, smug, even, the ham-headed son of a bitch.

A few minutes later, Stosh whipped out his cell phone, still swollen with smugness. He speed-dialed with his thumb, glancing over at me as if to say, Isn't that cool?

"Wow," I said with deep sarcasm.

"Budjynski," he muttered into the cell. "I got him. I'm bringing him in." A pause while the cell squawked and muttered. "Nah, not him. LoDuco. . . . Yeah, I know, but it's better than nothing. . . . Right. Be there in forty to fifty if I don't hit any traffic."

We did hit traffic, of course, and it was over two hours before we got to Riverhead. My bladder was bursting.

Stosh pushed me ahead of him into the bail-bond place. Canetti was sitting in his usual place behind the desk, reading a magazine. He glared at me, all mustache and bad mood.

"What'd you bring him in here for?" he asked Stosh.

"Had to get something, and I don't want him out of my sight for a second," Stosh said. "He's a tricky little fuck. And he has friends." He pushed me down in a folding chair and handcuffed my handcuffs to the back of it.

"Keep an eye on him, okay?" he told Canetti. "I got to take a shit. Be right back."

"I was just about to leave," Canetti protested, but the door was already swinging shut behind the massive bounty hunter.

Canetti eyeballed me in a disgusted way for a few minutes, then turned his attention back to his magazine. I was surprised to see he was reading *Modern Bride*; the cover story featured Cher, or someone who looked just like her, smiling in a frilly wedding dress.

There are many mysteries in life.

"What about me?" I whined to Canetti after it seemed to me I had been ignored long enough. I really had to piss now. Plus, the handcuffs had dug into my wrists and hurt like a motherfucker.

Canetti looked up from his magazine.

"What about you?" he asked mildly.

"Don't I get to piss?"

Canetti stared at me with a funny faraway look, as if I were a fishing worm that had started talking and he was trying to decide whether or not to put me on the hook anyway. Then he just went back to his magazine.

"Fuck you, LoDuco," he said to his lap. "Swim in it."

About ten minutes later, Stosh still had not come back. Canetti looked at his watch, cursed quietly. He glanced at me—not a real friendly look—then back at his watch.

"Fuck it," Canetti said. He jumped up and walked to the door. Instead of a good-night kiss, he gave me another long, hot-eyed glare.

Then he turned out the light and left. I heard his key jiggle in the lock, the bolt snick home.

I sat there in the dark. Slowly, my eyes adjusted. I could just make out desks, chairs, filing cabinets in the dim gray glow from the window.

Still no Stosh. Maybe he had fallen asleep on the toilet.

It occurred to me that now might be my only opportunity to get away. True, I was handcuffed to a fucking chair. But there was a solution to that; I held up the chair behind me like a loose pair of pants without a belt and waddled over to the door.

The door presented another level of problem. I tried to back up to it and turn the dead bolt with my cuffed hands, but the chair legs got in the way. Finally, I was able, by turning sideways, to hit the latch with a chair leg until it opened.

This trick would not work with the doorknob, though. I bent over and managed to turn the little lock nipple with my lips. Then I took the whole fucking doorknob in my mouth, turning it with my lips and teeth. It hurt like a son of a bitch. Finally, I got it to move, pulled my head back, and shoved a foot into the opening.

A few quick hops on the chair and I was out.

The door shut behind me. That was when I remembered that Canetti's bail-bond place was on the second floor.

I was on a kind of mezzanine with a cast-iron railing around it, dimly lit by overhead fluorescent lights. A staircase went down to a lobby-type area, where there was a double set of glass doors leading to the outside. I could see headlights going by, activity, freedom. I was almost there.

Somehow, I got downstairs without falling.

But the glass doors were not the kind I could open with my mouth. Or even with my hands if they'd been free. There was no knob, only a pull handle, and some kind of electronic security device on the wall next to it, little red digital letters flashing LOCKED.

Across from the glass doors, though, was hope: a short set of stairs leading down to a door with no knob or handle on it, only a push plate next to a little glass window with chicken wire in it. A basement door if ever there was one. I just hoped it opened out.

It did. I hopped and waddled down to it, carefully, pushed it open with the top of my head, and stepped inside.

That's when I slipped, or something. I think maybe the swinging door behind me gave me a whack. I don't know.

But whatever it was, I ended up bouncing down a concrete staircase in the pitch-dark, ass over chair legs.

I was out of it for a while.

The next thing I clearly remember was Stosh cursing to himself and dragging me up the concrete stairs.

When we got back up to Canetti's office, he stopped, panting and wiping the sweat off his divot cut with a forearm.

"You little fucker," he gasped at me. "Took me forever to find you. What'd you do that for?"

"I thought maybe you weren't coming back," I said, "so I let myself out."

"Should have left you down there for the rats." He bent over me and snapped a pair of handcuffs on the handcuffs that cuffed my handcuffs to the chair. Then he dragged me over to a water pipe

against the wall and locked me to it. I was lying on my side, bleeding quietly.

"Comfy?" he asked.

"Admit it, Stosh," I replied. "You fell asleep on the shitter."

"I sleep with my eyes open, like a cat," he said, so I knew I was
right. "I'm going to take a quick snooze now to recharge. Chasing
your ass all over Long Island has wore me out."

"No stamina, bro," I taunted.

"Don't go anywhere," Stosh said, and kicked me lightly in the
temple.

It's possible I passed out again. In any case, I opened my eyes
when I felt Stosh uncuff me from the pipe. He had changed out of
his ratty thief-catching clothes and was wearing a flimsy, sketchy
kind of suit, like the kind your chintzier funeral parlors bury people
in. All he needed was a Tyrolean hat to look completely ridiculous.

"I bet you got that suit in a Buffalo K mart," I sneered at him.
"It's got that Great Lakes, Cleveland-Toledo kind of look."

Budjynski ignored me. He didn't bother to hit me again, though
when he boosted me out of the chair by my still-handcuffed arms, I
nearly pissed all over both of us.

"Are we going bowling?" I gasped.

"We're going to jail," he said. "You're staying there."

"I need to piss first."

"Hold it." He pushed me toward the door. Then a thought occurred to him. "If you piss on my car upholstery, numbnuts, I'll wipe
it up with your hair."

Outside, the air was thick and humid, like maybe a thunderstorm
was coming on. I wondered what Patrice thought when she went out
to the car and found out I wasn't there. What would she do? Natu-

rally, she would assume that Worm Lips and the boys had come back for me.

Or—and this was an unpleasant idea—maybe she thought I'd ditched her, to get a head start on the bank account. I hoped she didn't think that.

I promised myself that as soon as Stosh got me to jail I would use my one phone call to call Patrice. Did they give you that one phone call when you were being recycled like this? I thought I'd ask Stosh; he would be glad to tell me, especially if the answer was no.

Then with a sick feeling, I realized that I didn't know Patrice's cell phone number, or house phone, either; I had never called her. I had a hard time remembering phone numbers anyway.

Stosh held me with one hand by my cuffed arms while he opened the passenger door of his car. It hurt like a son of a bitch, more when he suddenly whirled around, forgetting to let go of me. I whacked into the side of the car, hard, and would have slid to the ground if he hadn't kept a tight grip on me.

I saw the reason for Stosh's agitation. Somebody was walking up to us out of a little alley. You couldn't see his face, which was lost in the shadows between the buildings. But when the guy walked into the daylight, I saw that it was Carbone, the detective who had questioned me back in Vinnie's parents' garage.

"Hey." Carbone raised a hand in greeting. "What you got there?"

"Carbone, hey," Stosh replied. "Scared the shit out of me. What are you doing up so early?"

"Crime never sleeps," Carbone said. He peered at me, squinting his baggy eyes. "Don't I know this guy?" He pretended to be surprised. "Why, it's Johnnie Vinnie LoDuco McCloskey-Schmidt. Did I leave anyone out?"

"Who is Kenny Moleri?" I said. I wasn't being a smart-mouth, at least not much. I just wondered if he could tell me.

"That's right, Kenny," Carbone said. "I forgot about him. How is Kenny these days?" Then to Stosh: "Where are you taking this sorry piece of shit?"

"To county," Stosh said. "He's going home."

"I'm heading over there," Carbone said. "I'll take him in for you, you want."

Stosh considered this. I could see by the gleam in his eyes that he wanted to accept the offer. It occurred to me that maybe the suit wasn't for a court appearance or a funeral. Maybe he had a heavy date.

"My collar, though, right?" he asked.

"Sure," Carbone said. "I'll tell the world it was you."

"Just so long as you tell Canetti."

Somehow, I stayed on my feet when Stosh suddenly pushed me over to Carbone. "He's all yours," Stosh said. He shoved something at Carbone. "Here's the key to the cuffs. I was you, I'd keep 'em on. He's a tricky little prick."

"Do I get a piece of this?" Carbone grinned, taking the keys.

"You're out of your fucking mind. I'll buy you a beer."

"Deal. See you later, big guy."

"Thanks. Don't let the little weasel piss on your upholstery."

At least Carbone let me walk by myself and didn't drag me around like a rag doll the way Stosh had.

"Carbone," I said, "are we going to walk the whole way?"

"Relax. My car's just around the corner."

And he didn't try to handcuff my ankles to my neck, or any other cute bounty-hunter trick. He just pushed me in the passenger seat and slammed the door.

We drove through the Long Island morning for a while in silence. I felt like I was on my way to a party where I wouldn't know anyone, wouldn't want to meet anyone, and wouldn't be able to get away.

And the worst thing was, at this party I wouldn't be able to get shit-faced and pass out in the backyard.

We drove out of downtown Riverhead, out past the county jail and courthouse complex. I craned my neck around and watched as the buildings whizzed by.

"You missed your turn."

"I'm taking you to the county annex," Carbone said. "Out in Yaphank."

"I thought that was just administration," I said. Carbone didn't say anything.

We drove down past buildings that got shabbier and shabbier and were spaced farther and farther apart. Then just pine trees and sand.

Eventually, we jumped on the LIE.

"The cops'll be glad to see you, Johnnie. They want to talk to you, you know," Carbone told me after I had watched the pine trees zip by for a while.

I knew this. "I thought you were the cops," I said.

"Not for whatever bullshit you were into with McCloskey-Schmidt, I mean," Carbone said, as if I hadn't spoken. "They're looking for you. They want to ask you some questions about Joseph Colucci and Belinda Colucci-Hahn."

This caught my attention. "Huh?"

Carbone almost smiled, a gruesome sight. Smiling made his eye bags stretch sideways. "They'd like to ask you a few questions about how the bodies got in the chest freezer."

I sank down in the seat until the cuffs stopped me. "I had nothing to do with it. I don't know what you're talking about."

"LoDuco, you poor dumb shit," Carbone said. "They found your fingerprints on one of her fingernails."

"Oh." I tried to slump down lower in the seat, right onto the floor, but I was down as far as I could go. "Well, okay, I was there. But I didn't kill them."

Carbone seemed unimpressed. "Sure. But why did you put them in the fucking chest freezer? Did you really think nobody would find them there?"

I muttered something about buying time. Carbone shook his head in disbelief.

"It was a bitch getting them out. They were stuck together like frozen bait."

"Carbone, look," I began. He looked at me expectantly. "I didn't kill them."

"Sure. Nobody killed them."

"I mean, really. It was self-defense. Her or me. And it was an accident. I didn't mean for the garage door to come down on her. Old Colucci was fucking with the remote. It had nothing to do with me."

"Self-defense? Garage door? I don't know what you're talking about. Colucci died of a massive coronary. His daughter-in-law choked to death on her chewing gum."

"Chewing gum?"

Carbone nodded. "Wad the size of a softball, the coroner took out of her gullet. Don't know how she got it in her mouth."

The news sank in slowly, and I realized that old Colucci and Belinda had been worrying me, far down the list, of course. Still, I was glad to cross them off.

"So I'm not wanted in connection with Belinda Colucci-Hahn's death?" I asked.

"Oh, I don't know, there's got to be a charge in there somewhere," Carbone said. "Destroying evidence of a felony, public health nuisance, something. But no, there's nothing out on you over the Coluccis. Just answer a few questions, get the shit knocked out of you. Then when it's all over, everybody goes home happy."

"Great," I said. "When do we start?"

"Just be patient, LoDuco. We'll be there soon."

Something was nagging at my brain—well, a lot of things were. But out of the mess of things that didn't make any fucking sense at all, one piece swam to the surface.

"Carbone," I said, "If you knew old Colucci and his daughter-in-law weren't killed, what were you doing poking around Vinnie's parents' house?"

Carbone considered this. "Well, somebody had to check it out. But I was mainly out there looking for you."

"Me? Why me?"

"Somebody asked me to."

"Like who?"

Carbone wouldn't tell me, though I could guess.

"Just something I'm doing on the side," he said. "A little moonlighting."

We shot past the Yaphank exit, and my last glimmer of hope was extinguished. We were not going to the annex after all. Sadly, I watched the exit sign sink into the distance behind us.

"That was county annex back there," I said after a while.

"No shit?" Carbone said. He sounded mildly surprised.

"So if you aren't taking me to county and you aren't taking me to the fucking annex, then where *are* you taking me?" I was pretty sure I knew, but I felt this compulsion to ask.

"I'm taking you to see some friends of yours. Relax. We'll be there soon."

"What friends? I didn't think you knew any of my friends."

Carbone glanced over at me, that nasty smile weaving in and out through his jowl folds.

"I'm your friend, Johnnie. I'm the best friend you ever had."

"Carbone, you son of a bitch, you are not my friend. Don't tell me you're my friend. You're taking me to Malatesta so his thugs can rip my teeth out."

"Don't worry about Malatesta," advised Carbone.

I *was* worried about Malatesta. A lot. "Why shouldn't I worry about Malatesta?" I asked.

Carbone drove in silence for a minute, obviously wondering whether I needed to know.

"Malatesta's not a player anymore," he said after a while.

"What happened? Did he get fired?"

"You could say that. They put him through a feed mill and used him to fertilize the lawn."

"Whose lawn?"

"His lawn. That house of his, up in Nissequogue." Carbone shook his head. "Too much lawn for me. I'd hate to have to mow it. Take you fucking forever."

We rode in silence past a couple of exits. But I couldn't keep my mouth shut for long.

"So when did this go down?" I asked Carbone. "The yard work, I mean."

That made Carbone happy, I could see.

"Yard work, that's good," he said. "You're a funny guy, you know that? It's happening today, this morning."

"What, right now?"

He nodded. "Yep. They're probably putting him in the spreader as we speak."

I considered this.

"I guess he wasn't doing a very good job, huh? Malatesta."

"You can say that again. You and your friends out there, running around with heads and bags of money. It didn't look good."

Bags of money? I thought. More like a Baggie of money. It still didn't seem like enough money for everyone to be so upset.

"'Bags'? What bags?" I asked.

"Don't shit me, LoDuco," Carbone said.

It was a gray, foggy kind of morning, but the LIE is always well lit by powerful sodium streetlights, like at a stadium, and you can see everything, even if you don't want to. We were still heading west. When we got to the Ronkonkoma exit, Carbone cut across three lanes, horns honking at him, tires squealing, and made the exit— just.

"We going to the airport?" I asked. Carbone didn't answer. I didn't really think we were anyway.

We did head down toward the airport at first, but then Carbone started cutting off down narrow little streets between the pines, nothing on most of them but the occasional tire store or body shop. It was pretty lonely, rat-ass scrubby country, all pine trees and weeds, and it occurred to me it would be a good place to dump a body.

"Where are we going?" I asked again, but I was afraid I knew the answer. Some shallow grave in the Pine Barrens, probably, where I would lie until some pooch dug up a leg and took it back to the family picnic table. Or never be found at all, and be paved over when they finally expanded the LIE to seventy-five lanes. Or get built into the foundations of a new housing development.

"Carbone," I said, "would it do any good to tell you I have no idea what any of this is about and that I'm not responsible?"

He thought about it. "No."

"You wouldn't just stop the car, let me out, and let me walk away?"

"Uh-uh. Nope."

"I swear I'll go away and never come back."

"I don't give a shit if you come back."

"So tell me this." I was desperate by now. "Are you going to do it yourself?"

He finally looked over at me. " 'Do it'? Do what?" Then he broke into a grin, a big one this time, showing teeth.

"You think I'm going to shoot you. Relax. While I admit there'd be a certain enjoyment in the act, I am not going to shoot you."

"Is anybody going to shoot me?"

He shrugged. "It's possible. It's amazing to me, personally, that nobody shot you a long time ago."

I brooded on this. It was something I'd wondered about myself.

"Carbone."

"What?"

"Since you know everything, why not tell me what this is all about? I'd just like to know, before I get turned into a lawn treatment."

Carbone was loving me, I could tell.

"If I knew, Johnnie, believe me, I would tell you. But I'll tell you this."

"What?"

"Your friend Vinnie managed to piss off a lot of people," Carbone said. "A *lot* of people. Malatesta was nothing, a shitheel, a wannabe. Malatesta was just the beginning. No telling how far this thing reaches. This is big, you know."

"Yeah. I was afraid of that." I sulked for a minute, then asked, "How big?"

"Big. Bigger than I know anyway. This's global capital, big corporations, into everything, everyone. Truly serious money. Japanese, Russian, Colombian, who knows? It doesn't really matter where they're from anymore. They are just big."

"Bigger than the Mafia?"

"*The Mafia*. They own the Mafia. They use the Mafia as errand boys. The Mafia is the past. These guys are the future. They own everything, everyone. They have their own private armies, private gangs."

"Private police forces?" I suggested.

"Sure," Carbone said agreeably.

"Governments?"

"Governments." Carbone nodded. "Enough anyway so's they don't get in the way. But you, you stupid fuck, you got in the way."

We drove in silence, each of us meditating on my brainlessness and bad luck.

A thought came to me. "What about Worm Lips? What happened to him?"

Carbone frowned, looking confused. " 'Worm Lips'? Who?"

"Petey, Malatesta's little servant, lieutenant, whatever. The guy in the car coat."

"Oh, that little shit," Carbone said. I was glad to see we agreed about something. "He doesn't have a clue. He'll just end up working for the new guy and never know the fucking difference. Now that just goes to show you," Carbone said. "These new people, one thing they are not is wasteful. Malatesta fucked up, so they take out Malatesta. But they leave the help alone."

I was disappointed to hear nothing had happened to Worm Lips. "But what I want to know is who they sent. Who is replacing Malatesta?"

Carbone just shook his head. "Someone. The new guy."

Conversation faltered. The lights of the Veterans Highway flew past like fat yellow geese heading to the golf course.

A suspicion formed in my mind. I couldn't keep it to myself. "Carbone," I whined, "are *you* the new guy?"

Carbone smiled. I had to look away. But it would be just the kind of thing that would happen to me, if it turned out to be true.

"I'm taking you to meet him," he said after a few minutes of am-
biguous silence.

"Who?"

"The new guy. LoDuco, pay attention! Listen up! The new guy.
He's coming to take this shit over. And you, you lucky guy, you get to
meet him."

"Why?"

"He wants to meet you. He asked about you."

"So you've met him, this new guy? What's he like?"

I could see Carbone was considering whether it was worth it to
lie to me, whether it would be good for a laugh or just a pain in the
ass. Finally, he made his decision.

"Nah. I'm just a servant, a fucking dogsbody. Like your friend
Petey."

"Not *my* friend," I pointed out.

"I only know what they tell me, and they don't tell me much,"
Carbone went on. Was I supposed to feel sorry for him?

Somehow, by scooting through back roads and side roads in the
scrub, we had ended up driving east, back toward Yaphank. I was
getting seriously turned around.

"So if we're not going to the county jail, or to the annex in
Yaphank, or to the airport, and if you're not going to kill me, then
where *are* we going?" I asked.

I shivered. I still wasn't confident I wanted to hear the answer.

"Well, it's kind of a fuckup, really," Carbone said. "Your buddy
Bogdan is holed up in the Colonial Pines Shopping Mall. He's
taken hostages. And he's got a bomb, he says. And he's got the
head."

The head. "You know about the head?"

"I've known about the head for a while."

I chewed this over. Jennifer Smeals, bless her poisonous little heart, must have kept the fact that it was the wrong head to herself. Unless, of course, it wasn't the wrong head and she had been lying through her teeth at Bogdan's—always a possibility.

"Why does the head matter? I mean, what does it prove? It's just a fucking head."

Carbone shrugged again. He was going to sprain himself if he kept doing that.

"The fuck should I know," he said peevishly. "All I know is that Malatesta was hot to have the head. He wanted it. I don't know why. And now the people above Malatesta, the ones who put him there, they want the head."

"You don't know why."

"Nobody tells me a fucking thing." He took a sandy corner a little too fast and the car fishtailed around, scaring the piss out of me.

"Come on, LoDuco," Carbone said. "Let's go hang out at the mall."

CHAPTER THIRTEEN

THE COLONIAL PINES SHOPPING Mall and Low-Price Outlet Center stuck up from the acres of blacktop like a crash-landed UFO, a whole city from outer space dropped like a hot pizza in the middle of the Pine Barrens. If anyone had ever moved into the condo complexes and apartment buildings surrounding it, they had moved out now, since there wasn't anyplace to shop anymore.

The parking lot at Colonial Pines was something. You might go to Colonial Pines just to see the parking lot. It stretched out on all sides of the mall as far as I could see.

But the megamall was almost entirely abandoned, its anchor stores sucked away into another, bigger megamall just a few miles away. A few pathetic shops held on: a bagel place, a nail salon, a bargain clothing store, a pizzeria. I counted six cars in the parking lot on the way in.

Milkweed and tree of heaven were already springing up through cracks in the asphalt. Newspapers, soda cups, beer cans, and candy wrappers blew through the parking lot and up against the chain-link fence that kept the pine trees out.

There was some activity, though, way over by the main entrance to the mall, a line of police cars like early shoppers on sale day, waiting for the doors to open.

Carbone cut over toward them across the nearly empty parking lot. As we got closer, I could see uniformed cops milling around, a guy in a raincoat holding a megaphone, hatless cops pointing rifles across car hoods.

Carbone jerked the car to a halt, hopped out, and came around to my side. He pulled me out of the car and pushed me toward the line of police cars.

"Just stay with me, Kenny. Don't get lost."

"My name isn't Kenny," I told him.

Carbone smirked. "It is today. I'm telling you: Don't get out of my sight. It's for your own fucking good"—he smirked again—"Kenny."

The cop with the megaphone watched us walk up. The guys in uniform milled around nervously.

"Carbone," Carbone announced. "What's up?"

"Asshole's holed up inside," Mr. Megaphone said. "He's got hostages. And a bomb." He suddenly seemed to notice me. "The fuck is this?"

"Kenny Moleri, a good buddy of the guy inside," Carbone said. "We can use him in negotiations."

Megaphone Man looked at me as if he thought it would be better just to shoot me on the spot.

"You had any recent communications?" Carbone asked.

"I talked to the guy earlier. It's hard to follow him, but it sounds like he wants us to release some guy, Johnnie LoDuco, he says we have in custody. He also claims to have a head—whose head, he's not saying. He says he'll trade the head for LoDuco."

I was touched.

"We're not in contact at the moment," Megaphone Man said.

"The SWAT team's on the way, and the hostage negotiator. I'm sure he'll want to talk to your friend."

"Have you heard anything? You know," Carbone said mysteriously.

"Not a fucking thing, no. I can't raise Malatesta. I've been calling every few minutes."

So he didn't know. I opened my mouth to say something, then realized that Carbone was still holding on to me, because he twisted the handcuffs hard, cutting them into my wrists. I gasped and whined.

"What's the matter with him?" the cop with the megaphone asked.

"He needs to piss," Carbone said. Bless him for remembering.

"I do," I volunteered. "Bad."

"Well, take him over the fence. Better take the cuffs off, 'less you want to hold his dick for him."

"Perish the thought," Carbone said. "With half the cops in the county here and the SWAT team on the way, I guess we'll be safe with him loose." He snapped the cuffs off.

We didn't get all the way to the fence—it looked miles away—so I ducked behind a light standard for privacy. Pissing was such a relief, I didn't care now if I got shot. "He doesn't know about Malatesta," I said, zipping up.

"Just keep your fucking mouth shut till I figure out what's going on," Carbone said.

The cop in the raincoat was talking on a cell phone as we walked up, his megaphone under one arm. He held the phone out to Carbone.

"Carbone. Asshole says he wants to talk to you, only you."

"How sweet." Carbone took the phone and listened for a minute. "Ask him yourself," he said into the phone. "He's right here."

Then, to me: "Your buddy wants to talk to you."

I took the phone. "Hello? Bogdan?"

"Johnnie. How are you? You okay?" Bogdan sounded brisk and confident, completely in his element. I wondered if he'd done this kind of thing before.

"Yeah. I'm okay, I guess."

"Look, Johnnie, sit tight. I have this under control."

I looked around at the line of cop cars. The cops leaning on them bristled with rifles and shotguns. Just then, a helicopter made a low pass over the parking lot. It looked and sounded like Baghdad on a bad day. None of this looked like control to me.

"Bogdan, it's very heavy out here. You sure you know what you're doing?"

"I'll be out to get you in a few minutes," Bogdan said. "Be ready." He hung up.

I handed the phone back to the megaphone guy. "He's almost ready to negotiate," I told him.

"Good," the cop said. "The more he talks, the less likely we'll have to shoot his ass, maybe kill the hostages." He spat on the asphalt. "I really hate this shit, this standing around waiting."

But we didn't have to wait around long.

There was a tremendous crash of breaking glass, and a big Humvee with a full camo paint job came tear-assing around the corner of the mall. It looked like the real military deal, not a shrunkdown consumer Hummer. I couldn't see clearly, but I knew Bogdan must have been at the wheel.

The Humvee reached the line of cop cars before the cops could recover and start shooting at it. It knocked the end cop car right around, then started heading up the line, tearing off open doors and making the uniformed cops vault over the cruisers to get out of the way.

"Where the fuck is that SWAT team?" the megaphone cop gasped.

"Maybe they got stuck in traffic," Carbone said. He seemed pretty calm.

The Humvee reached us before the rifle cops could get a fix on it, though I saw them readying their guns, kneeling down, pointing them at us. Too many other cops in the way, I guess.

As the Humvee tore up to us, the driver's door suddenly flew open, knocking the megaphone cop on his ass. The megaphone went flying across the asphalt.

"Johnnie!" Bogdan looked down at me. "Get in!"

Carbone winked at me, made a stirrup of his hands. I stepped up, jumped in, and landed on Bogdan's lap. He pushed me off and roared away; I ended up in the passenger seat, head on the floor, ass in the air. That was just as well, because the rifle cops opened fire. Bullets twanged and splatted against the Humvee.

Bogdan let out a rebel yell. He seemed overexcited to me.

"H-one Humvee, full armor plate from the factory, bulletproof glass," he crowed. "We can take a hit from anything less than a bazooka and keep going."

I hoped the county cops didn't have any bazookas.

The Humvee whacked back through the line of cruisers, knocking them aside like toys. I had gotten myself turned around in the seat by now but was keeping my head down. I raised it enough to see out the windshield. What I saw was that we were headed straight for the wall of the mall building.

"Bogdan!" I yelled. "Holy shit!"

We crashed through the glass front of the mall and kept going.

I looked around the careering military vehicle. "Why are you taking me back inside? Why didn't we just drive out of here?"

"Patrice is in there, holding down the fort," Bogdan said gaily. He kept his eyes on where he was going, which made me glad. We were tearing down the center aisle of the mall now, going about ninety. We sideswiped a kiosk and went fishtailing across the floor.

I could see Gummi Bears, Swedish fish, and little soft chocolates stuck to the windshield.

"What happened to her? Is she okay?"

"She's okay," Bogdan said, and I heard something in his voice, a hesitation that made me wonder.

"Really? Everything is copacetic?"

"She's fine, she's fine," Bogdan said impatiently.

"What about Jennifer?" But the Bogman was strangely silent on this topic.

It seemed like the shooting had stopped behind us, but I couldn't be sure. I didn't feel like sticking my head out to be certain.

"Where'd you get the Humvee?" I asked Bogdan. I hadn't noticed it parked back at his mom's garage, and I think I would have. The vehicle stood out.

Bogdan smirked. "Got it off a guy in the service. A bunch of guns, too. He thought I was with al-Qaeda. I've been keeping it stashed in a garage in Patchogue. I knew it would come in handy someday."

The Humvee skidded to a halt.

Most of the storefronts we had passed along the main drag of the mall were empty, carpets folded back, electrical connections hanging from the walls. We had stopped in front of one of the few occupied ones. You couldn't see in the windows because they were painted black three-quarters of the way up. Two four-foot-high female hands were crudely painted on each window in flesh-colored enamel, big red fingernails spread out. In an arch over them, in lumpy yellow paint, it said LINDA'S NAILS. THE FINGER STALL. The door had gotten the same treatment, though of course the hands were smaller.

The shooting had stopped. I looked over my shoulder back down the mall, but I couldn't see anything but broken glass and little candies.

"Here we are," Bogdan said. "Come in and meet the hostages."

————

Patrice was standing on one side of the nail salon, a big black shot-gun in her hands. She was pointing it across the room, where a line of people sat disconsolately at the nail stations. They looked up as I came in.

"Hi Johnnie," Linda Scopolomini said. The guy sitting next to her, in some kind of Sheriff's Department uniform, didn't say a word. He stared back at me, looking plenty pissed off.

A kid in some kind of dorky white outfit with a little cap was sitting next to the uniformed guy. He looked like someone from the pizza-delivery industry.

But the prize of all were the three guys in orange Sheriff's Department plastic vests.

"Johnnie! Hey!" Bug Rankin waved; Hector and Alfredo grinned. They seemed glad to see me.

"What are you assholes doing here?" I asked.

"Picking up papers for the county, man," Rankin said. He was eating some kind of cake out of a cellophane wrapper.

"County? I thought you were going down on a felony."

"Naw, man, they knocked it down to a misdemeanor," Rankin said, crumbs falling out of his mouth. "Thanks to you, man."

"The mastermind!" Hector put in.

I couldn't take this.

"What about you, Linda? What are you doing here?" I hardly rec-ognized her; her big hair was down now—in a sort of jellyfish cut, with bangs and strands hanging down all around.

"This is my salon, Johnnie. You know how I always used to say I wanted to start my own? This is it."

I was nonplussed. "Well. Hey. Congratulations."

But something was bothering her; she frowned.

"What do you think of the name, though?"

"Well, I . . . Linda's Nails. Says it all."

"Not that part, the finger-stall part. That was Leon's idea. But I don't really get it."

"Ah, um, like a stall, in a market, I guess." I think I was blushing.

"Leon thinks it's funny, but he won't tell me why."

The guy sitting next to her laughed, though he didn't look much happier. I guessed that he was Leon.

Patrice looked good holding the shotgun.

"How've you been?" I asked her, though feeling a little constraint; the hostages watched us like hungry kittens.

"Johnnie, what happened? I was so scared when I got back to the car and you were gone! I thought for sure those goons had come back and taken you." While talking to me, she never took her eyes off the hostages. They returned the favor.

I tried to explain about Stosh and Carbone, but I felt myself skidding into pure incoherence right off the bat.

"I'll tell you later. I'm all right." According to a very stretched definition of *all right*, that is. Any minute, I expected SWAT teams to rappel down from the roof. "But what happened to you? What are you doing here?"

Patrice shifted the shotgun, causing a ripple to run down the line of hostages. She looked like she was about to burst into tears.

"I went to Bogdan's. When I got out to the car and you weren't there, I didn't know what to do. I needed help. So I drove down to Bogdan's." She glanced over at the big serial killer, who looked abashed. "Good thing, too."

"I'm sorry about that, Patrice," Bogdan said apologetically. It was weird and unpleasant to hear him use her name. "That was atavistic of me."

"I'll say."

"A temporary relapse. I lost control. In my defense, I was overstimulated."

Patrice nodded. "All those bodies. Still, I don't know why you needed another one."

Now I was seriously confused. "Will someone tell me what is going on?"

"When I got to Bogdan's," Patrice told me, "Bogdan's mom answered the door. 'Oh, Danny's down in his workshop,' she told me. 'He's always working away at something down there.' So I went down. And what did I see?" She turned to Bogdan, who still wouldn't meet her eyes.

"I saw Jennifer Smeals, bare-ass naked, tied to a sawhorse."

"Fuck," was all I could manage to say at this point.

"And what was our boy Bogdan doing?" Patrice asked rhetorically. "He was sitting there sharpening a saw."

"I wasn't just sharpening it," Bogdan protested. "I was setting it. I hadn't used it in so long, I was afraid it would bind."

"Whatever. You were getting ready to cut up Jennifer Smeals."

"I love her," Bogdan said simply.

Out in the parking lot, someone was yelling into a loudspeaker, yelling at us probably. You couldn't understand a single word he was saying, due to the distortion. It sounded like those announcements in Penn Station that you can never really understand but that make you nervous. This announcement would have made me nervous, too, if my nerves hadn't been shot to hell long ago.

"So what did you do?" I asked Patrice.

"I didn't think he'd listen to me," Patrice said. "I could see he was all worked up, all sweaty and nasty." She glared at Bogdan. "So I went back upstairs and got his mom."

Bogdan gave a groan of shame.

"She came back down with me. 'Danny boy!' she said. 'What's all this?' Can you believe it, all those years he'd been down there sawing off heads, and she had no idea!"

"What did Bogdan do?"

"Oh, he freaked out. He was making excuses a mile a minute. He cut Jennifer loose, took out the ball gag. . . ."

"Ball gag?" I rubbed my jaw, remembering the night in the motel. Served her right.

"Uh-huh. And there she was, drugged and naked. 'Bogdan!' his mom said. 'I will not stand for you consorting with loose women!' "

"Well, she *was* loose, after he cut off the ropes," I pointed out.

"Whatever. His mom stormed back upstairs and Bogdan went after her, bawling excuses."

"I'm sorry, Mom!" Bogdan sobbed, lost in the memory.

"So what happened to Jennifer?"

"Bogdan and his mom had to work it out. It took awhile. I got Jennifer's clothes for her, helped her get dressed, tried to talk to her, but she was still out of it. So I just went and watched TV in the living room. I figured Jennifer could take care of herself. When we got back downstairs, she was gone."

"Did she take the head?" I asked.

"I had it in a safe place," Bogdan said, wiping away his tears and getting back to normal. Normal for him, I mean.

"If she didn't try to take it, it probably *is* the wrong head," I pointed out. This was greeted by dead silence. Patrice and Bogdan stared at me curiously, then Bogdan lowered his gaze and slunk away toward the door.

"Anyway, Bogdan had an idea where you were," Patrice said. "He thought someone probably came by and conked you on the head and hauled you up to Malatesta's. I told him about Worm Lips, how the goons just drove away and left us, but he thought that was just a feint, to put us off our guard."

"His love for Jennifer was distorting his judgment," I said. "That's not like our boy."

"His judgment's not the only thing that's distorted about that guy," Patrice muttered.

"Wow!" Linda Scopolomini said, eyes wide. "That's some story!" We had forgotten about our audience.

"But how did you end up here? In the fucking mall?"

Patrice grimaced. "Bogdan thought he could rescue you from Malatesta's, or at least keep an eye out for you. He was going to drive up there to the house and try to find out where they were keeping you. I think he thought that Jennifer might be going there, too. But when we got to Malatesta's place, it was swarming with people."

"Lawn-care company," I put in.

"They didn't look like lawn guys. Bogdan tried to park where he could keep an eye on them without being seen, but it was ridiculous. You can't hide a big fucking Humvee behind a tree. Someone came up to us like he was expecting us. He told Bogdan that the cops had you in Riverhead and were going to send you back to jail. That was it for Bogdan; we took off."

"But that still doesn't put you in the Colonial Pines Mall."

"Wait, there's more. On the way out to Riverhead, a cop cruiser started following us. They gave us the lights, you know?"

I knew. "So what did you do?"

"Bogdan like wigged *out*. He wouldn't pull over, started driving really fast. More cop cars showed up."

"That ride of his is not street-legal," I pointed out.

"I wondered about that," Patrice said. "Bogdan told me it was hot—army but not surplus." She paused, looked at me confusedly. "Do you think he's really al-Qaeda?"

"I don't think so," I said.

"Anyway, he didn't want to stop. By this time, maybe a dozen cruisers were behind us. I thought they would do that strip thing, you know, like on *Cops*, and blow out the tires. Bogdan thought so, too, so we got off at the next exit."

"And that was here?"

"Close enough. Johnnie, that crazy motherfucker drove right

through the doors at the back of the mall. He had some kind of gun strapped to the ceiling of the Humvee. He took it out and opened up on the cops as they came up behind us. Made them back off all right. Then he dragged me in here."

She stared at the line of seated hostages, who looked back at her with glazed eyes and open mouths.

"You guys are better than the TV," Hector offered.

For someone who had recently taken such a hammering to his basic self-esteem, Bogdan seemed pretty calm, and I had to admire him. He was over by the black-painted windows with a cell phone to his ear. He looked like a businessman on a train platform, calling his office.

"Fuck!" he said. "No one's picking up."

"Who're you calling?" I asked him.

"The head cop. Not Carbone, the other guy, the one with the megaphone."

"You put him down, remember?" I reminded him. "Swatted him with the Humvee door. Maybe you broke his cell phone at the same time."

"That's too bad," Bogdan said. "I need to negotiate our getaway."

That sounded like a good idea, though not very fucking likely.

"How did you get his number in the first place?"

"He yelled it to me on the megaphone."

I thought for a minute. "I know! Call nine one one!"

This was pure genius on my part. Bogdan punched in the digits, waited, spoke, waited some more, staring into space.

Then he looked at me. "I'm on hold."

We waited.

"Hurry up, you guys," Patrice called over. "This fucking shotgun is getting heavy."

"I have to go to the bathroom!" Linda Scopolomini added.

All eyes were on Bogdan as he tried to raise the hostage negotiator. So no one noticed at first that Leon, the guy in the deputy's uniform, had pulled down on us with a little silver gun. He must have had it hidden in his sock or something.

"You're all under arrest," he said when he finally got our attention. "Just march out of here when I say so."

Patrice looked around in surprise, her shotgun barrel following her eyes. I thought we were going to see a repeat of the Frown episode. Never go up against a double-barreled shotgun with a tiny little automatic, I could have told Leon. But I didn't get the chance.

Patrice's shotgun went off, all right, but it wasn't pointed at the deputy or at anyone. It made enough noise and smoke for a howitzer. When the sound stopped echoing, a trashed light fixture bobbed down through the smoke and swung there over our heads.

In the smoke and confusion, Bogdan had slid up close to the deputy. Now he reached over and took the little gun out of the deputy's hands. The pistol disappeared completely into Bogdan's big fist. Leon didn't seem to realize what had happened for a couple seconds. He blinked and looked around at us.

"This is bullshit," he said. "I'm a cop. I can just walk out of here anytime."

"You're a hostage," Bogdan pointed out reasonably. "I can blow your head off anytime."

"I heard what you did to that woman," Linda Scopolomini put in, her voice quavering. "Are you going to cut us up, too?"

"I didn't cut her up."

"You've not going to cut me up," the deputy said.

"I'm not going to cut anybody up!" Bogdan was visibly losing his patience. He stared at the group at the nail stations, breathing hard.

"Look," he said, "you want to walk out of here?" The hostages all nodded their heads.

"I need a messenger," Bogdan said. "I don't think they'd let me live long enough to talk, the trigger-happy bastards. So I need someone to go out there and tell them we'll negotiate. Someone to convey my proposition."

No more nodding. Linda and Bug and his buddies and the pizza guy didn't seem eager to take Bogdan up on his offer.

"I'll go," said Leon. "I'm a cop. They'll listen to me."

"Good. Here's what to tell them. We'll give them the head, the bomb, and the hostages, in return for safe conduct to the airport and a plane to the Cayman Islands."

"Bogdan!" Patrice said admiringly. I felt a twitch of jealousy, just a little.

"Okay," the deputy said. He didn't sound very confident. "You give them the head—"

"Wrong," Bogdan told him. "They get us the jet first, and take us to the airport."

"And carry our luggage," I put in, but they all ignored me.

"Then we give them the head, the hostages, and the bomb. Got that?"

"Sure," Leon said, frowning. "But suppose they don't agree to it?"

"It can't hurt to ask," Bogdan said.

We huddled at the door to the nail salon, hostages and captors together, watching Leon walk toward the line of heavily armed, highly stressed, mentally challenged policemen.

The guard walked down the mall court toward the main entrance. I could see from the way his lips were moving that he was repeating Bogdan's message over to himself.

"He's not a cop, really; he's a corrections officer," Linda Scopolomini said, looking after him sadly.

"You know him?" I asked her.

She nodded. "He's my boyfriend," she said, and gave me a quick look. "You're not mad, Johnnie? You never come see me anymore."

"I'm not mad, Linda," I told her.

When he got near the entrance, Leon put his hands on top of his head.

"Men!" he yelled out. "Don't shoot! I'm a—"

They shot him to ribbons.

"Fuck!" the pizza guy said in an awestruck voice.

"I think they're nervous," I said.

"Impatient" was Bogdan's diagnosis.

"You hurt their pride, man, when you drove over them with the Humvee." This was Alfredo's contribution, only the third thing I'd ever heard him say. (The second was at the hearing, when he told the judge, "It was all LoDuco's idea to rob that store.")

"Why don't you throw the bomb at them or something?" I asked. "Then in the confusion, maybe we could get away."

"I don't have a bomb," Bogdan said. "I just told them I had a bomb."

"Why would they believe you?"

"You believed me," he pointed out. "Anyway, they can't take a chance on damaging the head."

"The head. Then they don't know it's not the right head?"

Bogdan pondered this. "I don't think so. Or else they would have just stormed in here and shot the living shit out of us."

Gunshots skipped and sang along the mall floor. Once in awhile, glass broke.

"They're shooting at us now," I said, pointing out the obvious.

"They must have liked doing it before," Bogdan replied. "Now they can't stop."

"Is there a back door to this place?"

Bogdan nodded. "How I got in."

I thought about this. "If you got in, they can get in."

"Probably there already."

"So what do we do now?"

Bogdan looked me in the eyes, taking the shades off to give me a better look at his soft-boiled blue ones. Standing there, bare-eyed, holding a big gun, another one shoved in his belt, he looked like something in a museum diorama.

"We negotiate," he said.

Patrice was back on guard duty, holding the shotgun. I went over to give her moral support.

"They'll listen to him, right?" she asked me.

I shrugged. "I hope so. You never know with these mob guys."

"Mob guys? What mob guys? I'm talking about the cops out there in the parking lot."

"So am I. I think these cops are not actually cops. I mean they are cops, but these cops are working for the bad guys. That may explain why they're shooting at us instead of calling in high-powered hostage negotiators."

"I can't believe Malatesta bought every single cop on Long Island!" Patrice wailed. The cops had stopped shooting at us by now, but every once in a while a piece of broken glass would come down with a crash.

"It's not every cop," I pointed out. "Only about fifty or sixty. Anyway, it isn't Malatesta anymore. It's the new guy."

Bogdan was deep in thought.

"Linda. It's Linda, right?" he said to Linda Scopolomini, who bobbed her head. "Linda, is there a security office here? In the mall?"

She bobbed her head some more. "Yeah, but there's nobody in it now."

"Okay. How do I get there?"

"It's right down there." She pointed. "A door with SECURITY on it. Past the bathrooms. But I think it's locked up."

"No problem," Bogdan said. "Here." He gave me the automatic rifle he was holding. "Spell Patrice. I'll be back in a jiff." In seconds, he was out the door, keeping low, watching out for any stray bullets.

Then he was gone.

"A *jiff*?" Patrice said in disbelief. "I never heard anyone say that before."

"Yeah," Bug Rankin said. He'd finally finished eating and was easier to understand. "What the fuck is a *jiff*?"

"Shut up, Rankin," I said, waving the M16 at him menacingly. I really enjoyed saying it. "Just shut the fuck up."

Suddenly, Bogdan's voice boomed out like the voice of an angry god from the tinny little speaker in the ceiling of the nail salon.

"Attention!" he boomed. "Attention, please! This is Hostage Taker One. I want to talk to Carbone."

"Hostage Taker One! That's tight!" Hector said. "He's a cool guy, your friend."

"He's a psycho," Patrice said.

From out in the parking lot came loud squeals, barks, static loud enough to break eardrums. Then, finally, we could hear Carbone's voice, only slightly distorted.

"This is Carbone, Hostage Taker One."

"They can hear him out there!" Bug Rankin said, wonder in his voice.

"They can hear him all over the mall," I said. "Can't you hear it? That echo?"

"They have speakers in the parking lot, too," Linda said thoughtfully. "They play Christmas carols in the winter. At least they used to."

"That is really *loud*," the pizza guy said. "Really fuckin' awesome! Can you imagine, like, running your sound system through that?"

"We are asking for transportation to the Cayman Islands for three people." Bogdan's voice boomed and echoed around the empty mall. "You will let us drive to the airport unmolested. At the airport, we will surrender the hostages and the head."

"We're working on it right now, Hostage Taker One," Carbone's amplified voice squawked back. Then, after a brief pause: "Window seat or aisle?"

"That cop has your sense of humor, Johnnie," Patrice said.

"Smoking or non?"

Bogdan rolled on, ignoring Carbone. "We will take one hostage with us on the plane to ensure compliance. This hostage will not be released until we safely deplane and leave the airport in the Cayman Islands."

Bug Rankin perked up. "Hey, can I go?" he asked.

"No, man, I'll go," Hector put in.

"Sit down," I said, "and shut up." I was so into being a guard.

"Not me," said the pizza guy. "I been there. It's fucking boring. Nothing to do all day but sit around in deck chairs."

Linda Scopolomini looked at the pizza guy admiringly. "You been to the Cayman Islands?"

He nodded. "With my parents. Man, it really sucked. But the babes were pretty." He smiled at Linda, his teeth as white as his stupid uniform.

"I think everybody should just stop talking so I can hear," I said, but they all ignored me. It was a ridiculous statement anyway; you couldn't keep from hearing. They must have been able to hear Bogdan's voice in Connecticut.

"You have ten minutes to supply what we require." Bogdan sounded like he'd been doing hostage negotiations all his life. "The bomb is set to go off in one hour. I repeat, one hour. If we receive an affirmative response, it will be defused."

This made the hostages look strained.

"*Bomb?* What bomb?" Bug Rankin asked.

"It's a bluff," I said.

"Johnnie, don't tell them that," Patrice warned.

"Yeah, but maybe it's like a double bluff," Hector said. "He's really got a bomb, but he just tells us he doesn't so we won't freak out."

Eyes darted around nervously, looking for likely bomb containers.

"What's that?" Hector asked, pointing. "Over in the corner, in that bag?"

A black plastic Hefty bag that could have been holding a bowling ball or something of around that size was sitting in the corner.

"Pretty small for a bomb," Bug Rankin said.

"It doesn't have to be big to do a lot of damage." Then, looking at me: "Hey, what's in the bag, man?"

"You don't need to know," I said. I wished I didn't know myself.

Carbone's voice cracked out of the megaphone. "You'll have what you asked for. We need some time to set it up. But you'll make your flight."

After a few minutes of silence, Bogdan slipped back into the nail salon.

"A lot of cops out there," he said. He was covered with sweat and fine white dust.

"Now what?" I asked him. He took his sunglasses off again—for effect, I guess, but maybe just so he could see. The lenses were covered with fine white powder.

"Now we wait," he said.

The silence got oppressive. No one was talking anymore. The cops had stopped shooting, and all of the broken glass must have fallen out of the frames already, because we didn't hear a single sound from outside. The only sounds were our group breathing and a vigorous fart from Rankin.

"Wasn't me," he said, looking around guiltily.

As if this was some kind of signal to start talking, Linda Scopolomini looked right at me and said, "Do you think there'll be TV cameras outside?"

Like I would know. I said, "Probably. By now, I imagine. Newspaper, TV, maybe even Hollywood scouts."

Linda perked up at this. "You think?"

"Sure." I nodded. "Events like this, there are always book and movie spin-offs. Especially if it ends tragically and a lot of people are killed."

All eyes at the nail stations had been on me; now everyone looked a little deflated.

"Jesus Christ, Johnnie," Patrice said. "Will you just cut it out?"

Squeals, honks, and incredibly loud feedback noises came from out in the parking lot. Carbone's voice came over the megaphone.

"Your ride's here," he said.

"The moment of truth," Bogdan whispered.

We looked at one another. No one was anxious to be the first one out the door. We all remembered Leon.

"Hostages first," Bogdan said. "Come on, don't worry, this is almost over."

"That's what I'm afraid of, man," Hector said. But he got up and walked to the door. "Come on, you pussies," he said to Rankin and Alfredo, who held back just a second, then got up and walked after him.

Linda Scopolomini turned her big round eyes on me.

"Be careful, Johnnie," she said, and walked out holding on to the arm of the pizza guy.

I was touched. Two dozen riot shotguns and high-powered rifles pointed at her, and she was worried about me.

Bogdan followed close behind Linda and the pizza guy, his pistol in his hand now, Patrice right behind him with her shotgun at port arms.

Just as we all got outside the nail salon, there was a popping sound from outside, and something whacked down and skidded across the mall floor. It looked like a big coffee can or something; after a second, it began pouring out clouds of white smoke.

"CS," Bogdan muttered, then, louder, so we all could hear: "Tear gas. We are betrayed."

There was another pop, from the back door this time, and another canister skidded along the fake marble, spewing out gas.

Great. They call it tear gas for a reason: My eyes were watering so fast, I couldn't see, and they burned like a motherfucker.

"You got any gas masks?" I asked Bogdan.

"In the Humvee," he yelled through the handkerchief he was holding over his face. But we couldn't even see the Humvee in the clouds of choking white gas.

"Back inside!" Bogdan, the squad leader, yelled, and we all tumbled back into the nail salon.

It was better inside, but not much. Tendrils of tear gas were floating out of the air ducts and slowly filling up the salon.

"I didn't even know those worked," Linda gasped. Streaky blue eye makeup was running down her cheeks. Everyone was doubled over, coughing and trying to shield their eyes.

Sadly, Bogdan pulled the pistol out of his belt and put it gently on the floor.

"This is over," he choked out.

Patrice laid the shotgun on the weapon pile, and after a second, I followed with the M16. I had really liked holding it, but clearly Bogdan was right.

"You can go now," he said to the hostages. "But don't run. Stay together. Put your hands behind your heads."

Everyone looked dubiously at the white smoke curling against the unpainted glass at the top of the salon windows. But the tear gas was getting thicker inside, too. Finally, Hector pulled the door open, put his hands behind his neck, and stumbled out into the swirling gas, followed by the others.

"Don't fucking shoot!" I heard Bug Rankin yell in the fog.

Patrice, Bogdan, and I all eyeballed one another.

"I'm sorry," Bogdan said. "I thought it would work."

"That's all right, Bogdan," Patrice said, patting him on the arm. "You did your best." She turned to me. "Come on, Johnnie. Race you to jail." She put her hands on top of her head and disappeared through the door.

"Well, Bogdan," I said, holding out my hand, "it's been fun."

He pumped my hand vigorously for a second, making it go numb. "Here, take this," he said, holding something out. I took whatever it was without thinking, staring out the window over the painted fingers at the wafting eyeball gas. But something about the heft was familiar. I looked down.

"Fuck, Bogdan, I don't want the head!"

But it was too late. Bogdan was out the door, his hands clasped behind his head, walking toward the cops through the swirling tear gas.

Outside the mall, there was a scene of incredible confusion.

I stumbled out the doors, skidding on pieces of broken glass, expecting any second to be hurled to the ground by a dozen cop bodies. Or else just shot to pieces, like Leon. I wondered what that would feel like, bullets tearing into you, coming out the other side, blood and meat bits spraying over everything.

But nothing like that happened, and after a little while, I took my hands down, opened my stinging eyes, and looked around.

Blue cop uniforms were swirling everywhere. The line of cruisers pulled up in front of the shopping mall was now surrounded by a longer line of cruisers. It took me awhile to understand what I was seeing: cops arresting cops, handcuffing them, throwing them in the backs of the second line of cruisers.

Suddenly, Carbone was at my elbow.

"Glad you made it, Kenny," he said, grinning horribly. "Come join the party."

Carbone steered me across the parking lot. A couple of ambulances had pulled up close to the mall entrance; I saw some paramedics humping a stretcher with a body shape covered up on it—Leon, I figured. A flash of blaze orange nearby told me that Bug Rankin and his buddies were getting their traumas straightened out. I hoped Linda was okay.

Straight ahead, there was a big gaggle of cops standing around pointing shotguns and rifles at two people lying on the ground, their hands handcuffed behind them: Bogdan and Patrice.

"Come on, get over it," Carbone said, elbowing his way through the crowd of cops. "Put those guns away. What are they going to do in handcuffs, spit on you?" Shamefacedly, the cops put up their weapons and backed off.

Carbone pulled Bogdan and Patrice to their feet, Patrice first, like a true gentleman. She glanced over at me and gave me a twisted smile.

Carbone was holding on to Bogdan by his elbows, looking him up and down, as if he were a long-lost brother.

"Bogdan! Bogdan O'Reilly! I never expected to see you again. At least not in handcuffs," Carbone said.

"Hello, Carbone," Bogdan said.

Carbone looked down at the ground, then back up at the mountainous form of the serial killer.

"You know, Bogdan, I've been wanting to talk to you for a long time. A long time. I think we have a lot to say to each other."

I never got to hear Bogdan's answer, because suddenly hands grabbed my elbows from behind.

"Come on buddy," a husky cop voice said in my ear. "Show's over." He tugged me away from the circle of cops around Bogdan and Carbone and pushed me in the small of the back. I stumbled forward, glad I wasn't handcuffed yet—I would have pulled a face plant for sure—and dimly wondering why I wasn't.

We walked over to a cruiser with all four doors hanging open, like a beetle about to take off. Another cop, pushing Patrice, pulled out from behind us and walked around to the other side. Patrice ducked her head down and got in the backseat. Oh well, at least I would get to ride next to her for a while.

I felt my police escort step away from me. I turned around, expecting the cuffs now.

"Get in the car," the cop ordered. He had his head down; all I could see was the top of his hat.

"You want this, I guess." I held out the trash bag with Vinnie's head in it.

"Just throw it in the backseat," the cop said gruffly. He kept his head down, scribbling away on a clipboard.

"The backseat?" I said. "Don't you want to refrigerate it or something?" But he walked away and got in behind the wheel. His partner came up behind me and gave me a shove.

"Come on, come on, get in the car," the cop said urgently. A woman's voice. It sounded familiar, but I was still dazed from all the running and shooting, so I got in the car and was sitting there with the head on my knees before the nickel dropped and I realized who it was.

"Jennifer?"

I wasn't completely surprised to see that one of the patrol cops was Jennifer Smeals, whose hair was cut short and dyed blond now. She made a nice cop.

I was surprised to see who the other cop was, though, the cop at the wheel. I was only surprised I didn't shit myself and start to whistle like a teakettle.

The other cop was Vinnie McCloskey-Schmidt.

Patrice was sitting beside me. She looked cute in handcuffs.

"You know these people?" she said in disbelief.

CHAPTER FOURTEEN

"SO IF THIS IS not your head . . . ," I began.

"Oh God," Jennifer Smeals said. She closed her eyes and put a hand to her face, as if she had sinus problems.

I persisted. "If this is not your head, Vinnie, whose is it?"

"It's Vinnie's head," Vinnie said.

I was ready for anything, but all the possibilities seemed to cancel one another out. My mouth opened, but I couldn't seem to make anything come out.

"Vinnie, my cousin, Aunt Teresa's kid," Vinnie explained. "He looks a lot like me, don't you think?" He squirmed around and grinned at us.

"Watch the road," Jennifer said, and Vinnie faced around again.

"What, cousin Vinnie the barkeep?" I asked.

"That's him," Vinnie agreed.

I had met Vinnie's cousin Vinnie more than once. It was true: They *were* a lot alike. I guess the resemblance was increased by having his teeth pulled out and the crabs eat parts off him.

Stunned is not the word for how I felt. I sneaked a look over at

Patrice; she looked perplexed, all right. She mouthed something at me, which I didn't get right away. Then with a kind of tape-delay effect, I realized she had just asked me, "Who is this guy?"

Not an unreasonable question.

"He was a real shithead, my cousin Vinnie," Vinnie told us. "I did the world a favor when I shot the motherfucker. But I only did it because he looked so much like me."

This confession filled the car like a nasty fart. Vinnie shut up, concentrating on his driving. No one else said anything.

"Actually, I didn't shoot him," he said after a few minutes. "He died of an overdose. Right in front of me. That's when I got the idea."

"Such a great idea," I said.

"We had planned to disappear. Me and Jennifer. And send for you when it was safe, of course," he added quickly.

"Of course."

"But when I saw Cousin Vinnie lying there with his eyes x-ed out, I thought, How much better if I could really disappear. Not just run away but die and be buried. Vanish from the face of the earth."

"Vanish from the lives of people who loved and trusted you," Jennifer added. I don't think Vinnie even heard.

"So you didn't kill him. Your cousin," I said. Vinnie shook his head.

"Hey, I did cut him up. That was a bitch. A lot harder than you'd think."

"You could have taken lessons from Bogdan," Patrice offered.

"This idea," said Jennifer, and her voice sounded sweet, cold, and dangerous. "What exactly was that about? Could you clarify this idea for me?"

Four cop cars barreled past, heading in the other direction, sirens

and lights turned up to the max. Four heads froze, resisting the urge
to swivel around and look after them.

"I'd kind of like to know, too, Vinnie," I said, rubbing my neck.
"I've been carrying your head around for maybe a month now. I've
been beat up, shot at, and blown up. I would really like to know
what the fuck this is all about."

"This Vinnie is that Vinnie?" Patrice asked. I would have nodded, but I was afraid my head would crack off.

"That Vinnie," I said.

That Vinnie shook his head, as if we were all too much, a bunch
of pushy, nosy children.

"I had my plan in place, perfect," he began. His tone of voice in-
dicated this was going to be a long explanation. It had better be, I
thought. "It was all set up. We were ready to go." He grinned at Jennifer Smeals. "In a few hours, I would have been where the law
couldn't reach me."

"Paraguay," I put in. Vinnie nodded.

"With you by my side," he said, giving Jennifer another tooth
flash. She was nonresponsive.

"Then I saw an opportunity. A chance to make things even better."

"A chance to keep all the money for yourself," Jennifer said bit-
terly.

"No. It wasn't like that," Vinnie said. "Jennifer, you should know
me better than that."

"That is exactly the problem."

"Wait a minute," Patrice put in, leaning forward and putting her
head into the force field between Vinnie and Jennifer. "First, could
somebody please take these fucking handcuffs off? There is, like, no
skin left on my wrists."

"Oh, I'm sorry." Jennifer went through her pockets and came up
with a key while Patrice twisted her arms around and presented the

cuffs. I was reminded of my backward cuff journey with Stosh, among other things.

"Okay," Patrice said, rubbing her wrists. "I could use some detail here."

"Couldn't we all?" I murmured.

"I mean," Patrice continued, "I know Johnnie was going to run away with you, that you had stolen all this money. Then you got killed, and it was all off. Right?"

"Right, Patrice," Vinnie said. Patrice stared at him.

"How do you know my name?"

"Jennifer mentioned it," Vinnie said.

"He knew," Jennifer said. "He already knew."

Patrice shook her head. "Whatever. But you didn't get killed."

"No."

"So where have you been all this time? Why didn't you tell us you were still alive?"

This, right there, was the question on all our minds. Leave it to Patrice to cut to the chase.

"I had to stay dead," Vinnie said. "To arrange things. To make them better. For all of us."

"How is that?" Jennifer asked.

"I can't tell you now. Soon."

"How soon?"

"Tonight. When we get where we're going."

"Where *are* we going?" This was Patrice.

"You'll see. We're almost there. Sit back and enjoy the ride."

But Jennifer was not in a riding mood. "I understand that part," she said. Her voice was dead level now, controlled. Maybe too controlled. "You already explained that part to me. I get it. You were going to disappear, go off by yourself. You were going to ditch me and your friend Johnnie, and go off and roll in the money like a pig in shit. All by yourself. But the one thing I don't understand is why you didn't."

Vinnie was shaking his head sadly the whole time Jennifer was getting this out, as if he couldn't believe what he was hearing, how deluded people could be.

"No, no, you don't understand a thing. I wasn't trying to ditch you. I was taking control, throwing off pursuit. I was working behind the scenes, all the while, to make this happen. I was helping you, helping us all."

Jennifer Smeals went off like a magnesium flare. "You *cock-sucker*! You son of a *bitch*! You let us think you were dead! Yet the whole time you were there, watching us, fucking with us."

She stopped, panting, out of breath. Vinnie shrugged, smiled modestly, scratching under his cop hat.

"It was all for you," he said. "For all of us."

This overflow of revelations was slowly soaking into my brain. There were still parts I didn't understand, of course. Big parts.

"Let me see if I've got this straight," I said. I paused, trying to organize the few thoughts I had left. Patrice and Jennifer watched me expectantly, like the hostages back in the nail salon.

"You killed yourself," I began again, "so you could blame yourself for everything, while you got away."

"Something like that," Vinnie agreed.

"But what I don't understand is this: What was wrong with the first plan? I mean, who were you going to blame everything on the first time? And what happened?"

Jennifer twisted around in her seat. "It was going to be you, Johnnie. You know that."

Vinnie smirked, his eyes on the road for a change. "Oh no," he said unconvincingly. "Not you. Never you, Johnnie boy."

"We were setting you up," Jennifer continued, ignoring Vinnie.

"We were casting you as the big guy, the brains behind us. Improbable as that seems."

Vinnie looked around almost guiltily. "Malatesta never met you, Johnnie. What did he know?"

"Thanks for the vote of confidence," I said.

"Malatesta would go after you. While we went to the Caymans. I thought that was the plan." She gave Vinnie a dead, unreadable look. "I was wrong about that."

"The Caymans?" I asked. "What happened to Paraguay?"

Vinnie shrugged. "Things change. Circumstances alter. It's like crossing a creek on stones."

"*What!*" Jennifer gasped. She seemed stunned by Vinnie's comparison.

"They look different when you're out there, jumping on them. The stones do. You have to change your plan to suit their configuration. A midstream course correction for each one."

"Vincent, for Christ's sake, spare me this *bull*shit!"

Vinnie smiled, a hurt little smile. "It's not bullshit, Jennifer. I'm trying to explain things to you. I wish you'd try and understand."

"But it's not believable," I protested.

"You got that right," Patrice muttered.

"Who would believe—I mean, I'm not a bad guy or anything. I think I'm pretty smart about some things. But who would believe that Johnnie LoDuco was some kind of financial mastermind?"

"No one," Vinnie said. "You're right. No one would have believed that. That's why I didn't tell them who you were."

"You didn't tell them? Malatesta seemed to know all about me."

Vinnie shook his head again. "I told them you were Kenny Moleri."

"Kenny Moleri? Who is Kenny Moleri?"

"He's behind all this," Vinnie said. "It's all his fault. He stole the money and hid it."

"He killed you and cut off your head," Patrice suggested.

Vinnie thought about this a moment. "No. I did that myself. You all know that."

"We know it now," Jennifer said.

"Kenny Moleri?" I asked.

Vinnie nodded. "Kenny Moleri."

I brooded on Kenny Moleri for a while. We all did.

"But Vinnie," I whined after a decent interval, "what happened to your plan? The credit card–skim scam?"

"Oh that." Vinnie looked slightly embarrassed. "That was an earlier version of reality. We're living a different story now, a much better one."

"Better? How much better?" I asked.

"Twelve million dollars better," Vinnie said.

That was better.

"But if not the credit card scam, then where did this twelve million come from?" I insisted.

"The money from the Web sites. The gambling sites, the porno. It all went into the bank I had created," Vinnie explained, as if it was fucking obvious. "The International Investors Bank of the Cayman Islands."

"And the money from the fake stock," Jennifer put in. She still sounded plenty pissed off.

"And the stock," Vinnie agreed. "I sold stock in the Web sites. It was very popular. I was doing a public service, really, when you look at how eager people were to buy."

"Vincent and his imaginary IPO," Jennifer sneered.

A memory floated past and I grabbed it.

"Jennifer, I thought you told me Vinnie didn't know shit from shinola about computers. You told me his secretary had to turn his computer on for him."

Vinnie was shocked into silence, a rare occurrence. But Jennifer shrugged it off with a smile.

"I didn't want you to look at that," she said. "I thought you might figure out what was going on. I realize now I had nothing to worry about."

Thanks a lot, I thought.

"The Web sites must have been doing well," I said.

"Not really," Vinnie said. "A very moderate source of revenue."

"If the Web sites weren't making money, why were people so eager to invest in them?"

"The future, Johnnie. The future looked bright. Everybody wants to climb aboard a winner."

"But if not the Web sites, where did the money come from? The actual, real, nonvirtual money?"

Vinnie shrugged. "I paid off the early investors with the proceeds from the later ones. Keeping a commission for myself, of course. And, too, I borrowed some money from Malatesta."

"A cheap fucking Ponzi scheme," Jennifer said. "They always fall apart. Then you embezzle something to keep it afloat, and that falls apart. Then you go down, and you're lucky if you just get prison time, and restitution, and nobody tries to take it out of your hide. That's always the way it works."

Vinnie nodded. I could see he was hurt by the "cheap fucking Ponzi scheme" part.

"All right. But the trick is to get out in the nick of time, before it all collapses. It's a dance, tap dancing on a house of cards. And the true beauty of what I did was to create the bank and to make Malatesta believe in it. That is where you were such a help to me, Jennifer." He gave her the benefit of a big white smile. She didn't even look at him.

Vinnie twisted around in the driver's seat. "Jennifer was my bank representative to the cartel," he said. "A physical representative of the virtual bank. She was very convincing. A meeting with Jennifer was like a week's Caribbean vacation." His dazzling smile was wasted on her. She not only didn't look up, she turned her head and stared out the passenger window at the strip malls whizzing past.

It was just as well Vinnie couldn't see her face. I saw it, reflected back in the window glass, and it made my balls shrivel up like I had just stepped into ice-cold bathwater.

Patrice spoke up. "Wait a minute, wait a minute. *Create* the bank? So the online bank, the International Investors Bank of the Cayman Islands, isn't real?"

Vinnie shook his head. "A virtual bank. It should be real, though, brick and mortar real, a Caymans tax shelter, a money laundry," he said. "Such a great bank. Someone should start it up someday. Maybe I will." He swiveled around to face me again; the cop car drifted back and forth from lane to lane.

"How did it feel, Johnnie? To be a millionaire, a twelve-times millionaire? I was very generous, wasn't I? We all got twelve million to start with—you, me, Jennifer, Malatesta." His glance swept over to Patrice and took her in like a psychic tentacle. "If I had known you, Patrice, you would have gotten twelve million, too."

"You mean the money in Johnnie's name's not really there?"

"There *is* no 'there.' But the money is real."

"Where is it, then?"

"Ah." Vinnie looked smug. "That's for me to know and you to find out."

We sped along in the cop car. It was getting dark, clouding up. Big wet drops began to attack the windshield. Heat lightning glowed suddenly, and after a while, like something you almost forgot to say, the thunder rolled out.

We didn't have much company on this part of the island, not many houses, only a few streetlights. Pine trees billowed up along the shoulder on both sides of the road. The island always looks best in the dark, when you can't see all the houses and malls and expressways very well. Now it looked shadowy and romantic in the storm, only the lights of an occasional diner or pizzeria throwing green-and-orange dazzle over the wet roads.

I felt very spaced-out, dizzy, way out of touch with any conceivable reality. I looked over at Patrice; she seemed the same way herself.

"Ecstasy?" I said to her. She looked at me in astonishment.

"Isn't that what you take?" I asked. "At like a rave or something? Ecstasy, LSD, something like that. You gave me something like that, didn't you?"

She shook her head.

"It's real all right," Vinnie said over his shoulder.

"Look, Vinnie, Jennifer, please, do me one favor. Take off the fucking hats. Please. I can't take it."

They obliged. Jennifer's lipstick looked black in the road light. With all her hair cut away from around her face, she looked a lot older. You could see her high cheekbones, deeply sunken cheeks, her lack of flesh, a blond skeleton in a cop uniform. It didn't help the reverberating cold sense of unreality that gripped me.

"Where *are* we going?" I asked.

Vinnie sighed, the exasperated dad again. "The Hamptons," he said. "I have a house there. Under another name. They all know me as Mr. Delicious. From the restaurants I own of that name."

"Mr. Delicious," I repeated. I had never heard of these restaurants.

"No one will bother us there, Johnnie," Vinnie told me. "We can stay there. All this will go away. And Johnnie?"

"What, Vinnie?"

"All the people you knew in high school will be there. Your fifth-grade teacher, Mrs. Veal, you always liked her so much. She's there, Johnnie. They're all there."

I felt like a cartoon character, badly drawn and tiny. I looked over at Patrice; she was tiny, too. The silhouettes of Vinnie and Jennifer towered in the front seat.

"Vincent, for Christ's sake," Jennifer said disgustedly.

We drove down toward the Hamptons but stopped south of River-head, somewhere just past Flanders, at what looked like an abandoned ice-cream stand. It was built mostly out of glass and stainless steel; an enormous sheet-metal and dead-neon ice-cream cone angled up out of the front like a Nike missile. There was a face on the ice-cream cone, big smiling mouth and demented eyes. The head was a swirl of soft custard, the hair a drizzle of chocolate sauce.

"Mr. Delicious," Vinnie said. He drove the car around the back of the ice-cream stand and into a garage that stood there, its door gaping open.

Vinnie got out of the car. "This used to be a gas station before it was an ice-cream stand," he told us, leaning in the window. "Built back in the twenties. Rumrunners used it during Prohibition. Watch."

He reached over and pulled some sort of lever hidden in the shadows. Creaking and grinding noises came from the garage floor, but I couldn't see a thing.

Vinnie hopped back in the cop car. "Hang on, kids!" He put the car in gear and drove it at the back wall of the garage.

This is it, I thought. This is the part of the story where Vinnie goes batshit and kills us all. I felt Patrice grip hold of me, and I braced for impact.

But there was no impact. The wall of the garage had disappeared, and the big dark space that took its place was permeable to automobiles. We drove down some kind of ramp, made a hard right turn, and rocked to a stop.

"Coney Island, last stop, everybody off!" Vinnie called out gleefully. He jumped out of the car while I was still reassuring myself I wasn't dead. Stark white light jumped from a big bulb hanging down on an electrical cord and lit up a small concrete room. Vinnie stood by the switch, grinning. Our front bumper was inches from a wall with a door in it.

Vinnie walked over to this door and pushed it open. "Almost home now, folks."

Patrice frowned at the open door. "You expect us to just march in there? You must be out of your mind."

"Sorry." Vinnie reached around the door frame and flicked another switch. Now we could see a long tunnel, raw concrete walls lit by overhead bulbs in little steel cages.

"Where does that go?" Patrice asked.

"The end of the rainbow," Vinnie said.

"You first," said Patrice.

We emerged from the narrow, smelly, damp tunnel like rats teleported to another planet.

"Where the fuck are we?" Patrice asked. Jennifer Smeals stood there impatiently, raking cobwebs out of her hair and wiping her fingers on the wall.

Vinnie had vanished in the dark up ahead. Then lights came on overhead, revealing a wall made of big smooth river stones, it looked like, and a staircase leading up, made out of whole logs, with half logs for the risers.

"Welcome to Duck Blind Lodge," Vinnie said proudly.

We staggered up the stairs into a big dark room that lit up as Vinnie tweaked a switch somewhere. Lightbulbs glared down from a chandelier made of deer antlers. There was a big pool table in the middle of the room, under the chandelier, with carved and decorated legs as thick as tree trunks. A pool table from the Middle Ages. On top of the pool table, in the middle of about an acre of green velvet, was a big bag made of some pale leather.

We looked at Vinnie. Honestly, I was afraid to ask what was in the bag, after the last few weeks. I was afraid I would open it and find my own head staring out at me.

Vinnie smirked. He walked over to the pool table, zipped open the bag, and pulled out a stack of banknotes in paper collars. I couldn't see the denominations, but I could see that there were a lot more of them in the bag.

"Merry Christmas, kiddies," Vinnie said.

There was a half million dollars in the bag, Vinnie told us. This was our getaway money. This was the bag Jennifer thought I had found. I could have told her it never would have all fit in a box of laundry detergent.

"Where did this money come from?" Patrice sniffed. I could tell she was still not warming up to Vinnie. She was a tough audience.

"I have Jennifer to thank for most of it," Vinnie said, smirking. "Her presentation as the stateside representative of the International Investors Bank of the Cayman Islands, Ltd., was so stellar that a decision was made to redirect additional revenue streams to it."

"The money from the Web sites, the porno and gambling sites," Jennifer explained. "Most of the money was from the fake stock. But the pages themselves did produce some income."

A memory rose to the surface of my thoughts like a used condom from a plugged toilet.

"Vinnie, you stole my books!" I accused him. "*The Sisterhood of the Tongue*. My stroke books."

Vinnie didn't flinch. "I introduced them to a wider audience. And here's the result." He swept his arm over the leather carry bag. "Your royalties."

"You were going to give them to me?"

"Oh come on, Johnnie," I heard Patrice mutter.

"Of course I was," Vinnie said, slightly hurt that anyone would think otherwise.

"Wow," I said. "What's my share?"

"You'll get what's coming to you. But not right away. This money is for the common good now," Vinnie said. He squinted, and I knew a philosophical lecture/sermon was building up and heading my way.

"Johnnie, you shouldn't think of money in physical, limited terms," Vinnie said. "As actual and particular dollar bills with your name on them. Money is speedy, Johnnie, faster than sound, and thinking of it in those terms just slows it down."

"Actual physical dollar bills not in Vinnie's bank account," Patrice put in helpfully.

"You have to let money find its own way, Johnnie," Vinnie said, ignoring the interruption. "You follow. If you try too hard to grab onto it, it floats away. But if you empty yourself out and just follow in the wake of money, it will accumulate faster than you can imagine. It's like so many things in this world. You have to take your ego out of the equation, and it all comes to you."

"You're really something, Vincent," Jennifer said, smiling. "You should bottle it."

"I've thought about going on the lecture circuit," Vinnie said seriously. "What has worked for me can work for others."

Jennifer nodded. "Ripping off Malatesta. He couldn't possibly kill everyone. Yes, I see what you mean. If enough people steal him blind, he wouldn't know who to shoot first."

I realized I knew something Jennifer Smeals didn't know, possibly a first. But before I could say anything one way or the other, Patrice yawned and changed the subject.

"All this shooting and driving and talking makes me so thirsty!" she said. "Is there anything to drink in this place?"

Duck Blind Lodge was pretty cool, even aside from its decor of leather bags holding vast amounts of money. It was an old-style tavern with a rustic feel, a clubhouse built for rich people sometime back in the 1920s. No ceiling; exposed rafters, rough but handsome woodwork, everything made out of tree parts with the bark left on, and stray pieces of wild animals. An actual duck boat was hung over the bar like a canopy, its blind of rushes dried out and falling to pieces, glued together by spiderwebs.

Another rough log staircase led up to the second floor, where the old guest rooms were. Vinnie told us he'd fixed up a couple for our night's stay. I have to admit I was looking forward to that part. It had been an exhausting day.

There was food at Duck Blind Lodge, too: fresh food, not ramen noodles and stale Cheerios. There were things to drink—beer, vino, booze, bottles of water. Vinnie had done well. He stood behind the bar, dispensing drinks and smiling. All he needed was a white jacket.

We sat around the room, eating and drinking. The leather money bag lorded it over the middle of the pool table, a wedding cake, an extra supersize party favor, the guest of honor. I think nobody wanted to let it—or anyone else in the room—out of sight for a minute.

Later, we all stood on a second-floor balcony, looking out toward the water, which we could see through the trees and waterweeds and rushes across the street. The Mr. Delicious sign was off to one side, silhouetted against the sky.

Vinnie looked out over the water, sipping his drink.

"All that water," he said, "and all those bodies."

"Bodies?"

"Drowned men. Bodies in sacks. Corpses dumped off boats. The whole floor of the bay has been a dumping ground for years."

"Body parts," I said. "Heads."

Vinnie nodded. "Arms, legs, feet. Mafia bodies, serial killers' bodies. Man kills his girlfriend; she's been fucking his best friend. What does he do with the body? Dumps her in the bay."

"Vincent, don't even worry about it," Jennifer Smeals said.

Patrice was smiling to herself, a little wry smile. I could see what she was thinking. She was thinking about Bogdan, and how he would never waste a good body by dumping it in the bay. Jennifer sniffed loudly and snubbed out her Marlboro on the deck railing.

"I don't believe it," she said. "How do you know this?"

"One night of the year, every year," Vinnie said, ignoring her, "all the bodies glow. They give off light. Blue light."

"Like glow-in-the-dark jellyfish," I suggested.

He nodded. "Something like that. They glow. Down under the water. If you go up in a helicopter so you can view the whole bay at once, you can see by the blue corpse light where all the bodies are. It's an impressive spectacle."

"You've seen it?"

Vinnie nodded some more.

"I think I heard something about that," I said. "Or read, or something. But I've never seen it."

"Not many people have. Seen it and known it for what it was, I mean. Known that it was the bodies of all those murdered people signaling where they were."

"Is it only murdered people who glow?" Patrice asked. "What about drowned people, accidental drownings? What about people who ran their boats into pilings, or got shit-faced and fell overboard and no one ever found their bodies? Do they glow, too?"

Vinnie said nothing. I could see he didn't know. Vinnie hated not having the answer to something. Finally, he made a sour face and poured his drink over the side of the deck.

"It's possible," he said. "I have no information on that subject."

Silence came down on us. Insects whirred and chirped in the woods behind the lodge. Occasionally, a car went past. You could hear the water of the bay surging and slapping out of sight.

After a while, I couldn't take it anymore.

"So Vinnie," I said, as bright and happy as I could be, "what's next? Where do we go from here?"

Vinnie stared into his empty glass. "Someone's coming for us," he said. "To take us away from all this."

Patrice nodded. "All this shooting and lying."

"Who?" I asked. "Who's coming? When?"

"Tomorrow," Vinnie said. "Tomorrow night. Eleven P.M., at the dock down behind the restaurant. I've arranged for a boat to come for us. We'll be taken to a safe haven."

"Where is that?" I really wanted to know.

"The Cayman Islands," Vinnie said. "I know some people there."

"Real people or virtual people?" asked Patrice.

"Real people. Good people. They'll take care of us."

"For a price," Jennifer added.

Vinnie nodded. "Why you can trust them. There are four berths waiting for us." He looked at me significantly. "That should prove my intentions once and for all. I've been planning this for years. All the little details are falling into place now."

"What will we do in the Caymans?" I asked.

"A nice Caribbean vacation for all of us," Vinnie said. "And from the Caymans, who knows? Brazil? Cuba?"

"Paraguay?" I suggested.

"*Paraguay.* Fuck Paraguay. The country's run by Nazis. There's no saltwater there. I would never live in Paraguay."

"I kind of liked Paraguay myself," Jennifer half-whispered. We all stared down into our drinks, swirling ice cubes thoughtfully.

Patrice broke the silence with a sudden loud yawn, like a police siren warming up.

"Excuse me! I am just so tired after all this . . ."

"Bullshit?" Jennifer suggested.

"That's it." Patrice nodded. "But if I go in and lie down, how do I know you're not going to come sneaking up in the middle of the night and cut my head off? How do I know I'm not going to get up in the morning and find that everybody's gone and left a pile of heads on the pool table?"

"Lock your door," suggested Jennifer.

"We're all in this together, Patrice," Vinnie said. His attitude now was one of righteously injured feelings, manfully put aside for the greater good. "No one's going to hurt you. Lie down, get some rest. We'll see you in the morning."

"I should go, too," Jennifer said, looking after Patrice. "I haven't slept in a couple days. I am completely exhausted. You'll be in soon?" This to Vinnie.

"In a few minutes," Vinnie said. "I want to talk to Johnnie some more."

Jennifer stopped in the doorway. It was clear she hated to leave us alone.

"You sure you'll be all right out here?" she said to Vinnie.

"Of course," Vinnie said, giving a careless wave of his hand. "Get some sleep. We have the big boat ride tomorrow."

Reluctantly, she closed the French window and went off to bed. I'll bet anything she sneaked off somewhere and put a wineglass to the wall, though. I would have.

———

The night was thick and heavy, with more thunderstorms in it, though it had stopped raining. Vinnie and I hung over the railing, staring out over wet trees toward the water.

"So Vinnie."

"Yo."

"Here we are, huh?"

"Here we are, Johnnie." He put his hand on my shoulder and shook me a little. "I always said we'd end up in the Hamptons, didn't I?"

"Flanders is not the Hamptons, Vinnie."

Vinnie shrugged. "It's the East End, isn't it? Anyway, there're too many people, too many fucking nosy people, in the Hamptons. I don't want to advertise my existence."

I could see why not. "This is a pretty cool house, though," I said, looking back at the main room of Duck Blind Lodge with its bar and deer antlers and bags full of money. "How long have you owned this place?"

Vinnie gave me one of his "significant" looks. "I don't own it, Johnnie. You do."

I can't say I was ready for this, but I had been shot at, terrified, and bewildered so much in the past twenty-four hours that I didn't have the resources to feel surprised anymore.

"How's that?"

"The owner of record is Kenny Moleri. Kenny Moleri is you. You are, according to your passport here, a Mr. Kenneth Moleri of Patchogue, New York." Vinnie took a blue U.S. passport out of his pocket and held it up, the way a magician holds up the magic card. He tossed it to me and I plucked it out of the air like a bat snapping up a mosquito.

"Who is Kenny Moleri?" I asked, not for the first time. The picture in the passport was me, without a doubt. It looked like my high school yearbook photo, but the expression was more worried.

"Computer programmer," Vinnie said. "He used to work for me." I knew from past experience that this little factoid was unlikely to be the whole story, or any of it. I wondered where Kenny Moleri was now, and how he got there. I could imagine his bones glowing bluely beneath about six feet of bay water. I thought about his skull rolling like a gutter ball down the deep channel that runs out Fire Island Inlet to the ocean. I didn't think I would have to worry about running into him.

"If I am Kenny Moleri," I said, "who does that make you?"

"The old Vinnie McCloskey-Schmidt is dead," Vinnie said. "Dead and buried."

"Actually, cut in pieces and chucked in the water," I said.

Vinnie didn't touch this. "Moleri killed him. He killed you."

"Who killed Moleri?"

Vinnie smirked. "I did. He was going to expose me to Malatesta, hand me in to save his own ass. He got scared, what we were doing. So I killed him. I told Malatesta he was really Vinnie McCloskey-Schmidt. I told him I was really you. Then I killed you."

"Thanks a lot."

"I erased the whole fucking blackboard so we could start over, without encumbrances."

"Like embezzlement, or murder."

"We rise from our graves," he intoned.

"Like zombies in a horror flick."

"And start our new lives. New names, new addresses, new accomplishments."

"New money," I said. Same old bullshit, I thought.

A car went by on the road below, sending up big rooster tails of water from the puddles left by the storm. Normally, I would have been standing on the curb and gotten a faceful. My normal luck, I mean. But now I was standing on the balcony of Duck Blind Lodge, looking down on it all.

Still, it seemed way too good to be true. My mind scurried around like a rat in a frying pan, looking for the flaw, the false bottom.

"Vinnie, what about the cops? They're going to miss us, right? When you don't show up at the station with us in chains. Are they going to come looking for us?"

Vinnie smiled sourly. "Don't worry about the cops. They've got Bogdan. That should make them happy. As far as you and your girlfriend, I left instructions with my lieutenants. My police contacts."

"Carbone?"

Vinnie nodded. "My main man."

I still wasn't completely relaxed about this. "What about Malatesta's guys? I mean, I know Malatesta is lawn food. Carbone filled me in. But aren't you worried this new guy will come after you?"

"I am the new guy," Vinnie said.

"You? *You're* the new guy?" My head had never really stopped spinning since this whole thing began, but it had slowed down some from fatigue. Now it cranked up to warp speed. "How can that be? I thought these guys were trying to kill you."

"I sold myself to them as someone who could undo the many mistakes of Malatesta. They hate failure."

"Do they know who you really are?"

Vinnie shook his head. "I wasn't frank with them. It didn't seem like a good idea."

"But how? I mean, didn't they recognize you?"

"Oh, no, they didn't know what I looked like. They didn't even know I existed. Malatesta never told them about me. He took all the credit for what I did. And when it fell apart, Malatesta did his best to cover up the whole thing. He thought he could put things right before they found out. So I never appeared in it."

"If they find out it's you who took their money, it's your ass."

"Oh, they know who took their money."

"They do? How did they find out?"

Vinnie smirked. "I told them. I told them they were ripped off by Vinnie McCloskey-Schmidt."

"You ratted yourself out?"

Vinnie nodded. "Part of my job," he said, then stopped for a moment. "My new assignment," he continued, as if that cleared something up, "my new assignment is to catch Vinnie McCloskey-Schmidt."

"So you're being sent to catch yourself."

Vinnie beamed at me, the lucky witness to his crowning achievement. But there was more to come.

"So who did you tell them you were?" I asked.

Vinnie stopping smirking and nodding. He got serious and stared at me for a moment before he answered.

"I told them I was you," he said.

Suddenly, it all became clear to me.

"That's why you dumped your cousin Vinnie's body parts in the bay!" I said. "So when they were found, the cartel would think you'd killed yourself!"

Vinnie watched me expressionlessly. "That's right," he said.

"But when I brought up the head, that was too soon." "That's right."

"So you wanted the head back to plant it again. So you could find it at the right time," I blundered on, then stopped.

There was quite a bit of silence for a while.

"You really fucked me up, Johnnie," Vinnie said. "But it's all right now. I forgive you. It was a challenge, really, to see if I could change course in midstride. But I did. I rose to the occasion. Everything's looking up. By this time tomorrow, we'll be on the high seas, heading for a new life."

"What about Vinnie's head?"

"We'll take care of that before we go."

CHAPTER FIFTEEN

I SLEPT LATE THE next morning. It seemed like I woke up every few minutes, covered with sweat. Patrice would be lying beside me, talking in her sleep and twitching.

But the last time I woke up, she was gone. Bright sun was pouring in the window. I was alone.

I jumped into my pants and went hopping out onto the landing, still pulling them on. Down in the big main room, Patrice, Jennifer, and Vinnie all looked up at me, grinning.

"Rise and shine," Vinnie called. "The big day is today."

"Morning, Johnnie." Patrice smiled. "Your fly is open."

Jennifer Smeals smiled, too, but didn't say anything.

Big waves of relief washed over me. I'd really expected everyone would be gone, leaving me not holding the bag. I thumped down the wide log staircase.

"Morning, everybody," I said brightly. "Tried to get a head start on me, huh?"

Nobody laughed, but at least they didn't get up and leave.

———

After a great breakfast—Vinnie was a good cook, no doubt about that—we all lay around the main room like fat, lazy dogs.

The bag with the money—Vinnie told us over breakfast it was genuine pigskin, cost a fortune in its own right—was discreetly zipped and snapped up, slumping in its own armchair like a passed-out party guest.

It was a scene of calm and golden domesticity.

Naturally, I couldn't leave it alone.

"So, Jennifer," I said, lounging back in my chair like a fucking pasha, "I probably shouldn't ask you this."

"Then don't."

"But I feel like I need to know. Just for the record. Did you know about this? This secret plan?"

Jennifer looked seriously pissed off. "You know I didn't."

"Just let it go, Johnnie," Vinnie advised, lying on the couch with his eyes closed, scratching his head. "Time for us all to move forward."

"But why did you save my ass? Why didn't you let Malatesta have me, or Stosh, for that matter? Was it my good looks or my jokes?"

Jennifer leaned forward in her lounge chair. She looked like she wanted to jump out of it and beat me to death, but politeness restrained her.

"When I thought Vincent was dead"—she shot him a look like twin ice picks—"I felt like I needed help. I needed you, Johnnie! You were the only place I had to go to."

"Plus, you thought I knew where the backup money was," I pointed out.

"I couldn't just let Malatesta and his goons kick the snot out of you," she said, but even I couldn't believe her.

"She needed you for the same reason they need you now," Patrice put in. "To blame everything on." She looked around the room. "Can't you see that?"

This seemed to be going in a bad direction. But before I could think of how to make things better, there was a sort of strangled yelp from Vinnie.

"God damn it!" He grimaced and clawed at his scalp.

"Vincent, don't scratch it," Jennifer said, momlike. "You'll pull them right out."

"Itches like a motherfucker," Vinnie said. "Can't you do something about it?"

"There may be some infection," Jennifer said, going over to Vinnie and looking very serious. She was obviously about to segue into her doctor persona.

"Let's take a look," she said, steering Vinnie into a chair. He sat down and leaned back like someone in a dentist's chair, scooting down so the top of his head was level with Jennifer's chin. She bent over, peering at his scalp, parting his thinning hairs with her long white fingers.

"Yes, it's infected all right," she said. "Sit tight. Let me get some things." Jennifer straightened up and left the room, walking fast.

Vinnie rolled his head over to me and winked. "Soon, Johnnie, soon. We'll all be out of here and living like kings."

"How do kings live?" Patrice asked. She didn't sound very happy about being a king.

"And queens," Vinnie said graciously.

Patrice shook her head. That was not what she'd meant, apparently.

"Kings always have to watch out for assassinations," Patrice said. "Kings have tasters so they don't get poisoned, bodyguards so they don't get stabbed or shot. Kings have to worry about the people rising up and cutting off their head. I'm just not sure I want to be a fucking king."

Vinnie sat up and turned around to face Patrice.

"I hear what you're saying, Patrice," he said, his tone very serious. " 'Uneasy lies the head that wears the crown,' right?"

"Whatever."

"But you don't have to be a king or live like one," Vinnie said. "With the money we'll have, you can be anything you want. Money is not about stuff, Patrice. It's about freedom. The freedom to be yourself."

I could tell Patrice was not buying this. She stared at Vinnie and looked like she was about to say something harsh. But before she could, and before I could butt in, Jennifer Smeals marched back into the room carrying a little black case.

"Vincent, lie back and I'll take a look at this," she said. She pushed him back in the chair gently but firmly.

Vinnie folded his hands on his chest and settled down, a little smirk on his face.

Jennifer opened the black case, pulled over another chair, and laid out some tools on a little white towel. I couldn't see them very well, but they looked something like dentist's tools. What do hair-replacement specialists use? I wondered. Big needles? Scalpels? I had no idea.

She bent over Vinnie's head, probing at the crown of it. "This looks bad," she said. "I'll have to lance the abscess."

"Will it hurt?" Vinnie asked, the big pussy.

"Hardly at all," Jennifer said. She picked up one of the silver instruments, one that looked like the pick thing a dentist sticks in your gums, but longer and thicker, and in one smooth, powerful motion drove it into Vinnie's skull, just at the point where the spine meets the cranium. She put some shoulder into it.

Vinnie's eyes opened up, big and round. His arms shot down by his side and his heels drummed on the floor. Little convulsions ran up and down his body. They stopped. His head flopped over to one side.

Vinnie didn't move anymore.

Jennifer leaned over him, felt his neck for a pulse.

Patrice and I were both on our feet now.

"You killed him!" Patrice shouted.

Smeals didn't look up from Vinnie's scalp. She was working away with her little scalpel now, removing strands of hair like seaweed and placing them in a little white enamel dish she'd taken out of her black case.

"Very good," she said with deep sarcasm. "Brilliant, just brilliant. Yes, Vincent is dead. Really fucking dead this time. And there's nothing you can do about it."

"What's with the hairs, Jennifer?" I asked. "It's a little late for a hair-replacement strategy."

That made her laugh. "You're so funny, Johnnie. If you really want to know, I can tell you." She lifted another hair carefully into the dish, as if it weighed a thousand pounds, then straightened up.

"These are synthetic hairs. I made them. They're like bank statements," she said. I must have looked a little confused, because she added, "Or ATM cards. Each one has account information coded into it, information I can read off them under a microscope. Information that will tell me where Vincent put the money."

"His money," I said.

"Our money," said Patrice.

"*My* money," Jennifer Smeals said.

"Why didn't you just write them down?" I asked. "The codes."

"This was Vincent's idea," Jennifer said, lifting hairs up from the enamel dish with her scalpel thingy and sliding them into a letter-size envelope. "He didn't want any record that anyone could get their hands on. At first, he told me he would hide the codes in one of his fake Web sites. You saw those?"

Patrice and I nodded.

"But even that was too exposed for Vincent. Then he came up with this brilliant plan. Why I went along with it, I will never know."

"Vinnie had that effect on people," I said, looking at his body all twisted up in the chair. He didn't look like he was asleep; he looked like he'd been fucking murdered and wasn't too happy about it.

Patrice looked sullen and pissed off. It was hard to blame her.

"Why did you have to kill him?" she said. "Don't you already know the codes?"

Jennifer shook her head. I could see this part bothered her. "Too many. Too long to memorize reliably. He dictated them to me as I made the hairs, then made me destroy the records."

"And you did?"

Smeals nodded. "It was for us, after all. For both of us."

"You trusted him," I said.

She nodded. "That was a mistake."

That was an understatement.

A thought occurred to me, a real motherfucker. That didn't happen that often, and I was eager to share.

"What makes you think those accounts are the real accounts?" I asked Jennifer. "They could be dummies, too. I mean, the coded accounts themselves could be a kind of code for the real accounts, just something to help Vinnie remember where the money really is."

I could see that this got to her. It would have been just like Vinnie to pull something like that, and she knew it.

I kept pushing. "Only Vinnie would know where the accounts were, but you just killed him."

Jennifer carefully sealed the envelope with the hairs in it, staring at me and Patrice as she licked the flap. She put the envelope in the little black bag, then began tossing her hair-restoring tools in after it.

"I know more than you think," she said, and I could see her confidence starting to come back. Too bad. "I know more than Vincent knew I knew. Not everything. Not the whole picture. But enough to do this by myself."

"So where do we go from here?" I asked. It seemed like a reasonable question.

"*We* don't go anywhere," Jennifer said. "*I'm* getting on that boat. *You* are staying right here."

"Where is this boat going? Is it for real?"

"It's for real. I think. You never know with Vincent."

"You're probably not really going to the Caymans, though, right?" I suggested. "I mean, that would be too obvious."

Jennifer Smeals shrugged. "What difference does that make to you? You're not going anywhere. You're staying right here for the cops to play with." She snapped her bag closed and smiled at us, a nasty tight-lipped lizard smile.

Patrice gave a funny half-strangled little yell and launched herself at Jennifer Smeals. Oh shit, I thought, this is where Patrice gets scalpeled to death, but Jennifer pulled some kind of move on Patrice I couldn't really see—it all happened so fast—and Patrice caromed off Vinnie's body, flew across the room, and smacked into the wall.

Vinnie slid off the chair and rolled onto the floor. His eyes were wide open and staring at nothing. The dentist's pick in the back of his head kept his face turned toward me.

Patrice bounced off the wall in what I thought was a pretty good move and came back at Jennifer, but Jennifer jumped up into a sideways kung fu–type kick and met her halfway with a boot heel. Patrice went down on the floor next to Vinnie.

During all this, I just stood there like a piece of shit on a stick. I know, I should have done something. But I was just frozen, all right? It all happened too fast for me.

Jennifer reached into her little black bag and came out with a small black gun. Worm Lips's piece, I thought. I remembered her picking it up after putting him down with her little lead pipe.

She pointed Worm Lips's gun at me.

"Well, Johnnie," Jennifer said, watching me carefully. "Here we are, alone together."

"Just you and me," I said. She didn't say anything, kept bearing down on me with the little piece. She held it the right way up, bracing her wrist with her free hand, shooting-range style.

"I can see why you had to kill him," I said. "He wouldn't have put up with this solo shit. He was a 'share the wealth' kind of guy."

Jennifer shot me a strange look. I know, I know—under the circumstances, any look would have been strange. But I knew that look. It said, I can't fucking believe how dumb he is.

I was right.

"You know, Johnnie," she said, shaking her head, "you don't get it, do you? You just don't get it."

She was right. I had no clue what she was talking about.

"Get what?" I said.

She stared at me some more, not saying anything. I think she was savoring my stupidity like a rare vintage.

"He was using you, too, Johnnie. You know that."

"We were going to South America together," I said. Even to me, it sounded stupid and unconvincing.

Jennifer ignored this. "He *was* you, Johnnie. Vincent became you. He was you right down to his fingertips. He stole you, Johnnie."

"What do you mean, 'stole'?"

"Your name. Your passport. Your Social Security number, your everything. Your personality, if that's what that is. Haven't you figured that out yet?"

"My record?" He could have had that for the asking.

As usual, Jennifer didn't pick up on my little comedy riffs. She took it straight. "That made him angry," she said thoughtfully. "It was like you were sullying his creation, getting arrested like that. But it was such penny-ante stuff, he decided it didn't matter.

"But he couldn't have two Johnnie LoDucos walking around." Jennifer paused again so we could both bask in the horror of this. "So he tried to kill you off."

I thought about it. "He didn't try very hard."

"He wanted it to get done, but he wanted somebody else to do it. Without getting his hands dirty. And Vincent really loved to manipulate people, get them to do things he wanted them to. He would get inside your head and steer you around like a big robot. Even if he didn't care about what you did, he got a big thrill out of making you do it. That's how he was. The little cocksucker."

I knew we were getting into personal reminiscence now. She looked down at Vinnie lying on the floor and gave his head a sideways soccer-style kick. I jumped a foot; the head didn't move much.

While Jennifer was preoccupied with Vinnie, I moved out of the line of fire, as much as I could. I also saw something Jennifer didn't.

Patrice rolled over and got up like a groggy fighter. She launched herself at Jennifer Smeals, wrapping around her legs.

Jennifer wobbled but didn't go down. She twisted out of Patrice's grasp, stepped back, and launched another sideways kick, a real good one this time. Her boot heel caught Patrice right in the forehead, in almost the same spot as last time. Patrice's eyes rolled up and she went down again.

While all this martial-arts action was going on, Jennifer Smeals held her gun up in the air, probably without thinking about it. She looked very stylish. But the crucial point was that the barrel was no longer pointing in my direction.

I stepped forward and took the gun away from her. We were both surprised by that.

Her foot came around in a wide head-high kick, but my unexpected move had thrown her timing off. I stepped back; she missed me by a cunt hair. I still had the gun. I pointed it at her.

Jennifer went into a sideways fighter's crouch, arms cocked and ready, moving like snakes. She looked up at me intently, eyes flat, mouth slightly open.

Then a smile slowly cut into her face. Her stance relaxed a bit.

"Come on, Johnnie," she said. "Put the gun down, all right? We don't have to do it like this."

"How do we have to do it?"

"The boat's on its way here, Johnnie," Jennifer said. "They're expecting two people. That can be you and me, Johnnie."

I shook my head. "They're expecting four people. Vinnie told them we were coming."

"Don't be a moron, Johnnie. Vincent never told them that. He never meant for you to come along."

"Bullshit," I said, and I meant it.

"Vincent put a lot of money in those accounts," Jennifer said, moving closer. "More than enough for two people to live on."

"I could just shoot your ass now and live off it myself," I told her.

Her grin got wider, revealing teeth.

"You wouldn't be able to read the account numbers. Only I can do that for you. Besides, I know you. You won't shoot me, Johnnie. I know that." She straightened out and took a step toward me, holding out her hand for the gun.

That's how much she knew. I shot her in the forehead, in just about the same spot her boot heel had caught Patrice. She went over backward, looking surprised.

———

After awhile, Patrice sat up, holding her head. She looked at Jennifer Smeals lying on the floor for quite a while before it sank in. Then her eyes got wide.

"Johnnie, holy shit," she said. "You shot her." She took her hand down. There were two little shield-shaped marks on her forehead where Jennifer Smeals's boot had whacked into her.

"You bet your ass I did," I said. I noticed that I was sitting on the floor. My hand was shaking badly. It was like looking at a hand and arm on a TV with really bad reception; I felt no connection to this arm. Worm Lips's little black gun was lying on the floor in front of me like an alien life-form. "I just got really tired of her kicking people in the head."

"Do you think it's true?" Patrice said. "About the boat?"

We were racing around Duck Blind Lodge like demented weasels, trying to scrape together something to travel in and taking care of some important last-minute business. Everything we had carefully packed was spread out all over the island, at Bogdan's, Aunt Vivienne's, who knew where. We had zip to wear.

Vinnie and Jennifer hadn't been any better prepared than we were. All we could find was a gym bag with dirty clothes in it and a cardboard box with some of Vinnie's clothes.

"I think so," I said. "You never know with Vinnie. Jennifer seemed to think it was for real. But we'll find out soon."

So far, our luggage consisted of the gym bag, a brown paper grocery bag (the kind with handles), and the pigskin bag with the half mil inside.

It would do.

Patrice and I leaned over the balcony railing and looked anxiously out at the water. It was getting dark already—it had been a really busy day.

"Johnnie!" Patrice whispered. "What's that light?"

Coming into view was a triangle of lights, green and white, with a boat's hull dimly visible, a ghost yacht skimming across the Peconic to carry us away.

As we stared at this shadow yacht, the top light in the triangle, a white light like a little star, blinked out, then on again. It did this three times. Then all the lights went out.

"That's it," I said. "Let's go."

Patrice went on down the cellar stairs, carrying our pitiful luggage. I picked up a squat red-and-yellow gasoline can, the kind you keep in the trunk in case you run out of gas. Unscrewing the cap, I laid a trail of gasoline back to the pool table.

Patrice had been surprised by the amount of gasoline we found in Duck Blind Lodge. "What was Vinnie doing with all that gas? Opening a gas station?" she'd asked.

I'd shrugged. "That restaurant used to be a gas station," I'd reminded her.

Patrice had given me a funny look. It was clear she felt sorry for me.

"You never give up, do you, Johnnie?"

There was a big pile of stuff we had put under the pool table, fireplace logs and bundles of newspaper, wrapped with string and soaked in gas. There were five-gallon jerricans of gas and kerosene and some kind of cleaning fluid I hoped was flammable. On top of the pool table were Jennifer Smeals, Vinnie McCloskey-Schmidt, and Vinnie's cousin's head.

Back by the head of the cellar stairs, I took out a matchbook and lit a match, looked at it, then set the whole book on fire, watching the match heads light up in quick succession. When the matchbook was burning nicely, I dropped it on the gasoline trail and closed the cellar door behind me.

Patrice was waiting for me at the bottom of the stairs. I hefted the pigskin bag and we took off through the tunnel.

As we were going out through the Mr. Delicious garage, I happened to notice a mayonnaise jar resting on a shelf by the window. I don't know why, but something in it caught my eye. When I picked up the jar and tilted it to the faint beam of streetlight coming through the dirty glass, I saw what was in it. The jar was filled with teeth, the roots all rusty with dried blood, a couple gold fillings showing.

I took it along.

The boat was there, all right, about seventy feet of gleaming white reality, moored in the moonlight off the Mr. Delicious dock. A rowboat was tied up to the dock itself, and two men were there, one sitting in the boat, the other standing on the dock, waiting, looking at his watch.

The skipper had one of those tough, Waspy faces you see sometimes—wide, thin-lipped mouth, chin like the business end of a tugboat. He wore a blue blazer and a captain's hat, just like a dentist on the bridge of his Chris-Craft. He carried it off better, though.

"Mr. LoDuco?" the guy in the captain's hat said, stepping forward and sticking out a hand as big as Bogdan's.

"That's me," I said with more confidence than I felt.

We shook hands. I had to put the pigskin case down first then shift the mayo jar of teeth to my other hand; I'd forgotten I was carrying it.

"Captain," I said in my best imitation Vinnie voice, "my two associates won't be able to make it after all."

The skipper looked slightly puzzled.

"I don't recall . . . ," he started to say, but I waved my hand.

"It doesn't matter. Here we are. May we come aboard?"

The captain stepped aside, and Patrice and I hopped off the dock into the rowboat, the guy in the boat helping us. The captain followed, and we shoved off.

The rowboat's oars stirred up the glow-in-the-dark jellyfish, which pulsed bluely.

"It's so cool how they do that," Patrice whispered, dragging her hand in the water.

"So long as it's just the jellyfish," I said.

The high side of the yacht loomed over us. We scrambled up a ladder, the rowboat guy handing up our bags.

"You had better get below," the captain told us. We ducked through a small door—I guess I should call it a hatch—staggered down a narrow ladder, tossed the luggage onto a bunk, and sat down. Almost immediately, the big diesels of the cruiser roared alive and the boat pulled off its moorings.

Patrice looked at me oddly. "What was all that about?" she asked. "Up on deck?"

I shrugged. "Just checking."

She stared at me, her expression one I couldn't read.

"You were good, Johnnie," she said after a minute or two. "You sounded just like him." Then she noticed the jar. "What is that? What are you carrying?"

I held it up. "Teeth."

"Uck. Teeth? Whose teeth?"

"Vinnie's teeth, I guess. The other Vinnie."

"What are you going to do with teeth?"

I had no idea.

"A souvenir," I said.

———

The boat was long and old, all wood, beautifully built, teak deck, brass fittings. It must have been eighty years old, a real yacht, not some fiberglass and plastic piece of shit.

We ran out of the bay without lights, the captain sweating and concentrating up on the bridge. (Bridge, bow, belowdecks—I learned this boat stuff quickly, like I was born to it.)

Patrice and I stood in the stern, watching the lights of Long Island fade behind us as we motored quietly out of Peconic Bay. Duck Blind Lodge was a little spot of orange fire on the distant shore. As we watched, the light died down and went out.

"Fire department must have come," Patrice said.

"Don't bet on it," I said. "Probably just the angle; something came between us and it. Duck Blind Lodge will burn forever. That wood was seriously dried out, like just waiting for a match." I shook my head sadly. "I hated to do that, torch that place. That was a great building."

"A nice funeral pyre for your friend," she whispered.

I thought about Vinnie and Jennifer, side by side on the pool table in the middle of the lounge area, the head between them, flames beginning to whoosh around them. I had to agree.

I went over to the railing and took the mayo jar of teeth out of my pocket. It stuck, and I almost lost it over the side, but then I got it out and took the lid off. Picking them out one by one, I dropped the teeth into the wake of the yacht. Some of them stuck to the side of the jar—from the blood, I guess—and I had to whack the jar with the heel of my hand like a catsup bottle to get them to come out. But eventually, they all rolled into the bay.

Patrice watched in silence. Nothing seemed to surprise her anymore, and who could blame her?

"Why did you do that?" she asked me when the teeth were gone.

I shrugged. "I don't know. An offering. To Vinnie. To the past. To just get this over with." I tossed the empty jar after the teeth.

"So long, buddy," I said to the white water streaming out behind the boat.

Back in the cabin, we sat on one of the bunk beds, like kids after a birthday party, stunned, tired, really crashing now from the adrenaline and sugar high.

"How much of what Vinnie said was true?" Patrice asked.

"We'll never be sure. But I tell you what."

"What?"

"The money's real."

Patrice put her hand over her mouth. "Oh shit," she said behind her fingers. "I bet it's not." She put her hand down. "Johnnie, let's look. Let's make sure it's not Monopoly money, or pieces of newspaper or something."

So we emptied the gym bag onto a bunk and unwrapped every stack of bills. They were real all right, every one of them.

Patrice sat down right in the middle of the pile. Her eyes were wide and stunned.

"I was never into money, you know?" she said. "I never really thought about it, never really cared. But this, there's so much of it!" She picked up handfuls and dropped them over me, over herself.

I reached over and gave her a push in the shoulder, not hard. But she went over backward into the money pile, her arms above her head, smiling up at me.

We rolled around in the bills all night as the yacht steamed south to the Caribbean. There is something about making love in the middle of half a million dollars, something we couldn't resist. Not that we tried that hard.

For months afterward, when I would pull out a bill to pay for something, rice or fish or fruit, this smell would waft out of the wallet, and the person at the market stall would look at me funny. The smell of us. I liked that. It made the bills seem less cold, less blood-covered.

Less Vinnie, more us.

"Money buys you the freedom to be someone else," Patrice says, and so far she's been right.

You'll want to know about our new island life. Not the Caymans—that would be too obvious, right? But not too far away. I'm not going to say where exactly. In the Caribbean somewhere. It's like Long Island, I guess, with the beaches and the water. Except everyone is black, and there are palm trees, and not nearly so many houses.

Patrice and I keep a low profile here. We take only so much as we need. Vinnie's pigskin bag is holding up well. The tourist credit card rake-off Patrice set up at the hotel where she works generally provides enough to live off without going into the bag too much.

After all the bullshit, we didn't keep the hairs with Vinnie's account info. No. We knew that would draw them to us, and then we would never be able to stop running. We weren't sure where to send them, but we ended up mailing them to Carbone, via Patrice's aunt in Florida. He would know what to do with them. Or not. Anyway, now it's his problem.

Sometimes we think about Bogdan. Not that we miss him, exactly. But you don't meet many people like Bogdan in your life.

We did hear something about him—Patrice read about it in some NYC papers she retrieved from the hotel recycling.

He got off, as it turned out. When the cops went to his mother's house, she wouldn't let them in. Something about not wiping their feet. Anyway, she slammed the door in their faces, and somehow it turned into a siege. The best theory is that one of the tear gas canisters the cops lobbed into the kitchen set some curtains on fire. The house burned to the ground; Bogdan's mom was incinerated. But every scrap of evidence burned up as well, and eventually they had to let Bogdan go.

The mall shoot-out never went to trial, for some reason. I think no one wanted to look too hard at that one. Half the police force would have had to testify against the other half.

Poor Bogdan. Now he'll have to start all over, from scratch, like us. Poor Long Island.

It's not a bad gig for me here, really; not what I ever thought I'd be doing, but hey. We have enough, and I don't have to work much. I hang around with the fishermen, play cards with them, do some work for them sometimes. They think I'm pretty funny. We get along.

We have a house—nothing extravagant. Just one room, a kitchen, some lizards.

But both Patrice and I are worried about a new parking valet at the hotel—he looks a lot like Stosh Budjynski, and not many people look like that.

And then the credit card thing—that's not going to last forever. We know that.

So we are thinking of pulling up stakes and trying it on somewhere else. We are nothing now if not transferrable.

Where to? Not sure. Guam maybe, maybe Malaysia.

Maybe Paraguay.